Safer Under the Stairs

Melanie Wyllie

ISBN 978-0-9956431-1-6

Book design by Barbara Wyllie

Cover image: Lower High Street, Southampton after the air raids of
30 November and 1 December 1940 © IWM (ZZZ 8205C).

First published as a Kindle eBook by Peach Publishing, 2014
This edition published by Melanie Wyllie, London, 2017

Contents

These Foolish Things

There was salt in a screw of greaseproof paper, marmite and meat-paste sandwiches, gritty with sand — an apple.
Sensible cardigans in case it was cold.
The sea ice-green — the dark shapes of the floating sea weed slimy against her legs.
Nanny disliked picnics.

The park seat was covered with pigeon's droppings.

The trees had the luminous green of the sea — the leaves not yet grimy and thickened by summer.

She had spilt coffee on the 50p Jumble Sale trousers.
It was a good thing they were brown.

A young Indian woman, her long greasy hair decorated with trinkets, a blue zipped jacket over her gold-trimmed sari sat on the next seat — the covers on the flimsy carry cot widely knitted pink and purple.
She ate a Crunchy Bar with quick furtive bites, staring straight ahead, rocking the carry cot with her free hand.

The sole of Hermione's canvas shoes had come away from the upper, unsuccessfully mended with sellotape. She must look out for another Jumble Sale.

They walked — their gowns catching the breeze — leisurely across the soft carpet of grass, dipping among the glowing flower beds and bending branches — to the Principal's Lodge for coffee.

They wondered what would become of them.

The war was soon to begin.
They were plunged into darkness.

Sharing toffees in the Nissen Huts inside the barbed wire fence.
The sentries calling out in the darkness.

The orange phosphorescence of lighted cigarettes — disembodied fireflies.
Borrowing precious stockings for a special date — and shampoo — and lipstick.
Scratched by the rough embrace of Air Force Uniforms.
The blackout a secretive cloak hiding the jagged and the ugly.

It had begun to rain — the promise of the early sun hidden by scudding clouds.

Her pockets were full of cigarette stubs she had picked up from the path.
The Council sweeper, unshaven, woolly-hatted, never came this way with his wide broom and rubbish cart.
She would extract the shreds of tobacco and roll them in the fine white cigarette papers in their green packet, licking the thin strip of gum.

Walking on the green springy lawns — breathing the scents of summer.
The black menace of Hitler's Europe — a hideous threatening spectre, loomed over them, waiting to pounce and tear their youth and dreams to tattered strips.

Counting with sick, quickened heartbeat the planes as they landed.
How many? How many? Please God!
Sending someone else to search the list of 'Missing', 'Killed in Action', pinned on the green baize board in the hallway by the dining room.

Praying that the loved one's name would not leap dazzling to brand their hearts.

The difference between happiness and despair, a line of type on a notice board.

Hilary lost Kes first.
Swollen-eyed, she continued to move the little flags on the flashing map — bright fragments denoting death and destruction— in their ever widening circles.

Hermione's turn came much later — his plane was 'Missing'.

She still thought of him as missing.
A word promising hope — possible life.

She saw him always young — the thick dark hair — the warmth of his hands.

Her mother lay in the high hospital bed — her flesh shrunken against the bones — patchy and sallow.
Her eyes fevered in their black sockets.

'I should never have called you Hermione,' she said. 'You should have been blonde.'

Hermione smelt the peppery smell of the carnations in the tinny hospital vase. A plate of half-eaten grapes, the stalks twiggy skeletons.
Her black plimsolls had holes in the toes. She folded her arms to hide the nicotine-stained fingers.

'You should pull yourself together,' said her mother. 'Letting yourself go like this. Stop moping. The war is over…' The words dried up. She closed her eyes.

The curtains at the Crematorium jerked squeakily across. The conveyor belt bore the coffin to the coke-fired furnace.

Uncle Patrick — a black scarecrow.
Aunt Edith — squat and shiny — her hat a black lozenge, sucking polo mints — stood disapproving.
They shook hands without removing their gloves, and went hastily away, fearing she might ask for assistance.

It was not madness — she had just given up on living.

The crowds jubilant and weeping — strangers embracing strangers — the roaring chorus of 'Keep The Home Fires Burning' — and the lights came on… the lights came on… The monster vanquished.

He was still 'Missing'.
She watched for the postman — jumped when the telephone rang — searching the crowds, always hoping.
She had written to his mother, but she had not replied.
They had never met.

The crump and shudder of bombs.
The deadly breath of the blast — stealthily moving curtains — shattering glass — wrenching people from their feet.
Swirling its unseen path.

The glittering glass ball turned above the dancers, sending spikes of coloured kaleidoscope light among them.
The safe warm beat of the band… 'These Foolish Things'… Faces touching, hands touching, closely moving.

Hilary had lent her a peach satin nightdress.
She descended the area steps with care.
They were broken, slippery in the rain.

The girl struggled with the pushchair. A miserable split broken plastic thing.
The child silent — sucking a piece of dirty rag — its face scabbed and reddened.
The girl's jeans were filthy.
She wore an outsize man's raincoat — the arms flapping loosely over her hands.
The thin bedraggled hair showing her pale scalp — her lips thin and bloodless.

They didn't speak.
Hermione didn't speak to people.

She rarely heard the child cry.
The girl made little noise — not like the young man who had lived there before, with the incessant, loud rock music.
His boots tramping the pathway over her head on the uncarpeted floor.

Her curtains hang threadbare, aged, grimed with city filth, perished with holes.

The walls of the toilet dark with mould, the high cistern noisy, the chain stiff and broken. The floor of the narrow passage carpeted with newspapers, covering the cold hard stone where the cooker stood, blackened and greasy, beside the chipped porcelain sink, its bowl finely webbed with cracks. Worn brown linoleum, holed to bare boards beside the bed with the bare mattress and stained eiderdown.

She wandered in her lilac silk, the hem wet with dew. The strawberries mounds of scarlet sugared fragrance. Crystal jugs of thick cream.

The fizz and bang of the fireworks — jewelled rain suspended in the velvet sky.

Rufus languid with his thin cigar... the band playing 'Night and Day'...

Her books stacked against the wall, the pages discoloured, bent with damp, the covers furred with mildew. Shelley and Keats, Henry James, Milton, Coleridge, Tennyson, Wordsworth...

They had eaten egg and bacon in the chill vaporous dawn light, and drunk champagne.
Rufus' thin sardonic face — his cynical wit — dropping his glass in the Cam.

> *...and now the Winter of the world*
> *with perishing great darkness closes in.*

He had been killed in the Desert.
His bones bleached as white by the burning sun, as the white expanse of moving sands that sucked them down.

She had kept her old wind-up gramophone — the small tin of worn needles — a few records. 'You've Done Something To My Heart', 'As Time Goes By', 'Moonlight Serenade'.

She passed the notice board with bowed head — not to see the ever lengthening list of names.
There was always someone to be comforted in the Nissen Hut.
Vi's Gerald — burnt beyond recognition — still alive in his fearful disfigurement.
Mary's brother torpedoed in the Atlantic — drowned in the oil.
Jolly pretty Clara's Guy, shot down over Italy…

She held her breath to prevent herself from crying aloud — the sobs gathered, knotted, in her throat.

The whole bus burst into song.
'It's A Long Way To Tipperary', they roared, standing swaying, laughing, crying, shaking hands.

After the euphoria, the Astonishment of Peace.

The maggot-stirring of the sprawled carcass, reluctantly loosening its putrid grip on the malarial swamps and suffocating sand — the peach-laden cliffs and icy wasteland.

Farewell parties, determinedly rejoicing.
Silent toasts to those who would not be coming back.
Goodbyes to those who had shared the torments of loss.
Resolutely turning away.

Hilary was married — still in uniform.
They gave her a slip and camiknickers made from parachute silk, a bar of scented soap, two pairs of silk stockings and a bottle of French perfume, bought on the Black Market. They all gave their sugar

rations for the icing on the eggless cake.

Her mother, returning to London, telephoned to say she had 'Absolutely nothing to wear!' and couldn't find a proper servant — only foreign girls.

She couldn't possibly have a foreign servant.
They were dirty and inclined to steal things — *and* pretended not to understand what you were saying.

Hermione shared an airy flat on Haverstock Hill with Megan and Brenda.
She got a job at the BBC.
They went dancing at Quaglinos — drank a lot at parties…
Blot it out — the pain and the memories — the ghosts who danced and drank with them.

She woke, startled by his voice — so near, so near — stretching out her arms in the darkness — to nothing.

It had happened gradually.
The strings that held her steady, snapping one by one.

One night at a party she had a great deal to drink, and responded to the kisses and caresses of someone dark and tall.
Turning her head she had seen his face in the light from the window… filled with horror she had fought him off, sobbing, scratching, kicking.
She was very sick in the mirrored bathroom with the gold taps and thick white towels.

She ran desperately after a departing figure… the walk… the way he held his head… only realising, breathing in painful gasps, it was not him.

*   *   *

She told her boss Algie Bates to 'Go to Hell', hissing through her teeth as he kneaded her shoulder whilst she typed.

Brenda said she should see a doctor. 'You've got frightfully thin,' she said.

Sir Benjamin Tyre, Assistant Commissioner at Scotland Yard, asked her to come and see him.
He had been at Cambridge with her father — Pembroke College. A constable brought tea and portions of crumby fruit cake to his office high in the cream and brown striped building.

'Your mother is worried about you,' he said. 'I understand you lost your young man — Airforce chappie…'

Hermione swallowed a mouthful of weak tea.
'He's missing,' she said.

'Well…' he said. 'My dear… life has to go on you know.'

He tried to be kind — sympathetic.
'You should take a holiday… the war has been hard on us all… we are all tired…'

Hermione walked down along the embankment up Villiers Street to the Strand, cutting through St Martin's Lane to Tottenham Court Road.
She walked all the way to Haverstock Hill, and shut herself in her room.
Megan brought her tea, leaving the cup and saucer outside the door when she didn't reply.
She didn't drink it.

The cats had been at the rubbish again. Stuff oozed, stinking, on the pavement.
Magda who had lived there before the young man, before the girl, had encouraged the cats, called them in her gutteral voice, putting saucers of milk on the steps.

Hermione had avoided Magda.
She was a refugee, her family destroyed, consumed in the dark abyss.
The pale blue eyes empty.
She shuffled about above on the bare boards, moaning, moaning.
She talked to the cats, lapsing into German.

The King was dead. Long Live the Queen.

The black-plumed carriage — dragging feet — the slow drum beat.
The icy February morning echoing the jangle of the horses — black veiled women.
The crown huddled silent with their thermos flasks — lining the Mall.

A wet June morning.
Red and gold uniforms escorting the golden coach. The white robed figure — stiffly regal.
The crowds, their spirits undampened by a night on the pavement, cheered themselves hoarse — eating their soggy sandwiches, singing 'Land Of Hope And Glory'.

Spent rockets fell from the sky into the thick dark waters of the Thames.

She left the airy flat on Haverstock Hill.
She left the job at the BBC.

Her mother had found the war most inconvenient.
She left her flat in Cadogan Gardens and took up residence at the Grand Hotel in Torquay, where she stayed playing bridge and Mahjong — walking on the front and going to sherry parties.

Despite the war there seemed to be an inexhaustible supply of sherry.

Occasionally she wrote to Hermione in her sprawling hand, complaining about the terrible food, pining for her customary winters on the Riviera. 'Here it is so *dull!*'

George had left her well provided for. She had no need for money.

Hermione irritated her.
Why couldn't she find a suitable husband?
There had been at least ten men to every girl at Cambridge.
Titles too!
It didn't do to be too clever. Men didn't like clever women. They made them nervous. Men liked to be admired, adored really. And her clothes! Surely she could make more of herself… She would never be a beauty, but she could *try* a bit harder. And now there was this tedious war… the supply of eligible young men threatened by death and injury. It really was *too* bad…

Hermione seldom replied.

Nanny got puffed walking up the steep cliff path to the hotel.
She carried the picnic basket and the towels.

Hermione clambering behind. Her bucket full of shells.

They had tea with her mother, on the immaculate lawn sloping down to the cliff top, round beds of lolling roses, — red and pink, yellow and white velvety-petalled— gently scented — viciously thorned. Her mother's dress of trailing chiffon, delicate pointed shoes, her face protected from the sun by the wide floppy brim of her silk hat. Far, far out to sea — a tiny sailing boat — motionless.

The waiter brought tea on a trolley… soft squares of tomato sandwich, sugared cakes, a big pot of tea.

She filled the dented kettle from the high cold tap. There was no hot water. The cooker smelt of gas.

She didn't like the look of the boyfriend. Weedy, shaven headed, spiteful mouth, dirty bitten nails.
'Do not touch me with your sticky fingers Hermione,' said her mother. 'Really Nanny! I'd rather Hermione didn't bring her bucket to the tea table!'

She wanted to show you her shells Madam,' said Nanny.

Her mother glanced briefly at the contents of the bucket.
'Very nice!' she said. 'Now please put them away.'

She lunched with Hilary in Dickins and Jones.
Hilary had some shopping to do.
She had put on weight, fleshy in the tweed coat and skirt, a brown felt hat with a feather.
She had two small daughters now.
She had photographs.
They had grapefruit juice and roast lamb.
'My treat,' said Hilary brightly, trying to avoid looking at Hermione, unkempt and shabby — out of place among the suited, hatted middle class lunchers.
Hermione ate with difficulty. She didn't eat meals — mostly currant buns and gin.
'You should be able to get a really good job with your Degree,' said Hilary.
There was a long pause. Finally she said, 'Life has to go on you know'.
Hermione didn't answer.
For you, perhaps, for you. The inner screaming, the awful guilt of being alive among so many dead — so soon forgotten… The Missing condemned to wander their No Man's Land — stumbling on the graves of their friends, uneasy in the blood-soaked earth.
No! No! Life should not go on… Life should cease.
How dare they say Life must go on…

'Smarten yourself up a bit,' said Hilary, wiping her mouth on the napkin, her lipstick leaving a red stain. 'You're very clever, and you've got lovely hair.'

Her meal tasted vomit in her mouth. She sipped the coffee, the dark shawl of despair wrapping her close.

She found the room in Keslake Road.
The lady from the Social Services was shocked.
She sniffed the air gingerly.

'It's very damp,' she said. 'I could put you on the waiting list to be rehoused'.
'No,' said Hermione.

Oh death, before I pluck my
brain away
Let me but sleep...

She would not leave him lost in the forest — the sinister grimness of the green-black pines, throttling each other with their whiskered branches, seeping sticky resin.

'You're entitled to Meals on Wheels,' the lady said, careful not to touch anything, 'and to a Home Help if you can't manage...' Hermione shook her head.

Perhaps you should see your doctor...' and then, brightly, 'I'll try and pop back dear, some other time — see how you're getting on.'

She got a job at Lyons Corner House in Coventry Street. She tidied herself up, found an old pair of stockings, her once good coat, still with the Utility label. Put up her hair.

In black dress and white cap and apron she served toasted teacakes and silver pots of tea to the large-footed, felt hatted, handbagged housewives, in town for the shopping, or a Matinee. Cream horns with jam. They licked their fingers.

The pay was bad. They relied on tips. Sometimes allowed to take home left-overs.

The plywood wardrobe wobbled on the uneven floor, the door kept shut with a wad of paper.

At the back she had his officer's hat, inside a linen pillowcase, in a brown paper carrier bag.

They had spent 48 hours leave together, walking on the Downs.

She could still smell the wind. So little time. The hotel bleak and deserted — the landlady suspicious. Lying in the dark they listened to the outgoing bombers. So close — already distanced.
She had taken his hat.
How to be happy with so many shadows.
They were exhausted with strain and long hours without sleep.

*...let light
Rise from the chambers of the east, and bring
The honied dew that cometh on waking day...*

Their last morning.

*   *   *

It was too tiring to get up.
She lay on the bed in her basement room, staring through the barred windows.

Nobody really believed Ruth. Nobody wanted to believe her.
They were sitting round the scrubbed wooden table of the kitchen in Clough Hall, eating walnut fudge cake Susannah Marchington had bought at Fitzbillies.

Strikingly tall and dark, her black hair wildly loose, wearing her old school Djibbah of red velvet, the clever face white and tense.
She told them of the incarceration — the systematic removal of Jews from their homes and jobs — the unknown horror of detention camps from which nobody returned.

Susannah was scornful.
She said it was nonsense. Propaganda. Lies.
Her boyfriend Hans studying Natural Sciences at Jesus was German.
His father had a high position in the Diplomatic Service.
She had spent Easter at their home near Berlin. A mansion with a water garden and orchard of cherry trees, foaming with pink and white blossom.
They were most cultured.

They had a musical soirée in the fringed salon, full of weighty furniture and ancestral oils, the chairs sturdily upholstered in magenta brocade.

A chubby thick-lipped tenor with black wavy hair, strangled in the grip of his wing-tied collar, sang songs by Schubert and Schumann. A fat lady in black lace with black coiled plaits accompanied him, banging with vigour on the strident-toned Bechstein grand — a black ribboned pince-nez on her long nose.

She was sure *they* had been Jewish, and they had eaten supper with the family after the concert.
Cold calves head in jelly — puréed celeriac — smoked duck with potato and caper salad — marinated oranges — brandy-soaked chocolate cake layered with whipped cream.

There was a sudden silence.

A slight shiver — a shaft of cold pierced the evening warmth.
A ragged cloud briefly obscuring the sun — a glimpse of bones — blood — flames.

The approaching conflict an ominous shape on the horizon — moving steadily nearer.

Ruth got up and left the room…

She wandered the streets — still searching — muttering and foolish. Tired she would slump on the pavement her head on her knees, the glossy dark hair, stringy and grey.

She washed up at the Athena Restaurant in Kilburn.
Fishing cockroaches from the soup — the heat and steam making her dizzy.

Madame Andreos, the proprietor's wife, exclaimed in horror at her chapped red hands, and bought her rubber gloves.

She was large and shiny — jewelled — the rows of pearls disappearing in her double chins.
She gave her some shoes — red with high heels — they were too big.

They bought the latest Super Deluxe Dishwasher.
She was no longer needed.
They gave her a cardboard box of Greek pastries, a pink mohair jumper and two weeks wages.

She sat in her broken chair, by the popping gas fire, and prayed…
for what…?
She was no longer sure.

Jeremy, a tail gunner had his left hand blown off.
A choral scholar at Kings — a talented cellist and composer.

She visited him in hospital, managing to obtain, at great expense, a bunch of thickly bloomed hothouse grapes.

She sat, not knowing what to say to this young man, his future as a musician shattered.

'Lucky to be alive really…' he said.

'You'll have to write lots of Symphonies,' she said.
She stayed a while and held his right hand.

Maisie, in the Canteen had hysterics.
She stood by the tea urn rigid and screaming.
Her mother and little brother buried under the bombed ruins of her home.

They drank at the King's Arms — close to the base.
A sunny lunchtime. Tables placed on the grass outside, under the leafy oak.
There was joking and laughter. Thoughts of fear and loss kept firmly in control.
They held hands tightly under the table.

There was so little time.

Cecil, debonair with his silk cravat, talked of the blue waters of the Mediterranean, the cool white wines, fronded palm trees.

He ordered a sandwich, lifting the slices of grey bread to peer at the yellow slab of cheese and spoke of fresh baked rolls, and real coffee, the pavement cafés in the Champs Elysées, the pretty girls with gay frocks and perfumed hair...

They drank to Peace, to Paris. When this ghastly war was over they would meet and drink Champagne...

His plane plunged burning into the ground near Rheims, the ashes scattered by the wind among the laden vines.

Her radio was very old — it crackled and wheezed — now there were programmes through the night. Unseen company to share the desolate dark.
Lying fully clothed on the hard metal bed in the Nissen Hut — too tired after the long night shift, to undress — too tired to sleep — someone quietly weeping — dreading the morning sun.

She swapped her meat coupons for gin at the off license.

Eyes were averted as the tanks rolled into Budapest — grinding the brave beneath their corrugated steel.

The world was weary of war. So many had walked jauntily on their last journey, their rotting bodies nourishing the weeds.

The gaily flashing lights of the Tickertape, rhythmically repeating Missing *** Missing *** Missing ***, red and white, red and white, interrupting her thoughts.

If only he had gone down like Cecil amongst the quenching vines, or in the shade of the whispering poplars...
Like Clare's Guy on the terraced silver Tuscan hills...

Not into the smoking pits of the poisoned country — the human abattoir, where only the vermin grew fat.

So life had to go on…
The little children queuing for their turn to die.

The girl came down the steps — bony feet slopping in the soiled fluffy slippers. She asked for milk… she had a plastic mug. 'It's for the kid,' she said. 'I've run out.'
Her voice was unexpectedly rough — her face so thin the joints of her cheekbones could be seen moving as she spoke.

She stood in the doorway smelling of mice cages.

Hermione kept her bottle of milk in a bowl of water. She filled the mug. It was not the child's fault.

'God what a hole!' said the girl. 'Jesus!'
She took the mug in white-knuckled hands.
'Thanks… thanks a lot…'

*   *   *

A legless serviceman with his tin on the corner of Shaftesbury Avenue, hoping for a few pennies.

A man with shaking hands, trousers secured with string, accosting people for cigarettes on the steps of the Underground at Piccadilly Circus.

An old woman in an Army greatcoat who wandered up and down the Haymarket singing Lili Marlene, pulling a battered tartan trolley stuffed with her belongings.

She was one of the lost — her shoes letting in the rain — her coat worn through to the grain of the cloth — she had striped socks — she had got two pairs for a shilling at the Church Jumble Sale — a lady in a green dress had given her a cup of tea and biscuits for nothing.

Those two days in the bedraggled wetness of an English summer...
They had poached egg on toast in a beamed Tea shoppe in Lewes.
The woman with crimped brown hair and floral overall told them
she kept chickens. 'Wonderful layers,' she said, pleased she could
offer them a treat.
There was sponge cake with home-made strawberry jam.
He had bought her an Anthology of English Poetry in the bookshop
next door.
There was so little time.
He flew into oblivion on a perfect summer evening — winging away
into the darkening sky, among the dusting of stars. A violet-blue
pool, still edged with sunset gold.

The day had been hot with a delicious breeze.
Some of the girls had sunbathed discreetly on the newly mown patch
of grass at the back of the Nissen Hut, the clean green smell of the
grass mingling with the spicy nasturtiums and lazy bending lupins
growing against the wooden walls.

They had not said 'Goodbye'.
She had been on duty all day in the still heat of the Ops Room.
It was just another mission.

The Red Cross patiently sifting through the piles of name tags —
making careful lists — notifying next of kin.
His was never found...

The doors of life clanged shut — heavy with bolts of guilt and
despair.

She didn't much like the look of the boyfriend's friends either.
One was a West Indian, tall and handsome — the other white and
ratfaced with a black leather jacket.

She saw them coming out of the house as she crossed the road
carrying the precious half bottle of gin in her old split shopping bag.
Her ankle was swollen — she had twisted it stumbling on the kerb.

They sauntered towards the Park — the ratfaced one lagging behind
— skinny jeans in heavy laced boots.

*   *   *

Hilary wrote on thick blue paper, the address printed in dark blue
curly letters.
It would be so nice to meet.

What about the Kardomah in Piccadilly?

Hermione pulled by nostalgia — the need to see a familiar face —
searched the wonky wardrobe for something to wear.

May could be quite chilly.

She had a navy woollen dress that she had worn to work at the BBC.
There were grey spores of mould on the sleeve.
She had no decent coat.
She would have to go bare legged — she had no stockings and could
hardly wear the striped socks.
She hoped it would not rain.

She went down Chamberlayne Road to catch the 6 from Kilburn
Lane.

Hilary was already there.

She stood looking in the windows of Hatchards.
She wore a blue dress and jacket.
She was slim again like she used to be.

Hermione saw her standing in the doorway of the Nissen Hut,
her eyes wide with distress, a hand clamped across her mouth —
shaking her head, shaking her head.
Herself stiff and speechless with terror — the hard rim of the
barrack bed hurting her legs.

She closed her eyes.
The haunted wings of rooks swooping blood red in the rays of the setting sun — glimpses of laughing faces hurtling past into luminous nothingness.

She opened her eyes.
The traffic inched jerkily forward — music clashed from open windows — fingers drummed on steering wheels.
The flags hung limply outside the Royal Academy.
A top-hatted doorman helped a woman with a large hat alight from a taxi in front of Fortnums.
She was jostled by office workers hurrying to make the most of their lunch hour.

She couldn't face Hilary.
Her life had gone on…
Did she ever think of Kes — buried in the overgrown ruins of the past? She couldn't speak to her — couldn't bear the pain of the brilliant sunlight.

She turned quickly — desperate to get away — back to Piccadilly Circus, down Lower Regent Street to catch the bus back to the familiar dim isolation of her room, where the sun never shone.

The top two stories of the house were boarded up — bomb damage had made the floors unsafe. It had been condemned, awaiting demolition.
Water poured into the hall when it rained.

There was a row with the boyfriend.
She heard raised voices — the sound of furniture being shifted, an object falling.

Iris had become pregnant.
Every morning she was sick in the enamel bowl in the wash room.
She tried everything to end it.
They boiled kettles to get enough water for her to sit in a really hot bath — filling it up as she sat, red as a lobster, crying.

Annabel flirted madly with the barman at the King's Arms to obtain a bottle of gin.

Clara produced some pungent liquorice-dark medicine she said would be bound to do the trick.
Nothing worked.

When it became noticeable she was discharged.
Her Terry was lost in a raid over Hamburg.

What had happened to Iris — and the baby?
She hoped she was able to keep it.

The boyfriend and ratface had an argument outside the on the pavement — laced boots visible through the railings.
There was a scuffle and shouts of 'Piss off' and 'Go fuck yourself!'
Ratface threw a cigarette packet and some screwed up paper down into the area to add to the accumulation of soggy debris. Blades of coarse grass pushed feebly through the cracked stone.

*   *   *

In the restless night of tangled dreams she heard crying.
She searched in the smouldering rubble among the forlorn remnants of domesticity — staircases holding defiantly to collapsing walls.
He was waiting for her. 'Don't worry!' he said, 'I'm fine'. He put out his arms — the sleeves of his uniform blue shreds. She struggled towards him through melting twisted metal, the bird-beat of her pulse throbbing in her throat. She couldn't reach him — she tried to cry out 'Don't go! Don't leave me!' but there was no sound.

Like a genie in a fairy tale he vanished, a vapid sulphurous spiral, into the black terror of a gaping crater.

> *Spare me the strength to leave you*
> *Now you are dead.*
> *I must go, but my soul lies helpless*
> *Beside your bed.*

She woke aching and cold on the damp mattress — the wall by the bed wet to the touch.

The child was crying — an urgent frightened cry.

*   *   *

Nanny said 'Big girls don't cry'.
She had grazed her knee falling on the smooth sweep of gravel round the circular bed of shrubs.
Tiny beads of blood spouting among the embedded grit.

Her mother's figure, a flimsy white reflection, appeared at the drawing room window.
'I would prefer it if you didn't bring Hermione round the front of the house Nanny,' she said, her voice sharp with annoyance.

'We were on the way to the village Madam' said Nanny, dabbing Hermione's knee with her handkerchief.
'You know you are supposed to use the side gate, Nanny. Please remember in the future.' She pulled the window shut.
Hermione could see the blues and pinks of the massed delphiniums in the tall white vase behind the glass.

The child was still crying.

She made a cup of tea.
The milk had gone sour — the smell of the cheesy bottle made her retch.

Oh God, why had it happened in summer?

They had lain in the high feathered grass, full of harebells and delicate hazy blue butterflies reflecting the sky — the hedges woven with convolvulus and wild roses.
Holding each other closely — inarticulate with love.

Grief forever associated with honeyed sunlight — the pain of the long light evenings — the fragrant air.

She drank her tea without milk.
The child's crying made her uneasy.

That night the Squadron lost four Spitfires — one limped home with a shattered wing — the crew mercifully unharmed.
One crew baled out over France, hopefully rescued.
The other two spun blazing to the alien earth — cutting a crimson pathway through the night sky.

Their time was running out.

The crowd at the King's Arms took their drinks out to the worn patch of grass and the wooden tables in the shade of the wide-branched oak — some sitting cross-legged on the ground.
They never knew which face would not be there tomorrow.

Oh God, why had it been summer?

Perhaps she should go and see if anything was wrong.
The girl might be ill…

Please God, that he had not suffered, had not been among the chained corpses dying as they worked on the shiny weapons of the remorseless war machine.
An empty skull at the barbed wire fence…

She mounted the steps slowly.
It was a hot day.
The bright sunshine harshly exposing the shabby, dirty, smelly street.
Nothing here to conjure up the rainbow of memories.

The curtains — tattered brown and yellow stripes — were drawn.
The light was on. She could see the fierce bulb glaring through the gaps.

She was pretty certain the girl was dead.

She lay higgledy piggledy — a floppy rag doll — her legs bent — a black mourning band tight round one arm — mottled and bloody — a fine sprinkling of white powder on the dark floor boards — a tarnished spoon — burnt and twisted — black powdery sticks of matches, scattered beside the open box.

A hyperdermic — the needle tipped rusty with dried blood, lying by her other hand. Pale eyes staring from the curdled face.

On the small square table stood the child's mug — the milk yellow and wrinkled, an open packet of custard creams, a tobacco box overflowing with ash and cigarette ends, two withered apples and a blackened banana on a plate, a little pile of dried-up tea bags.
The divan in the corner covered with old coats and magazines.
A plastic bucket of stinking nappies. Odd shoes. Broken toys. Empty beer cans and bottles. The child's hooded coat. A decrepit stained armchair. Dirty towels.

The child clung to the bars of its cot. The filthy little face puckered with fear, whimpering, the blanket caked with muck.

'It's alright,' she said. 'It's alright…'
She couldn't bring herself to touch him.
Her voice strangely distant.

The telephone in the call box on the corner hung broken and useless. She had to cross the road to the Newsagents and ask Mr Sarti to phone the police.

'Yes, we think she's dead,' Mr Sarti said to the 999 Operator.

He shook his head in sorrow.
He was not surprised. A hopeless creature. What a way to live. Stole sweets and crisps whilst he reached her a packet of cigarettes from the shelves behind the counter. Once he had caught her taking an orange from the fruit rack by the door.

He had said nothing, 'turned a blind eye, as you say...'
He shrugged, the child could do with a few oranges, poor little thing.

Mrs Sarti appeared from the cluttered back room — plump in a pink open-work cardigan over her peacock blue sari — plump brown feet in gold-embroidered mules — her round face anxious.
The shop smelt of curry and detergent.
She offered Hermione a cup of tea.
She said 'No thank you' — she should go and stay with the child until the police came.

She sat on a plastic stool, holding her breath against the animal stench, trying to avoid looking at the girl's disjointed body, the glass marble eyes.
She managed to murmur a few words to the child — sitting now — silent, picking at the blanket.

Life had ceased for this girl — would not 'have to go on' anymore.
In its own way a violent death.
A victim of peace, of a world which moved too fast, treading the weak underfoot.

Hurrying, hurrying, always hurrying, going nowhere, seeing nothing...

*　　*　　*

'Hurry up Hermione!' said her mother, impatient beside the Daimler, cool in her peppermint green linen and matching fine straw hat.
'You'll miss the train.'

Thomas stood deferentially, waiting to open the door, her blue school trunk fastened securely on the back.
'For goodness sake straighten your hat,' said her mother, 'and hurry up! Always dreaming...'

Hilary shook her awake — she was on the early shift.
'You'll be late,' she said. 'Better hurry...'

The cool dawn, sharp as lemons — she dragged herself from the refuge of the raven-hooded night to face another aching day — taut with unshed tears.

Hope was still fresh then.

Landing craft had floundered onto the beaches of Normandy.
The soldiers advancing step by step, forcing back the grey columns of the enemy — field by field, village by village — trudging forward through cheering crowds — waving tricolours, — snatches of song.

Automatic greetings.
'Hello! How are you?'
'I'm fine thanks. How are you?'
'Oh, fine thanks!'

Longing to rush back to the dim hut, and lie waiting for nightfall, the soothing merciful darkness.

With the first dream that comes with the first sleep
I run, I run, I am gathered to thy heart...

Hope trickling away.
A dried up river bed criss-crossed with jagged cracks.
The glittering roar of the waterfalls silenced.

The child had fallen asleep, its eyelids bruised with fatigue.

She sat stiffly, her mouth dry, waiting for the police.
They came, calm and competent, reassuring, gently helping her stand.
A sturdy young policewoman took charge of the child, carefully lifting the sodden little frame, encrusted with stale milk and excreta, speaking quietly to allay its alarm.
'There, there luvvie...! There, there!'

The street was filled with flashing squad cars.

She went back to the basement.
Someone would come and take her statement.

An ambulance arrived and took away a stretcher covered with a red blanket.

After a while a young policeman — they all seemed young — came to take her statement.
He balanced his hat on his knee, his face serious, and wrote in a black notebook.
He was polite, refused a cup of tea, brushed the seat of the chair before sitting down.
There was not much to tell. She didn't even know the girl's name.

After he had gone she went to the wardrobe and took out the brown carrier bag. She unwrapped the hat and held it. Sitting quite still in the broken-backed easy chair, the cushions flattened and dirty.

The numbing weight of grief was almost too much to bear, but she had to be there in case he came back.

Even now he could be on his way from some shadowy place — from the smoking chimneys, the sickening sweet smell of evil wafting across the fertile land, the rolling pastures of wheat and cream.

She must wait.
She must be there.
She cradled the hat in her arms.
He would always be with her.

Have you forgotten yet?
Look up and swear by the green of Spring that you'll never forget.

Tea with Julia

'We have to call grandmother Julia,' said Kate.

They were sitting on the old comfortable sofa in the nursery. Amanda put her feet carefully together and bent her knees slightly to one side the way grandmother said ladies were supposed to sit. She had admonished Kate for 'sprawling' in one of her deep armchairs. 'Good heavens, Kate,' she had said. 'Sit up properly and put your feet together, and pull your skirt down — doesn't your nanny teach you anything...?'

After their last visit to their grandmother when she had complained about their drab, dishevelled appearance — 'crinkled socks' — their mother had made an unprecedented visit to the nursery to speak to Nanny about their behaviour and their hair. 'Lady Morton was not at all happy with the children's hair,' she said. 'If Maison Antoine cannot cut it any better, we had better go somewhere else — Mrs Mackeson's children have their hair cut at Irene's, perhaps we should try there — and do make sure they call Lady Morton Julia...'

'She thinks it makes her old,' said Kate. 'To be called Grandmother — she doesn't want to be old...'

Their grandmother was expecting them this afternoon — for tea. She had a friend coming who wanted to see Harry's children.

They were wearing new lavender blue paisley dresses which had arrived this morning from Liberty in a big box packed with tissue paper.
Kate had wanted to wear her kilt, but it was red tartan.

Their grandmother was very specific about what colours could be worn. Only blues and lilacs in her drawing room and bedroom. A little pink was alright, so long as it was very pale.
Other colours, like red or yellow, were tolerated in the grand

drawing room, the library and the dining room — with reluctance in the music room which was predominantly pink — one could not really dictate the colour of visitor's clothing — but never green. Green was a very unlucky colour. It should never be worn indoors. If a guest unwittingly wore green she would greet them with frosty disapproval, distancing herself as far away as possible from the offending person. Once they had worn yellow twinsets and she had told Carstairs (her austere butler) to take them to the library — even though they had blue skirts. She had said she had a headache and he was to serve them tea in the morning room.

Nanny had bought them hair slides with velvet bows to match their dresses. They waited on the nursery landing in their blue tweed coats with velvet collars and matching velvet berets for Nanny to do a final inspection. Had they got clean handkerchiefs? And their gloves? Their grandmother always insisted they wore gloves — and hats. Ladies never went out without hats and gloves... Remember Lady Morton wished to be called Julia...

Amanda wished they were not going to their grandmother's for tea — wished they could stay in the nursery and make toast in front of the fire with the long toasting fork...

'She's a dowager now, anyway,' said Kate.
'What's a dowager?' said Amanda.
'When your husband's dead, your eldest son takes the title, and his wife takes your place...'
'Does that mean that Aunt Gwendoline is sort of more important than Grandmother?' said Amanda.
Kate said yes — now Aunt Gwendoline takes first place.

Amanda thought grandmother must be very cross — very cross indeed. The idea of Aunt Gwendoline in shabby tweeds, clumpy shoes and squashed hats being more important than their impeccably elegant grandmother was very difficult to believe.

Aunt Gwendoline and Uncle Clarence had a very grand house in the country, with a lake and deer. It had wood panelled passages and curving staircases and lots of little rooms and dusty cubby-holes where one could hide. They didn't go there very often. Uncle Clarence, an imposing figure, wore tweed suits and brown shoes, and smelt of tobacco and whisky. He didn't like visitors. He spent most of his time in London where he lived with their grandmother, spending his days at his club, or whatever else he did. Aunt Gwendoline didn't like visitors either. She hardly ever came up to London. She disliked London, considered their grandmother frivolous, a fact she did not attempt to conceal, and in any case spent a lot of time abroad in exotic tropical places collecting rare plants.

'South America,' said Kate. 'To the Amazon. The Amazon is a huge river with fish that eat you alive, and huge, huge jungles with hairy creepers and poisonous snakes that drop from the trees to strangle you…'

Amanda could easily imagine Aunt Gwendoline tramping through steamy jungles, hacking her way through grasping creepers, whacking at poisonous snakes with Uncle Clarence's large, striped golfing umbrella which always stood in the corner of the gun room.

Aunt Gwendoline didn't really like people at all. She was only interested in her plants.

When they did visit they had to take a train.
Amanda loved the train.
There were tables with lights with pink shades, and a waiter came with coffee in a silver pot for their mother, and glasses of orange squash for herself and Kate.
Their mother was always in a bad mood because Nanny didn't come, and she was 'in charge' of them.
Their mother was almost a stranger, finding them tiresome, never the slightest bit interested in what they were doing, seemingly unaware of how clever Kate was.

Aunt Gwendoline didn't eat meat.
In the gloomy panelled dining room, with a coloured glass window depicting a young man in armour brandishing a sword, Talbot, Aunt

Gwendoline's butler, presided over their lunch — dishes of roasted vegetables and colourful salads, fruit pies and jellies, and wine, Aunt Gwendoline liked wine.
Apart from themselves their was just Aunt Gwendoline and her assistant, Phillipa.
Their mother and father always referred to her, with a sigh, as poor Phillipa, not just because she worked for Aunt Gwendoline, but because she was impoverished. Her father had lost all his formidable fortune in the Wall Street Crash, and Phillipa had been forced to earn her own living. Thin, anxious, apologetic, she organised Aunt Gwendoline's life down to the last detail.

Kate said the Wall Street Crash was something to do with banks in America losing everybody's money — or something — and that some people were so desperate they had hurled themselves from the top of the Empire State Building.

Amanda had seen the pictures of the Empire State Building. She tried not to think of people jumping from the top — dark figures, arms outstretched, plummeting to earth.

Aunt Gwendoline always asked when Kate was starting school.
'Julia doesn't really approve of her going to school,' said their mother. 'She thinks private tuition is best for girls.'
'Rubbish,' said Aunt Gwendoline. 'Of course she should go to school. Is she learning Latin? And what about proper mathematics? And geography? And it's about time Amanda went to school as well...'
She would ask Talbot to bring more wine, and tell Phillipa to take them round the hothouses to see the new plants she had just brought back from Bolivia... or Peru... or Tibet... or where she had just come back from.

It was obvious that Phillipa disliked taking them to the hothouses, apprehensive that they might damage something — break a fat, leathery leaf from one of the shiny dark green trees sprawling dripping branches above them, or pick a waxy flower — or just break a flower pot, and that she would get the blame.

The hothouses were rather wonderful. Large glass buildings at the end of a long, grassy slope behind high, perfectly trimmed privet hedges before an abundant orchard. Inside they were engulfed in a warm mist among the dripping plants and strange, unreal flowers, all carefully labelled with unpronounceable names, where they came from and the date they had been found.

There were always several people working there. Students from Oxford, gardeners and serious men in shabby jackets.
Nobody really ever took any notice of them. An occasional vague nod, or a warning not to touch anything. Phillipa's hair would get limper than ever.

'Terrible clothes,' their mother would say. 'And her hair! Surely Gwendoline must pay her enough to have her hair done occasionally...'

Amanda thought that Aunt Gwendoline wouldn't really notice what anybody was wearing — except to look disdainfully at their mother's beautifully cut 'country' tweed coat and skirt — a small hat tipped at a stylish angle on her glossy waved hair.
Their mother did not care for Aunt Gwendoline and Aunt Gwendoline did not care for her, considering her as frivolous, or maybe even more frivolous than their grandmother.

They never stayed to tea. Their mother said it would make them too late getting home.
They had tea on the train — a silver pot of tea and square slices of fruit cake — trying not to spill the tea all over the place as the train swayed from side to side.

Nanny told them to stop dawdling, the taxi was waiting.

Taxis were another of Amanda's pleasures.
They always went in taxis with Nanny. Their mother said it was more practical than keeping a chauffeur, and she and their father had their own cars, and buses were out of the question — very unhygienic — 'Full of germs.'
Amanda always sat on the tip up seats, Kate only sometimes,

depending on what mood she was in. Today she sat on the proper seat next to Nanny.

'I hope we have smoked salmon sandwiches,' said Kate.

Nanny made a disapproving noise. She didn't consider smoked salmon sandwiches suitable for children. That is why Kate had said it — just to annoy Nanny.

'Contrary', Nanny called her.

'Just make sure you behave yourselves,' she said.

'And don't forget to call Grandmother Julia,' said Kate in her mimicky voice. Nanny ignored her. Sometimes it was best to ignore Kate.

Carstairs opened the door to them, bowing slightly as he always did.

'Good afternoon, Carstairs,' said Kate.

Amanda felt uncomfortable. She knew that this would upset Nanny. Nanny had no real status in their Grandmother's house — here she was just another servant.

'Good afternoon, Miss Kate,' said Carstairs. 'Shall I take your coats...?' And waving Nanny aside, he summoned a footman who whisked them away.

Nanny would wait for them in the Servants Hall.

Amanda wished she could go with her. It was always very jolly in the Servants' Hall — sometimes lots of buttered crumpets. Their Grandmother never had crumpets — much too messy and unladylike — and nobody minded if you didn't sit with your knees in a ladylike position.

Carstairs took them up in the gold cage lift. All the main rooms were on the first floor, even the dining room. Amanda thought it was just the ballroom on the ground floor, but the doors were always shut. They passed the grand drawing room, a sumptuous room, with large comfortable sofas and a thick, thick carpet strewn with silky rugs in jewel colours and patterns, like the pictures in the book of Ali Baba and the Forty Thieves they had in the nursery. There was a huge vase of burnished chrysanthemums on a table by the window, the heavy brocade curtains still undrawn on a navy blue sky. A red-shaded lamp glowed in the corner and there was a fire roaring in the grate, the spitting logs sending clouds of dancing sparks up the chimney.

There was nobody there — only the life-sized portraits on the walls. Their Grandmother in her tiara and Court dress, and their Grandfather who they didn't remember at all looking severe in some kind of gold-braided uniform, and other stern, dead relatives.

Grandmother had commissioned a portrait of Uncle Clarence, which would hang there as well. Amanda wondered if Aunt Gwendoline would also have a portrait, and what she would wear. Rubber boots and a squashy hat would look a bit out of place amongst all the ball gowns and medals.

They hardly ever went into the grand drawing room. At Christmas when there was a glittering tree reaching to the ceiling, and bowls of Christmas roses and jasmine, and wreaths of holly and mistletoe. And at Easter when there were vases of daffodils and narcissi tied with trailing green leaves, and china bowls of hyacinths and Easter Eggs. All kinds of Easter Eggs — chocolate ones wrapped in gold and silver paper, china ones painted with flowers, and decorative cardboard ones which contained packets of tiny sugar eggs.

Otherwise it was just to be 'shown off' to various friends and relatives, who were totally disinterested in them, barely acknowledging their presence.
Uncle Clarence was often there — bulky in his tweed suits — always smoking, with a glass of whisky clinking with ice, and Uncle Giles, handsome and immaculate, languid and drawling.
Amanda found him rather scary, like the foxy-whiskered gentleman in Jemima Puddleduck.
Uncle Clarence was scary too, but in an ordinary, grown up way.

Once 'shown off' they were quickly forgotten, and were often still there when Carstairs came with the cocktail trolley.
Amanda loved the cocktails — such pretty colours in such pretty, frosted glasses, with cherries and cucumber and little pleated parasols.
She decided she would have lots of cocktails when she grew up.

Uncle Clarence never drank cocktails.
He had his usual large tumbler of whisky with a splash of soda and lots of ice.
Uncle Giles drank cocktails, with his arm round a different, very glamorous, woman, every time they saw him.

They had tea with their Grandmother in her private drawing room. A very special room. All shades of blue and lilac, deep mauve to the palest harebell blue — silks and velvets — soft, soft chairs and sofas piled up with cushions and little blue silk bolsters, a blue silk chaise longue, the delicate pieces of furniture hand painted with flowers. The high windows overlooking the gardens hung with pale blue silk curtains — lamps with silk shades and bases of china flowers — even the pictures were of delicate flowers — and bowls of fat scented roses, even though it was winter.

Carstairs held the door wide open for them.
'Miss Kate and Miss Amanda, M'Lady,' he said.

Their Grandmother and her friend were standing at one of the windows looking out at the darkening gardens — the curtains yet undrawn.
Her friend was very tall and slim with dark wavy hair.
Grandmother was tall but she was even taller, in a dark blue coat and skirt, with a flashy diamond necklace and brooch on her shoulder.
She was very pretty, much prettier than any of the young women Uncle Giles put his arm round.
Their Grandmother was wearing powder blue — she nearly always wore powder blue, sometimes slightly darker blue or violet.
She had a silk blouse and long cashmere cardigan and her pearls — long rippling strands, almost to her waist.
'They call them ropes,' Kate had said. 'Ropes of pearls…'
Grandmother kept them wrapped in a silk handkerchief in a soft suede pouch in the drawer of her flower-painted dressing table with its rows of blue glass bottles in her blue bedroom, which they were rarely allowed to enter.

They made their way carefully across the thick pale blue carpet.

'Well, here you are,' said Grandmother. 'A little late, but never mind — Harry's girls, Esmé — Kate and Amanda. Children, this is Mrs Dupont.'
They said 'How do you do' politely and shook hands.
Esmé Dupont was very elegant and scented. She had long pale hands with scarlet nails and beautiful rings — diamonds and sapphires.

'My dear Julia,' said Esmé. 'Fancy Harry having girls.' And she laughed, a deep, throaty laugh.
Their Grandmother smiled a thin smile, and waved them to sit down. They sat as tidily and properly as possible on the edge of one of the very soft sofas. Esmé reclined in a deep armchair. Grandmother had her own chair.
She said, 'Mrs Dupont has just arrived from America on the Queen Mary.'
Kate started to say something, but their Grandmother continued speaking.
'You haven't seen Harry for a long time, Esmé, he has really settled down — no more gallivanting about...'

Amanda tried to visualise their father gallivanting without success. When he came to the nursery, which was seldom, he was always serious, and it was usually to complain — that they had been too noisy in the garden, or had left toys about — very annoyed that Kate had left her bicycle in the main hallway — 'Making the place look like a slum...'

'I'd like to see him,' said Esmé, taking a long gold-entwined cigarette holder from her bag. 'You don't mind if I smoke do you Julia?'
'Harry and Leonora have gone shooting at the Montgomery's place in Scotland,' said their Grandmother.
'Leonora! Shooting!' Esmé laughed again. 'That I can't believe...'

'No — no — Harry goes shooting, Leonora just visits. The Montgomerys are old friends. Kate would you ring for tea...?'
There was a bell by the fireplace, where a fire was glowing comfortably.
Kate bounded up to press the bell.

'There is no need to rush about,' said their Grandmother. 'Do try to be less guache...'

Esmé had black cigarettes with gold tips in a square gold cigarette case encrusted with diamonds, and lit her cigarettes with a gold lighter.
'Are they learning French?' she said.
'They are supposed to be,' said their Grandmother. 'But Leonora doesn't seem to be very competent at organising things. They have a governess who seems quite a nice young woman, and they are supposed to have French lessons twice a week with a Mademoiselle Simeon, but I don't know if she is a proper French teacher, or just a young woman who happens to be French.'

'Marcia's children have a French governess,' said Esmé. 'They speak French all the time.'

Kate and Amanda hated Lydia and Crispin Foster. They were very stuck up. They did not have a nanny any more. Lydia was too old and Crispin was going to prep school next year.
They lived in the country, not far from London, and had ponies.
Amanda was scared of ponies.
Lydia like to show off in her riding clothes, and Crispin pretended to love riding, but was really scared stiff too.
Mrs Foster was truly awful, very vain and patronising.
'You should ask your father to get you ponies,' she said. 'Lydia has so much fun with her pony. Of course you don't have a country place like ours, but there are plenty of riding schools in town.'

Their Grandmother considered Mrs Foster to be very common.
'No breeding,' she said dismissively. 'No idea how to behave — I think he made his money in bricks — or boxes — or something like that...'

Carstairs came with the tea trolley, carefully positioning the plates of tiny sandwiches — egg and cress and cucumber, little iced cakes, and a larger coffee walnut cake, already sliced, on a delicate fluted china cake stand — there was also a plate of thin, sugary biscuits —

on the low table between them.
'I think the fire needs attention, Carstairs,' said their Grandmother.
'And would you bring an ashtray for Mrs Dupont.'

Carstairs bowed slightly as usual, poking the fire and adding some more coal, and bringing a pale blue glass ashtray from a table by the window.

'That will be all, thank you,' said their Grandmother. 'We will serve ourselves...'

Amanda noticed she was wearing her special ring, a square diamond surrounded with little amethysts.
'Pass the sandwiches to Mrs Dupont, Kate,' said their Grandmother. 'And don't forget a plate and a napkin...'
There were large damask napkins so their laps were completely protected.
Esmé took two sandwiches, thanking Kate without looking at her.
'Whether the Fosters have a French governess or not is immaterial,' said their Grandmother, lifting the lid of the teapot and poking it with a spoon. 'Marcia is a vulgar little woman with no taste, and, I should imagine, very little French.'
Esmé laughed. 'That is rather unkind, Julia,' she said. 'I'm sure she does her best, I think she is going to send Lydia to Cheltenham...'

Their Grandmother poured the tea, a thin, pale scented liquid into the delicate cups.
'I consider a governess perfectly adequate,' she said. 'They can always go to Paris and stay with Charlotte and Xavier.'

Amanda would love to go to Paris. Mademoiselle had shown them pictures — lovely bridges with flying gold statues, fountains, avenues of chestnut trees with candelabra flowers, and little gardens with round flowerbeds and round ponds...
She had also shown them pictures of the Arc de Triomphe and the Eiffel Tower, and Kate had said she would like to go right to the top. Mademoiselle had said she must only speak French and Kate had sulked and broken the top of her pencil.

Mademoiselle was quite nice really. She didn't smile much, but at least was not as stuffy and condescending as the Foster's French governess.

'And what about gorgeous Giles?' said Esmé. 'A little more milk, please Julia — still entranced with the lovely Yvette?'

Last Easter Amanda and Kate had had lunch properly with the grown ups — seated according to their position.
Their mother and father at the top of the table with their Grandmother and Uncle Clarence — Aunt Gwendoline was, of course, absent — Uncle Giles and the lovely Yvette.
Kate was further down next to their cousin Bobby, Uncle Clarence's son. He was nearly seventeen, so very grown up. They didn't really know him. He was always away at school, or at some suitable establishment during the holidays, appearing occasionally at family functions. He was very quiet.
Kate had another young man in a brown suit on the other side.
Amanda didn't know who he was.
She was even further down the table between a dark young man with long white hands and a red spotted tie, and an older man with a large gold signet ring who called her 'young lady'...

It had been a lovely lunch. The table strewn with garlands of yellow and white tulips and little mossy pots of yellow and white crocus. There were beautifully decorated Easter eggs on each plate tied with gold ribbon, full of gold wrapped chocolates. The man with the signet ring gave her his egg — 'Better for you than me, young lady,' he said. 'I shouldn't eat any more chocolate...'

They had chicken in a creamy sauce and wonderful round crispy potatoes. Nanny would have been shocked at the amount she served herself from the platters brought round by the footmen — and there were meringues full of raspberries, and chocolate mousse in chocolate cases.

After lunch they went to the Music Room.
The Music Room had pink velvet curtains, a thick pink carpet, and

soft silky pink patterned rugs. There were a lot of small pink velvet armchairs and straight-backed chairs with pink velvet seats, and pictures of birds and girls carrying baskets of flowers.

Uncle Giles had opened the lid of the grand piano, and, lighting a cigarette, played a lot of runs and chords, and the glamorous Yvette started to sing.
It was all quite wonderful.
She sang 'It Was Just One of Those Things', leaning over Uncle Giles in a very provocative manner. She was wearing a floating flame-coloured dress with ruffles and frills. Then she sang something about being in the mood for love, and some other songs with really nice tunes. And then they sang 'In Your Easter Bonnet' together. Uncle Giles sang really well.
Everybody was very jolly, clapping and calling out 'Encore! — Encore!', and one lady with a diamanté cap and a dress with a lot of fringes got up and started dancing and then fell over, and had to be helped onto a sofa by the window.

Kate said had drunk too much.
'That's what happens when you drink too much,' she said. 'You fall over.'

Their Grandmother was very fond of music.
She promoted and supported all kinds of musicians, holding frequent musical afternoons.
Invitations to these events were much sought after.
Grandmother had a social secretary, Irma, who made all the arrangements, engaging the musicians, issuing invitations to the chosen few, making sure there were enough chairs with pink velvet seats, and organising the tea that followed the recitals.
Everything had to be discussed with Carstairs before she took the final plans to their Grandmother for approval.
There were, of course, always things she did not approve of, adjustments to be made, whether it was the choice of repertoire, the placing of the chairs, or the choice of sandwiches…

Irma was half Austrian, in her sensible grey coat and skirt, immediately recognizable as one of the staff, but not exactly a servant.

Amanda was rather sorry for her. It must be very difficult, if not impossible, to satisfy their Grandmother. She was always cheerful and welcoming, a strong young woman with thick curly blonde hair.

Grandmother expected them to come to her musical afternoons, dismissing protestations from their mother that they were too young. 'Nonsense, Leonora,' she would say. 'Of course they are not too young. One is never too young to appreciate music...'

Really it was because their mother did not want to be there. She found the recitals incredibly tedious. 'So boring,' she said, when she thought they were not listening. She made all kinds of excuses not to attend.

Nanny would bring them and leave them in the capable hands of Carstairs.

Amanda loved the musical afternoons.

She liked to watch the extraordinarily fashionable ladies with their smart pretty hats and smart pretty shoes, sitting sedately on the pink velvet chairs, clapping politely with gloved hands. The musicians were fun too, lady cellists with voluminous skirts, perspiring tenors, tightly encased in white tie and tails, fierce young women with shiny shoulders leaning over the piano keyboard, and wild-haired violinists swaying dramatically with eyes closed.

And afterwards the wonderful tea.

There were always smoked salmon sandwiches at these teas, and chopped ham or egg, and truffled foie gras on diamond-shaped pieces of toast.

They always managed to eat a lot of everything before Carstairs came to escort them downstairs to Nanny and a taxi home.

'I don't really know,' said their Grandmother. 'He always seems to be in France. He has an apartment in Paris and a villa near Cannes. He is hardly ever here. Are you planning to go to France?'

'The day after tomorrow,' said Esmé. 'I have a fitting with Balenciaga … he is absolutely the rage … and I have so many people to see … who knows when I might see him again — If there is a war…'

The words hung, a sudden shivering menace over the luxuriance of their Grandmother's exquisitely ordered sitting room.

War — was there really going to be a war? What would having a war mean..? What would happen if there was a war?

Trenches were already being dug in the parks for people to shelter in if there were air raids. Ugly brown scars cutting deep into the bouncy green grass, trenches that filled with water when it rained. Nanny said she didn't think they were very useful to the Barton-Clough's nanny when they met on their daily walk in Hyde Park. There were soldiers too — young men in uniform lounging on the benches smoking cigarettes.
Kate wanted to speak to them, but Nanny said it wasn't proper.

Next week Nanny was to take them to have their gas masks fitted.

'They make you look like a monster,' said Kate. 'And they smell awful…'
Amanda didn't know how Kate knew that. She always seemed to know everything. She had probably read it in Nanny's Daily Mail. They were not supposed to read newspapers — their mother didn't approve of them reading newspapers.
'They're smelly rubber,' said Kate. 'And they have to be frightfully tight so that the gas can't get in…'

Kate had asked Miss Tredwell, their governess, about the war, but she had got all flustered and said it had all been settled — there was nothing to worry about, and told Kate to get on with her sums.
But last time they were in the kitchen — sometimes, when it was raining very hard and they couldn't go to the park, Cook would let them come down to the kitchen and make jam tarts or fairy cakes. Amanda liked making fairy cakes best, because of the icing. Cook had told Nanny her nephew had already joined up, and her sister was

thinking of evacuating…
And why did they have to have gas masks, if there wasn't going to be a war?

Kate said Miss Tredwell was stupid. 'I don't think she knows much about anything.'

Amanda felt the war's sinister presence everywhere. At night it crouched, a dark, wheezing mass in the corner of the night nursery, by the chest of drawers — a pretty chest of drawers, painted with bluebells, to match the little table by her bed. It was always there, this fearsome, bloated thing inhabiting the darkness. Even when she buried her head under the pink silk eiderdown, she knew it was still there.

'I think we need another pot of tea,' said their Grandmother. 'And it is time the curtains were drawn — Kate, ring for Carstairs, and offer Mrs Dupont a cake…'

Esmé declined a cake, but took another of the delicious sandwiches. Carstairs came, unobtrusively, bringing fresh tea and closing the curtains against the inky darkness.

'So, what will you do if there is a war, Julia?' said Esmé. 'The Fosters are already making arrangements to go and live in America. Marcia has been checking on schools. They're thinking of Washington — Bernard has connections there…'

'I shall not be going anywhere,' said their Grandmother. 'Hopefully I shall be able to stay here. Harry and Leonora are looking for a place outside London anyway. Leonora has taken up golf. She is very keen, and they would like more room now the girls are growing older. They are looking for something round Sunningdale — there is apparently, a very good golf course there, and there are plenty of adequate houses…'

Nothing had been said about leaving London — of living in the country — of their mother's interest in golf. They saw her so seldom, they would not have known that she was interested in it. What would it be liking living in the country — would they have to learn to ride? Amanda did not want to learn to ride. She was always worried when they visited the Fosters that she would be made to get on a horse. Dancing class was bad enough, trying to remember the right positions for her feet, with Madame Irina clapping her hands — 'No, no, Amanda — the left foot first and the arms high — high! Do not sag — you are sagging!...' Kate loved dancing class, she liked to show off, pirouetting round and round until she got giddy and fell over, just like the lady who had drunk too much.

Madame Irina had a very heavy foreign accent which was very difficult to understand. Kate imitated her wonderfully, and the class would all get the giggles.

Perhaps Grandmother would consider riding unladylike, but she rather doubted it. Very grand people went riding, even the young princesses went riding...

Amanda wanted to look at Kate to see how she was reacting to this startling news that they might be going to leave the house in South Audley Street. No more daily walks in Kensington Gardens with its sparkling fountains and masses of yellow daffodils in the Spring, or taking bags of crusts that Cook had saved to feed the ducks on the deep, smooth waters of the Serpentine. Kate always wanted to go in one of the boats but Nanny said they were not allowed. 'Your mother wouldn't like it,' she said. So they would watch other people rowing out into the middle of the water getting muddled up with their oars...

But if she looked at Kate she might attract their Grandmother's attention, and she didn't want to do that, so she wiped her mouth carefully on her napkin and sat up very straight.

They could ask Nanny, but it was unlikely that she would know anything either.

Nanny might have to leave. They were really too old for Nanny now, but if Nanny left who would look after them? It was not the maid's job to look after them, and governesses were just for lessons.

'However,' said their Grandmother, 'I don't know how long it will

take for Leonora to tire of country living — after all, one can't play golf all the time.'
'And what about Harry?' said Esmé.
'Harry always indulges Leonora's whims,' said their Grandmother. 'It's the easiest thing to do — I think he quite liked the idea of playing the country gentleman, but I expect the whole enterprise will be very short-lived — if it ever happens...'

Amanda closed her eyes with relief — maybe they would not have to go to the country after all, would not have to leave all the safe, familiar places and things, and maybe Nanny could stay a bit longer, even though Kate was soon to have her own room.

'It would be safer in the country if there is a war,' said Esmé, stubbing out her cigarette in the carefully placed ashtray. She hadn't touched her sandwich. 'I'm surprised you are not thinking of moving away from London yourself. Charles absolutely refused to come with me on this trip. He said it was madness to come to Europe at this time. He even said the ship might be torpedoed — as if anyone is going to torpedo the Queen Mary...'

'Clarence's boy is going to Sandhurst,' said their Grandmother. 'They did not feel Oxford would suit him, so we shall have at least one soldier in the family... I don't know what will happen to Irina — maybe she will be interned — the Austrians are, after all, on the Germans' side. Anyhow, there may never be a war — Chamberlain seemed quite confident...'

Kate had said maybe Irina was a spy, but Amanda said what could she be spying on — Kate was very vague. 'That's the whole point of being a spy,' she said. 'People aren't supposed to know what you are spying on.' Amanda didn't believe that Irina could be a spy. She was much too busy arranging everything for their Grandmother to have any time for spying.

'Chamberlain is just a silly ass,' said Esmé. 'Everybody knows that war is inevitable. I am certainly not staying over here long. By the end of the week I shall be safely on my way back to America. I am really sorry I shall not be able to see Harry — I must say his girls do not look at all like him…'

And for the first time she turned to look at them. She had very lovely grey eyes, regarding them rather coldly — a critical appraisal.
'Kate has his colouring,' said their Grandmother. 'And, I think maybe round the eyes? Amanda doesn't really look like anyone…'

They were used to grown ups discussing their shortcomings in front of them. Too short — too tall— terrible posture— they really should stand properly — sit properly — maybe something could be done about their teeth — hair — clothes…
Hardly ever anything even the slightest bit complimentary. Aunt Gwendoline did go on a lot about Kate being a very clever child, but they didn't see her very often, and she was always in a hurry. They did overhear her once telling Grandmother that Leonora was a very foolish woman — and it was about time Kate went to school — they had not heard their Grandmother's reply.

'Harry is such a good looking man,' said Esmé, and sighed. 'Of course, if things had been different…' and she sighed again and twisted one of her flashing rings round her finger.

'Well, you did go off to America,' said their Grandmother. 'You couldn't expect Harry to wait around forever…'

Amanda knew Kate was longing to say something, but knew she must not interrupt their Grandmother or Mrs Dupont whilst they were speaking.

'I think it is time you rang for Carstairs to take you down, Kate,' said their Grandmother. 'It is getting late…'

The polite goodbyes — the polite handshakes — another lesson in good manners…
Pleased to be in the comfortable, solid presence of Carstairs.
Kate skipped into the gilded lift. 'Thank you, Carstairs,' she said.
'A pleasure, Miss Kate,' said Carstairs.

'Was Lady Morton's friend a nice lady?' said Nanny as they got into the taxi.

'She is very pretty,' said Kate.

'Very pretty,' said Amanda.

'And she talked a lot,' said Kate.

'And did you remember to call Lady Morton Julia?' said Nanny.

'We didn't call her anything,' said Kate. 'We didn't say anything…'

'Well, that's alright then,' said Nanny. 'Put your gloves on Amanda.'

Splintered

1

She must not walk on the lines — keep to the squares — keep to the squares. The Witch had her by the legs — pulling her down —her face hidden by the brim of her pointed black hat — her nails calcified yellow claws digging into her flesh.

She pulled her down — down onto the street below — a pulsating mass of crocodiles — open jaws grinning as they threshed the sick green water — steamy and clogged with slimy weeds.

The mournful wailing of the siren dragged her back — back to the mean bedroom, the iron bedstead with the lumpy stained mattress — the bare splintered floorboards — the curtainless windows — the fly-spotted light bulb hanging from the frayed wire.

'They said the war was over,' she said. 'Isabel — wake up. They said the war was over...'
'It is over,' mumbled Isabel. 'They're celebrating. They'll sound the All Clear in a minute — Go back to sleep...'

Eleanor didn't believe it was over. How could it be over?
The spider cracks widening into black chasms where the Witch stored her poisons — dessicated remains crushed to a powder — to scatter spotted venom — withering trees — birds, beaked balls of feathers plummeting to the sour earth, as she flew, cackling with delight — zigzagging among the criss¬cross beams of the searchlights — her yellow-eyed cat smirking behind her.

The war would never be over.

It had shredded their lives.
Turned the flowering orchards into twisted skeletons — booby-trapped by the Witch — there was no place of safety.

'Excuse me, Madam,' said the man in the tin hat, 'but you shouldn't be on the beach — War has been declared. The Alert has been sounded…'
'How ridiculous,' said their Mother. 'Why shouldn't we stay on the beach? I don't see any invaders…'
'Nobody is allowed on the beach during an air raid,' said the man in the tin hat. 'Didn't you hear the air raid warning?'

They had almost finished the sand castle.
Isabel was making the moat deeper.
Eleanor stood holding the bucket of sea water.
I'm sorry Madam,' said the man in the tin hat, 'but you will have to leave the beach…'

They were staying with their grandmother in Hove.
'Remember not to call Her Ladyship Granny,' said Nanny.
'What shall we call her then?' said Isabel.
Nanny fiddled with their hair ribbons. 'Just don't call her Granny,' she said.

From the balcony of their grandmother's flat they could see the sea — the heaving grey waves flecked with white — at the end of the Avenue.
Soon it would be fenced with barbed wire — floating with round, spiked mines.

On that day — that momentous day — everybody was huddled in the basement — grotesque in their gas masks, waiting for the first bombs to fall.
Nothing happened.
The All Clear sounded.
The worn elastic of anticlimax had made them weary.

It was too late for lunch.
Cook had to make sandwiches.
'I had to turn off the roast, Your Ladyship,' she said.
'Never mind,' said their grandmother. 'We'll have it tomorrow.'

*   *   *

Then there was safety behind the baize-covered doors that divided them from the elegant luxury of the 'proper' part of the house — from their mother and father — from the soft carpets and gilt-framed pictures — the polished furniture and overflowing bowls of flowers.
Their mother and father remote entities.
Their father making weekly visits to the Nursery on Sunday afternoons to play self-conscious games — admonished by Nanny to be on their best behaviour. Their mother in wonderful rustling dresses and glimmering jewels, coming to kiss them goodnight before going out with their father to dine and dance — a lingering fragrance — her necklaces swinging drops of cold glass against their cheeks.

Called to the drawing room to be briefly shown off to friends.
'Haven't they grown, Naomi?'
'Isabel is just like her father...'

'Thank you, Nanny — It must be their tea-time now...'
Smiling politely — feet together in white socks and patent shoes with buttoned straps — shaking hands politely before being led away.

On the other side of the baize doors they had their own lives with Nanny.
On rainy afternoons Cook let them make little cakes with blue and pink icing — piping squiggles all over the top.

They picked soft white mushrooms — pink-gilled parasols — in the neighbouring fields, and had them for tea on buttered toast, and filled bowls with blackberries from the hedges for Cook to make jelly.
They walked to the village where flopping bunches of mauve wysteria grew over the porch of the little shop, and bought packets of jellybabies and boxes of crayons, and threw stale bread for the ducks on the reedy pond on the village green.
They had warm clothes — clean and smart — velvet-collared coats

from Harrods — kilts and jumpers to match.

There were birthday parties with crackers and ice cream — dressed in stiff organdie frocks and pastel shoes — sandwiches cut in tiny triangles, and square-boxed presents tied with wide satin ribbon. The assembled Nannies ranged against the wall — on duty — alert to any sign of misbehaviour.

They had picnics in the beech woods, driven by the Chauffeur who unloaded the hamper — he had his own lunch in the car parked discreetly a little way off, whilst Nanny laid a white cloth, and they ate cold roast chicken and hardboiled eggs, and rolled down the slopes and got covered in leaves.

2

Their grandmother thought Nanny had their hair cut too short.
She had wanted them to have their portraits painted.
'I wish you would tell Nanny not to have their hair cut so short, Naomi,' she said. 'They can't have their portraits painted with hair like that. They look like orphans. We will have to wait until it has grown… it is really most annoying…'

Their mother was always fussy about what they looked like, what they wore, on the rare occasions they went out with her.

'I don't think that dark blue suits Isabel, Nanny,' she said. 'You know how particular the Comtesse is about clothes. She thinks the English have no taste — Put on their tartans…'

They didn't go to tea with the Comtesse.
Their mother went to tea with the Comtesse.
They, she, Isabel and Nanny, had tea in the Nursery with Jean-Phillipe and his Nanny.

The Comtesse didn't like children, offering her cheeks to be kissed in the formal French way, the briefest contact possible.

She wore beautiful clothes and sparkled with diamonds.
Her black eyebrows arched in permanent surprise.
'Jean-Phillipe is eagerly awaiting you in the Nursery,' she said.

Jean-Phillipe was never eagerly awaiting anything. He was completely disinterested in life.

He was sickly pale, with a web of cheesy blue veins under his skin.
'Pauvre petit,' said the Comtesse. 'He is so like his father.'

They had never met his father.
He worked in a gold and marble mansion in the City, and a gold and marble mansion in Paris.
Nanny said he looked after money — lots of money — other people's money…

The Nannies greeted each other warily.
Jean-Phillipe always had different Nannies.
This one was old and wore a grey uniform.
The Comtesse preferred grey.
'He should have more milk puddings,' she said. 'Get some fresh air — Madame La Comtesse says milk is bad for the sinuses, and that he is too delicate to play in the park — he has a weak chest…'
Their Nanny clucked sympathetically. 'Madam leaves me to decide what is best for the girls,' she said.

They had fish paste sandwiches and sponge cake with jam in the middle.
Jean-Phillipe broke up his food without eating anything, and spilt his milk on the cake.

Afterwards they played Happy Families.

3

Their grandmother's Rolls circled the park — the glass partition between the Chauffeur and the passengers closed.

Their mother had a pert black hat with a long feather. Their grandmother wore her mink coat — she always wore her mink.
Isabel sat on one of the jump seats, demure in her new cherry red coat and black patent shoes. They both wore hats — soft red velvet berets, the tops pleated into fat red velvet buttons. They had to wear hats when they went out with their grandmother.
'A lady never goes out without a hat,' she said.
'Won't a hair ribbon do?' said Isabel. 'I hate hats.'
'No,' said their grandmother. 'A hair ribbon will not do. Hair ribbons are frivolous…'

The air smelt of violets.
Their grandmother was very fond of violets.
She wore a bunch pinned to her mink coat, and kept a tiny bottle of violet scent in her handbag.

They passed a column of soldiers on horseback in wonderful uniforms — red coats and white breeches — white plumes swinging on their gleaming gold helmets.
The polished black horses stepping haughtily, bouncing their manes.
That's Buckingham Palace,' said their grandmother. 'That's where the King lives…'

It didn't look a very exciting place for the King to live. A flag fluttered from the flag pole on the roof.

'That means the King is at home,' said their grandmother. 'When the flag is flying…'

The sentries stood to attention outside their sentry boxes. Motionless in their black trousers and red tunics with brass buttons, and tall black furry busbies held with gold chains across their chins.

*They're changing the guard at Buckingham Palace — Christopher
Robin went down with Alice.*

'How long do they have to stand there?' said Isabel.
'Ask Cameron to go round again,' said their grandmother.
She had mauve doeskin gloves.
Their mother had a whole drawer of soft pale gloves, wrapped in
tissue paper.
They always had to wear gloves when they went out with their
grandmother.

Isabel slid the glass partition open.
'Once more round the park please, Cameron,' she said.
'Very good, Miss Isabel,' said Cameron.

*   *   *

They had lunch with Isabel's godmother, Aunt Edith. The Chauffeur
drove them.

They went without Nanny.
It was not suitable to take Nanny when they visited Aunt Edith.
They wore pink angora jumpers and coral necklaces.
'No green,' said their mother. 'Lady Cannon will not have green in
the house.
She says it is unlucky...'

Aunt Edith wore a great many necklaces and a lot of scent. She
allowed Isabel to choose the lunch — breaded plaice and mashed
potatoes and strawberry ice cream.
The dining room had heavy striped silk curtains and a china cabinet
with gold-edged plates and a tureen with a gold knob in the shape
of a rose. It looked out over a leafy square with a tennis court and a
summer house, flowering shrubs and round flower beds full of pink
and mauve Michaelmas daisies.

Even here the War had begun to gnaw the edges of their lives.
The Witch a faint shadow on the white damask tablecloth.

Aunt Edith recounted the ordeal of having her gas mask fitted.

They had all been fitted with gas masks — horrible black rubber things with a terrible smell that made you want to be sick.

They had tried to give Eleanor a Mickey Mouse one, but she had thought they were giving her a toy one — what use would a toy one be?

She had refused to put it on, fighting and screaming until they gave her a proper one.

Nanny had been very cross.

'No way for a young lady to behave...' and their mother had told Nanny that she must make sure that such a thing never happened again.

Nanny had made them practise taking them on and off.

'You have to be able to do it on your own — just in case...' she said.

'In case of what?' said Isabel, and crawled under the nursery table pretending to be a monster.

'That's enough, Isabel,' said Nanny. 'It's not a toy...'

Aunt Edith had had great difficulty getting a gas mask for her Pekinese Chowloon.

He had a jewelled collar, and ate with them — creamed chicken in a bowl decorated with gold flowers.

Gas masks were not supplied for dogs.

'I told them it was unthinkable that I would allow Chowloon to be gassed,' she said. 'Unthinkable. I had to get Reggie to speak to the Minister. You have no idea the red tape. In the end they supplied me with one for a baby — a sort of little house. Can you imagine the heaps of gassed dogs and cats — all the animals. There will be no animals left after a gas attack. Dr Marlow had to give me something for my nerves...'

She rang a little gold bell for the maid, a severe woman with frilled cap and apron.

'Bring the ice cream, Edna,' she said. 'Make sure Chowloon's is not too cold — it hurts his teeth. We will take coffee in the drawing room — and is there some chocolate milk for the children?'

Aunt Edith's drawing room carpet was so thick that their shoes almost disappeared in it — pink like the velvet curtains and sofa and Chowloon's special chair.

Aunt Edith smoked a lot — black cigarettes with gold tips, and offered chocolates from a huge round box with ribbons and gilt trimmings.

'One each,' she said in her strange husky voice. 'And one for my darling — Turkish Delight is his favourite...'

4

Isabel had started school.

She had a dark green uniform.

Sometimes she was allowed to have Sunday lunch in the dining room with their mother and father.

Eleanor longed to go to school — to have a smart green blazer with a badge on the pocket — a dark green tunic and a polished brown satchel with a pencil box of newly sharpened pencils and square white rubbers. 'Next year,' said Nanny. 'After the summer holidays...'
There was no next year. There was no school.

There was the War.
There was the Witch.

Their mother became ill.
'There must be no noise,' said Nanny. 'We must all be very quiet...'

A Nurse came in a crisp white uniform, a crackling apron and white-winged cap — walking soft-footed in white shoes across the thickly carpeted landing from their mother's room — through the baize doors to fetch trays from the kitchen — jellied consommé — a soup of finely pureed vegetables — a soft, sweet sponge pudding...
'She's hardly eating anything,' said the Nurse. 'She's very weak...'

'She's going to die,' said Isabel.

Eleanor said nothing. To die meant you were not here anymore — that you were never here anymore…
'Bring them later,' said the Nurse to Nanny, putting a quilted tea cosy on the pretty flowered teapot. 'We've had a bad night. She's sleeping now — I'll come and fetch you…'

And then there was no Nurse.
No one to smooth the sheets and plump the pillows — to ease the lacy nightgown over her head, and bring her medicine — a precise dose in a little glass.

The Nurse was called up.
She filled in the temperature chart for the last time — noticing the uncertain progress of the red line.
Soon it would be bandages and bloody broken bodies — no hushed dim rooms of the quietly dying…

5

Their house was requisitioned.
Soon it would be full of soldiers.
'Officers,' said Isabel. 'It's not big enough for a regiment — probably a General and Captains and things — and batmen…'
'What are batmen?' said Eleanor — were they going to play cricket in their park…
Isabel said she didn't know. 'All officers have batmen — they press their trousers — lay out their medals — polish their guns — bring them whisky and sodas — that sort of thing…'
There would be sentries at the gate, saluting khaki-coloured cars with flags on the bonnet — their tyres crunching the gravel as they swept up the drive…

It was sad leaving the house — there were so many cases and bags to label — saying goodbye to Nanny and Cook…
Their mother said they would come back as soon as the War was over — they might be home by Christmas…

They had been given very little time to find somewhere else to live.
Their father rented a house in Connaught Street.
A tall narrow house with three floors and a basement.
It smelt of London.
They had a bedroom on the top floor, and could watch the cars and people pass in the street below.
Where were they going? Where did they come from? Smart and shabby — old and young — black taxis and upholstered saloons…

'Why on earth are you moving to London?' said their grandmother. 'Everybody is leaving London — there is going to be bombing — Naomi is very unwell — the children — Really, Bertie, it's not very sensible…'

She was shutting up her house in Kensington Palace Gardens and going to stay with her younger son in Devon until the War was over. She hoped it would not last too long.

Her lilac silk drawing room was covered in dust sheets — curtains taken down and replaced by ugly black drapes. The windows crisscrossed with yards and yards of sticky tape — pictures stacked in the basement with the china and glass and porcelain lamps.

The servants dwindling daily — a weeping cook packed and ready to go to her sister's in Swansea — Cameron already gone to join a tank regiment.
What on earth was she supposed to do without Cameron?
How was she supposed to get about?
The Rolls carefully wrapped in padding like a giant parcel, in the garage.
Hired cars were virtually impossible to find.
She really couldn't use taxis. The drivers were erratic, drove too fast, always took the longest way round — and you never knew who had been in them before you…
This War was really a dreadful nuisance…

At least she would not need a chauffeur in Devon. Her daughter-in-law would take her wherever she needed to go, and it was most unlikely there would be any gas attacks in Devon…

She really couldn't wear one of those dreadful gas masks. They made one look like a hideous monster — ruined one's hair, and one would never get the dreadful rubber smell off one's skin…

She telephoned Harrods and ordered a quantity of silk underwear — one never knew if it would become unobtainable — or — horrors — that there might be clothes rationing. She ordered several pairs of silk-lined kid gloves, and a cashmere dressing gown as well — just in case.

No more first nights or balls or meeting friends in the Crush Bar at Covent Garden.
No more literary tea parties or intimate soirees in her elegant drawing room, where she gathered the artistic and the famous — civilised conversation — a little music — an illustrious guest persuaded to perform a Chopin nocturne — a Puccini aria — a brand new song from one of the latest shows — and even a little ragtime…

She felt nostalgic already, and telephoned Fortnums for a supply of China tea and Bath Olivers, and a case of their best pink champagne to celebrate when this dreary War was over. It really couldn't take too long to get rid of that common Hitler person…

'It's only just round the corner from Sophie and Alec,' said their father. 'Sophie will see Naomi is looked after…'

In their gigantic house in Hyde Park Gardens Aunt Sophie and Uncle Alec had managed so far to keep all their staff. The maids, the footmen, the cook and Giles the butler. Indispensable, totally reliable, Giles organised the household and Aunt Sophie whilst Uncle Alec spent most of his time being important in the House of Lords or at his club.

'I still don't think it's a good idea,' she said.
She had always thought Sophie was slightly mad, and Naomi was

probably dying. It was all most unsatisfactory. 'Can't you find someone to help?' she said. 'There must be someone who could come and help Naomi...'

The Witch was already perfecting her disguise — bottling toads — drying bunches of Deadly Nightshade over a fire of beetle's wings and the bones of rotten fish — throwing phosphorescent titbits to the complacent cat...

6

It was very strange to be alone with their mother and father.
No Nanny — no servants — no separate wing —just their mother and father.
Of course they didn't eat together, or sit in the drawing room together, but there was nobody else in the house.
It had been tried, with no avail, to get a maid or a nurse. Everybody was being called up, or going to work in munitions factories.

An agency had sent a very disagreeable woman who refused to clean — 'I'm not a charwoman' — or attempt the simplest cooking.
She was a parlour maid — parlour maids didn't cook. She remained mutinously in her basement sitting room until their father dismissed her.

They spent most of their time at Hyde Park Gardens.
'Naomi can rest here,' said Aunt Sophie. 'The maids will look after the children.'

Giles unsmiling, opening the heavy doors.
'Good morning, Madam.'
'Good morning, Giles.'
Leading them across the slippery marble floor to the gilt-caged lift which took them up to Aunt Sophie's drawing room.

Aunt Sophie telephoned constantly, sitting at the leather-topped desk, cluttered with silver horses and cigarette boxes, leather writing cases and pen holders embossed with gold leaf, and silver-framed photographs. Family portraits jostled on the walls over the squashy sofas and tapestry footstools. Herself when young, slim and arrogant in silky ball-gown.

The house was always full of guests — friends and friends of friends. Complete strangers.
The house absorbed them all in its vastness, to appear hungrily at mealtimes — served by footmen in the spacious dining room.

When the time came to convert the basement into a luxurious air raid shelter, it was full of luggage left by guests passing through.
Cabin trunks and hatboxes, bulging suitcases, golf bags, assorted umbrellas, walking sticks, a selection of tennis rackets.
'What shall I do with all the luggage, Your Ladyship?'

Aunt Sophie was instructing Isabel how to telephone for a taxi.
She had been shocked to discover Isabel didn't know how to use a telephone.
'We'll phone for a taxi...'
She had a whole list of numbers. 'We'll phone all of these...'
Isabel had to ask for a taxi to be sent straightaway, and then Aunt Sophie took the receiver and said that it would not be necessary. 'I'm just teaching my niece to use the telephone. Now try another one, dear...'
It seemed there were no taxis available.
Everybody was leaving London.
Everybody was telephoning for taxis.
'Really,' said Aunt Sophie. 'It is quite preposterous. What if we really needed a taxi?'

'The luggage, Your Ladyship,' said Giles. 'What do you wish me to do with all the luggage in the basement?'
'What luggage, Giles?' said Aunt Sophie.
She had no recollection of any luggage.
'I'll leave it to you, Giles,' she said. 'Whatever you think best.'

The maids looked after them whilst their mother rested, taking them up on the roof to see the elephantine barrage balloons, floppily silver, tethered to the ground, swaying over the park and the sand-bagged trenches.

They often spent the night in a discreetly opulent bedroom, with pink satin eiderdowns, and their own pink bathroom with large round tablets of scented pink soap and pink towelling bathrobes. There were frilly pink lampshades and silver-backed brushes, and a pink tin of biscuits by the bed in case they got hungry in the night. Draped in the pink eiderdowns they waltzed round the room guided by invisible partners — nodding to invisible guests.
'So nice to see you, Your Highness,' said Isabel.
'Who is that?' said Eleanor.
'Prince Herzog,' said Isabel.
'Who is he?'
'He is a Hungarian prince, stupid,' said Isabel.
She leant towards the mirror on the dressing table, and smiled at her reflection.
'My dear, you look ravishing tonight...' and then she twirled round and round so that the eiderdown stood away from her — a puffy quilted cloak
whisperingly soft.
'Keep an eye on the time,' she said. 'At midnight we will turn into pumpkins...'
'I thought it was swans,' said Eleanor. 'I'd rather be a swan.'
'They catch swans with wire,' said Isabel. They wind it round their legs, and when the swans try and fly away, it tears their feet off...'

They had breakfast in the vast dining room — hung with chandeliers — wedding cakes of dripping glass — a long damask covered table in front of the high, elegantly draped windows, laden with silver-domed dishes.
There was everything possible to eat.
Eggs — fried, scrambled, poached, little round omelettes — bacon, sausages, tomatoes, kidneys, kippers, kedgeree — all kept warm with little spirit lamps — fruit juices, tea, coffee, brown toast, white toast, rolls...
They sat in solitary splendour at the endlessly long table, white

clothed and napkinned, silver dishes of butter and marmalade, honey, and all kinds of jam. At breakfast they served themselves. The footmen came and went silently to replenish the dishes.
Their mother had breakfast taken to her room.

Aunt Sophie rounded up what guests were loitering, and organised a reluctant group to pick mulberries from the gnarled, drooping trees in the middle of the lawn, worn by deckchairs, overhung with magnolia, and edged with vibena and Canterbury bells.
'Cook can make mulberry ice,' she said, and pooh-poohed a thin blonde woman who complained about staining her hands.
'Nonsense, dear, lemon juice will soon get that off.'

7

Once a week they went with their father to Lyons Corner House at Marble Arch to buy their supper, and stood with him in front of the terraced slopes of pies — gold and shiny with crisp pastry battlements, decorated with flat golden leaves and flowers, sliced to display the pink meat embedded in jelly, the yellow and white of hardboiled eggs.
A fan of cooked meats, overlapping, scattered with parsley and cranberries. The man in a tall white hat, selecting what was required with his two-pronged fork.

After supper they went with their mother and father to the Odeon cinema — high in the circle — specks of dust dancing in the light from the projector — they battled in muddy fields, and flew their last mission — bandaged from head to foot in a hospital bed, the Nurse saying, 'I'm afraid there is no hope...'
Clipped-voiced people endured all kinds of suffering with dry-eyed stoicism — pulling themselves together, and carrying on — smartly saluting their superior officers as they flew off to certain death — 'Chocks away!' as the squadron roared into the sky.

They turned Isabel's bed into an aeroplane — sometimes a Spitfire, sometimes a Hurricane. Isabel was always the pilot — Eleanor a

gunner, a wireless operator, some other member of the aircrew who was killed or mortally wounded — the fuselage riddled with bullets...
'Lie down,' said Isabel. 'You're dead. Dead people don't sit up.'
'I'm only wounded,' said Eleanor. 'I'm shot in the leg.'
'No you're not,' said Isabel. 'You're dead...'

Their father was turned down by all three services as unfit. There were vague murmurs about his heart. He had hoped to join the navy.

The phoney war would soon come to an end.
The calm of the warm autumn days shattered by nightly terror, the dread wailing of the sirens heralding the German bombers, turning the blacked-out city into a monstrous bonfire.

They sat on the basement stairs, making shadow pictures on the wall with the light of a torch.
It was supposed to be safer under the stairs.
Among the heaps of rubble, twisted metal and crumpled walls, the staircases stood intact — going nowhere.

Their mother wrapped in an eiderdown, her slender pale hands gripping the silk.
'We'll go and stay at Hyde Park Gardens tomorrow,' said their father. 'You'll be comfortable there.'

'I think Bertie should take you and the children out of London,' said Aunt Sophie. 'I fear this dreadful bombing will get worse...'

They had spent the night in the newly equipped basement — family, servants and friends — in rows of sleeping bags, with quantities of blankets and pillows, trays of refreshments, flasks of hot coffee, tea and chocolate, bottles of whisky, gin, vodka, brandy, glossy tins of cakes and biscuits and plates of sandwiches.

Their mother, transparently frail, sat among Aunt Sophie's cushions on one of her voluminous, chintzy sofas. She didn't answer, her elegantly-shod feet light on the thick-piled rug.

Aunt Sophie, healthily robust, stood by the window.
'You could stay with Sandy in Oxted until you find something. They have plenty of room…'

In the subterranean cavern, the black walls slippery with green slime, the Witch tried on hats in front of a mirror framed with dried snake's heads — the forked tongues, stiff black thorns, protruding from scaly purple-tongued jaws.
Hats overflowed from a gold-banded chest — feathered and unfeathered, veiled and unveiled, wide-brimmed, narrow brimmed…
The cat replete with fish bones watching with sardonic yellow eyes.

8

Françoise was recommended by friends of their mother and father, who came one afternoon in a lollipop yellow sports car.

A dashing couple, she wearing a yellow silk dress, long silk gloves and pointed yellow shoes, her hair silky and golden. He, splendid in gold-braided naval uniform. There was much embracing and laughter.

It was 'chic' to have a French girl.
She came one afternoon.
She had a pale blue hat with a veil which hid her bad skin — later their father sent her to a specialist to have it treated.
Their mother was resting.
She came out on the landing in blouse and creamy slip, and called down to Isabel to show her into the cramped sitting room of the tall thin house, to wait for their father to arrive from the City.

Françoise always boasted that she had decided immediately that this was the man for her, notwithstanding he already had a wife.
Françoise knew she was dying but felt no necessity to wait until after this inevitable event.
She really didn't care.
She was engaged as 'mother's help', a terrible irony.

She was to start as soon as they went to Oxted.

The Witch threw off her cloak and tossed the pale blue-veiled hat into the spitting green flames of the reeking fire, where it dissolved in a flash of orange flame, and danced a jubilant gig...

The War had come.
The Witch had come.

9

Aunt Sophie's daughter Alexandra, her hair abundantly red, was a hearty young woman who wore gingery tweeds and tasselled brogues. She had recently married a Colonel in the Welsh Guards.

She had had the end of her garden partitioned off with wire netting to make a chicken run and enclosure for her goats.
She had white goats with bells round their necks, white hens and a noisy white cockerel.
She said they had to be as self-sufficient as possible. 'Digging for Victory, and all that...'
The gardener had already dug over the flower beds in preparation for planting vegetables.

They were not allowed in the garden, restricted to a small patch of grass at the side of the house, fenced with privet.

Françoise had joined them.
She had no specific duties, and did not seem particularly anxious to do anything at all, responding to their mother's suggestions that she should teach them a little French, take them for walks, help them to do some embroidery, with an expression of complete incomprehension, and shrugged contemptuously when asked to help Florence, Alexandra's elderly housekeeper, saying, 'I know nothing...', which was about all she did say.
Isabel said French people couldn't say 'th' or 'w'.
They can't help it,' she said. 'She probably could if she wanted to —

she's probably a spy — she's very nasty...'
Florence was very displeased at having to cope with all the household
chores on her own — and the cooking and Madam's ironing — and
now all these extra people!

All the younger servants had left to contribute to the war effort.
Annie, the parlour maid, came back in her smart ATS uniform to
have tea in the kitchen.
They were allowed to come and say 'Hello'.
They shook hands politely, and Isabel asked if she had a gun, and did
she know how to kill someone — had she already killed someone?
Florence, patting her rigid grey curls, poured out a stream of
complaints — a house full of children and foreigners — special
meals to be prepared for Mrs Bertie — having to take up trays — and
then the food untouched. She had to give it to the dogs!
She pointedly refrained from offering Françoise the seed cake.
'Overrun with lazy foreigners,' she said. 'No wonder the country is
in such a mess. Heaven knows what the Colonel would say!'

Alexandra had golden Cocker Spaniels.
There were sloppy bowls of water in the hall, and broken dog biscuits
and bits of bone on the Persian carpet. They sat in the best chairs in
the drawing room, snuffled legs under the dining room table, and
sprawled asleep on the embroidered silk bed spreads the Colonel had
brought back from when he was stationed in India.

'Please ask Alexandra not to let the dogs on my bed,' said their
mother.
She moved restlessly in the unaccustomed bed, the pitiless spread of
the cancer sapping her strength. 'And could I just have a boiled egg
and bread and butter?', pushing aside the plate of watery fish.

They were not allowed in the drawing room.
Alexandra didn't like children.
Florence didn't like children either. She disliked them almost as
much as she disliked foreigners.
They were allocated the morning room — where they had their
meals with Françoise who was also not allowed in the drawing

room, which made her very angry.
Françoise hated children, at least, she hated them.
She made no attempt to conceal the fact that she hated them —
walking round the table when they were doing some drawing and
painting — Aunt Sophie had given them beautiful boxes of crayons
— shoving them in the back and slapping their arms, ripping up
their drawings — taking away the potatoes, the jam sponge pudding,
before they could help themselves.

'I shall tell Mummy,' said Isabel defiantly.
Françoise just laughed. Not a pleasant sound.
Everything she did was threatening. It was like sitting with an
unexploded
bomb.
'Your mother — she is sick — malade — she can do nothing...'
She spat out the words with venom, grabbed Isabel by the hair and
shook her.

She had the afternoons off, so for a few hours they could lay mines
under the carpet, and use the armchair as a dug out, making sure
everything was tidy and in place before she came back.

They watched dogfights.
Tiny toy planes darting between the puffed clouds of ack-ack fire —
plunging stricken to the earth, trailing black smoke. Tiny toy men
dangling from tiny toy parachutes.

Alexandra suggested Françoise might help Florence in the kitchen.
'I'm sure you must be a wonderful cook,' she said. 'The French are
all wonderful cooks. Florence is a ghastly cook. Of course she isn't a
cook. It isn't her job to cook, but we all have to pull together in war
time...'
Françoise put on her blank look. 'I know nothing,' she said. 'I know
nothing...'

Sticks of firebombs fell on the street, setting houses ablaze,
illuminating the road and gardens with hissing sulphurous light,
spreading sheets of flame.

Alexandra in pyjamas and camel-hair dressing gown, red hair dishevelled, passed buckets of water and sand up the loft ladder to their father who was trying to extinguish the fire.

They stood in a shivering group on the lawn, watching flames shoot from the roof. The hedge was alight, so was the next door garage. The house opposite engulfed in flames.

'Where are their coats?' said their mother. 'Coats! Ou sont leurs manteaux?'
Françoise shrugged. She wore a red coat with a fake fur collar over her nightdress. They had dressing gowns and slippers.
Florence had a scarf tied round her head, bumpy with curlers — her handbag and a suitcase.
'Foreigners!' she said. 'What can you expect from foreigners!'

10

White mist choked the common.
Skeletal trees, haggard with cold.

Isabel read aloud Jeremy, by Hugh Walpole.
She had found it in the glass-fronted bookcase in the narrow hallway.
There were only grown-up books — Dickens — Trollope — Thomas Hardy — Trevelyan.

Below them in the kitchen their father and Françoise drank and laughed — the clatter of knives and forks on china — the background burbling wireless.

Along the passage their mother lay in the dim bedroom, propped up on the newly-bought pillows, in a special bed ordered from Heals with an extra soft mattress to ease the pain, eyes closed against the ugly furniture and dismal curtains of the rented house. Her bones luminous under the skin.

She stood in an empty echoing ballroom, holding a bouquet of roses and orange blossom — the rustling leaves of applause fading with the light, a trickle of cold wind lifting the hem of her silk gown.

Death paced impatiently, cracking his dry socket joints.
He did not have long to wait.

Occasionally their father brought coal for the fire — flickering feebly in the mean grate — stumbling on the stairs, uncertain with drink.

They had come when the picture postcard cottage was warmed by autumn sun. Late roses blooming on the walls, honeysuckle round the porch, facing the purple-heathered common, the surrounding trees showering the grass with burnished leaves.

A stage set for flowered-china tea parties — lace mats for the cake stand, silver sugar tongs.
The cut glass decanter of sherry with the nutcrackers and tin of fancy cheese biscuits.

Menace lurked — booby-trapped cosiness.

'Bertie,' said their mother. 'That girl told Isabel she couldn't have any breakfast…'
'I don't know anything about that,' said their father.
'Isabel has had no breakfast,' said their mother. 'You must see she has some breakfast…'
'I don't know anything about it,' said their father.

Their mother was anxious about their schooling — Isabel's schooling. Eleanor had not yet started school. All the good schools in the area had been evacuated. There was only Mrs Kelly who ran a small private school in her shabby house behind a shabby hedge, with desks in the dining room.
She took a mixed class of children, too 'posh' to go to the local school, whilst their parents considered evacuation, contacting lost relatives in Canada and America, wondering what on earth to do for the best.

Françoise was supposed to take them to Mrs Kelly's. She didn't. They could go on their own. Stupid little girls. She knew their mother was too ill to do anything about it.

'The Germans are right behind us,' said Isabel. 'Run!'
They ran, dodging from tree to tree, arriving breathless and dishevelled at the rundown house.

Mr Kelly appeared from time to time and threw furniture into the garden.
'He was on the Titanic,' said Isabel.
The children crowded giggling at the window, watching Mrs Kelly retrieve chairs from the bushes.
Mr Kelly had disappeared again.
He was probably in his usual place behind the kitchen door with a cup of pale tea and a biscuit.

'What's the Titanic?' asked Thomas. He was shorter than Isabel, the sleeves of his grey V-necked pullover neatly turned back.
'The biggest, safest ship in the world,' said Isabel. 'It hit an iceberg and sank…'
'What's an iceberg?' said Thomas.
'A huge lump of ice floating in the sea,' said Isabel. 'It made a great big hole, and all the water rushed in. Nearly everybody drowned. Lots of dead bodies in ball gowns and jewels turned to blocks of ice, floating about in the water — the band playing dance music as the ship was swallowed up…'
'Gosh,' said Thomas. 'Gosh!'

They learnt little, and as their mother became increasingly ill, they stopped going.

11

Their mother said she would like a piano.
'It would do me good, and Isabel could start lessons...'

Their black Blüthner grand that had stood in the corner of the drawing room by the French windows had gone, with the rest of the furniture, to be stored in a vast warehouse in the City that was subsequently destroyed in the bombing.

A mini piano was hired, cheaply wooden with shortened keyboard. It was put in the end room, which had been the drawing room, but was seldom used, becoming a dumping ground for any excess belongings they could not find space for, and there she played a little until she became too weak.

Eleanor desperately wanted to learn the piano, but their mother said she was too young.
'Next year,' she said. 'Perhaps next year...'

This year — next year — sometime — never — the prune stones lining the edge of the plate.
'Finish your prunes, Eleanor,' said Nanny. 'Don't play with your food...'

She played the piano anyway — picking out tunes with one finger and spreading her hands to hear the notes sound together, careful not to show any pleasure, otherwise Françoise would use it as a weapon to cause misery.

In the afternoons she would sit quietly by their mother's bed.
'Your father is always so cross with me,' she said one day, tears silently rolling down her face.
Eleanor was also silent — unable to comfort her — a sort of pain in her chest.
She was not yet seven years old.

Isabel refused to sit with their mother. Older, more aware, she couldn't bear to watch her slowly sinking into death.

'Why doesn't Isabel come and see me?' she said.
And Eleanor didn't know what to reply.

Spring did not reach the chill bedroom.
'The house is so damp, Bertie.'
She did not see the sharp white, green-veined snowdrops, pale-faced primroses, the tiny blue bells of the grape hyacinths.
A doctor came from London.
'We'll soon have you up and about,' he said cheerily.

Their mother, lonely in the No-Man's Land between life and death, twisted the sapphire ring that Bertie had given her with so much love — 'For ever and ever, my darling…' — and turned away her face.

They were sent to stay with friends of their father's in East Grinstead.
They had a big comfortable house of red brick, solid, welcoming.
They had hot baths and clean, warm beds.
When they returned to the cottage, their mother had gone.

'She's dead,' Françoise told Isabel — 'good riddance to bad rubbish' in her voice — 'And don't cry. Je déteste stupid people who cry…'

Their father told Eleanor — sitting in the kitchen by the old black Ideal cooking range.
Eleanor wasn't sure about death.
It meant she had gone away forever.
They would never see her again.

Nanny had said good people went to Heaven — a place of sunshine and flowers, where fluffy-winged angels played wonderful music on golden harps and trumpets.
Bad people went to Hell, where devils with pointed ears and tails like whips, poked the wicked with red-hot toasting forks beside pits of flame.
She was sure their mother had gone to Heaven.

They were not allowed to talk about her.
She was never mentioned, except in one of Françoise's venomous outbursts — 'Slut! Jewish slut!'
Her grave an unmarked weed-covered mound in the village churchyard.

They didn't even have a photograph.
Isabel had had one she put by her bed, but Françoise took it and tore it up.

All that was left were a few silken garments hanging in the musty wardrobe — a gold powder compact with her initials entwined — a mother-of-pearl fountain pen with a gold nib, rolled at the back of a drawer.

12

'You'll have to find the girls a governess,' said their grandmother.
She had been defeated by Françoise, seesawing between hysterical rage and snivelling self pity.

She had suggested the children should go back to Devon with her.
Sissy would look after them.
It was safer in Devon. There was a very good girls' school in Teignmouth. Now Naomi was dead the bad mannered ignorant French peasant girl could go.

Françoise had no intention of going.
She was already playing lady of the house.
The children had to remain to make the situation respectable.

She would not go. She would stay.

'Beastly woman,' said Isabel. 'Beastly, beastly woman. Why don't the Germans drop a bomb on her? Why isn't she put in prison with the other foreigners?'
'She's French,' said Eleanor. 'The French are on our side...'

Their grandmother took them to Bembridge to buy shoes.
'Their shoes are much too small, Bertie,' she said. 'Their feet will be deformed...'

She took them to tea at the Elizabethan Tea Shoppe, where they were still able to provide toasted currant buns.
There was a table occupied by a group of young men in air force uniform.
Only one of them had hands.
Their features shining stretches of scars.
They were making jokes through slitted mouths, struggling with stumped fingers, one with a steel hook, to eat their tea.
The one with hands helped, cutting the buns into small pieces and feeding the one with no hands at all.

Just outside Bembridge there was a hospital that specialised in treating these faceless young men who had fallen burning from the skies — grafting skin, constructing new ears and noses, fitting artificial limbs.
It was always shocking and disturbing to see them trying to cope with their dreadful injuries, knowing that their lives would never be the same again.

Isabel kicked Eleanor under the table, and hissed at her not to stare, but she was not staring, she was overcome with sorrow and an indescribable hopelessness, guilty that it was their courage that protected them every night when the bombers came...

There were a few governesses.
They were variously odd.
None of them stayed long — the cheques sent by their grandmother for their wages subverted into gin and black market goods.
They did their lessons on a card table in their bedroom — dictation, a few sums, a little geography.
Madame Slobanskaya was the last one.
She had a strange accent, and strings of wooden beads that swung and rattled.
She wore a drabbly striped inside-out jumper with pockets where she

kept bits of pencil, her handkerchief, and packets of nasty-smelling cough pastilles.

She told enthralling stories about her escape from Russia — the train trapped in a snow drift — a doctor performing an emergency operation, sterilising his instruments in the snow. Pursued by heavy-coated horsemen galloping beside the train, firing their long-barrelled guns in the air, brandishing curved swords,
uttering bloodcurdling yells...

'They stuck their swords through the flesh,' she said. 'Women, little children. Right through the flesh...'

She made jerky movements with her arm. 'It is the most terrible journey, the most terrible. When we arrive at the sea the boats are frozen in the harbour — we have always to keep hidden. We eat sour black bread and cabbage. It was so cold — so cold...'

Françoise tried to keep them apart, setting them unpleasant jobs — Isabel outside, digging the vegetable patch with an unwieldy spade she could hardly lift, piling the old cabbage stalks on a mound at the end of the garden — Eleanor raking out the boiler.

'Do it again,' she would say. 'Do it again...' — overturning the bucket of cinders — spreading the cabbage stalks back on the newly dug earth.

The never-ending washing up — hurling the dishes back in the sink. 'Do it again... Do it again!'

It was difficult to frighten or intimidate Isabel. She remained defiant and uncowed.

Eleanor walked in the Witch's shadow in a darkness spiked with terrors. The squares grew smaller all the time — the lines thicker and more dangerous — a stumble and they would trap her and drag her down into a black whirlpool...

Eleanor had to do the blackout.

Mourning shrouds blotting out the stars and the dawn light. Fearful of the hairy-armed demons that fidgeted beneath the beds, she rushed from room to room, trembling as she closed the doors behind her.

At this distance from London the intensity of the raids varied.

The nights were worst.
They went to bed half-clothed — ready to get up when the siren split the night with its searchlight wail —dragging out into the dark.
It was safer outside.
No buildings to be trapped in or buried under.

Up the lane to the top road, where they could watch London burn.
Livid — exploding — a pall of rosy smoke hanging entranced — ripped by red tracer bullets — black insect planes diving and tangling, spinning brightly to earth.

What was this dreadful war? Why did there have to be a war?
Their mother, remote and beautiful was dead.
Françoise called her a filthy Jew.
'Vermin,' she said. 'Poisonous vermin!'
Sometimes she thought it might be quite nice to be dead. She would be with her mother.
She would no longer feel fear, or the cold which split her fingers to the bone — oozing yellow fluid from the chilblains she suffered.
'No you can't have any gloves,' said Françoise, sending her out as darkness fell, to fill a sack with dead gorse to light the fires.
Out on the common of moving shadows and unexpected holes.

Grappling with the thorny branches of the dead gorse — her hands torn and bleeding — the darkness eerie and menacing — the Witch concealed by the sighing pines — her black cloak obscuring the moon…

She bent her knees up against the cold, trying to avoid catching the tear in the worn sheet with her foot.
Françoise had threatened severe punishments if the hole became bigger.
She never changed the sheets, but she would strip the bed to inspect the length of the hole.
Eleanor had folded the counterpane over her to get some extra warmth.
Françoise said she couldn't have another blanket.
'You're lucky to have a blanket at all,' she said.

The faceless turnip-headed orchestra was playing music from Les Sylphides.
On the dark stage the Witch waltzed round a cage of swans, their long necks folded against the lid.
Under the black rim of her hat she had thick clown's eyelashes painted on a chalk white mask, her mouth a gash of purple.
In her hand she held a photograph of their mother, which she tore into little pieces and threw high in the air — tiny fragments of their mother's face falling to the floor.

Eleanor tried to catch them, but they dissolved into gritty ash, leaving her fingers powdered grey.
She bent to release the swans, but the Witch, with a razor screech, kicked the cage across the stage.

The floor gave way beneath her, and she was thrown down into a cellar of rusty chains — rusty water running down the walls into pools of rusty-backed beetles...

Françoise was shouting at them to get up.
'We will leave you — hurry up — we will go without you.'

13

Sometimes the bombardment was so severe that some of the villagers from nearby cottages joined them — huddling in the hedge.

Hilda, their charlady, who came daily to clean, in crossover apron and carpet slippers.
Before she came Françoise would lock away the tea and sugar, and anything else she thought Hilda might steal.
'Those kind of people are all thieves,' she said.
The owners of the little shop which sold everything from bags of coke to birthday cake decorations.
Mr Mitchell who drove the local taxi, a decrepit old car, easily identified by his rasping cough, his garage a junkyard of broken bits of rusty machinery — car doors and rotten split tyres, slippery

patches of oil and scattered greasy rags.

He drove their father to the station every day to catch the train to the City, and fetched him in the evening. Small and wizened, cap forced on his head, a cigarette stub permanently stuck to his mouth, he drove erratically muttering oaths, urging the old car forward.

It was a mystery how he got the petrol for this low priority activity — it was unlikely he could play black market prices.

His grown up son who mooched round the garage was not fit to go into the army.

'He is retarded,' said Françoise. 'Stupid in the head — they are all stupid in the head — they breed retards…'

'She's the retard,' said Isabel. 'I don't suppose she even knows what it means…'

There were so many planes dropping bombs indiscriminately as they fled — chased by fighters — the searchlights picking them up in their beams — the sky a turmoil of smoke and flames.

'We'll probably be killed anyway,' said Isabel. 'Drilled through the head with shrapnel — I've got a whole box I collected yesterday…'

The ground was littered with shrapnel — small hard bits of nasty-smelling metal.

'I've got a boxful too,' said Eleanor.

14

Françoise sent them to their room without lunch.

Isabel had spilt salt on the cloth.

She hit them round the head as Isabel apologised.

She was always hitting them round the head.

'Cochons! Dirty — stupid…!'

Isabel fetched a toothmug of water from the bathroom.

'We are Prisoners of War,' she said, taking a sip of the water and passing it to Eleanor. 'Have some gruel, lieutenant…'

'What's gruel?' said Eleanor.
'Sort of watery soup they give Prisoners of War to eat,' said Isabel.
'Can't we escape?' said Eleanor.
'We don't speak German,' said Isabel. 'We'd be caught…'

They went across the wet and windy common to have tea with acquaintances of their father's, who had bought a farm near the woods. They bred horses, and kept a few cows, so that they could have their own milk, and make butter and cheese.
They had known their mother and had invited their father to dinner. He did not go.
Françoise had been hysterical. 'How dared they invite him without her — how dared they…?'
She had wiped out their mother — it was as if she had never existed.

They had said how sorry they were about Naomi — so sad. What about the children? How was he managing?
They understood he had a French girl to look after them. How lucky… Perhaps she would bring them to tea…?

She had not wanted to go.
Why should she take the children?
She didn't want to take them anywhere.
Their father said it would be nice for her to meet some other people.
Françoise didn't want to meet people — certainly not people who had known their mother.
Their father accepted the invitation.
He said they would love to come.
They are important,' he had said. They could be very helpful…'
Françoise was contemptuous. 'Snobs,' she said. 'What help are snobs?'

It was raining — a fine penetrating drizzle.

The Witch hovered impatiently in the folds of the lowering storm clouds — agitating the blackened heather to clutch and scratch their bare legs — pitting earth with roots and holes to trip them and twist their ankles. The cat was bored. It would have preferred thunder and lightening — forked lightening to cut the sky in two…

Françoise walked ahead.
She was wearing their mother's amber beads.
She walked fast, reviling their mother in a flat cold voice — each dreadful incomprehensible word a bruising blow.
What did those dreadful words mean?
She heard Isabel breathing — angry and hopeless.
It was better not to know.

There was a big man in the yard carrying a bucket of grain.
He wore corduroy trousers tucked into muddy boots, and a fair-isle sweater.
He did not shake hands.
He did not smile.
A woman stood in the window, wearing a blue twinset and pearl necklace.
When she saw them she turned away.

'You'll find Elsa in the kitchen,' the man said. 'Hans can show you the horses later, before you go home…'

They had taken in a family of Austrian refugees.
The wife, Elsa, cooked.
Hans helped with the farm.
He had been a laboratory assistant, and knew nothing of farms, detested the mud and the animals.
They had a daughter about the same age as Françoise.
It had been misguidedly thought they might become friends.

They did not know Françoise.
She didn't have friends.
She did not wish to make friends with anybody — certainly not with people from the kitchen.
How dared they make her have tea in the kitchen?
It was a wonderful tea — amazing cakes with whipped cream.
Elsa, a shapeless sad woman, served the tea.
Her husband in clothes too large for him, was morose and silent,

eating little.

The daughter, dark and very thin, seemed very shy, and only knew a few words of English.

Elsa spoke halting English, describing their nightmare journey, and their great good fortune to be taken in by these kind English people — how thankful they were to be alive, to be all together…

Nobody except Françoise smiled.
She smiled her chilling 'Come into my parlour' smile — 'You stupid ugly people. You do not deserve to be alive…'

Eleanor felt very old and very sad, and wanted to pat Elsa's hand and say everything would be alright now.
Isabel asked about the horses.
Hans took them to see them after tea.
They were the other side of the field.
There was a black one and two chestnuts.
Eleanor was glad they were on the other side of the field.
She was afraid of horses.

Going home Françoise pushed them roughly in front of her.
She was furious.
She had been snubbed by their father's friends, and sent to have tea in the kitchen with Austrian Jews.
'Jews,' she spat, shoving Isabel in the back so that she stumbled and nearly fell.
Françoise grabbed her by the hair dragging her to her feet.
'Don't you dare dirty your clothes…' She was viciously angry.

Falling in the mud would not have made much difference to their clothes anyway.
They were dirty already — and they were too small.
Their wrists stuck out of the frayed cuffs of their once smart coats — buttons missing.
Isabel had unpicked the hems to make them a little longer, but they were still much too short.

Eleanor wondered what their father's friends had thought of them —
a couple of scruffy urchins…

The daughter came once or twice to the house for Françoise to help
her with her English. Then no more.
'She is stupid,' said Françoise. 'A stupid slut looking for a British
husband. All she wants is a British passport. Who does she think is
going to marry her…?'

15

War encircled them snarling — crouched ready to spring.
A ravening wolf hungry for blood — stripping the bones bare.
Shuttered trains of condemned flesh trundling across Europe to feed
its insatiable appetite — laying waste to cities with its fiery breath
— acrid black smoke blotting out the sun — splintered forests grim
with graves.
A swaggering steel-helmeted conqueror.
'What big teeth you have, Grandmama.'

Françoise gave them curds and whey for supper.
She had let the milk go sour.
'Can't waste good food,' she said, tipping it out.
Ghastly grey fetid lumps in the willow-patterned bowls — oozing
rancid liquid.
'You can have a spoon of sugar — only one spoon…'
She scattered the meagre portion of white grains over the nauseous
mess.
The smell filled Eleanor's nostrils. She felt her stomach move up into
her throat.
'We can't eat this,' said Isabel. 'It's horrible.'
Françoise hit her round the head.
There's a war on,' she said. 'You're lucky to have anything to eat. If
you don't eat it now you'll eat it later…'

She sent them to bed — no talking — no reading — no light.

'Do you think Prisoners of War have to eat that?' said Eleanor.
'I shouldn't think even the Germans could think up anything so disgusting,' said Isabel.

Forbidden to speak to the village children, they climbed trees and pretended to be British Intelligence Officers parachuted into Germany.

Françoise set them impossible tasks, for which they were punished if they were not completed satisfactorily. They were never completed satisfactorily.

It was easy to deny them food.
No breakfast if they did not appear washed and dressed, beds made in fifteen minutes — then ten — then five…
No lunch either if there were any protests.
To be hit about the head for any reason at all — even for apologising — particularly for apologising.
'Give me your face,' she would scream.
Washing up returned to the sink to be done again, and again, and again…
Favourite things — books — feelings to be kept secret, otherwise they would be found, taken away, destroyed, ridiculed.
Eleanor shrank into herself, fearing the next inexplicable blow.

Their father, the Gentleman, whom nobody dared question, seeking oblivion in the dark green gin bottle, slobberingly compliant to the French girl's every whim.

Their father was seeing strange beasts rampaging through the prim and proper cottage.
Françoise sent them outside and told them to stay there. It was a cold winter's day.
They made a dug-out in the ditch, and roofed it with dead branches and twigs, and covered the damp earth with dead leaves.

This can be our HQ,' said Isabel. 'We are well camouflaged…' They sat crouched and stiff, hungry and cold.

'What's wrong with father?' said Eleanor.
'He's seeing pink elephants,' said Isabel.
There aren't any pink elephants,' said Eleanor. 'Except in fairy stories — how can he be seeing pink elephants?'
'He thinks he is seeing pink elephants,' said Isabel. 'And things crawling up the wall. It happens when people drink too much.'

Nanny used to drink lots of tea, but she hadn't seen pink elephants. She and Isabel drank a lot of water and they didn't see pink elephants.

'Gin,' said Isabel. 'Too much gin makes you see pink elephants…'

The doctor came in his big black car, and later another doctor in a shiny grey car.
They watched through the gaps in the branches.

Isabel said she would do a recce and see what the enemy was doing.
'I'll try and find some food,' she said.
She came back with some bread.
'There was some in the kitchen,' she said. 'She was upstairs with the doctor — father is making a terrible noise — We really should have a map to stick flags in…'

There were no squares left. The lines had taken over.
Now it was a question of speed — how fast could she go.
She would have to go very very fast if she was not to get caught.

The Witch, enraged, struck sparks from her cauldron with her broomstick, and conjured up a troupe of whispy dancing elephants of all colours — pink and blue — yellow and green — their long trunks tripping them up as they danced — falling higgledy piggledy into a multicoloured heap — a shrinking multicoloured ball, which she kicked for the cat to play with…

'Perhaps they'll take him away,' said Isabel. 'Lock him up — then she might go too…'

Darkness fell and a dank mist settled on the garden.

It wasn't really a garden anymore.
A garden of flowers where Mrs Turton had played croquet with her friends among bushes of lavender — now the bare stalks of curly kale and brussel sprouts protruded from the rough earth, and chickens roosted in her summerhouse.

'We'll have to take cover,' said Isabel as the siren wailed its nightly warning. 'We can't stay here — we'll have to run for it.'

There was no one in the kitchen.
Everything was quiet — except for the distant crump of bombs.
The stove had gone out and the room was cold.

Françoise was still upstairs with their father.
'They must have drugged him,' said Isabel. 'Given him masses of sleeping pills…'
She took some bread from the larder.
'Quick,' she said. 'We must get back to base before we're seen…' And they crept noiselessly up the stairs to their bedroom.

16

There was a superior boys prep school at the end of the lane which had been evacuated to the borders of Scotland where, it was hoped, the War would not reach.
The school had been taken over by the Ministry of Defence.

Their cottage was owned by the Headmaster's mother, Mrs Turton, who had accompanied them.
She did not wish to be left to the mercy of the German bombers — or even, maybe, to an invasion.

As the British troops straggled back to Dunkirk, weary and defeated, abandoning guns and equipment, and the German tanks rolled on to Paris, she had made an inventory of her furniture and packed her bags, pleased to learn that her cottage had been let to members of such a prestigious family.

She would have been shocked to know what was really going on —
at the state of her neat and tidy cottage — the drawing room a junk
heap — black market goods secreted under the frilled window seat
in the dining room — as the Headmaster would have been shocked
at his hallowed classrooms, well-ordered dormitories and smoothly-
mown cricket pitch being systematically laid to waste by its present
occupants, a completely unscrupulous bunch of Canadian convicts,
released to swell the Army ranks — dispensable troops, trained
for the most dangerous assignments. Theives — murderers —
blackmailers…

They filled the local pubs — openly selling stolen stores — great
blocks of butter and cheese, yard long tins of Spam, chocolate,
cigarettes, Rye whisky…

They drank and fought — breaking up the bars in the local pubs —
smashing the furniture — hurling bottles and glasses onto the road.
Two little girls murdered — found under sacking in the back of a
truck.

Eleanor made friends with one young soldier — dark and sleek
— who often walked up the lane — stopping to smoke a cigarette,
sitting under the young oaks.
He had a steel plate in his head. He had had his head smashed in,
in a fight.
He had been left for dead — 'bleeding all over the sidewalk' — he
still suffered headaches.
He allowed her to feel it — chillingly hard and smooth beneath the
thick dark hair and warm skin of his scalp.
His name was Mario.
He said they should be careful who they were friendly with — some
of the others were 'not very nice'.
They should not go near the grounds, or play in the rhododendrons
round the playing fields.

Isabel said she shouldn't sit out there with him.
'He might not be nice either,' she said. 'He must be the member of a
Gang. He must have been in a Gang fight. They are always having

Gang fights in America. They all have knives and guns…'

One afternoon when they were crawling among the heather, reconnoitring German positions, they found a soldier with pale blue eyes and dirty hands standing over them.
He said he had found a plover's nest, and taking Isabel by the arm, he pulled her to her feet. 'I will show you,' he said, and led her reluctantly away.
She came back running, breathless and shaken — grabbing Eleanor roughly — 'Hurry! Run!'
She did not say what had happened. She had a dark bruise on her arm.
'Never go out there alone,' she said. 'There are some nasty ones…'

'My sister says I shouldn't talk to you,' she said to Mario.
'OK,' he said. 'Your sister is a sensible girl. It's wise to be careful, but I would never hurt you. I don't go in for hurting kids…'

17

They did not go out in the air raids anymore.
There were patrols up the lane now, and sentries, and anti-aircraft guns on the school cricket pitch.
When the bombs fell near, the blast shifted the house — sliding the dressing table mirror, lifting the curtains — a sinister, unpredictable wind.

Beneath the bedclothes they read by the light of their bicycle torches, smuggled up earlier in the day.
Eleanor was struggling with Nicholas Nickleby.
Poor Nicholas Nickleby had an even worse time than they did.
Isabel said everybody should read Dickens.
There was a lot of Dickens in Mrs Turton's bookcase in the hall.
Isabel was reading Oliver Twist.

18

Françoise had devised a new twist to her 'Getting Up In Time' game.
They had got the five-minute deadline down to a fine art.
Françoise was not pleased.
Now it was to be whoever was last in the room would get no breakfast.
This was, of course, a deliberate attempt to set them against each other.
'She must think we're really stupid,' said Isabel. 'Beastly woman…'
They descended the stairs together and entered the kitchen in perfect step.
Her rage was total.
She screamed at the them to apologise — no food at all until they apologised… For what?
They did not respond.
She hit them round the head, and sent them to separate rooms.
All that grey cold day they were kept apart without food. As it got dark and the demons started to fidget, Eleanor muttered 'sorry', miserable for being a coward, miserable that fear and hunger had defeated her.

Françoise gave her some bread spread thickly with a jam that she hated — a dreadful homemade plum jam with slimy skins which made her heave as she tried to swallow.

Isabel did not apologise.
They were still kept apart — forbidden to speak to each other.
Isabel was made to sleep — still without food — on a shelf under the stairs.
Eleanor was choked with dread.
What might Françoise do to Isabel?
Walk on the squares — walk on the squares — but there were no squares.

That was one of the blackest days.

The bats had yellow eyes.
They followed the Witch as she skimmed the dark pines on her broomstick — squeaking — clutching a wig of wavy blonde hair in their torn-sharp claws...
'That's Isabel's hair,' she shouted, the wind echoing her voice. 'Isabel's hair — Isabel's hair...'

She saw Isabel standing on the edge of a cliff in her blue cotton dress. She wore a wide-brimmed hat with blue satin ribbons.
'Your hair,' she shouted. 'They've got your hair...'
But Isabel did not look up, staring down into the ravine where water clucked over smooth pebbles.
The wind laughed and shook the pines, showering the ground with green-bladed needles.
'Isabel's hair,' it mocked. 'Isabel's hair...'
The bats hung upside down, tangled in the blonde strands, blinking their yellow eyes, squeaking 'Isabel... Isabel...'
The wind swept the pines into a spiky cloud.
'Don't walk on the lines,' it moaned. 'Don't walk on the lines...'

19

They sat in the big oak.
The branches were so wide they could sit cross-legged.

They watched the soldiers in combat gear, snaking across the common on their stomachs, breaking into a crouching run, rifles at the ready. The Sergeant shouted incomprehensible instructions and insults, gathering them together and hurling abuse.
'We should report the troop movements to HQ,' said Isabel.
'The radio isn't working,' said Eleanor.
'We will wait until dark, and then go on foot to Marcel's and radio from there,' said Isabel. This is the spot they have chosen for the parachute drop... it would be a disaster...'

Their father was dangerously ill with double pneumonia.
He had caught cold fire-watching on St Paul's Cathedral.

City firms took turns to patrol the walkways at the top of the dome.
'Not much point,' said Isabel, 'when the place is on fire...'

They had to stay out of the house all day.
It was cold.
They fetched firewood and fed the chickens and sat in the big oak...
They had to keep out of the way.

Their father's condition worsened.
His breath came in laboured screams.
He was taken away in an ambulance.
Françoise went with him, and stayed at the hospital.

They were gratefully alone in the house.
It was good to be indoors.
They lived on leftover scraps, and bread from the shop on the road
where the convoys passed — khaki trucks of khaki soldiers — hour
after hour — going who knew where — on the quiet road between
high hawthorn hedges, wild cherry and crab-apple trees — now
spiky and leafless — brown twigs and thorns.

Perhaps they were going to Africa.
There was war in Africa.
They talked about it on the wireless.
War in the desert.
Eleanor saw all Africa as desert.
Nothing but sand — an ocean of sand, moving like the sea —
stretching far, far away, until it touched the edge of the sky.
How could they fight in the sand?
Everything would sink in the sand — be swallowed up by the sand.
Isabel said the desert was full of scorpions — like giant earwigs.
'They make a clicking noise with their tails,' she said. 'And if they
sting you, you die straight away — you go all stiff and die...'
Eleanor went to look 'Scorpion' up in Mrs Turton's dictionary
— a thick book with thin pages and small faint print: "Scorpion:
An arachnid of warm dry regions — having a segmented tail
terminating in a venomous sting."

She stood to attention at the gate, and waved at the endless convoy of lorries, jeeps and Bren gun carriers, praying they were not going to the desert. 'Please, God, don't let them go to the desert…'
Nanny said God always answered your prayers, but she did not think it could be true — why had their mother died? And she had prayed and prayed that Françoise would go away.

The Witch had probably stolen them, sweeping the sky of dreams and hopes and prayers with her bristling black broomstick, netting them in her black bag, woven from rat's tails, to burn on her putrid fire, sparking blue and silver stars among the smouldering remains of bugs and bones and mildewed stumps…

They were allowed one scuttle of coke a day for the stove, just to keep it alight.
They foraged in the ditches for bits of wood to eke it out and give them some warmth.

Eleanor's feet and ankles were swollen and split like her hands, rubbed into open sores by her Wellington boots…
They had no proper socks.
Isabel baked them potatoes from a pile in the shed, in the stove — charred — tasting of ash.
They were wonderful, and there was a bowl of dripping they spread sparingly on thick slices of bread.

The daylight shrank as winter closed in.

'There shouldn't really be Christmas in wartime anyway,' said Isabel.
She drew stars on a piece of paper, and coloured them in with yellow crayon.
The kitchen was dimly lit by an overhead light with a fluted glass shade, which cast lozenge-shaped patterns on the ceiling.
'The Jews have to wear yellow stars,' she said.
'What for?' said Eleanor.
'So everybody knows they're Jews,' said Isabel.
Eleanor was going to ask why, but she didn't — there were so many things she didn't understand.

They finished up a small piece of cold lamb.
'Perhaps we shouldn't eat it all,' said Eleanor, fearing Françoise's anger when she came back from the hospital.
'We have to eat something,' said Isabel. There isn't anything else…'

Their grandmother had sent them Christmas annuals — The Daily Mail and Rupert Bear.
They had expected her to come, but Françoise did not inform her of her son's illness until he was taken to hospital, and it was feared he might die.
She was very angry, and they had a very unpleasant conversation on the telephone.
She did not think she could make the journey.
Civilian travel was very restricted — trains erratic — frequently disrupted or cancelled.
There had been terrible bombing at Portsmouth and Southampton, and getting enough petrol and finding someone to drive her all the way from Devon was virtually impossible.

'If he dies,' said Isabel, 'we'll be orphans.'

They sat silent, each visualising life without Françoise.

Eleanor thought she would like to be an orphan.
No more Françoise — she couldn't stay if their father died.
It wouldn't happen.
Nothing good like that would happen.
He would come back, her willing slave, to bully or ignore them.
She would never go.
She would torment them forever.

He lived.

Returning from the hospital Françoise hit them round the head for finishing the lamb and leaving their annuals on the kitchen table.
She confiscated the annuals, and sent them to bed without supper.
'We have run out of rations,' said Isabel. 'There is nothing left to eat…'

They sat in the cold dark bedroom, wrapped in the stiff cloth of the heavy counterpanes.

'We can't go and look for food — the patrols are searching for us. We'll have to be very quiet...'
'How do they know we are here?' said Eleanor.
'One of the group is a traitor,' said Isabel.
'Who do you think it is?' said Eleanor.
'Perhaps the old man who works at the farm,' said Isabel. 'Or maybe Madame Cabot — she asked an awful lot of questions...'

20

The grim Christmas moved slowly to bleak, hopeless February.

After more unpleasant phone calls, it was decided that they should go to Devon for their father to recuperate.
With some difficulty, and at great expense, a car was hired.

They had stayed with Uncle Rick and Aunt Sissy with their mother as the first tremors of War sent shivers down the spine of Europe.
Their mother was already very unwell — unhappy to be without her nurse — unhappy to leave their home — unhappy that their father was in London.
She spent most of the day resting upstairs — coming down for a little while in the afternoon.
Slowly down the wide staircase — leaning on the curving banister for support.
They heard their grandmother tell Aunt Sissie that things didn't look too good.

Aunt Sissy took them to the beach.
She started to teach them to swim, and they went shrimping among the rocks, and had ice cream and sugary jam-filled doughnuts.
Their grandmother never came.
She sat in the garden in the shade wearing a wide-brimmed hat — or cut a few flowers for the dining room table, stripping the leaves from

their stalks in the cool of the garden room, and waited for someone to make the tea.

They loved the house.
It had a long veranda with comfy chairs, and a steamy conservatory thick with greenery and a little fountain, and lawns sloping down to a river with waterfalls, and a summer house lined with shells.

Uncle Rick was an artist.
He had painted a mural in the hall of ladies in long coats and high hats alighting from a carriage with polished trunks strapped to the roof.
There was another mural in the dining room. A picnic spread out on a white cloth on green grass. A whole ham — a cottage loaf — a triangular piece of cheese — apples in a bowl.

Uncle Rick worked in the ballroom.
It had a domed glass roof, the parquet trodden with paint.
It was full of billiard tables, their green baize covered with paints and jars of brushes and murky water full of dead wasps.
There were boxes of broken pastels and bits of canvas, a piece of wood ridged with hardened oils, smudged charcoal sketches and saucers of cigarette stubs.
There was a box of Napoleonic soldiers, and models of the Oxford and Cambridge boat race crews in their sleek polished craft.
There were billiard cues stacked against the wall, and wooden triangles of coloured balls.
He was never to be disturbed.
Aunt Sissy took in his meals on a tray, treading softly up the passage from the kitchen on the springy sponge-backed linoleum.
She made wonderful egg sandwiches with great lumps of egg, and proper lunch with gravy and roast potatoes.

Now she was head of the local WVS, driving everywhere in her green two-seater with canvas flaps — wearing her smart green uniform with red trimmings, or playing golf at the Warren in elegant tweeds.

This time their father stayed in the house so that he could have complete rest, and they went to a hotel with their grandmother and Françoise.

The Hotel was very grand.
It overlooked the sea — yellowish grey, rolling sloppy and salty against the cliffs — the lawns already decorated with yellow and purple crocuses.

Françoise was furious.
She wanted to stay in the house with their father.
Their grandmother said her place was to look after the children — although it was patently obvious she did no such thing.
'I wish to stay in the house,' she said. 'There are many bedrooms...' and without further discussion she moved in.

Their grandmother was at a loss as to how to deal with such behaviour.
If servants did not perform their duties properly they were dismissed.
She had always had a good relationship with all her staff.
This common French girl did not seem to understand her position.
She thought she was one of them.
Of course it was all Bertie's fault.
He had let her take over — to presume she was lady of the house.
She had not even informed her when he was nearly dying...
What on earth did he see in her?
She was ignorant, uneducated, and had terrible skin.
She did not know what to do about it.

She didn't want to upset Bertie when he had been so ill.
She stayed in the Hotel with them.
Horrified by their matted, unkempt appearance, their worn and dirty clothes, she gave up some of her precious clothing coupons to get them some new underwear, and a couple of second-hand woollen dresses.
It was disgraceful.

They had breakfast together in the huge almost empty dining room.
There were not many guests.

A few elderly people who had made the Hotel their home for the duration of the War.
Nobody had thought it was going to go on so long.

They ate tinned grapefruit segments and crisp toast with little curly pats of butter, served by a bent waiter in a musty black tail coat.

They had a large comfortable bedroom.
It was not as sumptuous as Hyde Park Gardens.
The curtains and satin eiderdowns were a rather drab beige colour, but the sheets were crisp and white, and there were plenty of pillows and three sizes of towel.

They pretended they were Russian princesses who had had to flee from the advancing German army, leaving their estate with the groves of silver birches and fragrant-fruited plum trees — the sand-coloured mansion with the golden weathervane and urns of flowers — the many windows mirroring the afternoon sun.

With velvet pouches of jewels strapped to their bodies — wearing ankle length furs and laced boots with little heels, they were driven away in their sleigh drawn by chestnut horses, through pine forest and across frozen lakes, wrapped in bearskin rugs, with chinchilla muffs to keep their hands warm.

21

Their grandmother didn't like girls.
She had four sons.
You knew where you were with boys.
She had been lucky with Nannies — except for the Irish woman who had rather overdone the medicinal brandy, and the one from Yorkshire who turned out to be a Buddhist — or was it a Mormon?
And then they were away at school...
And then they were away at university...
And then there were the daughters-in-law...
She didn't like any of her daughters-in-law.

Her eldest son's wife was loud and blonde — certainly not her natural colour.
She wore leopard skin coats, and drank too many 'Gin & Its'.
They lived in Florida, a convenient decision with the impending war in Europe — why stay to be bombed and rationed?

Bertie had insisted on marrying Naomi — he had been completely besotted with her.
She had done her best to prevent it.
A dancer — a chorus girl — Jewish.
She couldn't have been more unsuitable.
Of course her horrible illness and early death had been very sad, but it had opened up other possibilities — Lady Barnet's daughter Violet was still single — rather plain, but very steady — rich… Instead there was this truly unpleasant French girl.
Perhaps he would not marry her…
After all, he hadn't married her yet…

Her youngest son had already had a costly divorce, and was living with a married woman much older than himself. An Egyptologist — he knew nothing about Egypt.
Sissy was the least objectionable — cheerful and capable. She was managing marvellously with no cook and just a cleaning woman.
What a pity Bertie wouldn't let her take the girls.
That dreadful French girl was afraid she would lose her grip on Bertie, and have to leave.
She was going to suggest it again, but she really couldn't cope with any more hysterics — common peasant.

She didn't know what to do with the girls.
Isabel was easier — clever and pretty — always chattering.
Eleanor was plain — poor little thing — withdrawn and silent, her features too large for her small face.

She did her best.
She took them to the cinema.
She loved the cinema.
Sissy drove them in her green two-seater, with Isabel and Eleanor

squashed in the back — to Exeter or Teignmouth. They saw Dumbo, and The Last Time I Saw Paris. Afterwards they had tea in the Odeon tea room, with buttered toast and squares of sandy fruit cake.

Eleanor was unbearably saddened by Dumbo, and inexplicably miserable after The Last Time I Saw Paris, although she thought the music was lovely…

They turned up their coat collars, and with hands in pockets strode the paths of the Hotel garden.
'One day this city will be free again,' said Isabel. They sat on a garden seat and raised their glasses.
'To Victory!' said Isabel.
'To Victory!' said Eleanor.

Isabel tied her raincoat round her neck so that the arms flapped empty, and leapt from the Cedar tree.

They went to see Fantasia.
It made Eleanor uneasy.
She hated the pink elephants — the hippos with frilly skirts and ballet shoes dancing with crocodiles — the terrifying brooms and buckets — the black mountain and swooping black wings.
Perhaps these were the sort of things you saw if you drank too much gin.
'We shall hunt down our prey,' said Isabel. Tear it limb from limb!'

There were black birds perched on the Witch's broomstick — black birds with bald pink necks and cruel beaks.
They sat in front of the cat — ignoring its sardonic yellow eyes…
The Witch carried a Medusa's head of twitching snakes under her cloak to keep them quiet — stirring up the wind to hurl the window open…
Beating black wings filled the room — furry claws tearing the eiderdown — a snowstorm of feathers choking the air…
She found herself struggling with the handle of the wardrobe — the Medusa's head grinning at her from the dressing table.
'Whatever are you doing?' said Isabel, turning on the bedside light.

'Get back into bed...'

*　　*　　*

Aunt Sissy bought Cornish pasties for their supper — hot and crisp, juicy with meat and potato.
Eleanor ate slowly, savouring the golden pastry.
Soon she would be back being forced to eat the dreadful plum jam with its slimy skins, spread thickly on the grey wartime bread, with Françoise watching her heave as she struggled to swallow, knowing it would reappear until she had finished it.

22

Banished from the house for most of the day, they climbed trees — cut down paratroopers caught swinging in the branches — dug trenches and gun emplacements with bits of wood — rode their bikes, crouched over the handlebars — couriers carrying secret messages, their pockets full of hand grenades, guns and bullets hidden under turnips in their bicycle baskets. Isabel said the French ate a lot of turnips.
They practised salutes, and Zieg Heils, clicking their heels together, taking turns at being Germans.
Their grandmother was concerned about their total lack of schooling. Since Madame Slobanskaya they hadn't even had a governess. They have to have some education,' she said. 'If you insist they do not go to school, then you must arrange for them to have lessons at home...'

It was decided after much argument and more unpleasant telephone calls, that Isabel should go to weekly boarding school.
There was a boy's prep school just outside Bembridge, in wooded countryside, one of the few schools that had not been evacuated, and which took a few girls because of the war.

Eleanor was kept at home, hostage in the cause of respectability.
She had no lessons.
Occasionally their father would express horror at her ignorance,

setting her pages of formidable long division, or a lengthy poem to be memorised before
he came home from the City.

She worked desperately, trying to make sure all was learnt and correct before his return, terrified of his wrath.

The weeks were endless without Isabel.
She counted the days to each weekend — keeping out of the way — treading the squares with great care. Without Isabel she had lost her only friend and ally. She had no protection against Françoise's calculated maliciousness.

The Witch haunted the dark with her crooked decaying teeth and pale green skin — the yellow-eyed cat unblinking, motionless, ready with a swish of its black tail to gnaw its prey to the bone.
And every night the wailing siren — the roar of bombers — the whizzing thud of shells — the nightly terror a heavy black stone on her chest making it difficult to breathe.

She cycled precariously through the frightening woods to fetch milk from the only farm that still gave their father credit — scared of the lurking undergrowth — the rotting stumps and poisonous toadstools.
Sometimes there were soldiers — their tin hats stuck with leaves — jeeps churning up the mud.
She made sure she had her identity card — her gas mask bumping against the handlebars with the milk can.

She scoured the bookcase in the hall for something to read — A Tale Of Two Cities — Cold Comfort Farm — Villette by Charlotte Bronte — but the print was too small...

She seldom saw anyone except Hilda, but she hardly spoke to her — grimly on her knees scrubbing the kitchen floor, brushing the stairs with dustpan and brush, cleaning out the stove, stiff with disapproval of this lazy foreign woman who left the house so dirty. What would Mrs Turton think...?

There were scratches all over her polished furniture — her best blue vase broken — nasty stains on the carpets.

*   *   *

Their grandmother said Eleanor should have piano lessons.
Having failed in her attempt to send her to school with Isabel, she was determined to have some say in her education.
After all she was paying Isabel's school fees, and she had settled all Bertie's debts which were, as usual, considerable. She didn't know what he did with all his money...
'The woman who runs the little school — Mrs Kelly — she gives piano lessons. Eleanor can go to her...'

She went weekly.
Down the rutted lane, trying not to look into the leaning, sighing wood — sometimes there were army patrols — men with blackened faces dodging among the trees.

She had her lessons on a clattering old black upright in the corner of the classroom, in a fog of chalk, the desks crammed between the dining table and the sideboard, piled with booklets of multiplication tables, bottles of blue/black ink, and chalk-sodden dusters.
Mrs Kelly tense on her chair — alert to Mr Kelly's shuffling and muttering in the passage — fearful he might burst in.

She had to pretend to be reluctant to practise.
'Do I have to do half an hour?' she would say.
Françoise said she had to do an hour. 'Lazy little slut. A whole hour — not a minute less. I will time you. If your grandmother is foolish enough to spend money on piano lessons, you will not waste it — there will be no lunch unless I am satisfied you have practised properly...'

The rutted lane dissolved into a steaming swamp — bubbles breaking the surface — her feet sank in the moving mud.
Ahead, the dark shape of the Witch, arms outstretched, spread against the livid sky.

A root trapped her foot, coiling up her leg — as she struggled to free herself, it started to wail — sprouting fleshy leaves.

It was the air raid siren.
She sat up in bed — chilled with fear — cobwebs of nightmare clinging — clutching her cardigan round her for warmth.

The explosions were very near — the droning planes right overhead.
The windows rattled, and a whistling crash shook the house.

She huddled under the covers, trying to shut it out, and realised, with horror, that she had ripped the hole in the sheet.
Silently she prayed that Françoise would not discover it.
'Please, God, don't let Françoise look at the sheets...'

She found a photograph of their mother in a book of Chopin waltzes in a pile of music by the piano. A small square photograph.
She sat on a little wall beside a swimming pool — there were flowers in a carved stone pot — half-turned away, smiling.

She replaced it carefully among the waltzes, and put them in the middle of the pile.
It was safest to leave it there.
Françoise would never go through the music.
She would try and think of a really safe place to hide it, just in case Françoise decided to throw away the music.

23

She was alone in the house.
Françoise had gone to the hairdressers.
Every time she went out she said she was going to the hairdressers.
Once she went away for two days to the hairdressers.
Eleanor didn't care where she went, so long as she wasn't there.
She wished she would go away to the hairdressers for ever.
Isabel said she was probably a Fifth Columnist passing vital information to the Germans.

'The hairdresser is just a cover,' she said.

Eleanor didn't think she could have much vital information to pass on — unless she had been spying on the barracks — fraternising with the soldiers — smiling her mirthless smile to extract secrets — troop movements — the destination of the convoys — the position of the anti-aircraft guns.

The afternoon lay heavy.

The air murky and still as a stagnant pool.

The darkening sky leaning on the tops of the whiskered pines — grinning Medusa's heads hanging from the branches — the snakes tangled and hissing...

Dread spread a purple bruise inside her head.

She took the small cardboard suitcase from under the bed and placed her two precious dolls in it.

They were dressed in their best clothes — white muslin dresses with thin pink satin ribbons that Mrs Fraser had made them the first Christmas they were in the cottage.

Mrs Fraser was nearly a neighbour, but they did not see her anymore.

Françoise didn't encourage visitors.

She had come to tea with their mother.

They had it in her bedroom — their mother was too ill to come down.

Françoise had to take up the tray.

She had been angry at having to take up the tray.

She had slapped Isabel so hard that she left the imprint of her hand on her face.

She said she was in the way.

She had always hated Isabel.

She was too pretty and clever. Mirror, mirror, on the wall, who is the fairest of them all? Isabel — Isabel — Isabel...

The Witch polished her apples — red and shiny — appetisingly juicy — and piled them ready into the woven rush basket for later — for later...

Isabel was not frightened of Françoise.
'She's only a servant,' she said. 'Why should I be frightened of a servant?'
Eleanor wished she was brave like Isabel.
She knew she was a coward.
She was terrified of Françoise.

She crouched on the floor by the suitcase, tucking her collection of velvet ribbons in with the dolls and covering them with the silk scarf Aunt Sissy had given her.

At 3.15 a German bomber, in flight, released its destructive load on the centre of Bembridge, blowing a deep crater in the High Street.

The Odeon cinema took a direct hit — the few afternoon patrons, elderly couples, school children, the already mutilated airmen from the hospital, trapped beneath the toppled concrete.
Wendy's Wools was gutted — both the Miss Simms killed.
So were several people queuing outside MacFisheries.

Eleanor heard the shuddering explosion — the trees bending in the blast, dislodging the Medusa's heads — hurling them to the ground — smashed in pieces — broken shells dissolving into yellow toadstools.
She was still crouched on the floor when Françoise came home and started shouting for her.
'What do you think you are doing up there? Come down at once. The chickens haven't been fed. You will have no supper...'

24

The German bomber flew low over the common, its guns blazing, a stuttering clatter of machine gun fire.
It was too low for the anti-aircraft guns to bring it down.
It must have already off-loaded its bombs.
What was it firing at?
The common was empty.

It had flown over the barracks and the rows of camouflaged trucks, and the anti-aircraft guns on the school playing field.

Françoise said, 'Get away from the window, you stupid little fool. Sals boches — why is no one firing at it?'

The plane continued firing as it droned away into the distance — the swivelling gun searching for targets.

25

They were invited to a cocktail party at the Brett-Kirby's — friends of their father's.

They had left their home in Chelsea, and rented a house in Forest Row. Cosmo was 'something' in the Foreign Office so they had to stay within easy reach of London.

Madeleine Brett-Kirby had telephoned. She had really been their mother's friend. She was very upset at her death.

'My dear Bertie — I am so sorry,' she said. 'Devastated. So young, so beautiful. This dreadful war — I absolutely loathe being buried in the country — so dull. I yearn to be back in town…'

They were giving a cocktail party to welcome Dr Berg and his two teenage children — a girl and a boy — absolutely charming — to England.
Miraculously plucked from the black heart of Europe they had arrived with nothing, completely exhausted.
They had an absolutely dreadful journey,' she said.
'Helena is not with them — she was arrested — it's absolutely frightful. We have to help them as much as we can…'

She insisted they should all come.
'I must see the children,' she said. 'Poor little things. And do bring — er — you must all come. It will be rather spartan I'm afraid — it

is so difficult to get hold of anything with this beastly war. Cosmo should be able to wangle some drink — and I will just have to try and bribe the grocers…!'

Françoise didn't want to go.
She didn't want to meet the Bergs.
They were Jews — she wouldn't shake hands with Jews. She didn't want to meet the Brett-Kirbys either. Madeleine Brett-Kirby was a snob.
They were all snobs.
Jews and snobs…

Their father said Dr Berg was a well-known doctor in Germany — a specialist in heart disease.
It was amazing that they had managed to get here — although it was pretty bad about his wife…

Françoise had no compassion.
She would have been happy fuelling the ovens.
Isabel said they made lampshades out of people's skin — and boiled the bodies to make soap with the fat.
'The fat floats to the top,' she said, 'and then they skim it off…'
Françoise would have been good at making lampshades and cakes of soap…

Their father said Madeleine and Cosmo were very nice people — she could make friends with them…
Françoise didn't make friends.
'Interfering busybodies,' she said. 'Always poking their noses in other people's business.'

They went in old father Mitchell's 'taxi' which coughed and wheezed like old father Mitchell.

It was a big timbered house with a lot of chimneys, diamond-paned windows and timbered ceilings.

Madeleine had fine, gingery hair, set in fashionable waves with a

diamond-studded dragonfly clasp.
She was like a skinny bird — flapping beige crepe de chine and swinging ropes of pearls.
She embraced them in a cloud of scent — clearly taken aback by their shabby appearance.
They were wearing the woollen frocks their grandmother had bought them, which were already too small, and needed cleaning.

'My dears!' she said. 'My dears — and Bertie — how nice — and er...' extending her hand to Françoise, who pretended not to notice.
She was wearing their mother's mink stole and emerald earrings.
Madeleine made a funny clicking noise in her throat, and shepherded them to the other side of the room to meet the Bergs.
Tall, pale, dark and beautiful, the trio stood, awkwardly elegant in borrowed clothes, shaking hands, gravely smiling at the tweeded gentry who had come to welcome them.
The girl was particularly beautiful, with a single plait of thick black hair and wide grey eyes.

Madeleine had got two ungainly village girls, self-conscious in black dresses and white frilly caps to come and hand round trays of drinks and savoury titbits.

'It was frightfully difficult to get anything at all,' said Madeleine. 'I have cheated a bit — these are really only chopped egg and that awful salad cream — but I found some cods row — you must try one — and Cosmo has done wonders with the drink...'

She found them some grenadine.
She said they must come again.
They must come to tea.
She had hoarded some currants and icing sugar — they could have cake — she still had her wonderful cook. She was too old to be called up, thank goodness.
'You could come on the bus,' she said. 'It is not far to walk from the bus stop...'
Isabel said they would like that very much, but they both knew they would never be allowed to come — with or without Françoise.

Eleanor felt very miserable.
'Why is she so beastly to everyone?' she said.
'Because she's beastly,' said Isabel.
'She doesn't seem to like anybody,' said Eleanor.
'Well, I don't suppose anybody likes her,' said Isabel.
'She's horrible — and how dare she wear Mummy's things…'
'She can't wear her proper clothes,' said Eleanor. 'She's too big…'

<h1 style="text-align:center">26</h1>

Their father's youngest brother and his wife — or not quite wife, as Isabel put it, arrived, suave and debonair in a large shiny car.
There was much joking.
A splendid black market lunch of foie gras and roast beef was prepared and served in the dining room with a proper tablecloth.
There was much wine and music played on the gramophone.
Françoise wore a red crepe dress with a deep V-neck, its draped bodice unnecessarily revealing.
She played a record of Hutch singing 'Jealousy' over and over again, and tried to get their uncle to dance with her.
She fell against him, giggling.
They stood stiffly by the door, watching uncomfortably until they were sent away.
They had Spam and yesterday's cold boiled potatoes, and listened to the laughter in the next room.
'She's disgusting,' said Isabel. 'I hate her…'

Eleanor felt particularly sad.
These two handsome jolly people had hardly noticed them.
No kind words or smiles, just the polite 'Goodness, they've grown' and that was all.
There was a lot of washing up that day.

After they had gone Françoise was particularly unpleasant, criticising their clothes, their car, their lack of appreciation of the food.
'Snobs,' she said. 'Who do they think they are…!' and tipped the dishes back into the sink to be done again.

27

Françoise shouted for Isabel.
She was going to kill a chicken.
'Hurry up, you lazy slut,' she shouted. 'Come and hold the legs. I have to wring its neck…'

Isabel got up slowly, and moved towards the door like a sleepwalker. Eleanor ran — knocking over a chair — upstairs two at a time to the bathroom.
There was a bolt on the bathroom door.
She could lock herself in the bathroom.
She bolted the door with uncertain hands, and sat shaking on the bathroom stool.
She was petrified.
What if Françoise called her? What would she do? Please, God — please don't let her call me — she would rather be hit around the head and starved than help kill a chicken… she could never do anything so awful…
She heard Françoise shouting at Isabel. 'Hold them together — useless, stupid girl — tighter…'

She covered her ears with her hands, and closed her eyes, trying to shut out the frantic squawking — the hysterical clucking…

Muffled shouting. 'Pass the knife — the knife! Don't let go of the legs, you stupid fool…'

'She had to cut its head off,' said Isabel. 'With the knife — she cut its head off…'

There was a pause.
In the darkness Eleanor held her breath.

'It ran round the yard,' said Isabel. 'It ran round the yard with no head…'

Eleanor couldn't speak. Pain hammered her temples.

In the dark slimy cavern beneath the earth, headless chickens danced, their empty necks limply swinging.

The Witch, hunched in her black cloak, crouched by the green-flamed fire, throwing chicken heads into her black cooking pot — her pale, taloned hands spotted with blood, dry, black blood...
The cat sat beside her, its yellow eyes half closed — swishing its tail in anticipation of a tasty titbit...

28

Their grandmother came for a few days.
She didn't stay in the house.
Their father suggested she stay at the King's Head.
Before the war it had had a very good reputation — patronised by members of the golf club, supporters of the Conservative Association, the local doctor and his wife, the vicar and his sister...
It had had a very good restaurant which served sturdy English meals — steak and kidney pie, lamb chops, sole on the bone...
There had been a pleasant garden with blue and pink hydrangeas, where drinks and sandwiches were served in the summer.
Now it was full of rowdy Canadian soldiers and shady men in raincoats doing black market deals — gritty with cigarette smoke and jukebox noise — greasy with chip frying — the garden dug up and planted with potatoes.

She said she would rather stay at the Felbridge Arms, a respectable hotel outside Bembridge which had a better clientele — RAF officers, and nurses and doctors from the hospital.
The food was disgusting, the rooms and the water cold, but infinitely better than the squalor at the King's Head.
There was a limit to what one had to put up with, even if there was a War on.

She had been very lucky to get a lift from Devon.

Ellen Spencer had been visiting her daughter in Exeter, and her husband, a lieutenant colonel in the Guards, had sent his car down to drive her back to London.

It was an ideal opportunity.

She had to see her solicitor — her new solicitor — poor Mr Martin had died suddenly — probably the strain of this awful War — having to exist on a few ounces of cheese and a couple of slices of bacon...

Ellen was apologetic that she could not invite her to stay with them. Her son Conroy was coming home on leave, and her younger daughter Esme was coming — and Conroy's new girlfriend — Lucy Halbern — one of the Derbyshire Halberns — not very bright — rather horsey — but such a good family.
There was just no room.

Their grandmother was quite relieved — dear Ellen was very tiring — she never stopped talking, an endless stream of trivia — and the Lieutenant Colonel was a frightful bore.

She arranged to stay with Maud, Lady Osborne, who had taken rooms at Grosvenor House for the duration of the War.
'I couldn't run the house with no staff,' she said. 'Here everything is done for you, and the restaurant is quite good — no worry about eking out the rations...'
She still had one aged servant, who brought in the breakfast trays with hands that shook so much the china rattled, and the milk slopped on to the traycloth.
'I had to keep her on, poor old thing,' said Maud. 'She had nowhere else to go...'

Isabel wanted to know what it was like in London — whether the Lieutenant Colonel wore a Busby — whether his car had been camouflaged — had she seen the City burning, and the firefighters with their hoses — how did people find their way about in the blackout...?

Their grandmother said she didn't know if the Lieutenant Colonel wore a Busby — and no, his car wasn't camouflaged — and yes, there were a lot of buildings burning — and there didn't seem much point in having a blackout — the fires lit everything up, and she was sure the Germans knew how to find London — blackout or no blackout…

London was a very dangerous place.
She didn't know how Maud could go on living there.
The bombing didn't seem to bother her at all.
She slept soundly through the air raids, oblivious to the explosions and thudding gun fire, scorning the idea of going to the air raid shelter, comfortably furnished, in the basement.
'No ruddy Hun is going to get me out of my bed,' she said. 'Rather be killed…'

She was glad she only had to stay one night.
Just to meet Mr Cohen.
The windows of his office were boarded up, and there was rubble in the street.
He was a fleshy young man with crinkly hair firmly smoothed with brilliantine — excused military service because he was asthmatic.
He seemed very pleasant.
He suggested she let her house to some Arabs — a Prince — or Sheikh — or something or other.
He said she could make a lot of money. They were very rich…

She was not impressed.
She was very rich.
All the people she knew were very rich — or, at least, rich…
She didn't want to let her house to Arabs.
She didn't want to let her house to anybody.

Mr Cohen assured her the house was being very well looked after — everything was in order — no bomb damage so far…
If she would like to go and see?
She wouldn't.
She couldn't bear to see her house deserted — shrouded in emptiness — it was too upsetting.

'Very sad about little Naomi,' said Maud.
'Yes,' said their grandmother. 'Very sad...'
She didn't want to discuss Naomi with Maud.
She didn't want to discuss anything with Maud.
'I always thought she looked rather delicate,' said Maud. 'How's Bertie managing?'
'As well as can be expected,' said their grandmother — shuddering with kaleidoscopic images of Bertie sitting with the green gin bottle — the girls with their wrists sticking out of ragged coat sleeves — Françoise smiling her mirthless white-toothed smile — the dismal brownness of the cold cottage...
'This dreadful War,' she said. 'This dreadful War...'

She told their father about the Arabs.
'I said absolutely not, of course,' she said.
'I don't know why,' said their father. 'What's the point of having the house sitting there empty?'

Isabel said it would be exciting to have Arabs in the house — gliding about in white robes with gold daggers stuck in their belts — silent in sandalled feet — sitting cross-legged among woven cushions, smoking funny curved pipes and eating Turkish Delight out of gold bowls — and dates — fresh dates — not like those sticky brown things, on sticky brown twigs in the oval boxes that came at Christmas...

Eleanor sought refuge in the broad branches of the oak.
Not Arabs — not Arabs in grandmother's house...
Arabs came from the terrifying desert where soldiers vanished — smothered by the shifting tides of sand.
Whole armies vanished in the sand.
Giant scorpions with clicking tails patrolled the desolate sea of sand. In the deadly stillness of night, the cold white circle of the moon threw the black distorted shadow of the Witch onto the silver sand, as she swooped low to see if the chill night wind which ridged and humped the sand, had washed up any bones — white brittle fingertips — to scoop up in her black bag of gruesome trophies.

She spread her hands on the comforting roughness of the bark — opening her eyes on the softly rustling green of summer leaves above her head…

It was alright — grandmother would never let her house to Arabs. They were foreigners, and grandmother didn't like foreigners. She didn't want to let her house anyway.
It was alright.

29

Bertie needed another cheque.
A substantial cheque.
What did he do with all his money?
He certainly didn't spend any of it on the children.
She looked with despair at the girls.
Were these unkempt urchins really her grandchildren?

'What about their clothing coupons?' she said. 'What has happened to their clothing coupons?'

Of course she knew what had happened to their clothing coupons.
Françoise had used them for herself.
She was wearing a new green twinset — how she disliked green — so unlucky — and a tweed skirt.
And she had a camelhair coat.
How on earth had she managed to find a camelhair coat? It was impossible to get things like that now — quite impossible. One was lucky to find a rough woollen Utility coat — and that would probably take a whole year's coupons…
No doubt Bertie had bought it on the black market like everything else.

'Really, Bertie,' she said. They have to have clothes…'

Their father said there were no clothing coupons — they had had some pyjamas.

Françoise merely shrugged.

Last year they had had pyjamas.
Aunt Sissy had sent them pyjamas.

And what about Naomi's jewellery?
What had happened to Naomi's jewellery?
The pigskin jewel case with the gold monogram?
She had had some exquisite pieces.
The amber brooch Françoise was wearing looked very familiar.
She didn't want to think about it.
She couldn't ask Bertie about Naomi's jewellery.
It was never possible to talk to him alone.
Françoise was always there — a silent, malevolent presence.
It was all too dreadful.

She suggested Françoise should teach them French.
What was the point of having a French girl — she didn't like to say
maid, although that was what she was, a maid — what was the point
unless she taught the girls some French?
It was essential to speak a little French.
All properly educated people spoke a little French.
This is an ideal opportunity for the girls to become fluent,' she said.

Naomi had spoken fluent French.
She and Bertie had spent so much time in France.
They loved France.
Naomi had bought her clothes at Molyneux.
She was always beautifully dressed.
She had had singing lessons with an Italian soprano who had an
apartment on the Avenue Foche — lined with mirrors.
You could see yourself from every angle — very disconcerting.
She was a funny little woman with a moustache, dressed in dusty
black like a concierge — slopping about in bedroom slippers.
They had many French friends.

Goodness knows what had happened to them all.
There had been no news of the Comte and Comtesse with their

sickly little boy.
A vain woman — always wore too much rouge and face powder — or of the famous baritone — what was his name? Maurice something. Such a wonderful voice.
And what of the others?
Her pretty manicurist.
The chambermaid at Le Crillon where they used to stay. Really she preferred the Ritz, but stayed at Le Crillon when Bertie and Naomi were there.
The manager of the Ritz was such a charming man — filling her room with fresh flowers.
She supposed the Ritz and Le Crillon were full of Germans now.
Harry had always said you couldn't trust the Germans.

Europe was a German encampment.
A huge swastika hung over it.
Acquiescence cringed beneath its black folds.
Its gaunt hands scorched in the flames of resistance.

'It was so wonderful to motor to the South of France,' she told them. 'To get in the Rolls and drive through the scented countryside…'

From Paris to Beaune to stay with the Blanchards in their round-towered chateau among the vine covered slopes, and then down to the Mediterranean, taking the coast road from Marseilles to Nice.
To walk along the Promenade des Anglais in the evening sun, the sapphire blue sea striped with violet — smelling the salty air and the flowers — roses and carnations…
To sit on the terrace of the Negresco and sip champagne, and eat a little lobster with a wonderful sauce…
How she detested this dreadful war.

Isabel said the sea must be lovely and warm. 'Is the sea lovely and warm?'

Their grandmother said she never went in the sea. The sun was so very bad for the skin — terribly ageing, and salt water was terribly bad for the hair — took out all the natural oils…

'Were there yachts?' said Isabel. 'Super, grand yachts?' 'Yes,' said their grandmother. 'There were a lot of yachts...'

A great many yachts — elegantly superior — gleaming with fresh paint and polished brass rails — their crews impeccable in white uniforms with gold epaulettes. The guest lists a catalogue of European nobility — so many princes, dukes and counts, kings and ex-kings, and famous film stars to add a touch of glamour and excitement.
Nobility can be very dull — and, in many cases, impoverished...

'Do they have proper bedrooms?' said Isabel.
'I'm sure they do,' said their grandmother. 'And proper bathrooms...'
'Haven't you been on one?' said Isabel. 'Didn't you ever go on a yacht...?'
'I was invited,' said their grandmother.
She had had many invitations — Contessa Abrizzi — an impossible woman — the McKellans — American multi-millionaires — dog food or something — and Luigi, Prince Luigi Massimo — so charming and hospitable — what a pity they were now our enemies — this dreadful war.
That little upstart Mussolini, with his ridiculous hat, had caused so much trouble.
'I was invited by an Italian Prince,' she said. 'There were a lot of Italians on the Riviera before the War. They all seemed to be Princes...'

Eleanor wondered if the Italian prisoners who worked on the farms in their brown uniforms with large black circles on the back were Princes. They were always very jolly — calling out and waving from the back of the trucks that took them to the fields.

'Why didn't you go?' said Isabel.
'I never go on boats,' said their grandmother. 'I don't care for the water — boats are very pretty to look at — there were a lot of pretty boats...'

There had been so many little boats — their sails like white birds skimming the water — dipping and curling on the glittering aquamarine surface…

'I like to look at them,' she said.

She had tried to persuade Harry to buy a villa.
A villa overlooking the sea — where she could watch the boats and the froth of ice-white foam caressing the sharp black rocks — with a garden shaded by magical umbrella pines — where geraniums grew wild among fragrant bushes.

It seemed such a long time ago — another world.
A world of glamour — lavish parties on seductively warm summer nights.
Dining and dancing beneath an indigo velvet sky embroidered with stars…

Now everything was drab and difficult. Coupons and queues. Hoarding old scraps of lipstick and the last drops of scent. Listening to the nightly news bulletins of casualties and defeats — waiting for the siren and the first wave of bombers…

She told Bertie it was much safer in Devon.
It would be much safer for the children to be in Devon.
There were very good schools.
There was no response.

They were really sorry when she left.
She had bought sausage rolls and iced buns from a shop in Bembridge — homemade — very expensive — and had their hair cut properly.

'Oh well,' said Isabel. 'C'est la vie.'
'What's that?' said Eleanor.
'It means 'That's life' in French,' said Isabel. 'We're doing it in school now…'

Of course Françoise had refused to teach them French.
Not even a little French conversation.

She had come to England to learn English, not to speak French.
She refused to teach them anything.
Eleanor taught herself to knit with scraps of wool on two pencils.
They kept their books hidden.
Françoise hated them reading.
She only read magazines.
She said reading was a waste of time. If she caught them with a book, she would set them some particularly nasty chore.

30

The Blanchards had managed to escape, making a circuitous journey through France and across the Pyrenees to Spain, and then to England on a diplomatic flight with some Embassy staff returning to London.

They had had to leave the smooth stone chateau with the cellars of wine — their wine — Blanchard et Fils — Premier Cru — a black and white drawing of the chateau on the label — 'Bottled at the Chateau' — the ornamental ponds thick with creamy pink-tipped waterlillies and flashing darting goldfish.

Now it was the local German headquarters.
Black-booted sons of Deutschland clicked and strutted the length of the cool-tiled passages, and stood at ease among the manicured hedges.

They invited them all to dinner at the house their father had found them in the woods outside Bembridge.
They had been friends for many years — he and their mother had often stayed at the chateau — walking among the sloping vineyards and lunching on the grey paved terrace, trailing with flowering creepers — dishes of melon and raspberries — peaches and fresh figs — baskets of crisp rolls to eat with the many cheeses.

The house he had found for them was very primitive — no electricity or hot water, with tiny dark rooms.

It was only temporary — they were looking for a house in London — undeterred by the air raids.
They had not come all this way to be killed by a bomb in London.

Françoise had not wanted to go.
She hated meeting people who had known their mother.
She hated meeting anybody.
She hadn't wanted to take them, but the Blanchards had insisted.
But of course they must bring the girls.
They were looking forward so much to seeing them.
Their own children — a girl and two boys — would very much like to meet them.
They were all about the same age.

They had nothing to wear.
Aunt Sissy sent them two frocks she had picked up in one of the sales held to raise money for the WVS.
'They might be a bit big,' she wrote, 'but you'll soon grow into them…'
Eleanor's was plum velvet with puffed sleeves and a floppy lace collar. Isabel's an unflattering royal blue with long sleeves and a Peter Pan collar. They didn't fit anywhere.

'Nanny said it's what you are that matters not what you wear,' said Eleanor.
'She would,' said Isabel. 'Grandmother used to complain that she had green mould growing on her hat. Anyway, she wore a uniform…'
'She said it was really bad to be vain,' said Eleanor. 'People shouldn't spend lots of time thinking about how they look…'
'Well,' said Isabel, 'this terrible colour makes my face yellow. I look as if I've got jaundice. I don't think we could be accused of being vain. You look really stupid. If you tie that sash thing a bit tighter it might help. We'll just have to pretend we are wearing absolutely gorgeous dresses…'

Françoise wore their mother's black velvet wrap and her diamond and sapphire necklace and matching bracelet.
She had decided she was not going to enjoy herself, remaining sullen

and silent, refusing to join in the animated talk, even though most of it was in French.

Madame Blanchard was small, plump and pretty with short black curls and a lot of mascara.
She produced the most delicious meal from the cubby hole of a kitchen with only a wood burning stove.
Huge platefuls of cêpes fried in garlic and parsley, and a sumptuous apple tart with a thick toffee glaze.
It was a lovely evening.
They forgot their dreadful dresses — enjoying the warmth, the food and the friendliness.

'We are so lucky to be here,' they said. 'So very lucky… so many have not been so fortunate…'

*   *   *

Isabel spread a piece of paper on the floor.
'This is a map of the countryside near the frontier,' she said. 'We will drive as near as possible, leave the car, and go the rest of the way on foot…'
'What if we are seen?' said Eleanor.
'We can say we're picking mushrooms,' said Isabel.
'It's the wrong time of year for mushrooms,' said Eleanor.
'Well firewood then. We'll take a sack and say we're collecting firewood…'
'What about our papers?' said Eleanor.
'Jacques will bring our papers at nightfall. If we are stopped, we are to say we're visiting a sick aunt in Valain, that's a village close to the border. Jacques has arranged for a Madame Dauphin to be our aunt…' She folded up the piece of paper.
'We'd better get some sleep,' she said.

31

The Blanchards soon moved to London.
It was not difficult to find houses in London at that time — most people had left, fearing the bombs and impending invasion.
They bought a large house in Sussex Square with the money they got from selling jewellery they had managed to bring with them.

Françoise was painfully scathing about them, and their jewellery, but at least she could not accuse them of being Jewish.

They invited them all to lunch at the Free French Club in Cavendish Square.

Françoise objected to taking them.
'They're old friends,' said their father. They want to see the children...'
'What for?' said Françoise. 'What do they want to see the children for? Why do we have to take the children?'
'They're old friends,' said their father.

He made them wear berets.
It was not 'done' to go bareheaded.
They felt even more foolish with their outgrown coats over the 'too long' dresses and scuffed shoes.
'I don't think Nanny would want us to look as awful as this,' said Isabel as they tried to hitch their skirts up with belts. 'Refugees look better than this...'

Françoise had used their clothing coupons to get herself a black suit, and wore their mother's fox fur and pearls.

As they waited on the platform for the train to London Isabel said, 'We shouldn't be travelling in the same compartment, it's much too risky. You mustn't speak to me. Pretend you don't know me...'
She had rolled bread into pellets and given Eleanor one.
'If we are caught you must swallow it,' she said. 'It will kill you

instantly. It's a deadly poison…'

Eleanor had it in her coat pocket.
Travelling by train was dangerous.
She had vitally important papers wrapped in oilskin.
'I'm not going on a boat,' she said.
But Isabel said she must wrap them in oilskin — she might have to hide them somewhere — perhaps somewhere wet like a pond, or a well, or a lavatory cistern….

The train was halted just outside East Croydon because of an air raid.
The carriage shook with the thud of explosions — crumpled black clouds of shell fire hanging in the rain-heavy sky.

They took a taxi from Victoria.
Their father always took taxis.
He seemed unaware of the existence of buses or underground trains.

The Free French Club had heavy brown velvet curtains and greying nets — bright-eyed stuffed birds under glass domes and tarnished ashtrays on scratched brown tables.
A photograph of General de Gaulle, draped with a tricolour hung over the marble fireplace, in which there was a decorative arrangement of glass flowers on twisted metal stems, drooping tinnily in the sooty hearth.

The Blanchards ordered champagne, to celebrate their miraculous escape. Françoise didn't join in the conversation, staring fixedly at the crossed flags over a picture of the Arc de Triomphe behind the bar.

The dining room was very full, the tables almost touching.
Dapper men with trim moustaches and sharply-creased trousers, and women with sloppy mouths and high-curled hair, bent conspiratorially together.

'We have to beware Fifth Columnists,' said Isabel. 'They're

everywhere. Remember, "Careless Talk Costs Lives"...'

They had hors d-oeuvres of rolled soused herring, cubes of beetroot and vinegary potato salad, roast meat, and a kind of custard.

Madame Blanchard did her best to talk to Françoise, but she remained monosyllabic.

There was another alert whilst they were in the taxi on the way back to Victoria, and all the traffic was brought to a standstill.
They had to take a long way round to avoid bomb craters.

32

The soldiers had gone.
The school a deserted place of echoing dormitories and swinging doors — the walls scrawled with graffiti — banisters broken.
Convoys of camouflaged lorries and hooded guns trundled through the night.
There were whispers of invasion — the long-awaited invasion of Europe.
Rumours rustled the grasses, bending the purple-belled heather on the common.

The woods were silent as she cycled for the milk — invisible footfalls cracked the twigs and trod the fallen leaves.

Somewhere the Witch waited — in a clearing where the trunks of oaks lay rotting in the curling bracken — waited in the gingerbread house, the window frames glossy spirals of barley sugar — preening herself in front of the mirror, transformed into a blue-eyed blonde with wavy hair and frilled white blouse. Mirror, mirror, on the wall, who is the fairest of them all?
Isabel — Isabel — Isabel...

Her disguise falling from her — black cloak swirling round her spectral bones, she rushed from the house snarling, and smote the sky with upraised arms — startling the sentinel ravens, who rose in a black cloud over the roof of dark treacle toffee, and the cat stretched itself and smiled its self-satisfied smile.

Eleanor cycled as fast as she could along the uneven paths, bumping over protruding roots and through muddy pools, the rusty handlebars jarring her hands, brambles and sharp-edged grasses scratching her legs.

33

That summer, the summer of D-Day, she was finally allowed to join Isabel at school.

There had been several angry telephone calls with their grandmother, and Françoise had flown into a rage, banging about and cursing in French. She gave Eleanor more of the dreadful curds and whey to eat, which literally made her sick, and found her repellent jobs like cleaning the hen house, thick with muck and feathers, and the flour bin, which was alive with weevils...

There were only five girls who boarded.
They shared a bedroom in the Junior School, walking through paths of laurels to the Senior School for their lessons and meals.

It was strange being among so many people, sharing a bedroom with girls, who, apart from Isabel, she didn't know.
They were all very friendly, and one, Diana, helped her do her hair.
She had wanted to grow her hair, and had laboriously taught herself to plait.
Françoise said she couldn't have long hair unless it was plaited, and refused to show her how to do it.
Diana said she shouldn't scrape it back.
'It's not very flattering like that,' she said, and lent her some hairgrips. 'If you bring it up a bit on the sides it looks much better — sit still and I'll show you...'
It was a great improvement.

There was nothing much they could do about their clothes though. She had a second-hand box-pleated tunic which was much too big, a white cotton shirt that was too small, and an outsized rust-coloured jumper their grandmother had picked up in a jumble sale.
Isabel had borrowed a navy blue skirt and cardigan from Diana who seemed to have an endless supply of clothes, and bags of sweets which she shared. She had flowered pyjamas and a pale blue woollen dressing gown. She had a round face with big blue eyes and thick bobbed fair hair. She wasn't very clever, and Isabel helped her with her homework.

They were woken in the grey half-light of dawn by the roar of massed formations of Flying Fortresses passing overhead.
'It's the invasion,' said Isabel. The invasion has begun...'
Jumping out of bed, they leant out of the window, waving wildly in excitement, trying to count the planes, chanting 'It's the invasion — It's the invasion...'

The euphoria that the Allies had landed on the beaches of Normandy — that this was the beginning of the end of the War, soon faded. Hitler had unleashed his 'secret weapon'.

Miserably Eleanor was sent home with bronchitis.
She would rather have stayed at school.
Françoise didn't tolerate them being ill.
Of course the school didn't know that. They thought it would be much better for her to be at home. It was better for everybody to be ill at home, where they could be properly looked after. They were very short-staffed because of the War...

In the gloomy cottage on a day which seemed to have forgotten it was day — the sky dirty and unwashed — there were warnings on the wireless about a new threat — flying bombs — unmanned rockets packed with high explosives — lethal weapons.
It was expected they were to be launched in large numbers...

The announcer's voice was sombre and precise.
It was necessary to be prepared.

When the engines cut out, you had a count of seven to take cover, or, if that were not possible, to flatten yourself on the ground with hands behind your head to protect yourself from the blast.

This new horror — these sinister pilotless Doodlbugs as people called them, remorselessly spattering across the sky, opened up a new dimension of fear. Flames shooting from their tails, they proceeded, hideous and unwavering, Spitfires swooping and dodging in their attempt to shoot them out of the sky before they could reach London.

Waiting for the dreadful moment when the terrible gutteral clatter of the engine stopped, Eleanor often had to make the desperate choice between flattening herself on the ground and going home to Françoise with her clothes dirty, or risking possible death or injury. She always chose the latter.

One night whilst she was still at home, the school had the windows blown out by a Doodlebug which crashed in the neighbouring woods, setting the trees ablaze.
Isabel, fearless as always, organised the smaller children into an orderly crocodile, hands linked, and led them to safety.

Françoise didn't believe she had bronchitis.
She wasn't ill — she was faking — she was just a nuisance.
She couldn't even fetch the milk — their father said there were too many flying bombs.
Eleanor was sure Françoise would have been more upset at losing the milk than if she were blown up…
She must go back to school.

She was glad to go back to school.
Glad to be anywhere away from Françoise and their father.

34

They recruited Norma as a look-out.
She was not a boarder as her home was just across the fields.
It had been a farm.
Now the outbuildings were lop-sided and decrepit, with sagging roofs, broken beams and rotting hay.
Pools of stagnant water in the yard, spreading from blocked drains.
Norma's father was in the Army.
Her mother was never there.
Too tall for her age, with badly cut hair and bruised knees, she seemed as neglected as they were, with ill-fitting clothes and broken shoes.

During the afternoon when the boys played games, the girls had 'free time'.

They scrambled through the laurel bushes, and slithered down the muddy slope among the scrubby bushes and trees with roots sticking out, where the earth had fallen away.
At the bottom a stream flowed alongside a fence.
They were going to blow the bridge.
'Cut off their retreat,' said Isabel.
They tied string to a stone and lowered it into the water.
'Keep down,' said Isabel. 'We mustn't be seen…'

They had left Norma on guard at the corner of the box hedges by the playing fields.
If she saw the enemy approaching she was to whistle 'La Marseillaise'.
She wasn't much good at whistling.

She called down to them to hurry.
The bell's gone for Prep,' she said. 'We'll be late.

Norma and Isabel were in the same class.
They were both clever, getting top marks in all the subjects.
Norma was particularly good in Latin.

There was only one other girl in Eleanor's class.
She was a day girl, who came every day on the bus from Bembridge.
She had shiny brushed hair and spotless white blouses with little pearl buttons.

Their form master, an unpleasant bully, enjoyed ridiculing the girls, threatening to beat them if they did not answer his questions correctly.
They sat close together, gripping the edge of their desks, praying they would know the answers.

They had powdered egg scrambled for breakfast — yellow glutinous lumps sliding on the plate.
Eleanor had two helpings.
She was always hungry.
She managed to save some toast for Norma.

Norma's home was as decrepit as the outbuildings — dark, dirty and cold.
There were basins on the floor to catch the rain water which came through holes in the roof — the chairs were damp and sticky — the diamond-paned windows thick with grime.
There was no light — no fire — nothing to eat.
Norma seems to live on bacon rinds and cold porridge.
It was a good thing she had lunch at school.

She was always afraid her mother might come home and find them there. 'She doesn't like people coming to the house,' she said. 'Why don't you come and have supper with us?' said Isabel. 'It's macaroni cheese on Thursdays, and there's always masses…'

35

That summer — the summer of D-Day — the summer when the Doodlebugs terrorised the sky, and even the most stoical became nervous and apprehensive, they were allowed to go to Devon to stay with their grandmother and Aunt Sissy for the holidays.

It had been a battle, but this time their grandmother would not be defeated.

She accused their father of endangering their lives, and refused to take any notice of Françoise's tantrums.

'I insist,' she said. 'I insist that the girls come, at least for the school holidays...'

She did not add 'otherwise there will be no more cheques' — that would be blackmail. However, she made it clear that this time there were to be no arguments.

The train was full of soldiers.

The corridor was full of soldiers.

Their compartment was full of soldiers — weary soldiers laden with packs and rifles.

They were squashed among khaki knees and khaki kitbags.

Were they going to France — or coming back from France?

Their faces streaked grey with fatigue.

Some of them slept, heads lolling on each other's shoulders. Some smoked, or just sat, thinking of their last leaves — the last battle — the battle to come...

It was a long, slow journey.

The train kept stopping — jerking to a halt, quietly hissing — between embankments spread with tall white cow parsley, yellow buttercups and toppled trees.

Stopping at all the stations — the small ones deserted, the platforms of the large ones crowded with more soldiers, and sailors, ATS and groups of Red Cross nurses.

The soldiers had packets of sandwiches, slabs of fruit cake and bars of chocolate.

'Haven't you kids got any food?' said one. He had fair curly hair and looked very young. 'No,' said Isabel.

'Fancy sending kids off without any food,' said another, older, with nicotine-stained fingers. 'Here...' and he handed over a corned beef sandwich. 'Thank you,' said Isabel. Thank you very much...'

One of the others gave Eleanor a sandwich and half his chocolate, and another gave them some fruit cake. They were very hungry.

When they got to Exeter the soldiers helped them off the train with their suitcase and gas masks.
'Have a good time,' they said, and the young one waved as the train moved slowly out of the station.

'Where do you thing they're going?' said Eleanor.
'Plymouth,' said Isabel. 'They'll be going to Plymouth to go to France…'

Eleanor prayed silently. 'Please God, don't let them be killed. Please God…'

It was evening when they reached the house — calmly serene in the summer dusk.
Aunt Sissie welcomed them with her wonderful egg sandwiches.

Their room was so comfortable — the beds so comfortable — fine linen sheets — soft pillows — bedside lights — piles of magazines — a tin of biscuits — huge bath towels — scented soap —jars of bath salts.

Their grandmother and Aunt Sissy expressed consternation at the contents of their suitcase.
A proper leather suitcase with their father's initials stamped on the lid in gold leaf.
The contents, however, were pathetic.
Aunt Sissy was so angry that she left the room.
They heard her going down the stairs saying, 'That woman. It's a disgrace…' and their grandmother murmuring assent.

That summer the sun shone.
The days were golden and peaceful.
The waterfalls in the river at the bottom of the sloping lawn bubbled silken crystal water over mossy rocks.
The umbrella leaves of the plants on the banks spreading a green shade as they dangled their feet in the ice clear water.

Over the stone bridge, where the water tumbled wildly over rocks

in a tunnel of trees, to the kitchen garden, an abundance of fruit and vegetables. Long green beans hung among the leaves and little red flowers twined the bean sticks — fragrant warm raspberries — staining blackcurrants — translucent red currants — strawberries nestling beneath protective brown netting — sharp, milky-stemmed lettuce — fat-podded peas and sweet tomatoes — bushes of sage and mint, thyme and parsley.
The orchard of crusty-barked apple trees, and dwarf hedges of fat yellow pears.

Over the wooden bridge, overgrown with ivy, to the wooded paths, and little stream that ran all round the back wall, beside the beech trees — the paths crunchy with beech nuts.

They were free to go where they liked — to do what they liked.
They went to the beach and swam in the sea.
Aunt Sissy took them to her golf club and gave them golf lessons, and taught them to play bridge.
They went everywhere in her little green car.
To the cinema in Exeter and Torquay.
Their grandmother adored the cinema.
They saw Fanny By Gaslight and The Man In Grey with James Mason, and The Major And The Minor and Lady In The Dark with Ray Milland, The Bridge Of San Luis Rey and Love Story.
Their grandmother adored Ray Milland.
Isabel was crazy about James Mason.
Eleanor loved all the films and Aunt Sissy went to sleep.
Sometimes the would fetch golden-battered fish and thick chips from the Fish and Chip shop on their way home — or crisp shiny pasties, juicy with meat and potato...

The War receded — a daily crackling report on the wireless, between concerts and plays...

*　　*　　*

Uncle Rick never emerged from his studio.
Aunt Sissy took them in once to say 'Hello'.

They stood awkwardly among the stacked canvasses, loose golf clubs and piles of dog-eared books.

'Bertie's girls are here,' she said.

He took no notice of them, standing by his easel smoking a cigarette.

'Do you think he ever comes out?' said Eleanor.

'Probably when everybody's gone to bed,' said Isabel. 'Artists don't like people much…'

There was no place for the Witch.

Everything was too wholesome.

Even the outbuildings in the cobbled yard where the fig tree, laden with purple fruit, spread its branches on the white-washed walls, even the outbuildings were clean and tidy, smelling of last year's apples and freshly cut wood.

Enraged she conjured up a storm — spearing the sea with shafts of lightning — convulsing the water into high curling waves, breaking in a foaming mass on the promenade — hurling shingle on the road. Whipping the wind to a frenzy — dislodging tiles — painfully bending trees — twisting the branches — tearing the leaves — strewing the ground with unripe pears and apples and broken plums.

The rain a black sheet of sharp water filling the river to overflowing — flattening the flowers — shredding their petals onto the muddy earth.

Eleanor moved as fast as she could over the uneven pavement — the force of the wind preventing her from running.

Below in the stinking stagnant water, the crocodiles thrashed their tails, gnashing their greedy teeth.

She must keep to the squares, but the paving stones were cracked and wobbly and the wind made her lose her balance.

The Witch pursued her, her black cloak billowing in the wind — blotting out the light — trapping her in its suffocating folds.

Isabel said, 'Wake up — the storm's over — get the covers off your head…'

She got out of bed and pulled back the curtain.

The rain had stopped — the clouds puffily scudding across a pale moonlit sky.

The magic of the moon had been too strong for the Witch — banishing her with its silver light — soothing the turbulent waves — calming the wind.

It was over too soon that summer — gone too quickly.
In the slow smutty train back to London they saw the leaves had begun to fall.
There were no flowers on the embankments.
They shared the compartment with two WAAFS and an old lady.
This time they had their own food.
Aunt Sissy had made sure they had plenty of sandwiches and some sticky homemade honey cake.

'Back to War,' said Isabel. 'Back to the trenches…'

36

Despite the Allies inexorable advance, there seemed no sign the War was nearly over.
The daily wailing air raid sirens warned of guttering Doodlebugs and droning squadrons of enemy bombers.
People's hopes of peace before Christmas faded, and as the Allied armies marched into Germany, the Germans unleashed their monster secret weapon, a huge flying bomb which came with such speed that it was unseen and unheard
 until it exploded, wiping out whole streets — blocks of flats, shops and houses — swallowed up in vast craters.
All over Europe people scavenged empty-eyed among the ruins of their cities.

That winter it was very cold.
Bitingly cold.
With the chronic shortage of fuel, the school was drastically underheated.

They shivered in their beds, wearing underwear, socks and cardigans.
Diana brought her eiderdown, and had warm wincyette pyjamas, and cosy lined slippers.
They had the regulation blanket and cotton pyjamas, worn through at the knees and elbows.

Eleanor became ill again — really ill — shaken by a rasping cough.
Sent home, her temperature rocketed — even Françoise had to admit she was ill.

The Doctor was called, and ordered a fire to be lit in the bedroom.
'She must be kept very warm,' he said. 'It's certainly pneumonia…'

She lay in a daze of delirium watching the firelight flickering on the ceiling — drifting — drifting…

The cold white mist engulfed her — moist and suffocating.
She trod carefully among the coarse heather and vicious gorse — icy droplets running down her neck — her hair ragged and dripping.
Two German officers in black uniform stood on the path.
They had black motorcycles.
They had their backs to her.
She knelt on the wet ground, trying to hide.
It was sandy with little stones digging into her knees.
It sucked her down — she tried to grasp the bushes — tearing her hands on sharp spikes.
One of the Germans turned towards her.
He had yellow eyes gleaming under the peak of his black hat with the silver eagle — its silver wings spread ready for flight.
It had yellow eyes too.
Yellow eyes like the Witch's cat.
She could hear the Witch laughing — a screeching cackle as she fell — down — down — down into the swamp of crocodiles…

The fire was still alight — a friendly glow in the blacked-out room.
She would not sleep again — she did not want to dream — she would stay awake and watch the fire burning golden in the grate.
She wished there could always be a fire.

37

She did not go back to school.
Isabel did not go back to school.
They ceased to go to school.
The bills had not been paid.
Again, the money their grandmother had sent for the fees diverted, spent on other things — sirloins of beef, best back bacon and slabs of Cheddar cheese — green bottles of gin, cartons of cigarettes, perfume and silk stockings, a bolt of tweed cloth and a cashmere twinset. Anything could be bought on the black
market.

They were not able to say goodbye to Norma.
Eleanor thought of her alone in the miserable dark kitchen.
'Do you think she'll be alright?' she said to Isabel.
Isabel was reading about Napoleon's retreat from Moscow.
'They all froze,' she said. 'The soldiers froze to death. They fell as they marched — frozen to death — the horses too...'
'Do you think Norma will be alright?' repeated Eleanor.

'I expect so,' said Isabel vaguely. 'Do you want to be a cavalry officer, or one of the infantry...?'
'I'd rather be a Russian,' said Eleanor, thinking about Norma alone in the derelict house in the muddy lane, where the branches of the trees plucked at your hair...
They were living off rats...' said Isabel.
She was already riding with the Emperor, poring over maps in the red and gold tent, weighted with snow, the lantern swinging in the icy wind...

'She must be very lonely,' said Eleanor.
There were probably rats in the rotten outbuildings — rats in the yard — even, perhaps, rats in the house, tearing at the mouldy rush matting to make their nests, feeding their young on leather and bacon rinds...
She didn't like to think of Norma alone with the rats...

38

As the War progressed mercilessly to its end, Mrs Turton decided it was safe enough to return home, and they moved again to this house, nearer the village — near the church where their mother was buried.

Outwardly idyllic, in a hollow of shrubs and trees, with herbaceous borders and lupins and golden rod, and a small orchard of apple and cherry trees.

It was more hateful than the cottage.
It smelt damp and felt damp.
The sun, which burnt the grass biscuit brown, never penetrated the diamond-paned windows to bring any warmth into the gloomy timbered rooms.

They had the two servants' rooms next to the kitchen.
The sitting room had a table with a heavy brown cloth and several hard chairs.
It was airless, stuffy, and thick with dust.
They didn't care.
They were glad to be separated from the rest of the house — from Françoise and their father.

There was a spinney behind the tool shed, a tangle of small pines and rowan trees, Witch's trees, thick with nettles and brambles.
In the middle was a cesspit — the flaccid waters fizzing.
When the wind was in the right direction the sour smell invaded the house.

Françoise decided to breed rabbits for their fur.
She said you could make a lot of money from selling rabbit fur.
They spent their afternoons collecting sackfuls of dandelions to feed them with, wandering the lanes, hacking at the dandelions with blunt knives, and shoving them in the sacks with brown-stained fingers.

They must be fed up with dandelions,' said Eleanor.
'I expect they hate them,' said Isabel. 'I hate them. I hate her. I hate him. I hate this place. I wish I could leave and never see them again.'

No money was made from the fur.
The mothers ate their babies, and choked on fur balls.
They had a lot of rabbit stew.

Skinless rabbits frolicked in the field of yellow dandelions, singing 'Tiptoe Through The Tulips', the babies piled in sightless heaps.
The Witch swooped down, her fur cloak casting winged shadows on the bent grass — the rabbits vanished down their underground burrows — the dandelions crushed, oozing sour milky fluid.

39

They were sent with grocery lists to the village shops.
There were three that were possible.
One in the village, one at the crossroads, and one by the bus stop on the main road.
There were whispered consultations.
'I'm sorry, dear… you're not registered with us…'
'Can't let you have anything today, dear…'
The baker still let them have bread.
He did not speak to them, handing it over the counter, disapprovingly silent.
'Disgraceful,' said his wife, rattling the bead curtain. 'If it wasn't for those girls, I'd let them starve… supposed to be gentry.'

They had to do all sorts of extra tasks before Françoise would allow them to have a bath.
She had become even more cruel and vindictive.
The same miseries of endless washing up and cleaning repeated — the blows to the head — possessions confiscated.
No breakfast — no lunch — no tea — falsely accused of rudeness and slovenly behaviour.

40

Eleanor lay awake listening for the All Clear.
So now the War was over — was supposed to be over...
In the morning perhaps everything would be different now the War was over.

But nothing seemed different.

The church bells rang, and the people who had them, hung out flags.
There was not much rejoicing.
There was still the Japanese War.
Loved ones still hacking their way through jungles in the sweltering heat — shivering with fever — plagued by mosquitoes and dysentery — carrying their wounded on makeshift stretchers of bamboo lashed together with hairy creepers — soaked by the monsoon rains — advancing on swollen bandaged feet, to be cut down by whirling swords.
They had to leave their dead, alone in this hideous place, so far from home, so far from the comfortable countryside, the neat suburban gardens...

They did not transfer their imaginary games to the Japanese War.
They were too despondent.
They rode their bikes down the country lanes, and hid in their bedroom.
'It's probably nicer in prison,' said Isabel. 'At least you get regular meals...'

In the hot sultry summer weather the house smelt of mildew and sewage.

Gaunt emaciated men were seen in the village, returned from Prisoner of War camps.
Rationing continued, and the terrible revelations of the Death Camps began to occupy the papers.
Front page pictures of living skeletons, and piles of dead ones —

thrown higgledy-piggledy like heaps of rubbish.

Eleanor was sickened and horrified — the smell of death and despair confused with the scent of summer flowers and fermenting sewage.

Sometimes she managed to go to the churchyard to try and tidy her mother's grave, tearing at the long grass and weeds with bare hands.
She did not dare to take any tools.
She would get into awful trouble, and be forbidden to come again if she were found out.

She would go to the churchyard on her way to the village to fetch the bread.
She didn't like going to the bakers.
She knew they owed them money.
He was reluctant to serve her.
She had to say 'Would you put it on the bill, please…?'
She didn't look at him when she said it.
He would turn his back to take a crusty white loaf off the shelf.
'Just the bread,' he would say. 'That's all. Just the bread.'
He wouldn't let her have a currant bun.
'Just the bread…'

His wife once gave her a small sausage roll — an unheard of luxury.
'Shouldn't be allowed,' she said to her husband. 'They look worse than gypsies. It's a disgrace… Here dear, you eat this — looks as if you could do with it…'

Isabel was sweeping the yard.
She had been sweeping the yard when Eleanor had left to get the bread. 'Beastly woman,' she said, shoving the broom to and fro. 'Beastly woman… beastly woman.'

Françoise opened the kitchen window and shouted at Eleanor not to talk to her.
'Why have you been so long? Where have you been? Lazy little slut. Come in here at once. Now!'

They sat on the creaking springs of the mean beds, glum and weary.
They had to wash their underwear with Lifebuoy soap under the
cold tap in the basin, wringing out as much moisture as possible
before hanging it on the iron bedsteads.
When it had ceased to drip they slept on it to get it dry for the
morning.

Françoise did not let them have clean clothes.

'We should make a wax model of her and stick pins in it,' said Isabel.
'Lots of wax models — put a terrible curse on her — what could we
turn her into… ?'
'A slug,' said Eleanor.
'Then we could pour salt on her,' said Isabel. 'Salt is supposed to
dissolve slugs…'

The Witch screeched through the black sky on her black broomsticks,
the yellow-eyed cat smirking behind her.
In the darkness the giant slugs advanced, leaving thick slimy trails
on the dark earth, fleshy horns waving…

'Throw the salt,' shouted Isabel. 'Throw the salt…'

But the bag was empty, and she tripped and fell — down — down
among the thrashing crocodiles…

41

Françoise was to marry their father.
An inevitable awfulness.
'At least she won't want us to call her mother,' said Isabel.

She had been back to France to visit her parents, who had survived
the War, hungry but intact.
They went to Newhaven in a taxi to meet her off the boat, laden with
hats and things for her trousseau.
Her mother had sent them both hats for the wedding — felt hats with

grosgrain ribbons — navy blue and brown.
They looked absurd with their old, worn, outgrown coats.

Françoise chose a flamboyant hat, scarlet and black, with a veil, and tottering high heels.
Eleanor had a bilious attack — spots danced before her eyes, her stomach churned with nauseous curds.
She had to miss the small celebration their grandmother had reluctantly arranged at her flat in Hove, with the balconies overlooking the sea — wild and grey — the beach still fenced with rusty barbed wire, unsafe with mines.
She had managed to bribe a duck from the butcher, and Mrs Croft roasted it with sage and onion stuffing.
She ordered a small wedding cake from Zetlands — Mrs Croft wouldn't do Royal icing.

She gave Eleanor a Beechams powder, tucking her up with a lilac cashmere shawl on the soft couch in her lilac bedroom, and then went to her lilac silk-upholstered drawing room, the furniture painted with garlands of flowers, to greet her guests and toast the bride.

Nobody would have guessed how much she disliked Françoise, how angry she was that her son had chosen to marry such a dreadful person — a scheming liar — totally uneducated — unpleasant — and absolutely no breeding whatsoever.
Her father made cardboard boxes...
At least Naomi had been beautiful — poor little dead thing.

There had been so many really nice, suitable girls he could have married...

42

She was agitating again about their total lack of schooling.
'They're little savages,' she said. 'Really, Bertie, you can't let your daughters grow up like little savages.'
She had not forgiven Françoise for refusing to teach them French.
'They must have some grooming. What about a good boarding school…?'

It was decided they should go to the 'local' boarding school on the cliffs outside Brighton in January when it returned from its enforced evacuation to the Lake District for the duration of the War.
Their grandmother said it would be convenient, and she would be able to take them out at weekends.

Forms arrived.
A short exam had to be taken.
English — 'excellent'. Maths — 'needs attention'.

Then came the Clothing List.
They read it with much hilarity.
Never had they, or were likely to have, the items now compulsorily expected.
They barely had a change of underwear.
Eleanor had one vest and no uniform at all.
Isabel's Utility pyjamas were in holes — but she had a white blouse.
Somehow the Clothing List personified escape.
Somewhere there were people who actually possessed all these things.
Sports clothes — afternoon clothes — Sunday coat and skirt — night things — day things — socks and stockings — shoes for this, shoes for that — a Djibah.
What on earth was a Djibah?

It was a message from another world.
A world where you could breathe free and speak and live without fear.

Perhaps, at last, the War would be over.
The end of the War.
The end of the Witch.
Perhaps…

The end of the War.
The end of the Witch.
Perhaps…

Le Ciel Qui Pleut

The daughter looked older than her mother, her white anorak hardly covering her knees, her mousy grey hair, badly cut, the uneven edges hanging limply on the grubby collar. Her teeth should have been resolved as a child, now they clashed prominently, jagged when she grinned.

Hortense, her body corseted to thinness, hair a glossy red auburn, waved and highlighted. Her smart black costume with figure-hugging jacket. They walked arm in arm along the sandy gravel paths which circled the ponds of the Chateau.

It was Sunday afternoon. They had come with Clothilde and Armand in his canvas topped Citroen, with its deckchair seats. Clothilde, her lipstick a brilliant scarlet gash in her heavily powdered face, a perpetual cigarette hanging from her mouth, or between her long red-nailed fingers, worked in a bar in the Rue Belgrand. Leaning on the long silver chrome edged counter. Behind her a multitude of brightly labelled bottles. Ricard, Pernod, Sirop de Cassis, Pêche, Cerise, Framboise — all reflected in the long mirror which ran the length of the wall, lit with striped pink and green neon. She was always good to Adele. She had given her a cheap white plastic handbag with a mirror and purse inside, which she took everywhere. Armand had been her 'boyfriend' for years. He had his own charcuterie shop in the Rue de Bagnolet.

Hortense and Adele worked in L'Etoile, a two-star restaurant in the Boulevard Mortier.

Hortense in the lighted sentry box by the door, impaling paid bills on a red-cushioned spike.

She wore many large rings on her plump short-fingered hands. Adele worked in the kitchen, washing up the pots and pans. An impressive shiny white washing-up machine dealt with the plates and cutlery.

Hortense, liberally scented, presided autocratically over the cash box, entering the amounts carefully in her cash book.

Adele, hair and skin smelling of greasy dishwater, patiently scrubbed in her drab crossover overall, wrinkled stockings gathered in creases round her straight ankles.

The hours were long. They had one Sunday off a month when the patron's wife took over from Hortense.

They were given coffee and bread when they arrived at eleven, and then a good lunch at about half past three — soup, rillettes, cheese, salad and fruit, and wine if they wanted.

They then had the time until six thirty. They would go home and lie on the bed and have a little nap. Then back to the restaurant until midnight, when they had soup and bread and odd leftovers.

Today they had come to Chantilly with Clothilde and Armand. They had brought their own lunch. Thick slices of jellied fromage de tête sandwiched in crusty pain.

In the weedy moat the massed heavy fish floundered for the bits of yesterday's baguette.

They wandered slowly down the alleys of smooth-trunked, sky-fronded trees, stopping at the chipped statues, and standing aside for the horse-drawn carriages full of sightseers to pass.

Hortense bought curled, pointed icecreams from the gaily decorated carts, striped roofed, the ice cream scooped from under silver covers, the wafer cones stacked in glass jars.

Bernard Cronin, the Maitre d'Hôtel, flourished the red tassled menu as he ushered people to their seats, slightly bent at the waist. He had been sidling Adele into corners for some while now. Nothing had come of it. The restaurant was too crowded, the kitchens too busy.

Not understanding, she felt unexplainedly ashamed. She was supposed to respect Bernard in his black tail coat and winged collar, imperiously snapping his fingers for the wine waiter, complaining if the points of the tablecloths were not absolutely even, the table napkins properly folded.

She knew it was wrong that he was always trying to edge her into corners, but she did not know how to stop him. She was afraid.

He pressed her against the dank wall of the passage that led to the cellar steps. His soft maggot body trapping her as she tried to slide away. She tried to call out, whimpering. He was murmuring something.

Then she heard the merciful tapping of Hortense's high heels approaching. She was calling for her.

Bernard moved quickly, stepping to one side, smoothing his oily hair.

She shot past him, almost running, and opened the glass panelled door which led back into the kitchen.

Hortense was annoyed, where had she been? It was too late for games, she wanted to go home, her feet hurt. She helped Adele on with the too short white anorak, pushing her arms into the sleeves, scolding. Hortense and Adele shared the double bed in the cramped bedroom, untidily strewn with clothes, the curtained dressing table cluttered with bottles and jars.

It was Hortense's marriage bed — but Maurice had never come back from the war. She had waved goodbye from this window, and he had looked up raising his hand in farewell. He had been smoking. She remembered well the cigarette white in his fingers. She had lifted the small girl to wave too, weeping tears on the sparsely covered scalp.

Adele was a puny baby. Slow and awkward from the beginning. She had learnt to read simple books and write in a large childlike hand, grasping her pencil as if it were a knife, her mouth twisted with effort.

Hortense had been left to provide for her. She had been cheated of her youth, of her husband, and her marriage.

Gay and fun loving, she had spent her young years scraping and saving, hoarding coins in jars to pay the bills.

She had been at the restaurant for over twenty years, starting in the kitchens and graduating through waiting to the prestigious position of cashier. She had known some of the clientele since they were young men. Some flirted with her joking and nudging. At Christmas she received many presents and tips.

During the war the food was scarce, the chef had to use all his inventiveness to produce decent meals. The patron had an understanding with some of the lorry drivers who brought in supplies for the Germans, so things were not as bad as they could have been. They were patronised a lot by Germans.

Hortense took one of the German officers for a lover. She was propositioned by quite a few. She was a good looking woman, striking with her lustrous red-gold hair, silk-stockinged, curvaceous. They were mostly pleasant enough, some were too familiar, especially when they had been drinking, fondling her as she served at table.

The one she chose was a dull married man, she felt safer with him, she did not want to become too emotionally involved, also she had Adele to think of. He brought her extra food, cigarettes, silk stockings, scarlet lipstick, and sweets for Adele.

She put her to sleep on the sofa in the narrow sitting room when he came, bringing out her mother-in-law's monogrammed pillow slips and doily-ended bolster covers.

He was posted back to Germany, and she did not take another German lover. She did not want to be accused of collaborating with the enemy. She remembered those days nostalgically. There seemed to be warmth and hope then, people helped each other. She still thought Maurice would return.

When the Allies came, the restaurant was filled with Americans. She had an American lover. A tall husky married guy with cropped brush hair and khaki sleeves. He tolerated Adele.

She had grown gawky and gangling, shrunken into herself. She was no trouble. 'Elle est timide', Hortense would say protectively. He brought her tins of spam and chocolate, soap and shampoo, cigarettes, gum.

He took Adele to the park and pushed her on the swings on the small plot with broken slides and benches blistered by the sun, where the children scrabbled in the dirt trying to build 'sand' castles.

Everywhere there were flags and rejoicing, tinged with sad regret and bitterness, the little mounds of flowers on the corner of the streets where people had died. Sullen women with shaved heads conspicuously marked out as collaborators.

Hortense escaped that shame, nobody seemed to have known about Hans, she had been very discreet.

Dribbles of returning servicemen from the camps in Germany, or joyously with the Free French Army, proudly marching with De Gaulle up the Champs Elysees. A pandemonium of relief and excitement.

Her mother lived in a little village in the war trodden countryside north of Meaux. The village had remained implacably uncommitted to advancing or retreating armies, offering water and rough wine indiscriminatorily, regardless of uniform.

They remained isolated without power or telephone lines. Monsieur Cordeau the postman had to cycle to the next village to use the telephone if there was an emergency. That telephone too was frequently out of order.

As a child she had gone with her mother to the forest to gather mushrooms, brown spongy cèpes, frilly orange chanterelles, white mottled-capped parasols, scuffing her feet through the twigs and moss.

Her first boyfriend Robert's mother worked the level crossing outside the village, turning the wheel that lifted the barriers with a long heavy handle.

Robert had fair spiky hair slicked down with water and bony knees. They kissed gingerly in the rotten smelling shed behind his house, where his mother kept the paraffin and the winter potatoes.

Her mother was now an old lady, tending her small garden with its beetroot, cabbage and ragged tomato plants, a few hens scratching in the dust of the scrappy backyard.

Hortense rarely visited. It was a long walk from the nearest station, and there were few trains.

Maurice's mother lived in Crepy. She had always treated Hortense with disdain. She thought her uneducated, and was mistrustful of her abundant red-gold hair. Not the sort of girl she had wanted her son to marry. They had had a small wedding, she had worn a white dress of artificial silk, and a veil of coarse net with artificial flowers. There was a meal at the Cheval Blanc, pate, roast beef and cheese, attended by a selection of aging relatives with teeth problems. Maurice's mother had given her linen, and a fluted coffee set, grudgingly embracing her and welcoming her into the family. His father remained silent, sitting aside smoking foul smelling tobacco.

Her mother-in-law was bitterly disappointed with Adele. When it became apparent that the frail waxen baby was going to be backward, she blamed Hortense, making sour comments about peasant stock, and hereditary.

Hortense had not heard from her since Maurice went to war. If it hadn't been for Adele, she would probably have married again, she had had plenty of offers, but didn't want Adele's life to be disrupted in any way.

She had rejected Bernard's advances. She did not mix business with pleasure. Bernard's obsequious posturing did not appeal to her, and there was his aniseed-breathed complaining wife to be avoided.

Madame Cronin was 'nerveuse'. The floor space in the airless salon obstructed with small tables and spindly chairs. Every surface filled with ornaments, bowls, pots, curl-edged unused ashtrays, frolicking shepherds and shepherdesses, cute dogs, cats, naked cherubs, crinolined ladies. On the mantelpiece, next to the gilt carriage clock, an extremely ugly china parrot reflected in the large gilt framed mirror, leaning uncomfortably forward.

There was a faint smell of sick.

The bedroom spread with peach satin, thick nets shutting out the light. Here she lay most of the day, white and swollen, her rayon satin negligé loosely belted, eating sweetmeats, and leafing through magazines, petulant, complaining.

Hortense had almost married Marcel who owned the newsagent at the corner of the Rue Bertaux. His wife had died of cancer some years before, a thin ugly woman, unpleasantly amiable to all. It was a thriving business, and they would have been very comfortably off.

He lived in the room behind the shop, a dingy place divided by a curtain with one window high up in the wall.

He had been left with his old father-in-law, almost incapable following a stroke, who lay gurgling on a camp bed in the corner. Propped up he could manage to eat a little from a spoon, slurping noisily, and dribbling down his aged vest, his teeth short and brown.

Marcel served her sausage and noodles, cooked on the hissing gas cooker behind the curtain. They ate at the thin folding table covered in cracked oil cloth. The plates were none-too clean. He poured cheap rough red wine into tumblers.

One grey April day he took them both on the Bateaux Mouches. They sat in the 'lounge' on slatted seats, painted white.

Marcel's much-brilliantined hair gave off an overpoweringly rancid odour, which mingled with the diesel fumes. He wore an outmoded suit of toffee brown, double-breasted with wide lapels, the buttons struggling under the strain.

Adele was delighted with everything. Marcel had given her a transparent box of pink and white dragees wrapped in cellophane and tied with pink satin ribbons.

She would treasure this, putting it on the little table on her side of the bed, she would never open it.

She sat with her face very close to the window, so that she could watch the oily curdled waters nudging the side of the boat — and the sudden short darkness of the green-slimed bridges.

The fine rain hung, a fine veil in front of the looming buildings.

If Hortense could have been sure that the old man would soon pass quietly away she might have considered marrying Marcel seriously. She could remove him from the squalid back room. They would get a large flat, perhaps overlooking the Seine. She envisaged the entrance hall with a curly hat stand with a rack for umbrellas, and gilt-framed rose prints on the walls.

She would go to the Galeries Lafayette with Clothilde to choose stuff for curtains. Adele could have her own room with flower-sprigged counterpane and frilled lampshade on the bedside table.

For the moment her feet hurt. The new black patent shoes were really too small, but they had been such a bargain. She eased her feet out of them under the table and patted Adele's arm. She wished she would not sit with her mouth open.

The blurred towers of Notre Dame appeared on her left as the boat swung round the Ile de la Cité.

They had eaten the most indigestible meal. Salade of Gizzards, rather tough faux filet and chips, Camembert, pear tart and icecream. She felt slightly nauseated.

It was no use. For all its material advantages, she simply couldn't share a bed with Marcel. He probably never changed his underwear. She shuddered. He was very good to Adele, keeping her comics and chewy sticks from his shop, anyhow the old man would probably live for years.

She should have married Cyril after the war, but he had had no job, and Maurice had not officially been declared dead.

He used to pick her up and swing her round in his arms, dancing extravagantly to her record of Charles Trenet singing La Mer, or Piaf singing La Vie en Rose. She still had a wind-up gramophone. They would collapse breathless and laughing on the bumpy sofa. He had loved her hair, loosening it round her shoulders. He had made Adele laugh, playing childish games with her. Once he brought her a bottle of scent, which she still kept unopened in the drawer where she kept all her most precious things.

Adele was waiting for Hortense in the kitchen. She sat at the scrubbed wooden table in her too short white anorak, the white plastic bag cradled on her knees.

Vincent, the chef, had given her a bowl of chocolate mousse, which she had savoured slowly, spoonful by spoonful. She had got chocolate round her mouth, and carefully wiped it off with her handkerchief as Hortense had taught her.

Hortense was having a cognac with Mr Paul. He had been coming to the Restaurant regularly for many years. He lived in Lyon and came to Paris every few months on business. He always liked to have a drink and a chat with Hortense, showing her the latest photographs of his family, and having a moan about the modern way of life. Tonight he had ordered her a Baba au Rhum. The soft yielding sponge oozing golden liquid, sweet whipped cream softly mounded in the centre.

Vincent always kept titbits for Adele, a meringue, a piece of cherry tart, a round piece of Foie Gras with its charcoal-truffle middle. He was sorry she was as she was. He had two daughters, jolly, pretty lively girls, doing well at school, who would one day marry and have children of their own. Poor Hortense too, what a responsibility for a woman on her own. She was a good child, but she would always be a child. He supposed that was why Hortense had never remarried. She was a fine looking woman, with that wonderful hair — it was a great pity.

Hortense was a long time tonight. He asked Adele to put the empty vegetable crate out in the alley way that ran down the back of the restaurant.

It was awkward and heavy. Adele had a job to lift it. She had slipped the handle of the white plastic bag over her arm and it banged against her side. It was dark in the alley smelling of rotten cabbages and urine.

As she lowered the crate to the ground, she became aware that someone was behind her, half-turning she saw it was Bernard, coat unbuttoned. He moved quickly, pinning her to the wall, fumbling at her coat, pushing his heavy body against hers, his sour wine-breath on her face.

Bending her knees she sidled crab-like from under his slug-searching hands, and ran wildly knock-kneed, the white plastic handbag swinging against her legs. Silently she called for Hortense, the cries dumbly in her head, her breath coming in short gasps.

She came out of the alleyway, and, looking neither right or left, ran desperately across the Boulevard.

Monsieur Creton had had a good dinner at La Promenade. Escargots and filet of duck with green pepper sauce. They had had a good burgundy, liquers, and several pastis for aperitifs. It had been a jovial evening, and the business overtures were very promising.

He backed his car off the pavement between the small trees, which, during the day, shaded the dusty pavements and started down the Boulevard.

She came out of the alleyway straight in front of his car.

Mr Creton jammed on his brakes, leaping horror stricken from his car. He did not dare touch the white spread-eagled shape, the contents of the white plastic handbag scattered around it.

He ran, sobbing and incoherent, into the Restaurant.

Hortense was still sipping her cognac. Mr Paul was showing her photographs of his first grandchild, its red rubbery little face partially obscured by the ribbons on its blue knitted bonnet. It was vastly overdressed, with pompommed mittens and bootees. She made suitable clucking noises.

Bernard came noisily through the swing doors from the kitchen, letting them bang back against the wall. He already had his coat on. He went straight through the dining room, barely acknowledging Mr Paul with a thin lipped mouth smile, and met Mr Creton in the doorway.

Vincent was inconsolable. If he had not asked the child to put out the crate, he always thought of her as a child, she would still be alive. Something — somebody, had frightened her so badly that she had run away down the alley, straight into the path of Mr Creton's car. He sat at the kitchen table and wept.
The ambulance came and collected the pathetic heap. Hortense,

rigid with shock, sat beside the blanket-covered stretcher as it was taken to the hospital.

The police came. They questioned everybody who had been in the restaurant at the time, and search the alleyway. It seemed the young woman was mentally retarded and would have been easily frightened. The alleyway was very dark. They made no further enquiries.

Mr Creton had to be taken to hospital suffering from shock. He was gibbering and shaking, repeating that he hadn't seen her, she had run straight out in front of his car.

*   *   *

Hortense stood bleakly in her figure fitting black costume, a black hat with a veil hiding her red gold hair. She clutched a bunch of white roses to drop on the simple coffin after it had been lowered into the damp earth. It had rained throughout the service, little rivulets of water ran down the sides of the open grave. A young boy in black surplice held an umbrella over the priest as he muttered the correct words, making the sign of the cross.

Hortense was glad it was raining. A sunny day would have been unbearable. Clothilde and Armand supported her, other friends and acquaintances mistily around her. There were a lot of flowers. People had been very kind. The patron had told her to take a holiday, but she had been unable to bear being in the flat. She would probably return to work once the funeral was over. Tomorrow, perhaps.

Half her life had gone. Her heart was being buried now in the cheap wooden box with her daughter. The rain ran down her face mingling with her tears. Her smart black shoes spattered with mud.

Slowly she released the bunch of roses. They fell with a thud on the coffin. So be it.

The Meeting

The trunks had been sent on ahead.
They had only two small suitcases, Eleanor's Birthday cake in a fancy box, a bag with odds and ends for the journey, and their gas masks.

There were two other ladies in their First Class compartment. Two ladies in tweed suits — one with a jaunty feather in her high-crowned brown felt hat — the other wearing a squashed black straw, her cream pleated blouse fastened at the neck with a cameo brooch. They were deep in conversation.

Eleanor and Isabel had window seats.
Nanny had brushed their hair until it shone — as did their shoes — her last caring task before saying goodbye.

What was she going to do without Nanny?
She had had so little to do with the children.
She didn't even know what they liked to do — what they liked to eat — whether they slept well — did they wake at night...?
Isabel was engrossed in a book — Eleanor, her small, plain face peaky and worried, looking out of the window.
She had been going to join Isabel at school in the autumn — now Naomi didn't know where they would be, what school they would go to — whether there would be any suitable schools...

The man from the Ministry of Defence, in his pin-striped suit and regimental tie, had been very polite, almost deferential. He had gone to inspect the rest of the house with Bertie, whilst she remained in the drawing room with the Major — or was it Captain? — standing awkwardly with his gloves, had and cane under his arm.
'Won't you sit down?' she had said, and he had perched gingerly on the edge of one of the deeply comfortable armchairs.

They had been given hardly any time to organise their departure

— to arrange to have all their belongings stored. What about the paintings? The priceless china? The grand piano? The curtains and Persian rugs...?
There was nothing they could do.
The house had been requisitioned.

She had wanted to stay in London with Bertie at Uncle Alec's in Hyde Park Gardens, but Bertie had said it was better for her to go to Rick and Sissie — his mother would be there — whilst he looked for a house to rent.
She hadn't wanted to go. Sissie was always kind and thoughtful and Rick never left his studio, even for meals, but her mother-in-law did not approve of her — she didn't approve of any of her four son's wives — except perhaps Sissie, because she could boss her about.
She considered Naomi's illness a tiresome nuisance, as if it was not enough that there was a war on... refusing to acknowledge that she was, in fact, dying.
She knew she was dying. When Mr Simons had pressed her hand and said, 'We'll do out best...' and Bertie refused to meet her eyes, and talked about golf all the way to the station.
She knew it was hopeless.

The wolves came, silent on the silvered ground — patiently waiting for the flickering flame to drown in the melting wax — the frozen cobwebs of their breath motionless in the freezing air.

She had not wanted to leave the comfort and warmth of her home and all the familiar things she loved. She did not want to drift into death in a strange bed in a strange house.
Her nurse had been called up — the servants dismissed — nobody to look after the children... how could she look after the children? Increasingly frail, she could barely look after herself.
They were very well behaved. Nanny had done a good job — neat and tidy in their Liberty print dresses and jackets with matching piping.

The train was unbelievably slow, stopping at all the stations and between the stations — creeping and jolting along the tracks.

Isabel wanted to open the window but she said 'No', they would get covered in black smuts.

She had no idea how long the journey was going to take.
It was supposed to be an Express train.
There was no restaurant car and she hadn't thought to ask cook to make sandwiches.

The war was going badly. The British army was retreating — nearly to the French coast. There were rumours that France would capitulate — Hyde Park zigzagged with trenches and gun emplacements — the sky full of the shiny grey elephantine shapes of barrage balloons — their house requisitioned — and the tentacles of disease withering her bones…

Last summer on the soft sand of the beach at Le Lavandou the world was already changing.
The distant drumbeat of war mingling with the waves dragging the shingle, the little broken pale shells and polished stones shuffling back and forth, the swishing tread of armies marching…
Now the beaches would become graveyards — hot-barrelled guns aimed at the drowning.

The train pulled into Portsmouth, the corridor suddenly full of khaki and women and children struggling to find a place.
And their carriage was full.
A young woman carrying a small boy, two little girls, about the same age as Isabel and Eleanor and an older boy with a bandaged leg, the bandage blackened with dried blood.
They had dark curly hair, their faces yellow with fatigue, with shabby clothes and dirty hands, clutching bags and bundles, they squeezed themselves apologetically onto the seats.
The two ladies tut-tutted and drew themselves closer together.
The young woman sat opposite Naomi, cradling the little boy in her lap, his face milk pale.
'The boat,' she said. 'The boat made him very sick… it made us all very sick…'

Naomi fished in her handbag for barley sugar.
She always kept barley sugar when she was with the children.
Nanny had told her barley sugar was very good for travel sickness.
She held the bag out. 'Please,' she said. 'These are supposed to help…'
The young woman took one and unwrapped it for the little boy.
Naomi handed round the bag to the others.
'Thank you,' said the young woman. 'It is very kind…'

The lady with the feathered hat said 'Where have you come from?'
'Malta,' said the young woman. 'Many days on the boat. We are all sick — we leave everything behind…'
'Where are you going?' said the lady with the feather.
'Torquay,' said the young woman. 'We are to go to families in Torquay…'

Isabel said, 'Did you see any Germans — were there any submarines…?'
'One boat was torpedoed,' said the boy with the bandaged leg.
They all bowed their heads, and one of the little girls wiped tears from her face with the back of a grubby hand.
Naomi found her handkerchief in her handbag, leaning across to give it to the little girl, a small lacy square of fine linen.
'How dreadful,' she said.
'Some were rescued,' said the young woman. There were streaks of grey in her dark curls. 'Many were drowned. We were all very sick…'
Her voice faded.
These poor people had lost everything too — they had had to leave their homes — their country — they had nothing — at least she knew there were comfortable beds and hot baths waiting for them at the end of this interminable journey.
The little boy watched her with large dark eyes.

'The Germans are trying to push our soldiers into the sea,' said Isabel. 'They want to trap them on the beach so they can kill them easier…'

Naomi found her daughter's comments very disconcerting.
The school had said she was very grown up for her age — very clever

— imaginative — quick to learn…
'They fly their planes very low and machine-gun everyone….'
'That's enough, Isabel,' she said quickly. 'We don't want to think about things like that.'
She felt foolish in front of these people who had lost so much — whose future was so uncertain.

'My husband,' said the young woman. 'My husband works in the shipyards — they will bomb the shipyards — I had to bring the children away because of the bombing — they say we will be invaded…'
'They say that here too,' said the lady with the feather. 'We could be invaded any day…'

'Did you get shot?' said Isabel, addressing the boy with the bandaged leg.
He shook his head. 'I fell,' he said. 'The sea was rough — I caught it on a piece of metal…'

The little boy said, 'I want to go home…' and started to cry — big, slow tears.
Naomi searched for another handkerchief.
Eleanor got up and offered him hers.
'Don't cry,' she said. 'Please don't cry… it'll be alright…'

The pain had reached Naomi's legs. She would have to take one of her tablets. There was a small bottle of water in the bag with the children's books, drawing pads, and Eleanor's new box of crayons.
She couldn't swallow them without water.
The wolves moved restlessly beneath the frost-blackened bushes.
She wished that it was possible to get something to drink on this interminable train — anything — it was well past lunch time.

The corridor was full of soldiers with heavy canvas kit bags, smoking cigarettes, their rifles propped against the windows of the carriage.

The lady with the feather said, 'I wish I'd brought a flask — I never thought the journey was going to take so long…'

'We thought there would be a restaurant car,' said her friend. 'There's always a restaurant car on these trains…'
The little boy had stopped crying.
One of the little girls whispered in her mother's ear — the young woman shook her head, murmuring something back.
There was silence.

Naomi found her tablets and managed to swallow one with a small sip of water. She felt uncomfortable. All the children's eyes were on the bottle.
'I'm afraid this is all there is,' she said. 'Perhaps if we each had a sip…?'
She handed it first to Isabel, who said, 'I don't need any', and Eleanor took a tiny sip and passed it on to the little girls.
The hatted ladies waved it away. 'No, no,' said the one with the feather. 'Let the little boy have it…'

'What about Eleanor's cake?' said Isabel. 'We could eat Eleanor's Birthday cake…'

Naomi had asked cook to make the cake for Eleanor's birthday — she would be six the day after tomorrow — a special cake, to make up for having to leave their home and all their things, for having to say goodbye to everyone. How would they manage without Nanny…?
'We're going to miss them,' said cook, standing in the familiar kitchen with the heavy scrubbed wooden table and gleaming stove. 'Miss Eleanor to help with the mixing and shelling peas…'
She was going to stay with her sister — she would soon find another place — she was a very good cook and Bertie had given her excellent references.
'We shall miss you too,' she said.

'That's a very good idea,' she said.

Isabel was already standing on the seat trying to lift the box down.
Naomi knew she couldn't help her.
She didn't think she could stand.
She felt very faint.

The older boy got up to help, and between them they lifted it down.
'What are we going to cut it with?' said Isabel, opening the tin.
The boy had a penknife.
Naomi wiped it with Isabel's clean handkerchief.
She counted them all. There were ten including herself.
She carefully marked the cake into ten equal portions.

It was one of cook's lightest sponges, with a jam and buttercream filling iced with soft white icing with pink swirls and Happy Birthday Eleanor in curly writing, decorated with pink sugar roses. There was a little packet with six pink candles and six pink candle holders.
Naomi cut it into ten slices.
'We can use some paper from the drawing pads for notes,' she said.
Isabel got one of the drawing pads out of the bag and handed round sheets of paper.

'It's a very special picnic,' said Eleanor. 'We should make a wish — a special wish — though I haven't got the candles to blow out...'

The tablet made Naomi woozy. 'We can do something with the candles later,' she said, carefully wiping and closing the penknife before handing it back to the boy. He was very thin — the sleeves of his jacket too short, revealing bony wrists. 'Pass round the cake, Isabel,' she said.

There was a contented silence as they ate the cake. It was very good.

'You have to wish,' said Eleanor. 'Everybody has to wish...' She closed her eyes, her face puckered with concentration.

I just want to go home, thought Naomi. Like the little boy, I just want to go home... I expect that is what everybody is wishing — except perhaps Isabel — she is such a strange child...

'We should sing Happy Birthday,' said the young woman. 'It is your birthday and your cake...'
'I wish we could all go home,' said the older of the two girls.

It was the first time she had spoken — her face drawn and waxen with seasickness and lack of sleep.
'You mustn't tell your wish,' said Eleanor. 'It won't come true if you tell it...'

The little girl buried her head in her hands and started to sob.
Her mother stretched out a comforting arm.
'I'm sure it will be over soon,' said Naomi. 'The war — it will soon be over and we shall all be able to go home...'
The wolves had slunk away into the shadows. They would return when the pain worsened — they would come closer — always closer...

'It's Exeter,' said Isabel. 'We have to get off — it's Exeter...'

The hatted ladies got up to help them.
Naomi shook hands with everybody.
'I'm so pleased we met,' she said, and Isabel and Eleanor followed, shaking hands with them all. 'So nice to meet you' — 'so nice to meet you' — very polite. Nanny had been very particular about their manners.

'Hurry,' said the lady with the feather. 'You don't want to get left behind...'

Naomi shook the young woman's hand again. 'Good luck,' she said. 'I do hope everything turns out well for you.'

They pushed their way through the khaki mass in the corridor and out on to the crowded platform.

Eleanor turned to wave.
'Don't look back,' said Isabel. 'It is bad luck — you'll turn to stone...'

Naomi stood quite still — dizzy and weak.
Perhaps it would be better if she could turn to stone — at least she would no longer feel anything.
'Come,' she said. 'I'm sure Aunt Sissie will be waiting for us...'

What Dreams May Come

1

Fifty two
Fifty two dead.
On this spot fifty two men had died.

Fusillé.
The polished bronze plaque fixed to the uneven, crumbling stones of the wall which separated the orchard of lichened apple trees from the grassy slope to the village, almost touched by the spreading branches of the dignified oak weighed down with leaves thickening from the luminous lettuce green of spring to the dense green of summer.

On this spot — under these gently whispering branches, fifty two members of the Resistance were executed by the Germans on May 18th 1943.

There were no names on this simple plaque — just the stark record. On this spot on May 18th 1943 fifty two members of the Resistance were executed by the Boches.

The names of all those who died that day were carved on the stone memorial in the village square, with the names of the deportees and forced labourers who had never returned, and of soldiers who had died in the two World Wars. Wars to end all Wars.

Today, fifty two years later, there were many flowers laid against the wall and by the flag-draped memorial.

Today they were celebrating the fiftieth anniversary of the end of that dreadful war.

Gathered in the little square, the people of the village. Old men with medals — old women in black with empty faces — young women in bright cotton frocks — youths in jeans leaning on bikes, smoking

166

cigarettes — children politely quiet — children fidgeting to go and play.
There were men from the fire brigade — the Gendarmerie — soldiers…
The priest said a few words.
The mayor said a few words.
An old man, his jacket covered with medals, said a few words.
A young soldier played the Last Post on his bugle with the coloured cord.
The Marseillaise crackled from loudspeakers in the trees.
It was very simple and moving.

And then they all walked up the hill to the grassy slope, to where tables had been laid under the trees with crisp white cloths, and glasses of red and white wine, alternating, crisscrossing whiteness like jewelled bracelets among the little plates of almond-frosted biscuits and bowls of soft-petalled roses.

Gerard had not wanted her to come.
They had been invited to dine at the De Villiers.
They had quarrelled.

She could not bear the thought of dining with Hortense and Didier, in their ultra chic apartment overlooking the Seine in the glass-walled dining room.

They had a Vietnamese manservant, who was uneasily servile and silent.

She could not face the truffled foie gras — the lobster terrine, the roast veal à petits legumes — the bombe glacé — the Champagne — the wine…
The designer-clad couples — the women's skin tightened and papery — the dyed hair — the ostentatious jewellery, Hermes bags and expensive perfumes — Lust — Passion — Desire…
They talked about nothing at all.
The grim, bony spectre of past horrors hovering over the raised glasses.

Vive la France!

Gerrard said she should stop wallowing in the past.
'For God's sake — It was fifty years ago — Fifty years — half a century...'

It did not seem like half a century — more than half a century — since that dreadful day.

Her father had been working in the fields the other side of the village, with Monsieur Grigoire and his nephew Albert. He had taken his lunch with him — a slice of fatty pork and a hunk of rough bread.

Her mother, in her flowered blue cotton dress and blue apron, had been preparing the soup for supper with vegetables from the garden — carrots and peas, pale white turnips ringed with mauve, green beans.
The door to the garden was open.
There were pots of scarlet and pink geraniums on the grey stone step — warm in the evening sun.
She was seated at the kitchen table doing her homework — a page of arithmetic. They were doing multiplication...

First they heard the motorcycles — noisy and guttural — just like German — and then the lorry — the tyres slipping on the rough road — the gears grinding as it turned the corner.
Her mother stopped stirring the soup — standing deadly still — the ladle in her hand.

They heard the soldiers shouting commands — and then the gun shots — the terrible rattle of machine gunfire — and the birds rising in alarm — flapping like a gust of wind through the trees on the wooded slope — and then an eerie stillness.
More shouted commands, and then the lorry and the motorbikes came coughing and rattling down the hill and through the village and then — silence.
The village dared not breathe — frozen with unspeakable foreboding.

Her mother made a tiny sound — dropping the ladle on the floor, and sat down on a chair by the table.
All the colour drained from her face, tanned by the sun, leaving it stiff and waxen — jaundiced and shrunken — her hands gripping the edge of the table.

Cecile sat very still — clutching her pencil — panic rising in her throat — and waited…

Waited for the door to open, and her father to come in.
Waited for her mother to rise and stir the soup.
Waited for Madame Canneau's dog to bark — for Martin and Patrick Forgis to cycle past — free-wheeling down the hill — shouting to one another.
Waiting for something — anything — to end this paralysing fear.

As darkness fell there was a faint murmuring — a ghostly whispering movement — people began to go up the hill past the house.
Her mother hadn't moved.
She stared ahead with unseeing eyes — stiffly upright — as if she had died…

Cecile got up very quietly and moved the saucepan of soup off the stove.
The smell of the cooking vegetables filled the kitchen.
How could the soup smell so appetising if something awful had happened — surely nothing awful could have happened when the soup smelt so good?
Maybe nothing awful had happened after all.
Maybe her father was coming up the hill on his bike at this very moment.

She wanted to speak to her mother — to ask if everything was going to be alright — but knew somehow that she could not — so she sat down again and waited.

They found the bodies of their men — husbands, sons, fathers and brothers — heaped against the thick wall — the clumps of blue and

white flowers growing between the stones spattered with blood —
bundles of bloody clothes — legs and boots — arms outstretched.
Somehow they had to be carried and cleansed and buried.

Cecile heard the shuffling — the rustling breeze of weeping — the
creaking of carts coming and going outside — somebody coughing.

Later on she tried to feed her mother some soup — but her teeth were
clenched so tightly it just dribbled down her chin.

She went next door.
Madame Dubochet's face was swollen with tears — at first she just
stared at Cecile — unseeing…
'My mother,' she whispered. 'My father — My mother — She doesn't
move — she doesn't hear…'

Somewhere from in the darkened room Madame Dubochet's old
mother started shouting.
'Who is it? Tell them to go away — tell them to go away…'

Madame Dubochet took her hand, and they went back together to
the house where her mother sat motionless, gripping the edge of the
table with white-knuckled hands.

Walking up the hill in the sunlight with all these people in their
brightly-coloured clothes — young and old — the children waving
flags — talking and laughing — was very strange.
She had never thought she would come here again — to walk up the
hill past the house.
To stand on the grassy slope under the wide, comfortable branches
of the great oak — where her father and the others had been shot
dead…

The house was still there.
The middle of a terrace of small cottages.
First the Canneaus who had lost their son — then theirs — then the
Dubochets and Madame Dubochet's old mother in the blackened
hovel at the end, farthest up the hill.

Madame Dubochet had lost her brother…
The two middle houses had been made into one.
It had new windows and newly painted shutters and skylights in the roof.

There was a rose with fat, floppy pink flowers climbing up the wall where the two houses joined, and a bed of wavy hollyhocks by the front door.
A dark blue saloon car with GB plates was parked outside in the narrow street.

She sipped a glass of red wine and watched the children playing.
The sun was almost too hot.
The day after the massacre had been a hot sunny day like this.
She had been indoors with her mother.
She had not moved since the night before when she had helped Madame Dubochet prise her hands from the kitchen table and lift her onto the bed.
She had been very cold, and they had covered her with the warm quilt.
The quilt of gaily coloured squares.
Madame Dubochet came with bread and a piece of cheese and sat by the bed, whilst Cecile went into the hot, fragrant garden to pick a lettuce, crisply fresh with milky stems.
Her mother would eat nothing.
She did not speak.
Madame Dubochet managed to get her to take a few sips of water, slipping her arm awkwardly under her shoulders to raise her head.

Aunt Claudine came from Huberville.
A weary, bony woman in black.
Both her sons had been in the army, and she had had no news of them since France had fallen.
They could be prisoners of war.
They could be dead.

She had shrunk like a balloon, once buoyant with hope — gradually deflating to a shrivelled scrap of nothing as the hope seeped away.

The months turned to years — the flowers blossomed and died —
blossomed and died…
She did not notice the seasons any more.
She was permanently cold.
Now the War had taken her brother.

Her husband, Bertrand, a mechanic, worked at the local German
headquarters — servicing the trucks, and other vehicles.
It was a job — he was lucky to have it.
He was treated well.
So he worked for the Germans.
There was not much choice.
They still had to eat and pay the rent.

Huberville was about 12 kilometres from the village.
She came with the doctor.
There was no doctor in the village.
She came in his car — jerky, with faulty gears.
Doctors were allocated a certain amount of petrol.
He was a small man with thick black wavy hair, wearing a jaunty
spotted bow tie — red spots on yellow — and tan leather shoes.

Cecile was sent to 'play' in the tiny garden — the once neatly kept
patch, overgrown with weeds.
There were still raspberry canes and tomatoes — struggling among
the bindweed and nettles — and a few lettuces gone to seed — whilst
they 'talked' to her mother.

They could talk to her mother — but her mother wouldn't talk to
them.
She had not spoken since that dreadful night.
Cecile had to mash all her food and feed her with a spoon — coaxing
her like a baby.
She brushed her hair, and washed her face and hands.
She had to fill the basin from the outside tap, there was no running
water.
Madame Dubochet came to help wash her properly and change her
clothes — admonishing uselessly. 'Come along now Marguerite —

try a little — we have all suffered — what about Cecile...'
Her brother had been one of the broken bodies higgledy piggledy
against the wall. Her husband somewhere in the Army too, and she
didn't know if he were alive or dead.
Now she came to talk to the doctor and Aunt Claudine.

There were wooden benches and chairs placed on the grass.
The other side of the slope where the ground flattened into a straight
patch of grass, where there were no trees, a group of little children
stood with a young woman, holding white balloons, and two men
with wicker baskets of white doves.

At a signal from the young woman, the children let go of their
balloons, and the men opened their baskets to release the white
doves.

The balloons rose up into the empty, dizzy, blue sky — bobbing and
swooping in the breeze, and the doves flew among them with soft
white wings.

There was clapping and laughter and the clink of glasses.
The children looking up to watch the balloons floating away, their
little faces full of wonder and delight.

Aunt Claudine had not spoken to her.
She did not take off her cheap cloth coat.
She did not feel the summer heat.
She got back into the doctor's car and drove away.

Later an ambulance came with a nurse and a driver with a blue
peaked hat.
Madame Dubochet packed her mother's things into a bag, and
helped the nurse put her in the ambulance.
She did not look up.

Madame Dubochet took Cecile's hand as the ambulance drove away.
'She will be well looked after in hospital,' she said.
'They will look after her until she is better... It is for the best...'

She told Cecile she was to go to the Convent at Clermaison, twenty to thirty kilometres away on the hillside.
'The nuns will care for you — you can't stay here alone — the winter is coming — and your Aunt...' she shrugged.
'Your Aunt is not very well either...'
There was nothing she could do.
She had her difficult, demanding mother to care for, becoming more difficult and demanding every day, and now, with Charles gone — she did not even have time to grieve or fret over her husband's possible fate. Perhaps he would never come home.

The children were running now — running and dancing — waving their arms after the disappearing balloons — white dots — higher and higher — farther and farther. The white birds swirling together as they headed for home.

2

Gerrard said the brioche had an unpleasant texture — why did she not go to another boulangerie?

Cecile stirred sugar into her coffee.
Gerrard spooned honey on to the side of his plate, and spread it thinly on the slice of crumbling yellow.

His hands were thin and tanned.
As members of the exclusive Jeux des Anges sports club in the Bois de Boulogne, he spent most weekends playing tennis. There were squash courts as well, badminton, a swimming pool, and a gymnasium, where the wealthy tried to stay healthy and youthful, bending and stretching and lifting weights.

There was also a Michelin-starred restaurant, a bar for snacks — a coffee lounge — a shop selling designer sports wear and equipment, and a hairdressers and beauty salon.

Cecile enjoyed going to the Club.

She had always enjoyed going to the Club.
It was set in lovely grounds — shaded by towering chestnuts and frothy limes with their scented clusters of yellowy white flowers.
The railings hidden by magnolia and massed banks of rhododendrons — a tumult of colour in the Spring.
The lawns mown to a bouncy green carpet.
There were beds of shrubs and roses, and little pools with goldfish and waterlilies, with water bubbling from under the stones, and splashing fountains.
There was even a sundial.

She liked to wander in the grounds, and sit under the trees in the shade, or on the terrace and read — or just sit — listening to the comfortable plomp of tennis balls, and people calling to each other — little shrieks of laughter, disputes over the score...
And there was always the quiet luxury of the Club House.

They would often dine in the discreetly humming restaurant with friends of Gerrard's.

Hortense and Didier were members.
Hortense was having tennis coaching.
She had become increasingly enthusiastic since the advent of Henri, the new tennis coach, whose good looks had aroused a new dedication to tennis among the lady members of the Club.
She had taken up swimming and working out in the gym, to improve her physical stamina.
She had her hair restyled, and bought several new sets of sportswear — unable to decide between short pleated skirts and short-sleeved shirts, and sleeveless A-line dresses. Between all white — or white-trimmed with colour — or colours trimmed with white.

'You shouldn't wallow in the past,' said Gerrard, dabbing his mouth with his napkin. 'What is the use in wallowing in the past? What am I to say to Hortense, that you prefer to go to some God-forsaken village to celebrate with the peasants, than to dine with them? The Perrets will be there, and Ferdinand and Marie Kramer ... and Evelyn...'

Hortense was unbearable now Jean-Paul Perret had been made Culture Minister.
'Just a small affair,' she had said on the phone. 'Just a few friends — Jean-Paul and Thérèse — nothing formal...'

'I'm sorry,' she said. 'I have to go back...'

She could not go to a phoney celebration with Hortense and Didier and their superior friends.

Hortense had spent the war in England.
In the English countryside, riding ponies and attending a select girls' school.
Her parents had wisely left France whilst it was still possible, and her father had worked in the French Embassy in London.
Apart from sweet rationing, Hortense had been untouched by the War, and then she had gone to finishing school in Switzerland.

Didier's father had become very rich.
He had owned an armaments factory outside Lille.
The extent of his collaboration with the Germans would not stand up to much scrutiny.

She did not say this to Gerrard.
She said very little about anything to Gerrard.
They had nothing to say to one another.

Standing here on the grassy slope beneath the solid leafy branches of the great oak, watching the people busy with their celebration — the children trying to run after the disappearing balloons — the old men leaning conspiratorially together, deep in discussion — remembering — remembering...
She knew he would never understand, had never understood, her inability to escape from the shadows that haunted her — to shut and bolt the door — to walk away — not to look back.
To look back and turn to stone?
But she had already turned to stone, and the door remained threateningly ajar.

3

When the chill of autumn began to shorten the warm summer evenings, and cool winds blew flurries of gilded leaves on to the grass, she was taken to the Convent.
She went in the baker's van.
Monsieur Camil, the boulanger, was allowed sufficient petrol to deliver bread twice a week to the remoter houses and farms.
Clermaison was not in his area.
It was too far, but there was no other way of getting her there, and she could not stay alone any longer in the house with winter coming.

Madame Dubochet helped her to pack her things in a cardboard box.
Her few clothes — her school books and pencil case — some much-used crayons — a few bars of soap her mother had been saving — soap was very scarce — the jigsaw puzzle of Chartres Cathedral she had had for Christmas — her old rag doll...

She carried her winter coat which was already too small.

She sat next to Monsieur Camil on the front seat of his spluttering van.
The cardboard box with her coat had been put in the back with the bread.
He didn't speak.
There was not much to say.
Perhaps he had wanted to talk to her, but he didn't know how to begin.

They had to do the bread round first — bumping along the rough country roads — sounding the horn as they approached a village, or past houses or farms.
The people came to buy bread, looked at her curiously, and huddled to speak to Monsieur Camil.

At midday they stopped in a shady clearing and had something to eat — a stick of bread with some rough paté, and a bag of plums. Monsieur had some wine which he drank from the bottle, and some water for her.

They reached the Convent in the late afternoon.
It was high on the hillside — hidden by dark, silent pines — the road, hard rutted mud, a grey, austere building, the thick walls keeping out any warmth — the high, small windows keeping out the sun.

The nuns did their best.
They had very little.
There was a War on.
Finding enough food for them all to eat, and clothes for them all to wear, became more difficult all the time.

There was not room for many children.
The uncomfortable, unwelcoming metal beds with their thin mattresses of rough ticking, were crammed close together in the bare dormitory.
The cardboard box containing her things pushed under the bed.
One or two of the little ones had teddy bears propped against the lumpy ticking pillows, one had a felt dog with an ear missing.
A wooden cross hung above the door, and there was the obligatory picture of the Virgin in her blue dress, with a circle of yellow stars round her head, holding a very pink unwieldy baby on her lap.

The winter was bleakly cold.
In the refectory where they ate and did their lessons, there was a fire.
The huge fireplace piled with logs.
They all helped carry in the logs.
A man from the village came to cut the wood.
They all collected firewood — dragging fallen branches — filling sacks with snapped twigs.
There were two older girls — Anne-Marie and Nicole — the rest were under twelve, mostly under eight.
Altogether they were eleven children.
The nuns were not supposed to take children under five, or over fifteen, but in those extreme times nobody stuck much to rules.

Cecile was just eight.
She had had her birthday that summer.
Not a proper birthday.
Her mother lying with her face to the wall.

She had picked peaches from the little tree in the garden — downy-skinned — oozing sweet warm juice.
'Look Maman,' she had said, 'The peaches are ripe — they are really good...'

She had skinned one and cut it in little pieces, but her mother would not eat it.
She had taken the plate and sat on the hot, sun-bleached steps, the tears trapped in her throat.

Madame Dubochet had come fussing, propping her up firmly against the pillows.
'Come along Marguerite,' she had said, mashing the peaches with a fork. 'This fruit will do you good...'

She had not known it was Cecile's birthday.

After that there were no birthdays.
No special tea with little biscuits, and an iced cake with candles and Happy Birthday written across the top in pink icing — her friends laughing and singing, no crinkly, knobbly parcels to unwrap.

That first Christmas at the Convent they were each given a new pencil and a small bag of sweets, and they had roast chicken and apple pie for dinner.

The Mother Superior, a stern figure, tall and aloof, was, in fact, kindly and compassionate, known for her tolerance and hatred of the Germans.
She had taken in three Jewish children — two girls and a little boy.
The Convent did not take any boys — Jacob was an exception.
He was only three.
Everybody adored him. Everybody spoilt him.

Sister Agnes, who did the cooking, hoarded the ingredients to make him a cake for his third birthday — a sponge with a butter cream filling.
He had a small bed in Sister Celeste's room.

Their beds had been pushed even closer together, to make room for the two girls.

Jacob had been with a neighbour when his mother was arrested, and she had hidden him, telling the soldiers who came looking for him that he was away. She thought with his Grandmother. No, she didn't know where the Grandmother lived — perhaps in Lyons — or further south…
She had brought him to the Convent in the early hours of the morning, while the village was still sleeping.
Ruth, and Marthe, had come separately.
Ruth, who was thirteen, had been at school and had been told not to go home by her teacher. After hiding in the woods for a few days, living on sweets and a packet of biscuits, she had found her way to the Convent.
Marthe, who was ten, had been playing with friends when the soldiers came for her mother and father. The friends had hidden her until it was dark and then brought her to the Convent.

They had built a hideout for the Jewish children in the undergrowth on the thickly wooded slope behind the Convent, made of woven branches and bracken, supervised by Sister Constance who worked in the Convent garden, her long black habit tucked into black Wellington boots.

They all helped with the hoeing and weeding — digging potatoes and carrots — turning the soft, warm earth with heavy forks — putting the creamy, round potatoes and pale orange carrots into baskets to take to the kitchen.

4

There was a stall selling strawberries — the punnets of glossy, crimson fruit decorated with minature tricolours — the money raised to go to needy war veterans — or their families.

There was a red, white and blue collecting box, and a picture of General de Gaulle saluting, propped against it.

Sister Constance had not grown strawberries in the vegetable garden.
She did not grow frivolous things.
Strawberries were frivolous.

She grew sturdy, sensible things — potatoes and carrots — cabbages and turnips — haricot beans to be stored for the winter.

She couldn't prevent the cherry tree foaming with snowy blossom, producing a yearly abundance of glistening black cherries, or the plum's branches bending beneath the weight of the sweet, purple fruit, or the blackberries growing thick and wild up the wooded slope…

Sister Agnes bottled the fruit in glass jars, and made jams and preserves and sweet, delicious liqueurs.
They all helped to pick the fruit — their fingers indelibly stained with purple-black juice.

When the soldiers came on their regular visits, Ruth, carrying Jacob, and Marthe, would have to hide until they had gone.

They had tried to make the hideout safe and comfortable, and as waterproof as possible — always making a different approach so there would be no sign of a pathway.
There was always bottled water, a watertight tin of biscuits and dried fruit — some of the purple plums from the garden — in case they had to stay hidden for any length of time.

The Germans came at least once a week.
The soldiers in grey uniforms were not too bad.
They poked about a bit in the sheds and the dank shrubbery of dingy laurels and spiky holly, and took eggs and sometimes a chicken.

Sister Agnes was adept at hiding away supplies, but careful to let them find something — a few potatoes — knobbly cornichons — apples — a bowl of overripe tomatoes.
It was better to let them have something, than have them ransack the place.
The Officer in the grey uniform would exchange a few words with Mother Superior.
Sometimes he went into her office for a cup of herb tea — or a glass of one of Sister Agnes's liqueurs.

Mother Superior had given the young soldier two large bunches of carrots, which he held awkwardly against his tunic.

She said, 'They are nice grated — grated with parsley...'
She made a grating gesture with her long, bony, graveyard hands.
'Parsley,' she repeated, and bent to pick a handful — the broken stalks smelling deliciously tangy.

The soldiers in black uniforms were different.
They were the Gestapo.
Mother Superior didn't give the Gestapo bunches of carrots, or invite the Officer to have a glass of blackberry liqueur.

'Boys,' she said. 'We don't have any boys here...'

The Gestapo Officer tapped his boot impatiently with his stick.
'Where is the other Sister?' he said.
'We are all here,' said Mother Superior.
'You have four Sisters here,' said the Gestapo Officer.
'There are four here — three Sisters and myself,' said Mother Superior.
'I was informed there were four Sisters and yourself,' said the Gestapo Officer.

'Your informant was mistaken,' said Mother Superior.
'You only have eleven children here,' said the Gestapo Officer, indicating the line of children summoned to his presence.
'Why are there 13 beds in the dormitory?'
'We have places for 13,' said Mother Superior. 'At present we only have 11...'
'I'm sure I can find you another couple of little girls,' he said. 'If you wish, of course...'

They stood stiffly in a line.
Even the little ones didn't move as he looked them up and down — all praying that Ruth, Marthe and Jacob were safely in the hideout.
And what about Sister Clare?
She wasn't there.
Why had Mother Superior said there were only three Sisters? Sister Celeste taught them Maths, but Sister Clare taught them History and Geography, French and a little English. She was a very good teacher. She played the wheezing organ in the Chapel, and taught them hymns and anthems.
She was teaching Anne-Marie to play the organ.
She was much younger than the other Sisters.
Was she in hiding too?
Was she Jewish?

'There is an extra bed in one of the Sisters' rooms,' said the Gestapo Officer. 'Is that for the boy?'
'There is no boy,' said Mother Superior. 'The bed is there in case one of the girls is ill...'

After these visits, they all had to go to the Chapel and pray for the souls of their enemies, and for forgiveness for having to tell lies to protect their friends from terrible harm.

Somebody must have seen Jacob.
Somebody had tried to betray him.
Who would have done such a despicable thing?
There was the old man who came to chop the wood — but they were always careful to keep Jacob and the girls out of the way when he

was there.
Ruth was unmistakably Jewish…
Marthe, who was quite fair, would have passed unnoticed.

Every day Anne-Marie and Nicole wobbled down the hill on rusty bikes — the tyres flat — the brakes nonexistent — to fetch bread from the village.
Maybe one of them had let something slip…

'We have never said anything,' said Anne-Marie, her face twisted in distress. 'We never say anything — We just talk about the weather and get the bread.'
The thought that she had betrayed her beloved little Jacob was unthinkable.
She cared for him lovingly, taking him on her knee to tell him stories — burying her cheek against his curls.
And Nicole, who was painfully shy, never said very much at all to anybody…

Mother Superior said, 'We are among enemies. France is occupied by our enemies — they have spread fear and corruption everywhere. We have to be very careful — nobody is safe…'

They learnt that the Allies had landed from the postman — arriving, breathless with exertion — the hill to the Convent was very steep — with two letters for Mother Superior.
'The Allies have landed in Normandy,' he panted. 'They are advancing across France — We shall be free again — at last — free from the salles Boches…' and he went into Mother Superior's study with the other nuns, for a glass of Sister Agnes's plum brandy.

'This does not mean that the war is over,' Mother Superior told them. 'It doesn't mean that the Germans will retreat — we must be even more vigilant — like animals which are threatened, they will be even more dangerous.'

She wondered how many of these old people, gossiping and drinking wine in the sunshine, had been members of the Resistance — or

Collaborators…

They were starting back down the hill to the Village Hall, where a meal was to be served.

There was an English couple behind her.
They stopped outside the old cottages and called 'Are you coming Nigel? We're going to eat…'

They were heavy.
The woman's arms thick and reddened by the sun.
She wore a full floral skirt and a sloppy white T-shirt — her feet splayed in sturdy leather sandals.
The man, his stomach straining against the belt of his jeans, fetched something from the boot of the dark blue saloon.
The woman called 'We'll see you down there — don't be long — want to make sure we get the best of the food…'

5

Evelyn said, 'You're too thin —men don't like sleeping with bags of bones…'

Cecile didn't answer — watching Evelyn pour the tea — a thin stream of pale straw-coloured liquid from the spout of the elegant silver teapot into the Sevres china cups, patterned blue and pink with gold fluted rims.

She nearly said, 'But I've always been thin and bony…'
He had loved her as she was — thin and bony— at least, she thought he had loved her.
Perhaps it was only that he thought he could control her — and then, after many years, realised that he could not…

'Should I ignore it,' she said.
She had told Evelyn she thought he had a mistress, was pretty sure he had a mistress…

Sitting here in Evelyn's splendid drawing room she felt cut off from reality.

Since Hervé died, Evelyn had been obliged by financial difficulties to let some of the house. The ground floor was now occupied by a small publishing company — a very tasteful publishing company which specialised in Art books. The second and third floor were let to an Egyptian family, with three beautiful children. She had kept the first floor for herself — cramming as many of her things from the rest of the house into the rooms she had left.

The drawing room was hopelessly cluttered with furniture and 'objets' — sofas and a chaise-longue heaped with cushions, tapestry cushions, cushions with covers of washed silk, velvet boulsters — there were chairs and little tables everywhere. Little tables with straight legs and curly legs, inlaid with mother of pearl and ivory, covered with porcelain figures, bronze figures, silver boxes and ashtrays, faded photographs of faded relatives in silver frames, silver paper knives with jewelled handles, bowls of dusty dried flowers, dusty flowers of coloured glass — and lamps, standard lamps and table lamps, lamps hung with glass prisms and lamps with pleated silk lampshades, Art Nouveau lamps with shades of glass lozenges held by nymphs and disembodied hands.

Every space on the walls was hung with pictures, and there were pictures between the bookcases and glass cabinets, and canvases stacked against the bookcases and piles of books on the floor.

The study had become the kitchen, and Hervé's dressing room a bedroom for Evelyn's maid Micheline, ageing and frail, but determinedly loyal.

There was a plate of macaroons on the tray.
'I have told Micheline not to do any more baking,' said Evelyn. 'We eat very simply — I have told her it is time to take things more easily.'

Evelyn's once wondrous head of red hair had thinned and faded — like her yellow silk curtains — but her green eyes were still sharp

and unwavering — long white hands heavy with rings.
'Do you care?' she said. 'Gerrard has become so very pompous. What have you to say to one another..?'

6

The Boulangerie was still there.
It was smarter, with a striped awning and there were fruit tarts and eclairs in the window — round pain de campagne and croissants.

The café on the corner was still there.
It had not changed at all — the wrought iron tables and chairs in need of a coat of paint — on the dusty pavement — curling posters in the windows — and men drinking beer out of Stella Artois glasses.

The Village Hall was new.
A utilitarian structure which looked more like goods depot or a large garage.
There were tables down one side laden with food — cold meats and cheeses and bowls of salads.
There were tables in rows laid with cutlery and glasses, with carafes of wine and baskets of bread.
People were already queuing to help themselves to food.

The English couple jostled behind her.
'What a spread,' said the women. 'I don't think we need worry about there being anything left for Nigel and Lucinda…'

They had always had enough to eat — with the vegetables, fruit and eggs.
Sometimes the postman brought them a rabbit or a few pigeons — and sometimes, on special occasions, the old man who chopped the logs would kill one of the chickens, and Sister Agnes would roast it with herbs.

Sister Clare was teaching them about Italy when they heard Sister Constance calling from the vegetable garden — 'The Gestapo! …

The Gestapo!'

Ruth leapt to her feet and rushed to the back of the class to scoop up Jacob who was painting a picture of a boat, and ran from the room, shouting at Marthe to hurry.

Sister Clare stood as if frozen, by the blackboard, her hand with the chalk still raised — smudging the coastline of Italy somewhere near Naples, her face pallid with fear.

Sister Celeste came hurrying in — flushed and flustered. 'Hurry,' she said. 'Hurry — out the back...'

They piled Ruth and Marthe's books among their own as fast as they could — tidying Jacob's paints and brushes onto the shelf with the others — putting the picture with somebody else's.

'Sit down — quickly — ' said Sister Celeste. 'I shall take the lesson...'

She dusted the map of Italy off the board vigorously with the duster, and started writing some sums.
They bent their heads, carefully copying the figures from the board.

The car was already in front of the entrance.
They heard the motorcyle escort roar to a stop — exhausts exploding — and sharp exchanges in German, and Mother Superior greeting the Officer in his executioner's uniform.

They heard the thud of boots marching up the stone passage.

They were told to stand by their desks, whilst two small men in gaberdine raincoats and brown trilby hats inspected them carefully. One had sandy-coloured eyelashes and eyebrows, and pale watery blue eyes — the other was squat with heavy blueish jowls, glasses and bad teeth.
The Gestapo Officer in his black executioner's uniform stood by the door, tapping his black boots with his stick...
'We shall find them,' he said. 'And when we find them, it will not be

good for you — or the other Sisters...'

The stillness was the same stillness as the terrible night in the village
— her mother's white knuckles clutching the edge of the table...
The whole class held its breath and prayed.
'Let them get away — Please, God, let them get away...'

The soldiers in their black uniforms found Sister Clare hiding in
one of the outhouses, behind a pile of firewood, and dragged her
into the yard.

They tore off her wimple and her habit.
She was wearing a grey woollen dress with long sleeves and a white
collar, and she had short black curly hair.
She turned imploringly to Mother Superior who was standing rigid
and silent, one hand holding the heavy cross which hung from her
neck, the other loosely at her side.
'In the name of God...' she said — her voice unnaturally strained.

The man with the sandy eyebrows bowed slightly.
'A Convent is no place for a Jewess, madame,' he said.
'These vermin have no place in a house of God.'

He walked across the yard and suddenly, unexpectedly, struck Sister
Clare across the mouth.
The children instinctively moved closer to one another.
The soldiers were moving up the wooded hillside behind the
Convent, beating the brambles and bushes with their sticks.

'Take her away,' said the sandy man.
Sister Clare made an inarticulate sound, trying to say something, as
they forced her roughly into the back of the black Citroen.
Sister Celeste made a strangled noise, putting her hands up to her
face.
One of the younger children began to cry, and Anne-Marie hushed
her, holding her hand.

The soldiers were coming back down the hillside, their boots sliding

on the dry earth — dislodging stones.
They had found nothing.

The sandy man turned to Mother Superior.
'Now you will tell me where are the Jewish children.' His French was bad.
'There are no Jewish children here,' said Mother Superior, her voice studiously calm now, her face grey as granite.

He raised his hand as if to strike her, but instead, grabbed the cross and tried to pull it from her neck — but the chain was too strong.

He shouted at one of the soldiers who came at a run, and dragged it over her head, scraping it against her face.
'Now you too will come with us,' he said. 'Take her away… Schnell — schnell — We have wasted enough time here already.'

Two soldiers stepped forward and tied her hands behind her back with black wire.
She was pushed into the back of the Gestapo Officer's black Mercedes.
She did not look back.

Cecile heard herself scream — but nobody moved.
The scream was in her head — cutting through her head like a sharp knife through an apple — slicing her head in two.

They went on standing where they were — not daring to move — as if by staying still things would be alright.

And then Anne-Marie ran to the edge of the path, and was sick.

7

'You should take a lover,' said Evelyn, nibbling a macaroon.
She wore orange lipstick and a gold-flecked powder on her high cheek bones.
'You must come to lunch one Saturday. There are always interesting people. That writer Maurice Slavence was very attentive at Corinne's cocktail party. He is very cultured — though his books are very boring...'

Cecile remembered him without interest — small, with a pointed head — small fashionable glasses — small feet in pointed shoes — just small.

'I order the food in now,' said Evelyn. 'It is too much for Micheline. Antoine's provides a very good service — so long as you are careful with the menu — otherwise they always send salmon mousse — everybody is tired of salmon mousse...'

The dining room had been Evelyn's daughter Solange's bedroom — now the en suite bathroom was the guests' cloakroom.

Solange didn't take after her mother.
Sturdy and dark like her father — sallow skinned and square-jawed — she was very clever.
She had married an American banker and lived in New York.
She did not often come to Paris.
'She never made the best of herself,' said Evelyn.
'Terrible shoes — and always the wrong necklines...'

Evelyn had been in Paris during the war — thirteen in 1940 — living in the exclusive, leafy suburb of Neuilly — going to an exclusive, private girls school — beginning to fuss about their looks — and boys — listening to dance music — longing to be grown up.

In the exclusive leafy suburb, the war was hardly noticed.

They did not feel the shiver that ran up the spine of France as the grey-green army roared down the elegant boulevards of Paris in their monstrous tanks with swivelling turrets.
They did not witness the straggling lines of burdened people — the debris of their lives crammed into bundles and perambulators — trudging grey-faced and weary along the endless, straight, heat-shimmered roads, edged with silver-leaved poplars — going heaven knows where — a pathetically easy target for the marauding dive-bombers of the advancing enemy.

They heard stories of panic and chaos at the railway stations — of broken down trains and lack of petrol — of women and children machine-gunned by the roadside.

Mr Hubot mowed the lawn and trimmed the hedge, and Jacqueline shelled peas and made flaky pastry on the marble slab in the airy kitchen, and her mother lay in her bed amongst the lace-trimmed pillows, the lace-trimmed sheets ruffled, her breakfast tray, the croissant half-eaten, pushed to one side, petulant because the new blouses she had ordered had not arrived, and the shop was not answering the phone…

She still ordered her groceries from Fauchon, complaining about the erratic deliveries, and the lack of certain items — no pineapple — no bananas — a meagre, dwindling selection of tea — and coffee — dreadful coffee…

Her father, as always, absently soothing, preoccupied, too busy with his work to bother with trivial domestic matters.

He was a consultant at the Luis Berger Clinic.
A white building in lush grounds.
A hospital for the very rich — now mostly full of high-ranking German officers, their wives and mistresses.
He specialised in liver disorders.

It made no difference to him if his patients were German or French — or any nationality.

To him they were just patients.

Things were slightly different after Dr Muller was billeted on them.
Heinz Muller had met her father when he was studying in Berlin.
It was appropriate that Dr Muller should be billeted with them — so much in common — and near the clinic.
Her father spoke German.
Dr Muller had requested it.

There were advantages of course.
They were never short of food.
Fauchon suddenly managed to obtain all the items requested, although bananas were still a problem, and the quality of the coffee was variable.

Dr Muller was not a tall man — small boned — fastidious — with smooth blond hair and pebble grey eyes.
He wore glasses for reading.
His hands were large — the skin tinged with blue — the nails square and flat. They did not seem to belong to him.

He loved his food.
He was particularly fond of offal — brains — kidneys and liver — sweetbreads — giblets — stuffed heart...
He ate with gusto, mopping his plate with his bread, and drank quantities of wine.
He was very knowledgeable about wine.

Her mother didn't care for offal.
She picked at her food and drank too much wine.
Evelyn disguised hers with sauce. She didn't like it much either, but she was always hungry.

Heinz Muller would ask her questions about school — what was she learning — were they learning German — were the teachers good — what sort of music did she like..?

She was careful with her replies.

She could hardly tell him some of the teachers had mysteriously disappeared.
The Headmistress tight-lipped. 'I am afraid Mademoiselle Tercier will not be coming back — she's been called up — to do war work...'

And Mademoiselle Heron and Mademoiselle Sadler...

She had learnt to be careful what she said at school as well.
How many teachers were collaborators?
How many parents?

They heard stories of deportations — of trains leaving in the night for unknown destinations — cattle trucks with no windows.

It was true whole families had vanished.
Two in their street.
The Steins, whose mansion had electrically-operated gates, and a conservatory of tropical plants, and the Bergs who had a swimming pool with mosaic tiles, and gave wonderful parties on the fourteenth of July, with fireworks.

It was presumed the houses had been requisitioned as they were now full of Germans.
'Fancy not saying goodbye,' said her mother. 'Nancy Stein was always stuck up, but she could have said goodbye...'

Her father changed the subject. 'This is a very fine apple tart — remember to tell Jacqueline how much we enjoyed it...'

Heinz spoke good French, with hardly any accent — which was fortunate.
Her mother spoke no German, and her own knowledge was minimal, although she was learning it at school.
'Such an ugly language,' said her mother. 'Verboten this, and Verboten that... everything Verboten...'

She did not like having Heinz Muller in her house, always sneaking up on her — on the way to the bathroom — always having to make

sure her hair was tidy and her robe fastened — when she was writing letters, or getting ready to go out…
She didn't like having any German in the house.
She did not like eating offal — and great dollops of cream with everything…
She had no knowledge of politics.
She did not understand politics.
She wasn't interested in politics.
She read fashion magazines and listened to tuneful innocuous music on the wireless.
She didn't understand how France had been defeated by the Germans.

Evelyn's father went to work at the hospital every day with Heinz Muller in his staff car with the swastika pennant on the bonnet in a little silver holder.
He wore an officer's uniform, even though he was a doctor.
He was very polite — clicking and bowing — offering his car to her mother 'to take her wherever she wished to go'. 'At your disposal, chère Madame,' he said.

Her mother was flattered by his attentions — even though she didn't like him.
She was a beautiful woman — redheaded like Evelyn — slender, with porcelain white skin.
She was used to admiration.
She was bored with the war.
It might be fun to be driven down the Champs Elysees in a German officer's car.
Her father was not amused.
He forbade it — quietly but firmly, when Heinz was at a staff meeting.
'Absolutely not, cherie,' he said. 'Think how it would look — being driven about in a German staff car… You don't want people to think you are a German's mistress…'
Her mother said 'Rubbish'. She didn't see what was so wrong — people could think what they liked — it would be fun. The war was so boring. Everything was so boring. But she didn't go.

Her father told her that Brigitte must not come to the house any more, and that she must not go to her house.
'We have to be careful,' he said, meaning 'Heinz Muller is watching us'.

Brigitte was her best friend.
She was a very clever girl.
Her parents were very wealthy.
Her father was a lawyer, and her mother an accomplished pianist who gave lessons to a few, especially talented, pupils.
There was no need of her father's warnings.
Brigitte ceased to come to school.
The whisper that went round the class exploded in her ears.
Brigitte had been taken away.
The whole family had been taken away — to one of those camps — on one of those trains…

She had left the classroom abruptly — knocking her books to the floor — running down the echoing corridor — her hands over her mouth — retching — out of the glass doors into the gardens — taking deep breaths of the clean air to steady herself.

She inserted a cigarette into her long ebony holder — delicately inlaid with silver — and lit it with the gold lighter Hervé had given her.

After that things were relatively normal.
They became resigned to Heinz's presence.
They had plenty of food and fuel.
Her mother fretted and complained about not having new clothes — of having to pay exorbitant prices for shoes.
Evelyn was always needing new shoes.
She was growing so tall.

The leafy suburb remained untouched apart from the houses taken over by the Germans, who were seldom ever seen, coming and going in their smoothly-purring black cars, closing the gates firmly behind them.

Mr Hubot still worked in the garden — nurturing his beloved roses.
Jacqueline, placid in her kitchen, making liver paté — jugging hare
— reserving the blood in a brown pottery jug to make the sauce.
Heinz Muller was particularly fond of jugged hare.

At Christmas he gave them all presents.
A length of silk for her mother — cigars for her father — a silver
bracelet for her.
It was difficult to accept a present graciously from someone one
disliked so profoundly.

Sometimes her father and mother were invited to social functions at
the clinic, or sometimes at private houses. Once they were invited to
dine at the Berg's house.
'They used all their best china,' said her mother. 'The one with gold
crests...'
Her mother always lovely in her black lace evening dress, and black
taffeta cape — diamond combs in her heaped red hair.
She enjoyed dressing up and going out.
It was a pity there were so many Germans...

She really did not care for the Germans.
'Fat Fraus,' she said. 'So many Fat Fraus and Fat Frauleins —
guzzling — so much food — great slabs of foie gras — guzzle, guzzle
— they have no conversation — and the music! All Strauss waltzes
and dreadful drinking songs..!'

It is unwise to disturb the past,' she said.

8

Cecile moved restlessly in the deep soft-cushioned armchair.
It wasn't that she wanted to disturb the past.
The past disturbed her.
Behind the creaking door it waited for her...

The postman told Sister Constance that Sister Clare and Mother

Superior were dead.
They had been shot.

He propped his bicycle against the water butt and made his way gingerly into the middle of the vegetable patch where Sister Constance was planting cabbages.

They stood together — Sister Constance completely still and Mr Colombier gesticulating.

So far Ruth, Marthe and Jacob were safe.
They were being hidden separately in different places.

He warned her that the Gestapo would be back.

They knelt in the Chapel and prayed.
They prayed for Sister Clare and Mother Superior — that they were now at peace, with God.
They prayed that Ruth, Marthe and Jacob would be safe, and prayed for courage...

This time the black-booted Gestapo Officer came without the men in gabardine raincoats and brown trilbies.
He came in the long black car with the swastika flying on the bonnet — black-uniformed outriders, and soldiers in grey uniforms with machine guns in a grey truck.

He ordered them all outside.
Sister Agnes came from the kitchen — laboriously because of her bad leg — Sister Constance from the garden, her hands calloused and muddy.
Sister Celeste pink-faced and trembling.

The children were lined up and inspected carefully — their papers scrutinised.

Again the Gestapo Officer demanded to know where the Jewish children were, and again he was told there were no Jewish children.

They were forced down into the cellar at gunpoint.

The cellar was the storeroom — lined with shelves of jam and bottled fruit, and bottles of liqueurs.

The soldiers opened fire — raking the shelves — everything with bullets.

The jars and bottles shattered — their contents oozing, dripping red, purple, black pools of sticky liquid on the stone floor — like blood — fresh blood — congealed blood — spreading a dark glutinous stain on the white stones — the broken glass glinting among it like a carpet of rubies.

Sister Celeste started to sob.
The soldiers pushed them back up the steps and into the garden.
They were so close — menacingly close — that they could smell the hot cloth of their uniforms — see the hair on the back of their hands holding the guns — hustling them forward.

They dragged Sister Celeste, still sobbing, under the lofty copper beach, and shot her.

Paula was screaming, an hysterical, high-pitched screaming — and Anne-Marie tried to quieten her, putting a hand over her mouth — white and shaking and desperate.

Sister Constance ran towards the inert shape spread-eagled on the ground, her black robes billowing round her like some giant bird, and one of the soldiers struck her with his rifle.

'Do you have to go back?' said Evelyn.
'Yes,' said Cecile. 'I have to go back.'

9

She walked back to the apartment along the boulevard, the leaves of the plane trees a pale transparent green, casting dark green shadows on to the pavement, dappled with dancing patches of sunlight, and through the small garden with its trim box hedges and beds of flowers, and sat down on the stone bench beneath the acacia tree, already hung with scented clusters of white flowers.

The gardener was planting out begonias.
She didn't care for begonias, they were too careful — too cultivated — almost artificial.

There was a wheelbarrow of soft-faced velvet pansies — yellow and mauve, purple and dark red.

They had tried to put Sister Celeste's body into a wheelbarrow to take it to the Chapel.
Sister Constance and Sister Agnes had wanted to lay her out in the Chapel — to have a proper service — to give them time to dig a grave.

Sister Agnes fetched white sheets, and she and Sister Constance managed, with great difficulty, to wrap them round Sister Celeste's body.

Anne-Marie took the smaller children indoors to try and calm them. They were all very distressed.

Nicole and Yvonne, Jeanne and herself — the sturdier ones — struggled to help lift Sister Celeste's body into the wheelbarrow.
She and Jeanne held the wheelbarrow steady whilst the others tried to lift her.

It was useless.
In death her pleasantly plump limbs lolled heavy and uncontrollable, her head emerging from the white shroud — grotesque — shocking

— blood seeping through the sheets. Thick red sticky blood — thick red sticky jam — blood — jam — blood — jam…
They mingled in her head, sticky and red.
Even now she couldn't bear the sight of a dish of red jam.
Sister Constance's hands were covered in blood.
They had to stop.

Sister Constance said, 'May God have mercy on our souls — We will have to bury her here…'

Jeanne said, 'What if they come back — what if they come back..?'

Nobody spoke, filled with fear, and the two nuns knelt by the body and prayed.

She watched the gardener finish planting out the begonias.
The round bed in the middle of the garden was full of begonias now — bright pink and orange — red and yellow — perfect waxy blooms.

The gardener was young and dark skinned, probably Algerian or Moroccan, his hands and arms brown and strong.
He started taking the pansies from the wheelbarrow to plant them in the side beds, expertly digging little holes with his trowel and patting down the earth.

They had taken it in turns to dig the grave.
It had not been easy.
Two ageing nuns and four children in the glare of the afternoon sun.
The beech tree gave some shade — its luxuriant summer growth becalmed in the breathless heat.

They were terrified the Germans would return.
The air was full of the memory of machine gun fire — the smell of explosives and hot metal.
They might come back at any time — grey-green and black.
They might come back at any time.
They might kill them all — line them up against a wall.
Rat-a tat-tat…

Digging the grave deep enough was very hard.
The spades were heavy and unwieldy in their small hands.
They were bothered by flies, and horribly aware of Sister Celeste's
body untidily wrapped in the bloody sheets.

Anne-Marie brought them out water — but she couldn't leave the
little ones for long, so she couldn't help them with the digging.
Jeanne started to cry, and Sister Constance told her to go indoors
and rest.

It was early evening before the hole was long enough and deep
enough.
They stamped on the freshly dug earth to make it hard.

Sister Agnes fetched the wall hanging from Mother Superior's study.
It was a sombre tapestry of the Crucifixion.
The near-naked body of Christ impaled on the cross with giant nails
driven into his hands and feet — the head bowed beneath a bloody
crown of thorns.
It was old, and in some places worn through to the backing. half of
the Virgin Mary's head was missing, the sky brown and motheaten.

It had hung in the dining room until Mother Superior decided it was
too grim for the little ones, and had it moved to her study, where it
covered a whole wall.

'We will cover her with it,' said Sister Constance. 'When we have laid
her to rest...'

They had tried to lift her stiffening body, the sheet hardened rusty
brown with dried blood.
They wanted to lower her gently into the grave, but they couldn't
manage it.
They dragged her, and half pushed, half rolled her into the grave.

Cecile's knees gave way and she collapsed on to the trampled ground
— her head buzzing — coloured spots dancing in front of her eyes.
Nicole was weeping, the tears making clean furrows in her muddy

face, and Yvonne silently took her hand.

The nuns covered the body with the tapestry — tucking it round her as well as they could, and Sister Constance said some prayers.

The gardener had finished planting the pansies.
The wheelbarrow was empty.
He fetched a broom and began to sweep the path…

Filling in the grave had not been so difficult.
They all worked together — shovelling the earth back into the hole — gradually obscuring the pathetic remains of harmless, kindly Sister Celeste.

There were no flowers to put on the grave.
Sister Constance didn't grow flowers.
Like strawberries, she considered them frivolous.

They were too tired to climb the slope behind the Convent to pick some of the wild roses and convolvulus which twined and tangled amongst the bushes and brambles and draped delicate pink and white garlands along the sharp-twigged branches of the hawthorn trees.

It would have to wait until morning.
They were too tired to do anything now.
Too tired to eat the soup Anne-Marie had heated for them.
Too tired to notice the dull thud of heavy gunfire getting ever nearer — the night sky glowing red with the fires of bombardment.

Mr Colombier brought the bread and milk on his bike.
There was no post.
He said it was too dangerous for them to go to the village.
There had been hostages taken — eleven men — if you could count young Jean-Paul Terin and Yves Serrant as men.
They had gone to the Lubier's farm and gunned down everyone, including the old grandmother and the three young children.
The Resistance had hijacked one of their trucks…

It was terrible… terrible…
Pray God the Allies would reach them soon.

After the joy and excitement of the Allies' landing, they had expected them to sweep across France, the Germans retreating in disarray.
Instead the British and American armies were blocked in around Caen for over a month.
'Hardly off the beach,' Mr Colombier had said, shrugging in despair as the Germans increased the shootings and burnings, ever more frequent and haphazard.

For so many it was already too late.
Too late for Sister Clare, Mother Superior and Sister Celeste.
Mr Colombier didn't know whether Ruth, Marthe and Jacob were safe.
He didn't know where they were.
The deportations were still going on.
Only last week a mother and her small daughter had been dragged from their hiding place and taken away, and the old women who had been hiding them was shot — in her kitchen — by the stove…
'Someone must have betrayed them,' said Mr Colombier.
Perhaps it had been the same person who had betrayed Sister Clare — had seen Jacob…

She stopped at the Boulangerie to get a baguette for supper.

There was a young woman in the shop with a little boy. She was buying a strawberry tart.
The boulangère was packing it carefully into a square white box.
'He is growing so fast,' she said. 'It seems only yesterday he was in his pram.'
'He will be three next week,' said the young woman. 'Won't you, Henri?' and she bent and kissed him.

What had happened to them?
Had they got away?
How many times had she wondered what had happened to them?
In her dreams she saw them running.

'Vite … Vite … Hurry… Hurry…'
Ruth with Jacob in her arms and Marthe struggling to keep up.
Giant black boots trampling the undergrowth — waking with her
throat aching and dry…

'I'll take a strawberry tart as well,' she said.
Gerrard liked strawberry tart, and there was only fruit for dessert.

There was a message on the answering machine.
Gerrard was having an aperitif with André — they might go out to
eat — not to wait dinner…

She was relieved.
She did not feel like talking — laying the table — preparing the food
— melon — cold chicken — salad…
Gerrard always complained when they had cold meals.
He expected a hot meal.
'Perhaps you have been *too busy* to cook,' he would say.

She disliked cooking in this pristine kitchen — gleaming with
stainless steel and glass. Uncomfortable — unfriendly — everything
so precisely arranged.
It seemed sacrilegious to contaminate the spotless white surfaces
with anything as messy as food — cooked or raw — the necessity to
mop up all spillages instantly, dispiriting.
It had been designed by one of Hortense's many protegées — a young
designer.
Maurice may have been a genius, but he didn't have to do the
cooking.

The tart would keep until tomorrow.
She would get veal cutlets and mushrooms — they were not too
messy…

10

She was seated at the same table as the English couple. They ate with gusto, their plates piled high. They waved to another couple who had just joined the queue. They were tall, thin and bony. The man was bald and wore glasses. The woman had black hair streaked with grey, scraped back and tied untidily with a black ribbon.
'Must have had another row,' said the woman.
'She's neurotic,' said the man. 'Doesn't know what she wants — hopeless — He should have stayed with Sue…'
The thin man picked up a tray and cut himself a slice of paté. She held the plate.
They both wore thick-soled trainers and jeans.

At last the Americans came.
Their jeeps revving up the rough track to the Convent, the tyres spitting stones.
An American officer leapt out of his jeep and saluted Sister Constance.
He was accompanied by a French officer, his uniform crumpled and stained.

The soldiers spread out fast — running crouched — guns at the ready.
'We have to check for Germans, madame,' said the French officer. 'We have had trouble with snipers…'

'There are no Germans here,' said Sister Constance. 'Not now…'

The American took off his helmet and shook her by the hand. He was young with blonde curly hair and very white teeth. There was a ring of dirt where his helmet had marked his forehead.
He looked very tired.
The three of them stood, heads bowed, as Sister Constance spoke, turning slightly to glance at the newly dug mound of earth covered with wilting convolvulous, where Sister Celeste was buried.
At the sight of the soldiers, the little ones started to cry, huddled

together by the wall.
They were too young to differentiate between friends and enemies
— they were just more soldiers with guns.

They came back from their search, walking now — calm,
unthreatening — and pronounced the place 'all clear'.

The officer replaced his helmet, and saluted again.
They jumped back into their jeeps, and with much churning of dried
mud and twigs, were gone.

So that was that.
For them the War was over.
Not for the soldiers wearily slogging their way through fields of
ripening wheat and long, coarse grass, perspiration soaking their
tunics — the sun cracking the earth — briefly cheered by flowers
and flags and kisses, as they trudged through shattered towns and
villages — gratefully sheltering in the dense quiet forests.
For them there was a long way to go.
A winter of boots heavy with mud, and icy rain scarring their faces
— numbed hands fumbling with rifles and billy cans — feeble fires
of smoky damp wood — and horrors and more horrors...

But for them it was over.
There should have been a celebration, but nobody felt like celebrating.
There was not much to celebrate.
Not much to celebrate with.
Sister Agnes made an omelette — there were nearly always plenty of
eggs — the hens were good layers — and they had boiled potatoes,
salad and fresh plums.
They would have had fried potatoes, but they had nothing to fry
them with.

There were extra prayers — thanking God for his Mercy and Love,
and so on and so on...
Kneeling with her eyes tightly shut, she mouthed the words.
She didn't believe in God.
No loving God could have allowed all these terrible things to

happen. Her father dead — her mother sick — her aunt sick — her cousins missing — Mother Superior dead — Sister Clare and Sister Celeste dead — and who knew what dreadful things had happened to Ruth, Marthe and little Jacob — and that was just in this little bit of the world.

So where was this God of Love?
Sitting up among white clouds in his white palace with gold spires.
Lying back on white cushions — eating grapes from a golden bowl — surrounded by white-winged Angels.
Looking down on his people — bleeding to death — starving to death — crying out for His Mercy...
She didn't believe in God then, and she didn't believe in God now.

She had refused to marry Gerrard in Church.
Gerrard's mother had been very displeased.
'Everybody gets married in Church,' she said. 'It isn't necessary to be religious...'
But Cecile had been adamant.
She would not swear anything before God.
She did not want God's blessing.
God did not exist.

Later there had been another Convent.
A severe place with high smooth grey stone walls, and locked iron gates.
A place of rules and regulations — of serious learning and serious worship.

She had been in the Choir.
She was lucky to have a good voice.
The music a candle flame of light in the cheerless regimented days.
There were anthems to learn, and psalms and hymns — so many services...
One of the Nuns played the organ — thundering out the Jubilates and Hallelujahs — joyous sound reverberating in the dusty rafters.
Sister Francesca who took the Choir, was small and plump and kindly.

She reminded her a little of Sister Celeste except that she lived in fear of the Mother Superior, not the kind who would have sheltered anybody, who would appear silently from the darkened body of the Chapel to criticise their performance.

Sister Francesca, filled with enthusiasm for the music, conducting eagerly on tiptoe, her face pink with exertion, was instantly chastened and miserable.

'Bach is the Church's lifeblood,' she would murmur, as the Mother Superior complained that the music was not suitably devout, terrified that Mother Superior might suddenly, out of spite, ban Bach from their repertoire.

It was a gloomy place. The enclosed environment seething with jealousy and pettiness. The long dark passages, dank and chilling, the crevices mouldered with the loathings and frustrations of those who hurried past — hands clasped — heads bowed in prayer.

It was not the slow tranquil place of the old Convent — so cruelly disrupted.

They were taught well though.

She had become fluent in English and Italian.

They had wanted her to learn German as well — 'You have an aptitude for languages — you will be able to get good jobs...' — but she had refused.

German, an ugly language for an ugly people. A language personifying cruelty, fear and death. No. She would not learn German.

11

She left the car at the end of the track.

It was very overgrown. A tree had toppled, its branches splayed and rotten across the path, thick with years of brown decaying leaves.

The Convent had decayed too. The stones crumbled, the garden a wilderness.

There was high soft-seeded grass entwined with tiny purple flowers, like miniature sweet peas, and little white starry flowers, and thick-stalked daisies where Sister Constance had grown her neat rows of vegetables. The fruit tress misshapen. Their trunks encrusted with lichen had a few scabby apples forming among the split branches. The beech tree was more magnificent than ever, soaring shimmering against the opaque summer sky. Under its satin-leaved branches a bed of angry nettles obscured the place where they had buried Sister Celeste. The wooden cross which Nicole had so painstakingly made would have rotted away.

One of the barns, where the hens had been kept, had collapsed in a mound of crumpled stone, and ivy obscured the heavy oak door of the convent and clambered over the roof covering the narrow windows of the dormitory where they had slept, knees drawn up against the cold, in the solid indigo stillness of the night.

When the weight of summer had become burdensome, and the long evenings had begun to shorten, Uncle Bertrand came in his rickety van.

They were to visit her mother.
It seemed such a very long time since she had left her home — the bunches of herbs drying by the stove — her quilt with the coloured squares — the warm peppery smell of geraniums — such a long time since her mother had been helped, unseeing, into the back of the ambulance.

The awful empty void.
Her father gone for ever into the night — her mother shut in her own blank world — hiding from the unbearable knowledge of her father's death.

Perhaps her mother was better now — perhaps she could come back to life — perhaps they would be able to go back to their home and be together.
She did not think so.
If God existed — if he was truly merciful — then perhaps it would

be possible, but from what she had seen, she did not believe it was possible.

They drove to a dusty little village, and sat at a café in the shade of a chestnut laden with spiky green conkers. The chairs were metal — sharp and uncomfortable.
Across the street two old women in black gossiped outside the boulangerie, its dusty windows pasted with ragged posters. Bread was still scarce, tough and grey.

'Your Aunt isn't very well,' said Uncle Bertrand. 'She would have come — if she was well…'

He lit a cigarette, staring down at the metal table.
'She will be better when the boys come home…'
He was a kindly man, but awkward, not knowing what to say.
He had ordered a grenadine for her, and a beer for himself.

A fat woman with a grubby apron and sloppy shoes served them.
She brought a plate of biscuits.
'The child looks hungry,' she said.

Uncle Bertrand thanked her.
'Your mother isn't very well either,' he said. 'The doctor said it would be nice for her to see you. You musn't expect too much — she's been very ill… Now the Germans are gone it is easier to get about…'

He stopped talking.

Now the Germans had gone he had no job.
Thank goodness Claudine still had her jobs cleaning at the hospital and the school.
He did not know what they would do if she was not earning a little money.
How would they manage?
It was good for her too — gave her something to occupy her a little, otherwise she would just sit at the window — watching the road — waiting for the boys to come home.

They drove up an avenue of trees — the road rutted — full of potholes.
The central rim of grass so long it dragged against the bottom of the van.
Either side the trees rose high, their thick trunks bulged and calloused with age, the leaves already beginning to turn gold and crimson — rustling in the fidgety autumn breeze.

The hospital had once been a chateau, facing squarely into the sun, the paint on the shutters flaked and peeling, the grey stones pitted and cracked, the gravel sprouting weeds.

The bell rang sonorously in the distance, and after a lengthy pause, the heavy door was opened by a diminutive nun in white.
She ushered them into the hall and told them to wait.

The hall was suddenly dim and chilly after the light and warmth outside — large and bare with grey pillars of rough stone.
There was a statue of the Virgin with her head demurely bent over her folded hands, and a wooden bench against one wall, beneath the inevitable crucifix.

It smelt strange — a mixture of disinfectant and the sickly sweet smell of madness.

There had been a girl at school in the village who had smelt like that — weirdly silent, or shrieking and banging her head against the walls or the desks, or anything…
She had been sent away.
A tall, gaunt nun, also in white came.
She spoke briefly to Uncle Bertrand, and they followed her along a corridor of uneven flagstones into a large room.
There were easy chairs, well spaced, and small tables, and rugs on the stone floor.
There were large vases of flowers — golden rod, and a bell-like pink flower and white lilies by the huge empty fireplace and the French windows, which opened onto a terrace with steps leading down to a lawn which stretched and dipped towards a distant wood.

An old man was endeavouring to mow the grass with an old hand mower.
There were a few people walking on the lawn, and sitting in chairs on the terrace.

It was quiet and peaceful, and pleasant, apart from the strange sweet smell which pervaded the air.

At first she didn't recognise her mother — huddled in a large armchair by the window.
The black wavy hair — thin and straight, and peppered with grey — motionless — the capable hands thin and pale — the knuckles protruding painfully as she clutched them together.

The nun bent and spoke to her, and Uncle Bertrand said 'Hello Marguerite... It's Bertrand... How are you feeling? We should have come sooner, but there was no petrol...'

Her mother didn't respond, clutching her hands together more fiercely.
'Cecile and I have come to see you...' his voice tailed off, and he sat down on a chair opposite.
She stood awkward and uncertain.
She felt sick — should she approach her — speak to her — what should she say? She had an urge to run away, through the windows, across the lawn — far away to the distant safety of the woods.

'It's Bertrand,' said her Uncle again. 'Bertrand and Cecile... go on — say something to her...'

She took a step nearer the chair.
'Maman,' she said. 'Dear Maman — we have come to see you...'

Her mother lifted her head and looked at her — a look of indescribable pain.
Cecile thought she was going to scream.
The greyish pallor of her skin became tinged with yellow like an old bruise.

She started to whimper.

Uncle Bertrand tried to soothe her, but she became even more distressed — pushing herself back into the chair — rigid — lifting her hands as if to ward off a blow — her arms stiff as a mechanical doll.

Cecile felt completely hollow — empty with misery.
This was not her mother — this thing in a shabby cardigan and skirt and brown woollen stockings, cringing in the chair — this pathetic creature.
This was not her mother with her capable hands, rolling out the pastry for apple tart, tying ribbons in her hair. The mother she knew was gone forever.

The tall white figure of the nun came swiftly across the room.
'There, there,' she said, taking her mother's hands in her own and rubbing them. 'There, there, Marguerite, do not upset yourself.'

They had to leave.
The nun spoke to Uncle Bertrand — and they left.

As they drove away in the rickety van he said 'I'm sorry... Your mother is still very unwell — it is sad — this war — it has gone on too long — done so much damage...'

As he left her at the convent he said, 'I'm sorry you cannot come to us — your Aunt Claudine — she couldn't manage...'

12

It was a terrible winter — punishingly cold.
Ice gripped the land, and hung long stalactites from the trees.
The water froze — the handle of the pump welded solid, draped with sheets of ice.
They ran out of paraffin, using up the scant supply of altar candles to give them some light.

There were worse shortages than when the Germans were still there. Railway lines and bridges had been blown up, roads reduced to rubble, everything was scarce.

Fortunately there was always plenty of wood, branches broken by the wind, the slope behind the convent a mass of rotting logs and fallen trees.
They had potatoes, carrots and apples stored in one of the sheds.
They ate a lot of soup, and apples baked in the woodburning stove in the kitchen.

It became so cold that Sister Constance let them sleep downstairs in the refectory where there was always a fire burning.

Some of the little ones became ill — two so seriously that Anne-Marie had to go to the village to get the postmistress to telephone for the doctor.
She had to go on foot as snow had made the road almost impassable.
When the doctor finally came, he had to leave his car at the end of the track, and with the help of Anne-Marie and Sister Constance carry the sick children, wrapped in blankets to his car to take to hospital.

The sky lowered itself towards the earth — an impenetrable wall of sleet and snow.
The wind hurtled through the trees, tearing off branches, prising slates from the roof of the chapel, and hurling them on to the stones below.
One day, whilst preparing the soup, Sister Agnes had a stroke, keeling over by the kitchen table, scattering potatoes on to the floor.

It was then that they were disbanded — relocated to other convents.

A priest came with a lady wearing a pinstripe suit with square shoulders, and high-heeled shoes.
She carried folders and asked a lot of questions.
They were both very serious and unsmiling, looking disapprovingly at the children in their ill-fitting clothes — the dog-eared books —

the general disorder.

Sister Constance wandered restlessly about, talking to herself, praying. The tall figure in her gumboots, digging and planting, filling straw baskets with pearly new potatoes, and crisp sugary peas, hoeing and weeding among the neat rows of feathery carrots and juicy ripening tomatoes, this strong woman, who they had all held in awe, was now like a ghost, a wandering spirit, her gaze fixed on other things.

'You must ask Mother Superior,' she told the pinstriped lady. 'Mother Superior is in charge of everything. You must speak to her...'

13

Gerrard sat next to her, distantly hostile — uncomfortable on the gilt-meshed chairs of the Salle de César.
On the stage a young man with black shoulder-length hair veiling his face, swayed dramatically over his violin.

The accompanist, also a young man with a red crew cut, was visibly sweating, his pudgy face twisted with the effort of keeping up with the accelerating pace of the violinist.

Classical music irritated Gerrard — particularly when trapped in this kind of claustrophobic situation.
Jerome, now frantically doublestopping, was another of Hortense's proteges.
Cecile was not listening.
She saw his bow flashing faster and faster, aware of Gerrard impatiently looking at his watch.
These occasions were always trying.
Afterwards there would be a reception, and Hortense would drag the embarrassed young man round like showing off a prize puppy.

There was applause.
Cecile prayed there would not be an encore.

Gerrard was already half out of his seat.
'I hope they've got some decent whisky,' he said. 'Next time we must have a really good excuse…'

It was difficult to think up a completely genuine-sounding excuse. Having a headache — being suddenly called away to a sick relative — an important business meeting — all were transparently false, and it was unthinkable to offend Hortense and Didier.
Cecile would not have minded if she never saw them again, but to Gerrard they were very important — socially and professionally.

Hortense had over-lacquered her hair.
It rose stiffly above her pale forehead like a classy haystack — L'Herbe d'Or — the newest shade — the colour of hay.
She had matching lipstick, which, with her over-moisturised skin, gave her the appearance of a boiled pudding.
She wore a black tuxedo with satin lapels, and a four-stranded diamond choker.

'He is so talented,' she said. 'Absolutely brilliant…'
She had come straight over to where Cecile was standing with Evelyn.
Evelyn leant on her silver-topped cane. She was having trouble with her hip.
She wore a flowing kaftan of limegreen silk with several ropes of pearls, her flame-coloured hair cut in short curls.
'My dear,' she said. 'You are so good at finding new talent — it is quite amazing…'
Any waspish sarcasm was lost on Hortense.
'It is a gift,' she said. 'One has to be so sensitive — sometimes I feel I am too sensitive — You will have to excuse me, I have to go and speak to the Baron…'

She disappeared amongst the careful coiffeurs and jewels of the other guests.
Didier and Gerrard were in a corner with a group of black suits, talking business.
'She is an extremely silly woman,' said Evelyn. 'Vain and stupid. She

makes herself look ridiculous. Didier shouldn't indulge her...' and turning to Cecile, 'you are looking very wan,' she said. 'The country air didn't do you much good. However, you wouldn't have enjoyed the evening with Hortense and Didier. Pretentious — pompous — very, very dull — it would have made you very angry...'

Gerrard had drunk too much.
He had flirted with Zsa Zsa Smetterlin, whose strapless red satin dress had not been designed to conceal her considerable attributes. Gerrard was still very goodlooking, and he could be very charming if he wished.

Cecile could have driven home the same evening, but she would have arrived very late, and had an uneasy apprehension that she might find someone else in bed with Gerrard.

Instead she had gone to find the place where her mother was buried — a little churchyard near the hospital.

Her mother had died that awful winter, the year the war finally ended.
In the February when the punishing cold — snow and frost — had brought the country to a standstill, and when the children at the Convent had been divided up and sent to other convents after Sister Agnes had her stroke, her mother had died of pneumonia.

The news had been slow in reaching her.
A short, badly written note from Uncle Bertrand finally arrived several weeks after Cecile had been in the new convent.
It had not been possible to grieve — there was so much grief — everywhere there was grieving.
'It is God's will,' the new, forbiddingly cold Mother Superior said, holding Uncle Bertrand's note as if it might carry some infectious disease. 'Your mother is now in His care in Eternal Peace... You may go to the chapel for half an hour, and pray for her...'

The churchyard was very overgrown, the gravestones toppled and broken.

More angry nettles blocked the pathways between the graves, surrounded by precarious trees choked with ivy, their starved, leafless branches drooping, grey with fatigue.

Somewhere here her mother had been buried, hastily, in some lonely corner.
In the loneliness of dying she so hoped someone had been with her.
The nuns at the hospital had seemed kind.
Maybe someone had held her hand — had stayed with her.

14

Evelyn sipped her champagne.
She would have preferred brandy.
Her hip ached. She didn't know if it ached more if she sat down or remained standing.

She watched Pamela Masterson, the wife of an attaché at the American Embassy talking to Cecile.
She wore a red jersey jacket and skirt edged with gold braid, and had a red satin shoulder bag with a gold chain and red shoes trimmed with gold.
She was very animated, gesturing, spreading her hands with long red scrabbling nails, to illustrate what she was saying.
She was shorter than Cecile, and had to throw back her head to look up at her as she talked.

Cecile was tall and slim — thin now — too thin really. She wore black with no jewellery — always austerely elegant.

She remembered when they had first met.
Gerrard had brought her to one of their picnics.
Hervé had loved picnics. He liked to organise the food and the people — stylish picnics with silver cutlery, white linen cloths and napkins — chilled drinks and delicious food, all beautifully packed in creaky hampers, and a wind-up gramophone to play the latest dance tunes.

They had driven out to the woods at Compiegne, where the pines dropped a spiky green carpet on the silky white sand, sinkingly soft and hot to the touch.

Gerrard had come in his dashing new dark green sports car with his new girlfriend — Cecile.
Gerrard had a seemingly endless number of girlfriends. Girls who giggled and fussed with their makeup, existentialist types with chalky-white faces, green eyeshadow and oversize earrings, and knowingly curvy blondes pouting shiny scarlet lips.

Cecile did not fit any of these categories.
She didn't giggle or pout. She wore no jewellery of any kind, and very little makeup. Tall and slim — simply and elegantly dressed, with pretty dark wavy hair.
She had a coolness, a remoteness, that Gerrard found irresistible.
Gerrard had to control his women — to be in charge — to order his affairs to his liking — to seduce and discard as he fancied.
Cecile did not seem to be bothered. She remained aloof, detached, it did not seem to matter to her whether he was there or not.
She didn't wait by the telephone, or rush to his bidding. The less concerned she was, the more frantic Gerrard became.

He proposed to her out of desperation.
It had become imperative that he should possess her.
As his wife she would 'belong' to him. He would be able to control her, to discover and manipulate her innermost feelings.
Of course it hadn't been like that.
Cecile revealed nothing of herself. It was probably impossible for her to do so. She had spent all her life concealing her feelings.

Gerrard's mother had not approved of the marriage.
'We know nothing of her family,' she said, prowling restlessly around Evelyn's exquisitely arranged salon, picking up things and putting them down again. 'She has no parents...'

'That's hardly her fault,' said Evelyn. 'They were killed in the war...'
Why couldn't Geraldine sit down? She was sure to drop something...

to break something… 'Most unfortunate,' said Geraldine.

They had, like Evelyn's family, not been particularly inconvenienced by the war.
There had been a nasty moment when it was suspected that André's grandmother might have had some Jewish blood, but that was quickly resolved, and André's law firm had continued to practice without too many problems.
She had even occasionally entertained some of the German officers, clients of André's.
They had been most charming and polite, sending her little notes of thanks and bouquets of flowers.

At least they had stayed put, not like some people, the Rosens for instance, who had just vanished into the night…

Their comfortable house in Enghein had been untouched by the bombardment and the retreating and advancing armies.
There had been some skirmishes with the Resistance before the Allies finally arrived, but nowhere near their house, set well away from the road, surrounded by a high wall, with wrought-iron gates locked securely against intruders with a brass plaque warning of 'Chien Méchant'.

Gerrard's schooling had been uninterrupted, although the headmaster was deported, and several of the older boys had been sent to 'work' in Germany.
Only one had returned after the war, permanently sick and unable to work.
Of course terrible things had happened.
But it was a long time ago.

'We don't know how they died,' she said, peering at a yellowing photograph of a stern gentleman in a top hat.
'Her father was in the Resistance,' said Evelyn.

She wished Geraldine would stop pacing about. She had the unique ability of being agitating and suffocating at the same time. Nobody, except perhaps Royalty, would be good enough for her precious Gerrard.

'I believe her mother died of pneumonia,' said Evelyn. 'In the dreadful winter of '45…'

'She has no dot — nothing,' said Geraldine, inspecting a silver cigarette box, turning it upside down to read the inscription on the base.

'She's done very well,' said Evelyn. 'She is an excellent linguist, and has a very good job…'

'He could have married Agnes Duchamp,' said Geraldine. 'They have a wonderful place near Carcassonne — in the mountains. Quite spectacular. Or Irene Martineau — her family is incredibly wealthy. So many really suitable girls…'

The wedding had been very modest.

No church ceremony, which had also caused consternation, a luncheon of crab mousse and roast veal at the Hotel des Pyramides in the Bois de Boulogne.

15

They had been young and carefree then.

Hervé spoilt her completely.

Her days taken up with dress fittings and hair appointments — little lunches at smart restaurants — drives into the countryside — to Versailles for tea in the cobbled courtyard — to Chantilly where friends stabled their horses — to Longchamps where the hats were more talked about than the horses, to drink champagne with one's high heels sinking into the turf.

Solange had a nanny.

She hardly saw her, occasionally popping into the nursery for a new toy that had taken her fancy.

She was a plain child, plump and solemn, not the sort that could be dressed up and displayed to visitors.

She had a cook and a housekeeper.

All she had to do was select the menus for the day.

She liked to give cocktail parties and dinner parties.

They holidayed in luxurious hotels in smart places, or with friends in sumptuous villas.

She decided to sit down — take the weight off her hip.

She would go home as soon as possible.
It was at times like this that she particularly missed Hervé. He had always managed everything so well — except at the end, when she found how little money there was left.

Cecile was coming towards her.
She had finally managed to extricate herself from Pamela Masterson.

Evelyn didn't care much for Americans now, coming in coachloads — middle-aged, middle brow, with waterproof hats and cameras. Tourists acquiring instantly forgotten information — or the young, brashly loud in their uniforms of jeans and T-shirts, chewing gum and obstructing the pavements with bulky backpacks.

It was different then.
They brought life and laughter to a weary city, uneasily occupied for so long, beginning to wonder if the war could ever end, as the Germans settled in more comfortably, subtly tightening the oppressive screws, ready to obliterate any sign of dissonance or dissatisfaction.

That summer when the swastikas were torn down, you could almost taste the relief.

Then the Americans were everywhere, whizzing about in jeeps and khaki limousines, stars and stripes flying. Cheerful and generous, handing out gum and chocolates to the children, nylons and lipstick to the girls.

Officers moved into the Bergs' house, the Steins' smaller and dishevelled — the Germans had torn down the shutters and smashed the windows and the stone urns and statuettes on the terrace — became offices.

Soldiers descended with ladders and tools, and set about making everything spick and span.

The officers gave lots of parties — big, noisy parties.
The drawing room was cleared for dancing, Leah Berg's black baby grand — a Bechstein bought in Vienna, on which Clara had reluctantly practised, stripped of its maroon silk fringed cloth and framed photographs of Leah Berg's grandparents, Mr Berg's moustachioed father, and Samuel as a fat baby in a romper suit — became the centre of the dance band, the lid strewn with sheets of music, cans of drink, overflowing ashtrays and the trumpet player's mute.

The heavy mahogany dining table laden with food, the polished surface scratched and scarred by glasses and bottles and careless knives and forks.
They jived and smooched the nights away.
There was a sense of abandonment — people drank too much — made love to complete strangers — fell in the swimming pool — threw each other in the swimming pool — it was all strangely unreal.

The war was not over.
There was still fighting around Dijon and Nancy, and it wasn't until November when Strasbourg was finally liberated.

At first Evelyn felt awkward among the familiar over-stuffed furniture, using Leah Berg's monogrammed china and elaborate silver, to eat hot dogs and French fries.
The ugly poolside chairs and loungers and over-colourful towels, where they had splashed about and drunk fizzy lemonade, whilst Leah Berg sat squatly under a parasol urging little Samuel to swim. Now girls in skimpy bathing costumes sprawled in the sun, and strong young bodies thrashed in the water, and lay around drinking ice cold beer.

They had never been very friendly with the Bergs, or the Steins. Her mother said they had nothing in common, deploring Leah Berg's

accent and her lack of chic, and complaining that the Stein's house smelt of mothballs and lineament.
Evelyn had been invited occasionally with Brigitte, whose father had business connections with them.
they were certainly very wealthy, and considered themselves to be very important.
The Bergs had two maids, a chauffeur, and a governess, and Mrs Stein had her own personal maid and a nurse for the boys.

What if they came back?
But of course they never came back.
After many years two of the Bergs' cousins came from Israel and started a long legal battle to have the house returned to them.
Nobody came for the Steins'.
Brigitte and her family never came back either.

She and Brigitte had made fun of the Bergs. Leah Berg like a shiny boulster with her heavy bosom and satin blouses, the many rings on her fat hands — too much powder and rouge — the diamond necklace disappearing into the folds of her neck — and Mr Berg with his thick-lensed glasses and gold watch chain.
The children went to the Jewish school.
Clara, who was their age, had a faint moustache and heavy eyebrows.
The little boy, Samuel, played the violin — not very well.
The Steins — stiff and dusty — the two boys peeky — the younger one asthmatic.

She was ashamed of having made fun of them.
How had they managed?
Herded like animals into filthy crowded freight cars.
Hours and days of terrifying darkness.
A horrifying journey to an unspeakable death.
And Brigitte with her bright face and tumbling curls, who was afraid of the dark, and suffered from travel sickness.

She shuddered.
Even now it was painful to remember.
Cecile had her dark memories too. She never spoke about them, but

they were always with her.

Her mother became hysterical and had to be sedated.
She had always refused to believe the stories of deportation and death.
'Gossip — scaremongering gossip,' she said, fussing over some triviality. She had no matching shoes for her new dress — the ersatz shampoo had ruined her hair. 'Propaganda — of course there are no death camps — what nonsense…'

Now, faced with the inescapable truth, she had screamed at her father for bringing wicked filthy Nazis into their home, and collapsed weeping onto the sofa.

With all the distractions of the Americans moving in — the prospect of parties — of dancing — she soon recovered.
Even though she still found the truth hard to believe, expecting the Bergs and the Steins, and all the others who had 'left' suddenly, like Dr Schwartz, one of the doctors at the hospital, a brilliant man, to come home.
But these unpleasant things were soon forgotten.

At last she was able to dress up again and go out, and dance, and flirt — so many gorgeous men…
After years of dismal dreary evenings being polite to boring Germans — although she had to admit, some of them had been very goodlooking too — trying to eat rollmops and heavily spiced sausage without removing her gloves, whilst a stodgy collection of musicians played waltz after waltz, just being among these easygoing affable Americans was bliss — the music was bliss.
It was all just wonderful.
She went a little crazy with it all.

In their exclusive, leafy suburb, they were unconcernedly unaware that France was still reeling from years of occupation and the war of liberation that had ravaged the countryside and reduced their cities to rubble.

Their generous American neighbours showered them with gifts —
there was an abundance of food — chickens and ham, steak, butter,
tea and coffee, freshly baked bread and cakes...
They had nylon stockings and underwear and an endless supply of
soap.

The people of Paris were still queueing for their bread ration.
There were shortages of everything — queues for everything — even
for their tiny meat and cheese rations.
Some shops ran out of food — filling the empty windows with
cardboard replicas and paper flowers.
And as the winter came, the power cuts became more frequent.
There was a terrible lack of fuel.
People sat in their houses in their overcoats, wrapped in rugs to try
and keep warm.

Whilst they danced cheek to cheek to the music of Glenn Miller
and Cole Porter in the Bergs' old drawing room in front of a blazing
fire, with hot punch, bowls of thick soup and juicy steak pies, the
majority of Parisians, those who could not afford to buy goods on
the Black Market, ate soup which was barely more than hot water
with an occasional lump of potato or chunk of carrot, and shivered
beside meagre fires on which they burnt anything they could find
— scraps of paper, old chair legs, even floor boards and bannisters —
often in the darkness of the frequent power cuts, trying to preserve
the last stubs of candle as long as possible.

Cecile smiled and sat down beside her on a small red velvet sofa,
above them hung a very much enlarged photograph of Ravel at his
piano.
'I'm afraid Nancy tends to go on and on,' she said. 'Shall I get them
to get you a taxi, or would you like another drink? I'll ask if they
have some cognac...'

16

Cecile took her coffee into the drawing room.

It had the same hygienically untouchable air as the kitchen.

The white leather sofas and chairs solidly uncomfortable, defying you to sit on them, to spoil the symmetry of the room.

Everything so carefully positioned — the glass-topped tables on the shaggy white carpet — the stunted Bonsai trees in their grey-pebbled tray...

She had objected to the Bonsai trees. She imagined their roots being bound tightly, like the feet of the Chinese women, to prevent growth. 'But cherie,' Hortense had said. 'They are delightful — so petite — so charming...'

And the paintings — bad abstracts — migrainously zigzagged — the sort of paintings hired out for the waiting rooms of dentists and solicitors to show their appreciation of 'Art'...

In the corner by the windows, a standard lamp with tubular antennae drooped towards the floor, the silver bendable tubes, like long-necked birds with illuminated beaks reaching for water.

She crossed the room to shut the windows — the breeze had caught the folds of the voluminous gauze curtains, and they billowed inwards, enveloping the miniature desert of cacti in a white shroud.

There had been curtains like these in the bedroom of the hotel where they had spent their honeymoon.

Long French windows opening onto the balcony where they had had their breakfast.

A balcony with camellias, and dark wooden boxes of purple violets and iris.

The waiter bringing their breakfast on a gold-knobbed trolley — warm rolls and croissants wrapped in a white napkin — a silver dish of butter — coffee in a silver pot — fresh orange juice in a crystal jug — a bowl of polished fruit.

She had a robe of very fine wool — pale lilac with satin piping.

Beneath them the hotel garden sloped down towards the sea — the

glittering wondrous sea, gently ruffled, sparkling, as if handfuls of diamonds had been scattered on its surface.
The clear acidulated sapphire water streaked with amethyst where hidden seaweed clung to rocks.
At dusk a dense salt green.

The scents of the garden lying still on the warm night air.

Gerrard in white slacks, the sleeves of his dark blue shirt rolled up — 'Shall we take a boat trip today?'

Shirts.
She had to go to Sancerre's and get the shirts he had ordered — hand made — fine Egyptian cotton — two white — a fine stripe and a pale blue.

He was going to Geneva tomorrow.
'I really need the shirts,' he had said. 'And Hortense wants to know when we shall be going to the house. She wants to invite the Perrets...'

Many years ago they had bought a house together near Vence.
Gerrard had liked the idea. Didier considered it a good investment. To Hortense it was another possession — always greedy for possessions she was enthusiastic.
Cecile would rather they had bought a house of their own. She didn't want to share a house with anyone. She didn't want to share a house with Hortense and Didier, but it was a long time ago when she and Gerrard were first married, and she hadn't wished to be difficult.

They had spent many summers there when Hortense and Didier's two sons were young — so well behaved with their strict nurse — a sturdy blonde from Alsace, who believed in discipline and routine.
Hortense was very particular about servants. They had to wear uniform. The boy's nurse in a crackling grey dress with stiff white collar and cuffs, grey stockings and sensible black shoes.

The cook-housekeeper, Seraphine, who had to keep the house in immaculate condition at all times, wore black in the winter and white in the summer, a concession to the extreme heat. Her husband, who did the garden, was never allowed in the front entrance or anywhere in the house, unless engaged on a necessary activity, like bringing in logs or changing light bulbs.

It was impossible to avoid Hortense. If you were not there for her to yabber at she would search you out. Didier would don his khaki shorts and beige leather sandals and disappear for the whole day into the hills.
Gerrard would arrange fishing trips and horse riding, and Cecile would be trapped on the terrace being yabbered at by Hortense, who had vacuous and superficial opinions on nearly every subject.
Sometimes there would be other guests, and Seraphine would have extra help from the village to prepare and serve the meals, and Hortense would inspect the girls' finger nails and make them tie back their hair. In the summer she had given up insisting on stockings — Didier had said she was being unreasonable. 'It's much too hot — their legs are brown anyway…'

She would be expected to accompany Hortense on superfluous shopping expeditions, for Hortense to buy yet another bathing costume, sun hat, or ugly 'fun' shirts for her sons, and nasty rubber shoes she made them wear for swimming.

As the boys grew older they managed to extricate themselves and go to the beach alone — even invite friends — uncomfortably — for lunch, when Hortense would interrogate them on their families, schooling and ambitions.

Then they got old enough not to come at all, developing keen interests in camping and hiking, anything that took them as far away as possible.

Guillaume refused to go to university.
He grew a beard and went to live in an artists colony in Mexico.
It was best not to mention Guillaume to Hortense. She was very touchy about Guillaume.

Olivier had a good job at the Bourse — seen very seldom and very briefly — smart designer suits and silk shirts.
He lived with an Algerian girl which horrified Hortense, although she was somewhat mollified on finding out that she was a very successful business woman, and probably earned more than Olivier.

Now Hortense consoled herself with her many protegés who were much easier to control — their livelihood depending on her approval. So the Maurices and Jeromes flitted through her life — writing second class poetry, designing monstrous furniture and unsuitable clothing — hair stylists and fitness gurus, artists and musicians of varied talent, and of course, interior designers.

She didn't know why Gerrard should expect her to tell Hortense when they were going to the house. He always decided when they should go.
He liked to go when Hortense and Didier were there.
He and Didier belonged to the tennis club at Vence, and there were always tournaments.

She would like to go when no one was there — to be alone in the lovely house with its arched doorways and little fountain in the stone-flagged hall, splashing a crystal necklace of cool drops into the mosaic tiled pool with plump goldfish lazing among soft-fronded weeds.

She would be able to sit in the scented garden, and watch the distant sea change colour — and walk among the shrubs and rocks and bent olive trees...

She would be able to eat what she liked — when she liked and not be involved with the constant argument about what they were to eat.
Hortense always with some new fad — insisting on bits and pieces of colour-coordinated food on large gold-rimmed white plates — no red meat — no shellfish — and Didier demanding steak and lobster — bouillebaise and stuffed aubergines.
Didier invariably won on questions of food, sweeping aside Hortense's protests — 'When I am not here, cherie, you can eat what

you like. When I am here we eat proper food.'
And then Hortense would sulk — pushing her food around on her plate and complaining that the steak was tough, the aubergines fatty, the cheese dried up, the white bread indigestible.

Gerrard would have to phone her. She only wanted to boast about how friendly she was with the Perrets.

She should have got the shirts yesterday, but she had been delayed by Gerrard's mother, who phoned almost daily with a liturgy of complaints.

At 88 she was still very fit and active.
Since André's death ten years ago she had lived in an exclusive and very expensive apartment in a converted mansion.
All her needs were catered for — a communal dining room serving excellent meals — a bar — a lounge — TV room — beautifully kept grounds with graceful trees, and a herb garden with neatly-trimmed box hedges.
Her apartment was light and airy. She had her own furniture and washed Chinese rugs — but she always found something to complain about.

17

She saw Geraldine as if through a distorting mirror, her image swelling and shrinking, the features squashed and elongated — and instead of Geraldine, overheated with food, scraps of cream and pastry from her strawberry mille feuille sticking to her upper lip, she saw Madame Dubochet's old mother in her blackened hovel, sucking her soup noisily through toothless gums, whilst delivering a stream of complaints about her daughter — her daughter's husband — her son — her grandsons — 'leaving her to rot' — hobbling out of her warped doorway to shout at the Forgis brothers on their bikes — remaining silent only when the German patrols passed — so old — her skin waxen yellow — the nails black and brittle...

Whilst Madame Dubochet's old mother gnawed and dribbled over the last bit of gristle on a chicken bone, Geraldine, then a handsome young woman, was tucking greedily into her Black Market pork, charcuterie and patés, so easy to obtain from her father's business, inviting Vichy officials and German officers to share in suppers of foie gras and fromage du tête.

She felt sure that her 'little suppers' had helped to influence the local Vichy not to investigate further in the matter of André's grandmother — they had conveniently found no further papers or other evidence to corroborate their suspicions.

They were both greedy and selfish.
Madame Dubochet's old mother had not ceased to shout and bang her stick and complain, even when her son's cap and bloody jacket were returned, confirming that he had been among the dead on the grassy slope beneath the leafy oak that dreadful night.

Hortense was the same — completely self-absorbed, concerned only with herself.

They had never like each other.
Geraldine thought Hortense vain, spoilt and stupid, tolerating her only as Gerrard's friend Didier's wife.

Hortense thought Geraldine common and nouveau riche — the daughter of a charcutier who married money — spoilt and ignorant. She only tolerated her because she was Gerrard's mother.

Cecile also had to tolerate her because she was Gerrard's mother.

Geraldine had been quite happy to be friendly towards those who held their country in a slowly tightening garrotte, so long as she could ensure her supply of meat and cheese — wine, petrol, coal and extra clothing coupons.
André was not happy about it.
He had never been happy about it.
He was caught in a poisonous web. Every movement entangling him further in what he despised.

Cooperating at work — cooperating at home. He was truly a collaborator.

Collaboration never worried Geraldine.
She enjoyed the little suppers — priding herself on the abundance of food and drink, the dishes of boudin blanc and pig's trotter with onion sauce — pig's trotters were Lise's speciality.

Her cleaning left much to be desired, but she was a very good cook — and very discreet.
She valued her job — the comfortable room and plenty to eat — too much to gossip about her employers or their guests.

Gerrard, watching from his bedroom window, saw them arrive in their sleekly silent staff cars, the chauffeurs leaping out to open doors — the smart Nazi salutes — Heil Hitler! — the officers with their immaculate uniforms — peaked hats tucked under their arms as they bent to kiss his mother's hands.
They often brought sweets and chocolate for him.
He would lie in bed and listen to the talk and laughter downstairs.
An SS officer sometimes came to tea — chilling in his black uniform and glassily polished black boots — leaning back against the golden velvet sofa cushions, smoking small cigars.
When he came his mother wore her best blue dress and pearl necklace, and there were chocolate eclairs.
He spoke careful, clipped French, and once brought him a model tank.

He was careful never to mention the suppers or the SS officer's teatime visits to anybody.
He was uncomfortably aware that it was unpatriotic, and that to be known to be consorting with the enemy would be very unpopular, and even dangerous.
He was also not at all sure that his father knew of the SS officer's visits.

Cecile didn't blame Geraldine.
That was how she was.

She had thought it perfectly alright to behave as she had.
It had been her way of protecting herself and her family.
She remembered the war as a small nuisance that she had overcome,
and that, apart from the occasional twinge of nostalgia for her role
as an admired hostess, had since forgotten.

'They gave me damson jam,' her furious voice crackling down the
phone. She always held the receiver too close to her mouth. 'Damson
jam with stones — I could have choked — I told the girl to take it
away at once and bring me some honey — she said there wasn't any.
No honey! And the croissants were stale — yesterday's — tough and
chewy. I demanded to speak to Madame Thesiger immediately. She
came back with blackberry jelly and said Madame Thesiger was with
the doctor — Madame Davide had been taken ill...'
Geradline hardly paused for breath. 'There is nothing wrong with
Madame Davide. She is a hypochondriac. Madame Thesiter doesn't
want to talk to me. Gerrard must speak to her. He must insist that
she speaks to me, otherwise he will have to take the matter up with
the Governors...'

'She is probably just very busy,' said Cecile. 'There must be so much
to do...'

She could sense Geraldine's exasperation.
She had always thought her ineffectual and unnecessary.

'I will speak to Gerrard myself,' said Geraldine. 'I will phone him at
the office' — meaning — 'You are utterly useless...'

18

It was always a pleasure to got to the Rue des Merles in the small
streets behind the Place de la Madeleine.
A street of chicly expensive shops and boutiques.

A milliners with a single, glorious hat resting on a curved wooden
chair. A cartwheel of creamy tulle, with a crown of creamy silk roses.

A chocolatier with a window full of small mountains of truffles, stacks of assorted boxes tied with satin ribbons, and little heaps of sugared almonds, pink and white, strewn like pebbles on the draped white cloth, and bunches of sugar flowers in delicate, fluted vases.
There was a jeweller with two oval windows lined with dark blue velvet, displaying snakes of diamonds and a single square cut sapphire on dark blue velvet cushions.

Sancerre's was at the end of the street, next to the café with bright yellow umbrellas, and yellow flowers on the round white tables, and tubs of bushy conifers edging the pavement.

Before that was a gallery where Hortense bought pictures and small pieces of sculpture, which she quickly tired of and resold.

They had been to a preview there quite recently — one of Hortense's proteges, Georges Ballardin, had had an exhibition.

His paintings were strange — queasily unpleasant — blobby blotchy figures and blobby blotchy landscapes — a lot of grey and green and vermilion splodges.
There was much talk of uterine imagery, and references to the Life Force and galactic visions…

Gerrard, dismissing them as 'total rubbish', disappeared among the crush.

There was the usual preview mixture of high-heeled young men with multiple earrings and sooty mascara, the sober suited, firmly corseted in a variety of plain and patterned waistcoats. 'Arty' women with fringed shawls and necklaces of large beads, standing squarely in thonged sandals or very old espadrilles, and the 'soignée' in sharp sequinned miniskirts with puffed out designer hairstyles.

The waiters struggled through the throng with trays of champagne and orange juice, stuffed vineleaves and miniature tarts of anchovies and black olives.

Hortense and Georges Ballardin made a bizarre couple. Hortense with her glittering jacket embroidered with silver thread and greenish metallic discs, her skirt too short, the heels of her diamanté-trimmed shoes too high, arm in arm with Georges in his old orange tweed jacket, white trousers and grubby white poloneck.

Didier was nowhere to be seen.
He might not have even been there.
He tended to avoid these occasions.

She glimpsed Gerrard in the far corner, where the steel spiral staircase twisted up to the floor above.

He was talking to a young woman.
At least she looked young.
Her back was turned, and her light brown hair tumbled, curling, onto her shoulders.
A jewelled hand held a glass of champagne — the sleeve of her black chiffon blouse ruffled at the wrist.

Gerrard was very close to her.
He had a hand on her arm, his head almost touching hers.
He looked serious — even angry.
Perhaps this was his mistress.
The thought barely touched her — mildly curious to see what she looked like.

She had said to Evelyn that perhaps it would be best if they had a divorce.
'Absolutely not,' said Evelyn. 'A divorced woman has no status — no status whatsoever. For a man it is different — there is always a place for a single man — but for a woman, nobody wants an extra woman at their table. You would be cut off — uninvited. First you must find yourself another man…'

They had met for lunch at l'Escargot.
Evelyn ordered consommé and fillet of sole, which she didn't eat.
Cecile had a salad with prawns.

Evelyn drank champagne.
Cecile drank Perrier water.

Apart from two young women with flirty hats eating smoked salmon at a table by the window, the restaurant was full of older men with young women, ordering frivolous things like soufflés and flambées and pink champagne, and older men with older men, eating solid dishes of beouf bourgignon and blanquette de veau, helping themselves generously from the cheese board, washing it all down with dusty bottles of Bordeaux.

Evelyn liked to come to this restaurant.
She had often come with Hervé — the old proprietor, now sadly retired, had been a good friend — always the best table, and a centrepiece of beautifully arranged flowers — and once before they were married, with her mother and father.
Her mother had behaved very well.
She had managed not to smudge her makeup — drinking unobtrusively — perfectly steady — walking to the Ladies' Powder Room with the precisely careful steps of a practised acoholic.
Nobody would have guessed that she had been drinking all morning.

She had started drinking heavily when the Americans came — partying every night at the Berg's old house — Manhattans and martinis — bourbon on the rocks.
'Now the beastly, boring War is over we must celebrate,' she said. 'We have lost too many years already…'
She loved to dance — she loved the flattery — she loved to be among so many young men.
She was hardly ever home.
Evelyn sensed the widening gap between her mother and father.
Her father spent longer and longer hours at the hospital.
At the rare meals they had together, her father stayed silent, whilst her mother prattled, nervously, incessantly — gulping her wine, desperate to fill the empty space. Her father now slept in the spare room — maybe listening in the dark for the sound of her mother stumbling on the stairs in the early hours of the morning.

Her father, white with misery and lack of sleep, demanding to know where she had been all night, and her mother, wrapping her damson satin housecoat tightly round her, 'Don't shout, cheri — I have a headache. You must have been asleep — I came in very quietly — it was very late...'

And when the Americans left, as they had come, in a swirl of khaki limousines and jeeps, stars and stripes flying, and the Military Police, with their white helmets and armbands, firmly locked the freshly painted gates of the Berg's and Stein's properties, her mother locked herself in her room and wept and drank, and drank and wept, and played dance music endlessly on the gramophone.

She too had been sad to see them go.
She had had several boyfriends among the young soldiers briefly stationed there.
The only one whose name she could remember was Gus, with corn-stubble hair and very blue eyes.
He had given her six pairs of nylons as a parting gift — which was probably why she remembered his name.

None of them were there long.
Passing through to join the tortuously slow advance — the final effort — slogging their way among dark forests and Wagnerian mountains — cautious in the disfigured cities, where snipers hid among perilous buildings, and booby traps waited to blow their legs off.

For her mother it was different.
The more senior personnel remained until they all moved out — when the Russians had reached the outskirts of the blackened, festering skeleton of Berlin.

It was generally supposed she had been having an affair with Colonel Brockmeyer — Chuck Brockmeyer — so assured — so handsome...

She pushed her sole away.
Her hip ached.

The chairs at L'Escargot were very elegant, but not very comfortable. She would have a cognac with her coffee.

Perhaps she was starting to drink too much — perhaps she would end up like her mother, a drunken sodden creature, nauseous and nauseating.

'In any case,' she said, 'Gerrard hasn't mentioned divorce. He doesn't want a divorce — because he has a mistress, does not mean he wants a divorce… On the contrary, the situation may suit him very well…'

19

There was only one picture on the pale varnished wood of the display platform inside the window of the Galerie Sarthe.

A large, unframed canvas, the paint applied so thickly that it made ridges and hollows in the swirling mass of browns and greens — the dense browns and greens of forests — trees and undergrowth crushed and welded together — secretive and impenetrable.

She smelt the freshly trodden earth — nutty and warm — thick with twigs and leaves and brittle nut kernels — piling curly young green fronds of bracken into a heap. Sister Constance, sturdy in her old rubber boots, chopping down saplings and the lower branches of young trees to make a framework. Anne Marie fussing that it would be too damp for Jacob — Sister Celeste, puffed with exertion, assuring her they would never have to be there very long, not long enough for Jacob to catch cold, and Jacob gleefully rolling down the slope calling, 'Watch me! Watch me!'

It had been such a fine day — the soft spring light casting primrose patches among the new, transparent leaves, clusters of milky wood anemones and bluebells among the briars and blackberry bushes, sprouting crisp green shoots — delicate whitethorn blossom, like a captured flurry of snowflakes.

But there was already blood on the sun.

The sharp-clawed predators with their grey army of faceless followers — creatures in black boots, trampling bloody, broken limbs — already lurking in the shadows — cold shivers of wind their shallow breathing.

She closed her eyes to shut out the picture — feeling the pavement move.
Was she going to faint?
She opened her eyes, trying to steady herself — looking down at the square white card neatly positioned by the bottom of the picture.
'The Hiding Place' by Jacob Kaminski.

She had to sit down.
Somehow she reached the café.
She asked for coffee and a glass of water, clasping her hands beneath the table to control their shaking.

He had lived.
Jacob had lived — had grown up — had become an artist…
The relief was so profound that she couldn't take it in.
He was alive.
She must find him.
She had to find him.
Sister Celeste's blood was sticky on her hands — the earth heavy — the heat crackling with fear.
She had to find him.

She stood again in front of the disturbing, forceful canvas.

Had he been afraid — cowering in the dark makeshift shelter, hearing the crashing movements of the black-booted soldiers as they trampled the twigs and broken branches, beating the undergrowth with their heavy sticks — the coarse bracken tearing their legs — guttural commands — the sudden metallic terror of gunfire — the startled flapping birds — the silence — being bundled from here to there — clinging to Ruth's shoulder.

The girl in the gallery was smoothly beautiful — the short black skirt — endless, long, pale-stockinged legs — her blonde hair cut in a short, bouncy bob.

She was sorry — Monsieur Sarthe was in Mexico — he would not be back until next week — she was standing in for his Personal Assistant who was on holiday.
She had no information about the painting or the artist.
She thought it was on loan.
She looked through all the desk drawers, and found the name and address of the owner of the painting.
Paul Selignac.
The address in a small village near Tours.
She wrote it down on a white card.
She was very polite.

20

She reached Tours at about 11 o'clock.

Gerrard had left at 6.30 for the airport.
He would not be back until the weekend.
She wondered vaguely whether the girl with the tumbling curls would be going with him.

She could only think about finding Jacob.

She had almost forgotten the shirts, and that they were to dine with an important client.
Gerrard had rushed in, late from the office, with just time to shower and change.

He poured himself a large whisky on the way to the bathroom, and said she must surely have some jewellery.

She stared blankly back at herself in the mirror, a thin stick of black — her dark hair flecked with grey — her face bleak and tired.
'Jewellery doesn't suit me,' she said. 'It never suited me…'

He knew she never wore jewellery — apart from her engagement ring, a small, square diamond, and sometimes earrings when she was younger.

Hortense had tried to get her to colour her hair.
'Just to get rid of the grey,' she said. 'You would look years younger — men don't like women with grey hair...'

Cecile refrained from saying that she was not really interested in whether men liked it or not, and that colouring her hair would not stop Gerrard from straying.

Hortense had telephoned at lunchtime to ask them to aperitifs — the Perrets were coming, and bringing the Brazilian soprano Carmel Mendes. 'They're great friends — such a fantastic voice — she is going to sing Traviata at the Opera in October — she is only here for a few days — staying with Jean Paul and Therese...'

Cecile said unfortunately they were going out to dinner — one of Gerrard's clients — Robert Binoche...

'Oh, darling,' said Hortense. 'Poor you! Robert is such a bore — He is in the middle of divorcing his perfectly splendid wife to marry a girl half his age, with half a brain. Silly old fool! So he goes around moaning about his digestion — his children refusing to speak to him, and the money it is all costing...'

She had so wanted to tell someone about Jacob.
She almost phoned Evelyn — but Evelyn knew nothing about Jacob — or about the convent — the nuns hiding Jews — or about any of the things that had happened — the terrifying things that still painfully wound her throat with wire, imprisoning the silent screams...

The girl at the gallery had written down Paul Selignac's phone number as well as his address, but somehow she couldn't bring herself to phone him.
She had to go herself — speak to him face to face.

What if it was not the same Jacob Kaminsky? It could be someone else with the same name…
But it had to be him. Who else would paint woods like that? Their woods…

It had been an uncomfortable meal.
The girl had long straight blonde hair, held back with a jewelled butterfly, a strapless white dress and gold dust sprinkled on her shoulders. Her face was disappointedly peaky. She spoke little, drinking champagne as if it were lemonade, and nibbling at her food like a rabbit eating a stick of celery.

Gerrard and Robert talked business — discussing property deals, and the difficulty of obtaining building permission for certain sites. It seemed Robert was in the process of constructing a block of luxury flats in Cannes.
He was soft-bellied with an unhealthy, indoor pallor — looking nervously about as they were led to their table, as if expecting his 'perfectly splendid wife' to materialise — relieved to sit down — to order importantly from the lengthy menu for himself and the girl.

She could sense that he irritated Gerrard.
He was irritated already.
His mother had phoned him twice at the office during the day — once about the damson jam, and once about the wine served at lunch, which had been a very poor quality — rough and acidic.
'They want to make us ill — so we will have to call the doctor, and they can make more money out of us,' she had said. 'You will have to speak to Madame Thesiger…'
He had told her she was perfectly capable of speaking to Madame Thesiger herself, and that they would try and come and see her on Sunday — if he was back from Geneva…

How many Sundays — how many birthdays, anniversaries, lunches and dinners, had they spent with Geraldine — trying to be festive.
In the dark heavily shuttered house in Enghein when André was alive.
André getting quieter and quieter — sinking into his chair —

fiddling with his glasses, which hung round his neck on a chain, whilst Geraldine became more vociferous and argumentative.

The food was always very rich — slabs of foie gras embedded with black truffles — roast duck — roast goose — cream sauces — cream pastries.

Cecile felt no hunger — revolted by the excess.

When she was young, before she had encountered Geraldine's gluttony, she was always hungry — but she had lost her appetite, stifled by the heavy lace cloth, the heavy silver cutlery — the dishes heavy with food — Geraldine piling her plate — her squat hands heavy with rings. She could hardly bring herself to eat anything.

Inevitably there was a row — about anything — about nothing.

Geraldine on the attack — Gerrard becoming increasingly tense and angry — she and André remaining mute — sickened —invisible.

When André died, Geraldine had presumed she would live with them, or more precisely, they would move to Enghein and live with her.

She had never forgiven or forgotten Gerrard's firm unequivocal refusal, never missing an opportunity to remind them that they had abandoned her, blaming Cecile for her son's unaccountable behaviour — as if Cecile had ever influenced Gerrard's decisions.

It had to be Cecile's fault — Gerrard would never cast aside his mother — that's what came of marrying someone with no family — they didn't understand family responsibilities — and with no children of her own, could not possibly appreciate the sacred bond between mother and son… and on… and on…

Gerrard told her to take no notice.

He had no intention of living with his mother.

Now they had meals in the airy dining room at Le Refuge, with long French windows opening onto a terrace overlooking the gardens.

Geraldine refused to sit on the terrace, resentful and petulant — complaining about everything and everyone — insisting on taking coffee in her room with the windows tightly shut whatever the weather, so she could continue her liturgy of disapproval — lipstick didn't suit older women — only maids and schoolteachers wore black stockings — and, when she was younger — only streetwalkers wore heels that high — wasn't it about time she had a child? — soon she would be too old — everybody she knew had grandchildren…

Cecile wished Gerrard would go on his own to see his mother.
Geraldine didn't want to see her.
She would suggest it.
When he came back from Geneva she would suggest it.

Robert and the girl ate lobster, and there was a lot of fussing, with Robert helping her manage the silver lobster pick.
Gerrard had trout — dissecting it like a surgeon — very deliberately to conceal his irritation.
She had fillet of sole, which was easy to eat and quite plain. She smiled politely, trying not to notice Robert's asinine behaviour. For once Hortense was right — it was ridiculous. The girl was half his age, with half a brain. She opened her small pink mouth for Robert to pop in a morsel of lobster, and chewed it up in a rabbity way before opening her mouth for more.
Gerrard buttered his bread with swift, furious movements, and asked if he had come to an agreement with the architects.
Robert said they were going to Cannes next week to find out exactly how things were progressing, and would like Gerrard to join them as soon as possible to sort things out…

She felt an overwhelming desire to leave — to escape from this sleek, smooth place, full of sleek, smooth people — from Robert and the girl's embarrassing idiocy — from Gerrard's disdain, to get up and go — to drive away into the night to find Jacob.

She slept fitfully, menaced by dreams.
In the threatening blackness behind the creaking door, the voices of the lost clamoured for her attention.
The murky waters of the consuming whirlpool sucking them down, choking them into silence — a reverberating silence — metal screeching on metal — a silence prickling with horror.

She woke suddenly, cold and alert, to the grey dawn, the curtains lifting ghostly shrouds in the chill morning breeze. She heard Gerrard in the bathroom — the sound of running water, and got up to make coffee before he left.

She had no trouble finding the village, a street of shuttered stone, a boulangerie, post office, a gendarmerie, and a Café des Sports.
There was no one about.
She went into the post office to ask the way.
The post mistress, round and friendly in a shiny blouse with wide stripes of brown and orange, came to the door to show her. 'Such a lovely house, madame,' she said. 'Monsieur Selignac is a real gentleman…'

The countryside was very pleasant, rounded comfortable woods, and fields of sunflowers and maize.
The house was some way off the road, hidden by a field of young poplars, filling the air with silken whispering.

She felt very nervous and apprehensive.
Perhaps she should not have come — perhaps she should have telephoned —not just turned up.
There might be nobody in — they might be busy — not want to see her…

21

The house was of soft grey stone — long and low, with a neat square of gravel to park the car, and a fig tree spreading along the wall by the open front door, the figs already purple among the glossy dark green leaves.
She stood a moment, steadying herself before she rang the bell, closing her eyes briefly, remembering the picture, the swirling browns and greens — the heavy weight of leaves…

The man who came to the door was tall and thin, with close-cropped grey hair. He wore jeans, a dark T-shirt and espadrilles.

He looked annoyed, as if he had been disturbed.
He said 'Yes?' briskly, in a 'What the hell do you want?' tone, and

held the door with one hand as if about to shut it.
'I wondered if you could help me,' she said. 'I'm looking for Jacob Kaminsky.'

The man's demeanour changed instantly.
He dropped his hand from the door, and his face relaxed — he had a nice face.
'I'm sorry,' he said. 'I thought you were selling something…'
He gestured for her to enter. 'Please, come in…'

The hall was cool with a floor of old terracotta tiles, which led into a long room with French windows opening onto a terrace with nasturtiums covering the low wall, and urns and pots and troughs of flowers — a profusion of flowers — fat pink daisies, phlox, petunias, columbine, sweet williams, marigolds — so many flowers she didn't know all their names.

He asked her to sit down, and said he would go and fetch some coffee — unless she preferred an aperitif?
She said coffee would be very nice.

She was relieved to sit down.
The chair was deep and comfortable. She was weary, unutterably weary.
The past flashed by like the scenery from an express train —half seen — half remembered — sudden jolting images — brief glimpses — a solitary pine — a toppling of blue rock — a vine-covered hillside — the criss-crossing girders of a bridge — lonely stations — a hand — the side of a face — the corner of a building — swans flying in elegant symmetry, white necks stretched, high up in a hazy blue nothingness — a kestrel hovering over a field of clover — a blind, crawling tank, grotesquely camouflaged, lumbering through a field of long-stalked daisies and tall-seeded grass — a sentinel staircase in a landscape of rubble…

He had come back with the coffee, and sat down opposite her, and she began to apologise for turning up without warning — telling him about the picture — of having to find Jacob.

'I knew him as a little boy,' she said, and he ran across the grass, hiding in the folds of Sister Celeste's black habit, as Anne-Marie tried to catch him to take him to bed — ginger hairs on the backs of the Gestapo man's hands...

She saw he was looking at her.
It was a curious look — compassionate, yet somehow stern.

'I'm afraid I do not have good news for you,' he said. 'Jacob is dead. He has been dead a long time, almost twenty years...' He paused, looking down at his hands. 'He committed suicide.'

The noisy darkness closed in on her.
Anne-Marie's stifled weeping — the spitting death of machine gun fire — Sister Celeste crying 'Hurry! Hurry!' Sister Clare naming Italian cities — Rome — Venice — Naples — The clatter of the spoon from her mothers' cooking pot on the stone floor of their kitchen — the urgent bubbling of the neglected soup — wheels skidding on gravel — revving engines — guttural commands — her own internal screaming — sticky red jam spreading on the cellar floor among the shattered glass — her hands sticky with blood — heavy clouds that obscured the bloody sun — incinerator ashes of the damned...

From a long way off she heard his voice.
'I'm sorry to have given you such a shock — let me get you something — a cognac — a glass of wine...'

She opened her eyes.
He was leaning towards her — concerned — apologetic...
She stared unseeing at the open door, despite the soft fingers of summer warmth reaching into the room, she felt icy cold, unable to move.
She did not close her eyes again, afraid that the darkness would engulf her.

Paul came back with a glass of wine.
He said she must stay and have a little lunch — they could eat out on the terrace — it was such a lovely day.

'Drink a little wine,' he said, 'it will make you feel better...'

They sat in the shade of an umbrella on the terrace. A solid woman in a flowered overall served their meal.

Slices of pink ham overlapping on a fluted white dish, a golden omelette, a salad of crisp curly lettuce and flat-leaved herbs — a wooden board of cheese — a bowl of peaches — purple grapes in a basket lined with vine leaves.

Paul said, 'Come — eat a little — Annette will be most hurt if you do not eat...'

It was very calm and quiet, there was a wonderful scent of flowers and newly mown grass. She began to feel less cold. She drank a little wine, and ate a little. The food was delicious — simple and delicious.

'It is very kind of you,' she said. 'I should not have turned up like this — I'm sorry — it was very rude...'

'Not at all,' he said. 'One needs time to talk about important things...'

He cut slices from the long crusty baguette and passed it to her. 'Jacob was always troubled,' he said. 'I first met him at an exhibition in Paris — an exhibition for new artists. He had several pictures on show, and I was very impressed. We became friends — I have a gallery in Tours, and he sold many paintings there — but he was always troubled...'

22

'Be still,' Ruth had whispered, breathless from hurrying, scrambling among the clinging brambles, sap-filled branches whipping their faces. 'We must stay very quiet...' her sallow face tense, a lock of dark hair falling over her forehead.
She put an arm round him.
Marthe, eyes punched purple bruises in her pale face, blue and

wizened with fear, huddled against them.
Jacob held his breath as long as he could, anxious in case his breathing made a noise.
They must not make a single sound in their hiding place of woven branches and scratchy bracken.

Grey wolves — sour fangs savaging the earth — hunting them down — sharpening their bony claws on the smooth fibrous bark of the beech trees — breaking the bushes — ripping away the curtains of milky convolvulus and apple-pink wild roses scattering the ground like confetti from a forgotten wedding.
He covered his ears to shut out the terror.
He longed for his mother — his sister — for the comfort of his home — his father, a dimly-remembered figure, who had gone chalk-faced with the men in black — the same men who had unleashed their wolves to hunt them down.

Nobody came to say it was 'All Clear' to go back to the Convent, where Anne-Marie and Sister Celeste would fuss over him, give him his supper and tuck him up in the little bed beside Sister Celeste.

Nobody came.

They stayed absolutely still and quiet, not daring to move.
The darkness enveloped them like a velvet cloak, and he had fallen asleep when a man came and led them out of the wood.
He carried Jacob on his back — the girls followed behind, Ruth holding Marthe's hand.
They were hidden in a hayloft.
He did not know for how long. A young boy brought them food, mostly bread and wrinkled tomatoes, sometimes a hard-boiled egg, or a bit of cheese, water and clean clothes.
None of them were the right size, but they were clean.

Ruth said, 'We have to call you Jean now — You must remember your name is Jean...'
She was upset. She had been sick, and sat in the stifling loft, shivering. 'Your real name is a secret — you must not tell anyone

your real name…'
Marthe had said, 'I want to go home — when will we go home?
When will we ever go home?'

And then they were separated.
It was not safe for them to be together.
He had to say goodbye.
They had to wait until nightfall.
There was a moon — a crescent of silver in a sky carpeted with stars.

Ruth's hands were winter cold — her face stiff.
She brushed his face with icy lips, unable to speak, and Marthe knelt
on the hard muddy stones of the yard whispering 'Goodbye', her
little face puckered in the effort not to cry.

He never saw them again.

He heard the soldiers come into the yard, crouching in his hiding
place in the old barn, among piles of logs and sprouting potatoes,
stacks of old wine bottles and bundles of straw.
Madame Claudine and her old father Pépé had made a space for him
to sleep, and found him scraps of paper and pencils, even a few stubs
of coloured crayon, so he could draw.
He did not know how long he had been there.
He was very lonely and frightened, especially at night, and longed
for Ruth and Marthe to comfort him — longed to run out into the
sunlight — to see his mother…
These soldiers were not speaking the frightful, frightening language
of the soldiers who spread terror and panic.
There was laughter and whistling, and Madame Claudine came
rushing in and picked him up in her arms.
There were tears running down her face.
'Les Anglais,' she said. 'The English have come — we are safe…'

These soldiers wore unthreatening khaki battledress, and sat about
in the yard, with sleeves rolled up, and smoked cigarettes.
They were tired, their faces streaked with dirt, but they were
cheerful and friendly.

One of the officers spoke a little French.
He said things were going well — it would soon be over — the Germans were retreating — very slowly — but they were retreating…

They did not stay long — climbing onto their khaki trucks — waving and calling out as they disappeared in a cloud of dust down the rough road into the distance where the heat hung like water and black smoke billowed up from a little town — the Church spire glinting in the sunlight.

Madame Claudine said she was sure he would soon be able to go home to his mother — in a little while, when the Germans had gone. It would not be long now, like the nice English Captain had said.

But the winter came, and he was taken to another place — to sleep and eat, with lots of other children — to do lessons and play games, and his mother did not come. Nobody came. Perhaps they did not know how to find him? He had another name now.

It had taken him years to get his name back — to find any evidence of his family — where he had come from.
He had to retrace his steps — going from place to place — asking questions.

He knew he was Jacob Kaminsky — not Jean Tivier.

At last he found the small town where they had lived — the house where he had thought he was safe — would always be safe — tiny fragments of memory — jagged splinters — his mother calling him — his sister pushing him on the swing with fraying ropes — he had always wanted to go higher. Blue and white plates on the table — a bowl of shelled peas — a red ball — the men in black leading his father away.

The bird's nest in the kind lady's garden.
She had called him to come and see it — to see the speckled eggs.
The bird's nest had saved his life.

When the men in black came for his mother and sister, she had shoved him in the cupboard under the stairs among the boxes and brooms.

'Not a sound,' she said. 'We will play hide and seek...' She put a finger to her lips, 'Not a sound...'
Cowering in the darkness he heard the fearsome knocking — the harsh interrogatory tones — clicking boots — black boots...
His heart beat so loudly, he thought they would certainly hear it...

Later through the dark wood — the trees leaning like old men with grasping hands — the path knobbled with unseen roots, hurting his feet. She had carried him, soothing him with soft words...

She had saved his life.

He had found their names, with sickened horror, amongst the roll call of the dead — the files with worn buff covers — columns of black spidery writing and uneven typing — a silent testament of unspeakable horror — his sister too, Sylvia Kaminsky, aged six years...

The gnarled mulberry tree still spread crooked branches across the patchy grass — squashed ripe fruit staining the earth like coagulated blood — their blood...
There were cabbages and french beans growing in the vegetable garden, and two children's bicycles propped against the wall under the kitchen window.

He had gone back to Paris to carry on painting — transferring his sadness, anger and terrible loneliness onto his canvasses.

Paul had met him then.
'A very nice looking, amiable young man,' he said.

They had moved to sit under an oak tree, which roofed the garden with gentle green shade — Agnes had brought coffee.

'His paintings were so very good,' he said. 'He began to be known, selling a lot. Later I will show you the ones I have left...'

He did not give up his search for Ruth and Marthe.
It was not so hard to find the Convent.
It had to be within walking distance of his home, surrounded by woods.
But it was derelict — a crumbling ruin, strangled with ivy, the grounds overgrown, the weeds and grasses waist high.

The village had suffered.
The old men in the Bar des Sports spoke of treachery.
They had been betrayed.
So many shot — men, women, even little children — farms burned to the ground — destruction everywhere.
Someone had betrayed them.
They raised their glasses, clinking them in a toast.
'May his soul rot in Hell...'
'It could have been a woman,' said one.
'We shall never know,' said another.

The Germans were convinced the nuns were hiding Jewish children. Two were taken and executed — the Mother Superior, much respected, and a young nun who turned out to be a Jew.
That hadn't helped.
They went back and searched again, but found nothing.
They shot another nun in the grounds of the Convent, in front of the children, but they never found any Jewish children.

Yes, it was sad to see the Convent now — a ruin — the roof of the Chapel fallen in...
They had helped many people.
After the Germans had gone, one of the remaining nuns had had a stroke and the other went off her head.
The children had been sent to other convents.

They knew nothing of Ruth and Marthe.

Dreadful business war. War was a dreadful business. The Germans were a despicable people.
Now they came in expensive cars to occupy the country as tourists — staying in the best hotels — spreading their flabby white bodies in the herb-scented Mediterranean sun — lolling by palm-fringed swimming pools — slurping the fine wines — guzzling the wonderful food…

'They were full of envy,' said one, his face weathered brown from working in the fields. 'They envy us our beautiful country — they are greedy — they wanted it for themselves — they have always wanted it…'

They shook their heads and emptied their glasses, pushing back their chairs, and went out blinking into the bright sunlight.

23

'He was very depressed when he came back to Paris,' said Paul. 'He became very withdrawn — hardly left his studio. He had many friends, but he didn't want to see anyone…'

He started a systematic search of all the places within easy reach of the Convent — going through all the records — checking all the Jewish families — speaking to any who were still alive.

He found Marthe's family first.
There was an aunt and a cousin.
He spoke to the cousin on the telephone.
They arranged to meet during her lunch hour.
They both worked. She in the Tax Office, her mother in a bank. She would bring some photographs — her mother would not come — she never spoke of that terrible time — it made her too upset.

She was tall and thin — fair skinned and fair haired.
She looked washed out — wrung out — colourless and drab, waering a limp grey jacket and skirt.

There was a blue vein in the middle of her white forehead, and blue veins on the backs of her hands.
So like Marthe, pale little Marthe, with her skinny blue-veined arms and legs.

Neither of them was hungry.
They ordered croissants and coffee.
He had told her on the phone why he had been trying to find Marthe.
She said her mother had taken her south to Marseilles where her grandparents had a flat.
It was safer to be in a big city — people didn't take any notice of you.
In the country everybody knew everybody. It was very dangerous.

Marthe's mother was supposed to have joined them with Marthe, but she was taken before she could make the journey. They had hoped Marthe had been saved.

They never talked about it. The memories were too painful.
Her mother had lost her husband, her sister, her brother-in-law, and her niece.

Marthe had been picked up almost immediately after they had parted. The Germans had intercepted the van taking her to an isolated farm, and found her hidden under some sacking.
The driver had been shot.
Marthe was deported.

Thinking of Marthe he found it difficult to breathe — feeling her fear shiver in his bones…

She took some photographs out of her handbag.
Two little girls smiling.
'Me and Marthe,' she said. 'Just before…'
A group — two young women, a man, sitting on a bench with two little girls on the grass in front of them.
'My mother and father — Marthe's mother — me and Marthe,' she said, pointing at each one in turn with her pale blue-veined hands.

The faded grainy figures smiled out at him — dissolving into a heap of jumbled bones — skeletal fingers pointing accusingly.

He spilt his coffee — the dark liquid spreading on the white cloth.

She knew nothing of Ruth.
Marthe had been alone.
Alone — her terror ricocheted round his head — a spiked ball of panic — shredding the sunlight — making him giddy and nauseous.

24

And, at last, Ruth.

In the files of the Mairie at Herbeville, a calm small town on the banks of a slow flowing weedy river, with a curved stone bridge, hardly wide enough for two cars to pass.
A pretty town with hanging flower baskets and a fountain in the cobbled square.

It was market day, the stalls piled with cheeses, star-leaved artichokes and fat-podded peas, glossy purple aubergines and aromatic branches of tomatoes, iridescent trout and orange-clawed crayfish — great bunches of parsley...

The pavement cafes were full of people eating steak and frites — baskets of bread — carafes of wine — children in bright summer clothes playing round the War Memorial.

The Mairie, a grand building with tricolours flying, and stone lions either side of the door.

Here, among the rows of metal filing cabinets, sitting at a worn chipboard table, the sunlight illuminating the layers of dust, here, in these musty dog-eared files, the catalogue of atrocity — neatly documented.

Her father, Dr Weiner — his wife Therese and son Nicholas — aged
13 years.
Deported 10 March 1943.

And below, separately, in a different spidery hand — Ruth Weiner
— aged 11 years.
Deported 17 August 1944.

The last transport.

Goblins with yellow-starred wands, waltzing their oom pah pah of
hate, and balding hags nodding over their knitting as swollen bodies
swung in the wind.

He had driven the end of the pen so hard into the palm of his hand
that it broke the skin, and a drop of blood fell onto the dusty table —
scarlet and shining in the sunlight.

The last transport.

As the Germans began their jerky retreat from Paris — swaying
lorries of glum soldiers — the officers in long grey limousines with
their wives and mistresses fashionably coiffed and clothed, weighed
down with leather trunks and crates of champagne, flanked by
motorcycle outriders, and the Resistance started to hang tricolours
from the windows, and pepper the departing enemy with sniper fire,
the sliding doors of the last transport in the siding at Drancy were
slammed shut, the human freight shocked into stupefied silence,
even the little children made no sound, their little bodies stiff with
fright.
It was not yet dawn — the cold mist of night still hung over the
wagon sheds.
The trucks jerked and clanged as the engine was coupled on —
shunting forward — sleepers groaning as the signal dropped — the
points engaged — picking up speed — speeding forward to their
Golgotha.

The driver felt the bile rise in his throat, and rummaged in his jacket

pocket for his antacid tablets — pain gnawing at his stomach.
His wife said it was the bread. Goodness knows what it was made of.
She had been very excited — getting up in the darkness of early morning to make him a flask of coffee — or what was supposed to be coffee.
The Germans were leaving Paris.
They were moving out — convoys clogging the roads out of the city — the Porte de Vincennes — the Porte de la Chapelle — the Porte des Lilas.
The Allies were getting nearer and nearer.
Any day now they would be here.
She hoped he would not miss it.
She hadn't wanted him to go.
It was dangerous enough with the bombings and sabotage…

He chewed three tablets at once.
He had tried to change his shift.
He did not want to be part of this abomination.

The train bristled with soldiers.
They had two in the cab with machine guns.
Yves, the stoker, kept his face hidden under his cap as he shovelled the coal.
Nobody wanted to drive this train.
Nobody wanted to be seen driving this train.
The ones who had been brave enough to protest had been shot — falling across the lines — arms spread — in the middle of a sentence…

The soldiers with their guns made him nervous.
He did not want to be shot.
What would happen to his wife and children?
They knew nothing of this abomination.
There were lots of rumours — dark stories — whispers — but the true scale of the horror could not be imagined.
They must never know.

When they had arrived for the first time at their desolate destination, with the single track and wooden platform — splintered — sprouting weeds — it was like arriving at the gates of Hell.

A pall of thick gritty smoke hung like a madman's vomit over brown trodden earth and shrivelled bushes.
SS men in their executioner's black uniforms stood arrogantly on the ramshackle platform with their dogs and whips, ready to torment their victims.

The soldiers had jumped down and broken open the doors of the trucks, and a pathetic straggle of people stumbled out, hardly able to walk, shielding their eyes from the light after days in darkness — young and old, men, women, children, babies — the soldiers shouting 'Schnell! Schnell!' hitting them with their rifle butts.
The SS dividing them with their whips — old, weak, children and babies one way, young and fit the other...
The bodies of the dead dragged out and hurled onto wooden carts.

And the smell — the smell of the place was overpowering — a sweet, rotten stench — a smell that lodged in the nostrils and throat, and soaked into clothing.
He never took his jacket home.
He could not hang this jacket in this house.
When he put it on the smell of death and fear cloaked him with horror.

He had been sick — climbing down from the cab, sitting on the footplate on the far side of the engine, out of sight of the executioners and the snarling dogs — his head between his knees.
Yves, beside him, eyes closed, crossing himself, his lips moving in prayer.

They never spoke about it.
Nobody at the depot spoke about it.

It wasn't the bread that gave him pains in the stomach, and prevented him from sleeping.

25

Jacob had thought a lot about the train crews.

He painted many pictures of them.
Powerful paintings — the faces luminous green — no eyes — no mouths — bulbous fingers splayed over their ears.
The smoke from the coal-fired engines and the smoke from the flesh-fuelled camp furnaces twisting together in a hideous, putrid embrace, a lurid spreading stain in an azure sky — blotting out the sun — weeping sooty tears on fields of golden corn…

It was these paintings that the German collector had wanted to buy.

Tall and distinguished, his silver hair straight and sleek — blue eyes coldly dispassionate — fashionably tanned — immaculately dressed — pale blue silk shirt — Gucci brogues — a thick gold link bracelet…

'Wonderful paintings,' he said. 'Inspiring…'

Gabrielle clasped her hands together with delight.
He wanted to buy them all.
She had four of Jacob's paintings in her little gallery in Montmartre, three were train paintings, and one of a gnarled mulberry tree laden with ripe, purple fruit, the base of the trunk heaped with broken toys.

'He wants to meet you,' she told Jacob, breathless with excitement. 'This afternoon — about 4…'
She did not say he was German.
She was aware that Jacob did not care much for Germans, but, all the paintings! He wanted to buy them all!

'I went with him,' said Paul. 'I didn't know either that he was German — Gabrielle meant well — she is a sweet person — but — well, she had no idea…'

As soon as they entered the Gallery, Jacob saw the man was German.

Gabrielle moved to introduce them. 'Monsieur Kruger,' she said. 'He is so looking forward to meeting you…' She took Jacob's arm. 'And this is Jacob Kaminski — the artist himself…'

The distant rumbling of the avalanche grew to a thundering roar as it hurtled its suffocating destruction — engulfing all before it.
He felt the approaching weight bearing down — already burying him in a frozen grave — and then the silence — an icy, indifferent solitude.

'They are not for sale', he said.

*   *   *

'Do you think they'll find us?' whispered Marthe, her face as white as the milk the boy had brought Ruth.

'They won't find us,' said Ruth. She coughed her painful cough. 'They won't find us…'

The goblins played Blind Man's Buff with Marthe — taunting — prodding her with their yellow-starred wands.
She stumbled, bewildered and frightened — skinny white arms outstretched.
Small men with small eyes signing documents of death.

Figures in black, masquerading as men — crushing heads and limbs with their polished black boots — grinding faces, pulped and sightless with their crimson-trimmed heels…

In his head the spotlight swivelled.
He could feel their heat — smell their sweat.

Astride benches in the stone-flagged hall of a plundered chateau, the walls hung with the hairy-snouted heads of wild boar, and grinning foxes, they gorged themselves on boudin noir, prepared to an authentic recipe — one and a quarter pints of thick cream to five pints of blood, bulging in the intestine skin — and sliced brains, sautéed and sauced with black butter...

The small men with the small eyes, podgy-paunched evil, at each end of the long rustic table, burrowed by worms, heavy and dark with ancient rivalries and betrayals, beneath portraits of smiling Adolph and sneering Heidrich.

The goblins banged their tambourines, leaping and somersaulting in triumph at a good day's work done.

He tried to dim the spotlight and the bats came — blocking the air with black-webbed furry wings and high-pitched squeaking, and as he raised his arms to beat them off, they shrivelled into heaps of papery black ash.

He could hear his mother weeping.

Ruth said, ' Do not show you are afraid.'
A black-guantletted hand held the blade of a bayonet to her throat — a tiny trickle of blood making a thin red line on her dying skin. 'Never let them know you are afraid...'

Madame Rabelais came with his bread.
She was worried — was he ill? Did he need anything?
He asked her to bring coffee tomorrow — and perhaps some fruit — apricots or plums — perhaps a few grapes...

He ceased to paint — stacking the canvasses neatly against the walls — cleaning his brushes — tidying his sketches into piles.

He must leave everything in order.
It was time for him to go.
It was time to join the others.
He was filled with an overwhelming sense of urgency.
They had been waiting long enough.
He must go now.

He longed to be with them.

He threw open the shutters, and lay on the divan, to wait for the darkness, the merciful night, to come.

They walked towards him through a field of frothy grasses, yellow-faced daisies, ragged-edged cornflowers and nodding poppies — delicate-winged butterflies darting and dipping among them.

They were all smiling. Mother Superior imperceptibly, a tall angular figure, hands folded on her chest, chubby Sister Celeste beaming with joy, strong Sister Constance in her rubber boots, carrying a basket of vegetables, Sister Agnes with an elaborately iced cake on a gold-rimmed plate, and Sister Clare, who was not a nun at all, in a blue woollen dress and lilies in her dark curly hair.
His mother in her flowered dress, weeping with happiness, his father holding her arm — Sylvie waving excitedly.
And Ruth, even Ruth was smiling.
He couldn't remember ever seeing her smile.
She was holding Marthe's hand, and Marthe was smiling too, and behind them a procession of people he did not know, carrying flowers and candles, curving away into the distance.
A river of wondrous light in the gathering dusk, as if the stars had deserted the sky to form a magical pathway for him.

He went to meet them — the grass springy beneath his feet, feeling the warmth of their welcome reaching out to him.
The search was over.
His anguish was over.
At last he was content.

26

The shadows lengthened across the freshly-mown grass — cool, mint green shadows — the flowers, warmed by long, lazy hours of sunshine, filling the air with fragrance.

'I was away,' said Paul. 'I had to go to Milan on business — My assistant phoned to tell me. She was distraught. Madame Rabelais had found him. She said he looked so peaceful she thought he was asleep. He had taken an overdoes — I took the first plane...'

He paused. 'He had left a will, properly witnessed by Madame Rabelais and the boulanger, leaving everything to me, with a list of people he wanted me to help or give gifts to, and stipulating that none of his paintings should be knowingly sold to Germans... He had refused to see anyone after the business at the gallery... He often shut himself away when he was working, so no-one was unduly worried...'

*   *   *

It was late when she got back to Paris.
Paul had suggested she stay — or go to a hotel in Tours, but she wanted to go home.

He had shown her the few paintings he had in the house — most of them were in his gallery in Tours. She could see them another time. Like the painting in Paris, they were dense and impenetrable, the paint applied in thick, swirling strokes.

He said he had some photographs somewhere. He would find them and send them to her.
She was overcome with sadness, and an indescribable sense of loss.
Not even the two little girls had been saved.

There was no end to the nightmare.
No waking to find the morning sun dancing on the ceiling.

The nightmare was reality.

They had been put to death — a hissing, choking, horrific death.
Her mother crazed with grief.
Her father a broken bundle of bloody clothes.
Sister Celeste's blood still on her hands, as they tried to heave her body into the makeshift grave.
Jacob must have hoped, as she had hoped, that at least Ruth and Marthe had survived — having feared and verified the deaths of his mother, father and sister, had hoped — surely — that the girls were still alive…

She understood so well how he had been unable to bear the burden of grief and guilt — could no longer live with the knowledge that they had all perished in terror and humiliation…

There were messages on the answering machine.
From Gerrard — curt — he would not be back until Sunday evening — make sure she told Geraldine they would not be coming…
From Hortense — peeved. Where had she been? They had to discuss dates when they were going to Vence — the Perrets needed to make arrangements…
From Evelyn — It was such lovely weather — they should have a picnic — she would order food from Antoine's…

She made a sandwich of ham and lettuce, and ate it standing in the pristine kitchen.
It was late and she was so tired — completely drained.
She would see to everything in the morning.

In her dreams her mother carried an armful of white lilac.
She said, 'Hurry up — Your father is waiting — we shall be late…'
Her aunt running, flatfooted in her worn cloth coat.
'They're here — they've come — my sons — my sons…'

Martin and Patrick Forgis on their bikes — waving flags and shouting 'Vive la France', and under the comfortable, rustling shade of the dignified oak, Jacob, a small figure, standing quite still beneath the cascading green leaves, his little white face stricken with fear…

She called, 'I'm coming, Jacob, I'm coming…'
But she couldn't reach him, however hard she tried, she couldn't reach him.
She tried to tell her mother to wait, but she had disappeared, and gusts of wind lifted the broken lilac blossom, buffeting it against the stone memorial, showering the figure of the First World War soldier — standing squarely, rifle at the ready, staring unseeing eyes into the distance, the scented flowers covering his helmet and the sturdy hands which held his gun.
She could hear her aunt wailing, 'Give them back to me — give me back my sons…' and she turned towards Jacob, but he had vanished too, and where he had stood was a pile of shoes, all kinds of shoes — workmen's boots, smart high heels, sandals, sensible lace-ups, shiny patent peeptoes — scuffed and polished, old and new — and babies booties of the softest doeskin — blue and pink — and a pair of red satin slippers…

The branches of the majestic oak were suddenly bare, silhouetted against a darkening sky — black clouds racing across the bloodshot dusk — a hangman's gibbet swinging in the wind…

27

Evelyn had everything necessary for a super picnic.
She had hired a chauffeur-driven car to take them to Versailles.
'You look too tired to drive,' she said. 'I want you to enjoy the day…'

She had recently sold a rather valuable painting — one she had never really liked — of people riding in the Bois de Boulogne. The women rode side-saddle, and the men had moustaches. Hervé had liked it. He said it represented an era, but she had thought the horses wild and the women ugly…
She could afford a little extravagance.

There was a folding table and chairs — a white damask cloth and silver cutlery — Champagne in a bucket of ice...

'You look exhausted,' she said. 'Why don't you go down to the house in Vence for a while — on your own — before that awful woman Hortense is there...'

'She wants it for the Perrets,' said Cecile.

'You should speak to Gerrard,' said Evelyn. 'It's your house as well — tell him you need a rest...'

Cecile could imagine Gerrard's response to that — what did she need a rest for? What did she need rest from? Her life was a perpetual rest — she hardly ever even did any cooking...'

'Would you like me to speak to him?' said Evelyn. She had known Gerrard since he was a child — a spoilt child — the dreadful Geraldine had spoilt him — dreadfully...

There was ratatouille and cold chicken, prawns in aspic and tomatoes dressed with oil and herbs — fresh raspberries, with raspberry coulis and raspberry sorbet.

Evelyn said, 'I remembered it was your birthday next week, and thought it would be nice to have a pre-birthday lunch...'
She passed a little package across the table, beautifully wrapped in pale blue paper with little silver stars.
'Happy Birthday,' she said. 'I hope you like it...'

Cecile wanted to speak to her about Jacob, about Paul, but she didn't know where to start — so she said nothing.
The package contained a delicate porcelain egg — a Fabergé egg — very pale blue, exquisitely painted with forget-me-nots.
She had often admired it among Evelyn's many precious 'objets'.
She started to protest that it was much too valuable, but Evelyn stopped her.

'When I am gone,' she said, 'Solange will sell everything — she has no time for these sort of things — her mind is like a calculating machine — these sort of things are just so much clutter. There will be plenty for her without this one — I want you to have it — it will give you pleasure.'

28

Paul sent the photographs with a little note to say he hoped they would meet again soon.
She spread them on the kitchen table.
Photographs of a young man sitting with friends in a café, smiling — leaning on the bridge by Notre Dame — in a heavy overcoat outside the Jeu de Paume — arm in arm with a pretty girl walking by the Seine.

She could recognise the boy Jacob in this smiling young man — the wide dark eyes and curly dark hair.
She looked at them a long time.

It was strange that they had both lived in the same city — walked the same streets.

When she and Gerrard were first married they lived on the first floor of the Comtesse de Tressilly's shambling mansion on the Left Bank, its elegant façade cracked and pitted by bullets and shrapnel from the last battle for Paris, as the Allies advanced on the Hotel de Ville. The fighting had been particularly fierce in Montparnasse, St Germain des Pres and the Palais de Luxembourg, from where the Germans took deadly aim up the Rue de Seine.
The whole building had been severely battered. The remaining balconies perilous, the carvings mutilated.

It had been Hortense's idea.
There had been problems with the lease of their apartment at the last minute.
'She really needs the money,' she said. 'They lost everything...'

There had been high-ranking German officers billeted in the house during the war.

The Comte had been interned soon after the occupation of Paris. He had never recovered.
He came home not really knowing who he was, or why he was there — unable to sleep — eating only soup and bread — wandering round the house opening and shutting doors, and out onto the street — losing himself among the crowds — being brought back by friendly Gendarmes — and dying quietly, sitting in his chair by the window, where he liked to watch the people passing by.

The Comtesse spent the war years in a cheap hotel nearby, with all she had managed to salvage in two cabin trunks and a hat box, which filled the small, shabby room, eating questionable stews and drinking acidic wine in the grubby dining room.

The Germans ransacked the house before they left — taking anything they thought might be of value — pictures — silver — small pieces of furniture — occasional tables inlaid with ivory and mother-of-pearl — delicate Louis XV chairs and Aubusson rugs — breaking up and burning what they couldn't carry in the marble fireplaces — leaving them scorched and blackened.

The Comtesse lived on the ground floor.
Her few bits and pieces of rickety second-hand furniture dotted around the vast space of the Grand Salon, where the famous and fashionable, aristocrats and artists had gathered to eat and talk and dance. Now single, feeble bulbs hung from the chains that had supported the glittering chandeliers — the high ceilings webbed with cracks, the mouldings crumbling bunches of fruit and flowers — odd bits of carpet, worn through to the webbing, on the splintered parquet floor.

The house was full of ghosts — jostling on the marble staircase and gathering in the domed hall — wandering arm in arm — dancing in the Grand Salon — long-gloved hands poised on smart-suited shoulders — bubbles from the glasses of champagne rising in a sparkling mist — snatches of music — the sharp exact rhythms of trumpet and saxophone, whispering melodies of violins — a babble of voices, of laughter and argument — and the shuddering shadows of dagger-tongued vampires leaving a trail of blood and spittle on the flesh-white marble — smothering their victims' cries with silk-pleated cushions.

Grotesquely made up — dressed in pre-war evening dresses of satin and ecru lace, second-hand cardigans, trailing wraps of perished chiffon and ostrich feathers, the Comtesse moved among them, smoking continuously with a long ebony cigarette holder, drinking brandy from a cheap tumbler, shuffling from empty room to empty room.

She could be heard complaining loudly to her femme de menage, stolid, long-suffering, and frequently unpaid, who came daily to tidy up, do the washing, and prepare a meal in the cavernous kitchen in the basement, her husband dealing with the aged boiler and any other odd jobs.

Convinced that Gerrard was a German officer, she would appear from the shuttered emptiness to berate him — 'Salles boches — cochons — You are all pigs — ignorant pigs...'

Above them Madame Sokolova gave singing lessons — the sound of wobbly arpeggios and strangulated high Cs filtering down into the domed hallway, where flaking cherubs cavorted amongst beribboned clouds in a faded blue sky, their garlands drooping with fatigue.

Hortense had taken a perverse pleasure in the Comtesse's condition — the scraggy scarecrow with wirewool hair, slopping round the empty rooms in 1930s finery and old tennis shoes, muttering to herself.

Her father had not been sufficiently high up in the Foreign Office to be invited to any of the intimate suppers, stunning balls and musical soirées for which the Comtesse was famous.

Now she could feel superior, clicking across the marble floors with her stiletto heels, chicly compact in her braided Chanel suits.

Looking at the photographs of Jacob spread out on the kitchen table, Cecile remembered how intimidated she had felt — by Gerrard — by Hortense and Geraldine, and the lurking Comtesse — escaping furtively to the market with her straw basket, unable to decide what to buy, hesitating between the slithering silver-scaled fish lying on a bed of cracked ice and bubbled seaweed and plump chickens among bunches of tarragon, blue and white bowls of purplish gizzards and speckled brown eggs, usually opting for the butchers in the Rue Conté, where the butcher would present her with two perfectly-trimmed chops of pork — or veal — or lamb — or a tender steak, expertly wrapped in greaseproof paper.
Safe and simple.
Gerrard was not easy to please. Used to his mother's elaborate meals, he would find fault with everything. Why was they no sauce of green peppers to go with the veal? The steak was overdone. Herrings were for peasants. The Camembert was chalky...

Cooking was not easy either in the high narrow kitchen — an inadequately converted anteroom, papered with hardly discernible trellises of roses — a single gilt tap over a cracked basin decorated to match the abundantly floral wallpaper.

Hortense thought it delightfully quaint.
Geraldine's first horrified reaction tempered by the cachet of informing her friends that her son had an apartment in the Comtesse de Tréssilly's mansion, safe in the knowledge that they were never likely to know what a state it was in.
Perching cautiously on the edge of one of their new steel and canvas chairs which Hortense had insisted they buy from one of her protegés — 'Futuristic,' she said. 'He is so innovative...'
She sipped Cecile's coffee with disdain and suggested she should go to the hairdressers, and was she sure she was preparing proper meals for Gerrard? 'You should not dine so late,' she said. 'It is bad for the digestion — a sure way to get stomach disorders...'

The chairs, glass-topped table and sofa upholstered in black with white squiggles and dots, looked incongruous in the stately decrepit room — ugly and uncomfortable.
Gerrard said it amused Hortense, and Didier was happy when Hortense was amused.
Somewhere in the surrounding streets Jacob lived and moved and painted.
She may have passed him in the street, bumped into him in the market, or seen him sitting at a café drinking with friends.

They had not lived there very long.
Indulging Hortense for Didier's sake was one thing, but Gerrard was not prepared to put up with the perpetual draughts, the thin stream of tepid rusty bath water, the Comtesse's nocturnal wanderings and the ridiculous furniture.

She picked up the photographs one by one, and carefully put them back in the envelope.

She smelt the strong scent of ivy thick on the hot stones of the Convent — the sandy-haired Gestapo man with his dirty fingernails strutting in front of the row of little children flattened against the wall, and Anne-Marie, her neck bones taut with fear, holding the smallest one's hand — the terrible sounds of the soldiers' boots as they trampled the undergrowth where Jacob, Ruth and Marthe were hiding.

And in the flickering, stuttering images of a black and white film — jerkily, in slow motion, with gaping mouths and outstretched arms, they watched the soldiers raise their rifles and shoot the dumpy, fleeing figure of Sister Celeste, the bird's wings of her black habit flopping uselessly around her as she fell…

*   *   *

She went down to the Rue des Merles to look again at the picture before it was taken to Tours to be part of the exhibition, but it had already gone, in its place a twisted metal sculpture entitled 'Flight'.

The strangulating wire tightened round her throat. 'Flight'. What flight? Whose flight?

The vicious silent coils of barbed wire, hung with fragments of flayed skin, like torn remnants of cloth.

The unseen razor wire that sliced into ankles and wrists, severing veins.

The empty husk of her mother's head, floating, sightless, in an empty void, lit by hollow pumpkins with grimacing mouths, bobbing sulphur orange in the darkness…

She backed away — she would go and have a coffee — watch the people busying themselves with life — everyday things…

Gerrard had his back to her — the young woman's head was bent, dark waves of hair obscuring her face. Gerrard reached across and took her hand.

Instinctively, Cecile moved to greet them. 'Fancy seeing you! How nice,' stopping herself just in time. Stepping back quickly, she turned and walked back up the street, averting her eyes from the tortured metal in the gallery window, hurrying, light-headed, her thoughts scattering — blown powder puff dandelion heads caught in the wind — pirouetting corps de ballet performing their grand finale.

29

She sat on the terrace at the Club, drinking tea with lemon.

Gerrard was playing doubles with Hortense, Didier and Juliette Meyer, a forceful business woman, firm fleshed and vigorous, her springy curls held back with a wide towelling headband.

Gerrard and Hortense against Didier and Juliette.

Gerrard was a much better player than Didier, Juliette a very much better player than Hortense, who, despite extra coaching from the gorgeous Henri and an expensive new racquet, remained feeble-wristed and slow.

'You should play,' she said to Cecile. 'Do something with Gerrard — show some enthusiasm…'

Cecile thought Didier would probably prefer to play with one of the younger more agile members of the club, than be stuck with Hortense's double faults and useless backhand.

'You should make more effort,' she had said.

They were in the Ladies Powder Room, and Hortense was applying a thick layer of black mascara to her pale eyelashes. They stuck out in sooty surprise under her plucked eyebrows. 'I need a new curler,' she had said. 'This one is useless…'

She probably knew about the young women, dropping hints about improving her appearance, the importance of keeping one's husband's interest, being more involved…

Cecile could just see the edge of the courts, and could hear the voices of the players — laughter and exclamations — and the pleasant twang of racquets hitting the ball.

The grass at the Convent was coarse and lumpy.

The old man who came to saw the logs sometimes cut it roughly, and the sun withered it to a biscuit-brown stubble.

They were playing rounders with Sister Clare, running, happily breathless in the sunshine. The ball was old and squashy and it was not easy to hit it with the improvised bat — an odd-shaped piece of wood with a flat side.

The plane skimmed the top of the trees spluttering and coughing, a desperate dying struggle — a khaki plane with white stars on its wings — a brown dummy slumped in the cockpit — the tail streaming a flaming banner of scarlet-flecked gold.

In an instant it was gone, hidden by the wood, and then an explosion shook the earth and the air, and a thick pall of black smoke filled the sky, blotting out the sun, and it was suddenly nightfall.

In the chapel they said prayers to the deaf God in his remote gilded kingdom, and somebody's son's charred corpse lay in a corn field thousands of miles from home.

'Reconnaisance,' the postman said. 'American. Nothing left when they got there — made a big crater in George Girodet's field…'

Mother Superior gave him some plum brandy.
It was very hot, and the air was tense — alert to every snapping twig and tumbling acorn.
'Patrols,' said the postman. 'Gestapo…', and the air trembled, and fear touched them lightly with its icy fingers.

Gerrard said, 'We're going to shower and change — we'll meet you in the bar…'
He stood in front of her, casting a shadow over the table, the gold-rimmed china with the impressive logo, the dish of pungent shiny lemon — mopping his face with his towel.
He looked tired and strained.

30

The boat slid forward in the water, rippling the satin surface, a wide sash of topaz and plum, spangled gold and silver, and patched with inky black shapes, constantly changing like the shaken magic of a kaleidoscope.
There were pink cloths and chunky pink candles in glass dishes on the tables, and vases of pink roses. The whole boat strung with multi-coloured fairy lights, shiny sweets hung from a silver thread.

Gerrard was not please, hardly bothering to conceal his irritation.
Why had she wanted to celebrate her birthday on a Bateau Mouche?
'For goodness sake,' he said. 'Why not the club?'

It was so easy to arrange at the Club.
A quick call to Edouard, the Maitre D', and a table would be specially prepared, with flowers and tiny boxes of chocolates, and at the appropriate moment a cake, ablaze with candles, would be borne aloft and placed in front of her, amid a little round of applause, and the glasses filled with champagne.
He had already told Hortense and Didier, Evelyn, the Perrets…

Why had she suddenly insisted on a Bateau Mouche? The food was mediocre, and it would be full of tourists…
Did she want to celebrate her birthday among a noisy crowd of camera-clicking Americans and Japanese?
They had often entertained clients for dinner on the Seine. It was pleasant to discuss business gliding past the floodlit beauty of Notre Dame — the Swiss were particularly appreciative.
Cecile would never come if there were Germans, pleading illness. It was not possible for her to sit at the same table with Germans.
Gerrard did quite a lot of business with Germany.
Her refusal to make an appearance on these occasions made Gerrard very angry.
'The whole German nation were not SS stormtroopers,' he would say. 'They'll all be dead now anyway — or in their dotage. You are being ridiculous.'

They had asparagus, and stuffed breast of chicken with tiny new peas.

She said, 'I think we should talk about the future…'
'Why should we talk about the future,' he said. 'What is there to talk about?'
'I saw you,' she said. 'At the café in the Rue des Merles… also at the preview of that unfortunate exhibition.'
She sipped her wine, looking down at the iridescent ribbon of the river.
'She looked very pretty and very sad…'

Gerrard put down his knife and fork.
'You are making something out of nothing,' he said.
'No,' she said. 'It is not nothing. You are not happy with me. I only annoy you. We do not have to do anything dramatic — just go our separate ways — see how things work out…'

In the end it had not been so difficult — this moment she had been dreading. It passed quite quietly, a stray pebble hardly disturbing the surface of the gleaming water that frothed against the side of the boat.

31

'I hope you know what you are doing.' Hortense stood by the window, looking down into the street. The traffic was at a standstill. She was wearing red.
It made her look old, the cossetted skin puffy and unnaturally smooth. 'It seems incredibly foolish…'

'We are only going to live separately,' said Cecile. 'Nothing dramatic.'
'So, what if she wants marriage — children — what if he had a son?'

Cecile put the tray of coffee down carefully on the glass table top. She was surprised that Hortense had bothered to come and speak to her at all — she was aware that she had always thought her stupid, stupid and difficult.
Hortense moved away from the window, bending to inspect the small desert of cacti, spikily defiant in their sandy, silver-fenced enclosure.
She sat down on the white leather sofa and crossed her legs.
She was wearing black gilt trimmed shoes with very high heels.
'Didier has had a mistress for years — he has her tucked away somewhere in a flat near the Bois de Vincennes. I believe she is quite a personable young women. He thinks I don't know. He had another one before, but she didn't last so long. Men are so stupid. How could I not know?'

Cecile was truly amazed by this revelation — that the strictly proper, impeccable Didier should have mistresses…
That domineering, opinionated Hortense should acquiesce was even more amazing.
'We still share our marriage bed,' said Hortense. 'Go through the motions. I have no intention of divorcing, or being divorced. I make sure I get all that I want. That my bank account is plentifully replenished. What can you possibly hope to gain? A woman on her own has no social value whatsoever…'

Evelyn said, 'I know you are not happy — but I do not want you to be alone. It is not good to be alone...'

She thought of her mother, spurning her father, lying on her bed in the darkened room, watching television and drinking. And then, when he died, the grief, the hysteria, the descent into drunken despair. 'I cannot be alone — I have never been alone...'
She wanted light — all the lights in the house had to be turned on — never turned off — day and night the house was ablaze with lights — dancing with an unseen partner in the stiffly upholstered salon — tripping on the hem of her nightdress — turning the music up louder and louder until it filled the room with a throbbing mass of sound.
They had found her in a crumpled heap, among sharp shards of broken glass — the Persian rug sodden with cognac...
Would Cecile be able to prevent the ghosts that she struggled to keep at bay from finding their way in — from inhabiting her life? The burden would crush her — drive her to madness...

She didn't know what she would do if anything happened to Micheline.
She didn't think she could manage alone — not with this hip. She didn't want to be alone — but she didn't want to give up all her treasures.

'You should sell,' Solange had said on one of her infrequent visits.
'Look at all this stuff. You should sell everything that is not absolutely essential and move to somewhere like Gerrard's mother. She has her own things and is very well looked after. I believe it is a lovely place...'

Evelyn didn't listen.
She never listened to Solange.
It was a preposterous suggestion...

'Are you sure this is what you want?' she said.
She poured herself another brandy. Cecile was drinking Perrier water.
'Try one of these cheesy things — they are quite delicious. As I have

said before, being a wife is better than not being a wife. You will be uninvited.'

Cecile said she had thought about it.
'She looked so unhappy,' she said. 'And it doesn't matter a jot to me...'
'It is her fault she is unhappy,' said Evelyn. 'Not yours. It is your husband she is having an affair with...'

'I don't think I was ever a good wife,' said Cecile.

If she had been able to shut out the restless phantoms that lurked behind the creaking door — ever wakeful — ever vigilant — the thin grey vapour of guilt which found its way through the smallest cracks — a strip of stony cloud across the eggshell dawn — then it might have been possible.

She had tried to do the things she was supposed to do — feel the things she was supposed to feel — sometimes she almost convinced herself that she had succeeded — and then the flock of birds would rise in a terrified wave of beating wings — and the brutal tread of black boots snapped brittle bones like twigs on the weary earth...

'I really was no good as a wife,' she said.

'My dear,' said Evelyn. 'You must have a good lawyer. I will give you the name of my lawyer...'

Geraldine was convinced they had done it specifically to annoy her — to make her life even more tiresome.
'There was definitely something wrong with the fish yesterday,' she said. 'And it was full of bones. As if it was not enough that they are determined to poison me, or choke me to death, you and Gerrard have to start gallivanting about. Who is going to come and see me? I suppose you won't be calling anymore, and I've told Gerrard he can't bring this woman — whoever she is. I shall be left entirely to their mercy — unprotected. I always said you didn't look after Gerrard properly, and now look what's happened...'

32

She met Paul outside the Jeu de Paume, and they walked into the Tuileries Gardens down the gravel slope and passed the round pond where the childrens' boats with their colourful sails skimmed confidently in the frisky breeze.

He had phoned to say he had come to Paris to do some business. Could they meet — have some lunch? He had suggested various restaurants, but she said she would prefer just a café in the Tuileries Gardens — if it was fine.
It was particularly lovely at this time of year — the trees splashed and trimmed with yellow and red, the paths mounded with soft yellow leaves — the woody scent of autumn — the summer crowds diminished.

They ordered ham baguettes and coffee.
He told her the plans for the exhibition were going very well.
They had designed a really nice catalogue with a short biography.
She asked him about his family.
He had an older sister — Catherine.
She lived in Lausanne — had two grown up children — a son and a daughter — and two grandchildren, both boys.
He did not see them very often. He usually went for Christmas and the New Year, and sometimes if he had business in Lausanne.

They had lived in a small town, St Augustin, not far from Angers.

His father, a professor of French literature at the University in Angers, spent his life with books.
The house was full of books.
In his father's study the heavy dark wood desk was piled with books and papers — books on the floor and on the chairs.
He was a true academic — totally immersed in his work — his teaching and writing.

The war, at first a distant annoyance, became suddenly an

overwhelming threat, the tremors of impending catastrophe sending shock waves across the continent.

The usual animated conversations at the dinner table, where all the daily events were discussed and argued over, became more subdued as the war came ever nearer.
Europe was being engulfed by a black-booted, goose-stepping army, shrouding their countries in a gigantic swastika.

After Czechoslovakia was swallowed up with hardly a murmur, they went down like ninepins.
Poland surrendered — Denmark surrendered.
As he and Catherine played in the spring sunshine, hunting for birds' nests, and collecting flowers to press in her special book, the German army was crossing the borders into France. Then the Dutch surrendered, and, as they were being taken in the blue and white school bus for their first swimming lesson in the new public swimming pool, the British army were being driven back into the sea. Then the Belgians surrendered.

The conversation at the evening meal became almost monosyllabic.
Their mother served the food in silence.
Norway surrendered.
There were whispers of an armistice.
Their father was bereft. The shame that their country had given in without a fight.
'To save Paris,' people said. 'We had to save Paris...'
The Germans were already in Paris.
The armistice was signed.
Hitler made a dawn visit to Paris — a quick appraisal of his ultimate prize — the city of Napoleon.
Strutting beneath the Eiffel Tower with his henchmen — greatcoats slapping their legs — dismissing the elegant, sophisticated boulevards with a disdainful flick of leather gloves.
The humiliation was complete.

'We should go into mourning,' said their father, stirring his soup so fiercely it spilt on the cloth.

'Maybe it's for the best,' said their mother. 'We don't want war.'
'We shall live in shame,' said their father. 'Prisoners in our own country.'

He had been right.
Very soon the notices started going up — instructions on behaviour — orders to be obeyed.
They queued for Papers and ration cards at the Mairie — details of their parentage, their property, their professions, all meticulously noted.

A German officer and a team of German bureaucrats came to the University, and went through the library removing books they considered politically or theologically unsuitable.

'They're after the Jews,' said their father, tearing his bread into pieces until it was reduced to crumbs. 'That is what it is all about, Adele — the Jews — and the Communists. They are like a malignant virus — spreading everywhere — infecting the country — infecting thought — trapping us in cages...'
And their mother said, 'Don't get so upset, George. Maybe it won't be so bad. Maybe it will become easier — more relaxed in a while. At least we are not at war...'
'Maybe there are worse things than war,' said their father.

That summer they did not go to the seaside at Pornic for their holiday, to paddle in the magical stretch of aquamarine water, and build castles on the beach, scramble among the rocks, and run on the soft white sand among the glossy fairytale pines.
There were corpses on the beach.
The swollen bodies of English soldiers, drowned when their ships had been sunk off St Nazaire.

'The bay is full of bodies,' Madame Besson, the boulangère told their mother when they collected their bread — everything was rationed now. 'Terrible. All those young men drowned...'

'It was particularly difficult for my father,' said Paul. He had finished his sandwich, stretching his long legs out in front of him. 'He was used to being head of his department, lecturing and discussing any topic he chose, encouraging the students to argue, exchange ideas...'

He was presented with a list of forbidden subjects, forbidden authors, modes of acceptable behaviour — all essays to be submitted to the director, to be checked for subversive opinions.
Jewish students were expelled.
Two of his colleagues — eminent professors — Jews — were summarily dismissed.

He was enraged.
A mild man, rage was an alien emotion.
He paced his study, and paced the garden. He got up in the night, unable to sleep, and paced the kitchen.
'They have no other livelihood,' he said, poking the stuffed tomatoes with his fork. 'What are they going to do?'

'We children were very scared of the German soldiers — especially the armed patrols and the motorcyclists with their helmets and goggles and black gauntlets. They were really scary...'

He had two very good friends — Christophe and Armand.
They always played together — sat next to each other in the classroom — visited each other's homes — and then Armand stopped coming to school.
After several weeks he asked the teacher where he was.
Anxious and flustered she said she thought he was not well — and — had he finished his sums...

One day he had been with his mother to the bank in Angers.
It was opposite an old grey building which the Germans now used as one of their headquarters, with swastikas hanging from the balconies and armed sentries.
His mother stopped outside the bank to speak to an acquaintance, and he watched horrified as a man was half lifted, half dragged from the building by two soldiers. One of the sentries stepped forward and opened the doors of a waiting black van.

As the soldiers started to thrust the man into the back of the van he turned a white face, streaked with blood.
It was Armand's father.

He grabbed his mother's arm, desperate, starting to sob, trying to show her, without pointing, without drawing attention to himself.
They both turned, his mother and her friend, just as Armand's father was shoved into the van and the doors slammed shut, and it reversed sharply out of the courtyard and drove past them up the street.

'That was Monsieur Tivier!' said the woman. 'Oh my God — that was Monsieur Tivier!'

He was sick all the way home.
His mother tried to comfort him —he could feel her shaking.
For days he refused to go to school.

Paul paused. 'We never saw them again — Armand, or his brother, his father or his mother — a jolly little woman, always smiling, handing round sweets to everyone. She always had a big bag of sweets...'

After that things just got worse.
There were shortages of everything.
Anybody who had a bit of garden grew vegetables — kept some chickens — rabbits — even goats. People bartered food for services — eggs for petrol — a leaking pipe fixed in exchange for cheese — a bicycle repaired for a box of vegetables — a rabbit for mending a roof...

The chemist and his wife, who worked with him in the shop, wore yellow stars — and then they too disappeared.
The librarian was arrested for allowing Jewish people in the library. She was never seen again.

Their father came home one night haggard, unable to speak.
Their mother, sitting him down, rubbing his hands, speaking to him

like a little child. 'There, there, George. Whatever has happened? What is it, George? You are shivering. Shall I get you some brandy?'

There had been hostages taken — many hostages — in reprisal for the killing of a German officer in Nantes.
The orders had come from Berlin.
One hundred and twenty-three hostages.
A massacre.
Two of his students had been among those executed.
Some of the gardeners at the University had been rounded up to dig the graves.
He had seen them being marched off, carrying spades.
He was inconsolable.
That dark winter was the lowest point.

The rules and regulations — the posters ordering this and that — forbidding this and that — continued to appear. The strictures against the Jews becoming so restrictive they really had no right to do anything.

Banned from public places — cafés, cinemas, theatres, concerts, museums, parks, even telephone boxes — only allowed to shop between three and four o'clock in the afternoon, when the scant supplies had gone. It was a preliminary to arresting them and dispatching them, clutching their pathetic bundles of belongings, trainload after trainload to some unknown destination from which they never returned.

'We were too young to know what was going on,' said Paul. 'We were lucky — we were protected by our parents, and, of course, we were not Jewish — but we all lived in fear.'

It was later, when the war in Africa turned in the Allies' favour, and the Italians began to waver, that their 'cousin' Jeanette came to stay.

Their mother prepared the spare room and told them cousin Jeanette was coming to stay for a while — a distant cousin of their father's who needed a holiday.

Their mother was very nervous.
'What about rations?' she said to their father at supper. 'Will she have a ration card? There is little enough for us, even with extra milk for the children…'

And later when they were supposed to be asleep, they heard her talking, her voice raised, almost hysterical…
'It's too dangerous, George. What about the children? We will all be shot if she is found out. What about the children?'
They couldn't hear their father's reply — trying to soothe her.

'She must be a spy,' Catherine had said as they crept back to bed. 'I don't think she is our cousin at all…'

She was young and pretty — rather serious and quiet — spending a lot of time in her room, or walking in the nearby woods.

Strange people came after dark — conversations conducted in whispers — stopping altogether if he or Catherine appeared.

'She has a radio,' said Catherine. 'I've heard it — she's sending messages — she's a spy…'

And then one day she was gone.
When they came back from school she was not there.
Their mother was in the garden digging potatoes.
'Jeanette has gone home,' she said. 'She was feeling better…' and she sat down on a muddy stone and started to cry.

Soon after she went to bed and lay with the curtains drawn day after day, oblivious to those around her.

We were a bit older then.
Catherine was twelve — so we managed.
Our father had long holidays from the University, and the neighbours were very kind.

'I don't remember exactly how long she was like that, but it seemed

a very long time.
She was never the same.
My father became increasingly reclusive — suddenly old — all his enthusiasm for his work, for his life — gone.

So that was my war.

Shall we walk a little whilst there is still sunlight?'

33

They sat either side of the wide stone fireplace — wide enough to smoke a ham from the sturdy blackened hook that hung in the chimney, above the hinged door of an old bread oven.
The fire an orange-gold mass of collapsing logs.

She was tired, but content.
The warmth of the fire making her pleasantly sleepy.

They had just finished a delicious meal — a perfectly roasted chicken, dauphinois potatoes, a caramelised apple tart.

It had been raining when she left Paris.
It was early, and there was not much traffic.
She had wanted to be in Tours by lunchtime, to meet Paul at the gallery, and see the final preparations for the preview tomorrow.

She was still in the flat.
She had begun to look for somewhere else, but so far had seen nothing she really liked.
There was no hurry.
Gerrard had left.
He had taken a hold-all and his briefcase — he would fetch the rest of his things later.

They had stood facing each other across the impersonal white room — the white leather sofas and shaggy white carpet — the glass-

290

topped table with a bowl of polished stones Hortense had given them for Christmas — a pewter vase of white orchids.

He had said, 'I'm sorry about all this...' He looked tired and drained. She had said, 'I am sorry too...' and then he had picked up his bags and he was gone.

Paul phoned several times a week.
She came to look forward to his calls — there always seemed so much to talk about.

He had invited her to stay for the preview — it was too far to drive back to Paris afterwards — it would be late — they were to have a small dinner party — there were people he wanted her to meet. If she came the day before she could see if she approved of the way the pictures had been hung — Annette would be delighted to have someone extra to cook for — there was plenty of room.

She had been sleeping better — the phantoms that stalked the night trod more quietly — the charred stumps of trees and sucking mud shrouded in white mist, muffling the feeble beating of dying hearts.

Paul had warned her it might be distressing. 'They are very intense,' he said.

She walked into a haunted forest.
The sunlight caught in the grappling, whiskered arms of sombre pines. The heat driven down into the thick brown carpet of fallen pine needles. The smell of heat overpowering — the pungent smell of hot resin weeping sticky tears down the twisted trunks — hot earth — hot jam — hot cloth — hot blood — hot scented flowers.
It whirled around her — hot, hairy hands clutching her clothes.
Sister Celeste cried out, 'Run — run — hurry — hurry...' her body rolling, helpless, lifeless, wrapped in the bloody sheet, across the hot, sunburnt grass.

The ground gave way beneath her, and she felt herself falling...

Paul was holding her hand.
She was propped in a chair in his office.
Hélène, the gallery assistant, stood, scarecrow-like in her skinny jeans and skinny top, her hair an unruly mop of corkscrew curls, nervously holding a bottle of water.
'I'm so sorry,' she said. 'I don't know what happened…'

Paul said he was sorry too, he should have realised it might be too much for her.

He took her home, with Hélène following in her car.
Annette produced wonderful thick vegetable soup — a plate of cheese — a bunch of purple grapes — clucking about Hélène being too thin — checking Cecile's bedroom to make sure it was warm enough.

Paul said she must rest — he had to go back to the gallery with Hélène and finish the hanging, make sure all was ready for tomorrow.

She lay on the comfortable bed, under a warm, patchwork quilt.
Outside in the garden, the mauves and pinks of michaelmas daisies, the reds and yellows of dahlias — a magic carpet of muted, mingled colour, submerged beneath the fine, soft rain.
Annette had placed a white jug of fine-petalled michaelmas daisies on the dressing table.

Annette had been Paul's housekeeper for many years. Her brother-in-law looked after the garden.
She was a widow, and had worked for the doctor and his wife in the village — cleaning the surgery, tidying the magazines, sometimes preparing lunch for the children.
She had been delighted to come and work for him. She had her own apartment the other side of the kitchen. It gave her much pleasure to keep the house spotless, and cook wonderful meals.

Paul had asked her to come when he was living with Claudine.
They had lived together for nearly twelve years, although she had spent a lot of time in Paris where she had a flat.

She did not really like the country, except for weekends — in the summer — to invite guests and eat on the terrace — or for New Year. She travelled quite a lot, working for Lancôme — checking the merchandise, the staff, the displays — in countries all over Europe.

She had wanted him to move to Paris — to open a gallery in Paris — but he didn't want to live in Paris — there was too much pressure — it was too expensive.
She was not interested in domesticity — cooking, cleaning, she loathed cleaning.
The house had become an increasing mess of unmade beds, unwashed dishes and discarded laundry.
He was travelling quite a bit at that time as well.
It had been depressing to come back to a dirty house and last week's greasy remnants on the stove.
Annette had taken over.
It had eased their relationship, which was not very good.

Claudine had gone to art school — had wanted to become and artist — but, though her paintings were competent and her drawings carefully accurate, she did not have the talent.

She had never really accepted this.
It made her resentful — thwarted.
She was ambitious.
She was never contented — always restless.
Expecting more from him than he could give.

They had drifted apart.
It was quite painless.
It was quite a long time ago now.
He had never felt the need to replace her.
Had never met anybody he cared enough about.

Cecile dozed.

The nuns danced a stately pavanne on the grass beneath the layered russett petticoats of the magnificent beech.

Jacob said, 'I think they understand — I hope they understand — I had to join the others…'

34

Paul got up and put some more logs on the fire.
They spluttered and sparkled, flying up the chimney, glossy and gleaming, like the tail feathers of a kingfisher caught in the sunlight.

He said, 'Would you like another coffee or a liqueur? Annette makes them herself — plum — walnut — blackberry — they are very good…'

She shook her head quickly to stop the glass shattering — the purple liquid spurting — the children bunched in terror against the dank cellar wall, their heads distended in silent screaming…

Paul said, 'You don't have to come tomorrow — I don't want it to upset you…'
She said she would be alright — it had just been rather a shock.

She owed it to the others — to them all.
She hoped, as she had hoped so many times, that the other children had grown up to find happiness — had had homes and families — that Anne-Marie had had her own little boy, to love and care for, as she had loved and cared for Jacob.
Jacob's paintings were a testimony to what they had suffered — a reminder of the horrors and humiliations of that dreadful time, which, in the end had defeated him, and which still held her in its choking grasp.

Paul said, 'I have to go to Geneva at the end of the month. I was wondering if you would like to come?'

She felt the tension, the fine puppet wires of strain relax — a sudden warmth. 'Oh, yes,' she said. 'I would like that…'

She, too, would like him to come to Vence with her, to be able, at last, to enjoy staying there in that beautiful place, without Hortense's incessant trivial yattering — Didier's indifference — Gerrard's boredom — to walk in the sloping scented gardens, distantly trimmed with violet ocean, among the lush plants and vivid flowers, and sit on the warm-stoned terrace by the round pool with the fat stone fish dribbling cool prisms of water onto the pebbled stones and clumps of emerald reeds…

To feel at peace like she did here.

'You have such a lovely house,' she said.

Paul looked down at the richly coloured Persian rug in front of the fire.
'I would like to share it with you,' he said. 'To share my home — to share my life…' he paused. 'You don't have to say anything now — just think about it…'

She felt the warmth spread — an unaccustomed feeling of complete pleasure. The ache across her shoulders — her neck — easing. 'Oh, yes,' she said. 'I don't have to think about it. I would be honoured to share your life — very honoured…'

At last she might be able to live with her ghosts — to distance herself from their agony — to find some peace — some happiness — a word — a feeling she was completely unfamiliar with…

'Yes,' she said. 'We should be together. There are so many things to see, to do. It would be so good to do them together…'

He leant forward and took her hand. 'Thank you for being here,' he said. 'Thank you for finding me…'

She laughed. 'We have to thank Gerrard. If I hadn't had to fetch his shirts I would never have seen the picture and come to see you.'

To know someone cared for you made you strong — now she could

Patsy would complain.
'I can't take time off whenever I like,' she would say, tossing her blonde hair, stiff with hairspray.
'After all, he's old enough to go on his own.'
Speaking to her father she raised her voice, using slow measured tones as if conversing with the retarded.
'The bus goes right to the hospital.'

Ernie was neat and clean. His tie carefully knotted, his collar standing away from the turkey-neck. The strands of hair combed thinly across the freckled scalp.

The doctor said it could be his kidneys.
She saw them piled in the white dish, sleek and shiny.
Doug wiping the bloody knife on a cloth — slicing away the membrane with one sharp cut.

There was not so much to do in the shop nowadays — people went to the supermarkets to shop, filling their cars with multi-packs — the meat hygienic in its transparent wrappings.
Most of Doug's work now was preparing meat for the restaurants he supplied.

*   *   *

Patsy's flat was high in the tower block.
The kitchen small and narrow, surfaced with beige melamine.
She had bought a mock leather sofa for the lounge in a darker beige, the carpet brown swirls.
The television chattered in the corner.
The metal window frames rusting.
She had a view over the river to the old Battersea Power Station — the railway lines swerving across to Victoria Station.
At low tide the river regurgitated remains — handles of perambulators and bicycle wheels — tins and shoes — chair legs — bits of clothing, saucepan lids, the occasional dead cat…

She had started eating the Indian takeaway she had bought on the

way home — chicken curry — when May phoned.
'No I can't,' she said. 'Mr Prescott will be away on Thursday and I have to be in the office.'

She worked cramped among files and boxes of dusty paper clips — her polished nails tapping out reports and contracts on the new IBM.
It was only a small firm, with a small staff. Just her and Debbie, and Gerry, prematurely bald with hairy hands.

She had turned the sound down on the television whilst she answered the phone. She had thought it might be Geoff. She had been watching the second part of a three part series about India at the time of the Raj. There was a lot of galloping about, and turbans and princesses with pearls in their hair. The hero saluted the passing horsemen. His helmet had a spike. He turned and swaggered after them — bandy-legged — the edge of his tunic rucked up in his belt.

'The bus stops right outside the hospital,' she said (again) listening to her aunt's worried voice.

She had spilt some coffee down the front of her new satin blouse — it was terylene really, but it looked like satin.
She had bought it last Saturday at Richards in Oxford Street.
She was annoyed — she hoped it would not leave a stain.

'No,' she said to her aunt's query. 'I won't be coming over this weekend — Geoff and I are planning to go to the coast. I'll ring you on Thursday after Dad's been to the hospital.'

She absently picked her teeth with her little finger nail — dislodging a fibrous bit of chicken, which she swallowed.
The remains of the curry congealed on the plastic tray on the little table in front of the television.
She would have to heat it up again in the microwave.

A group of white-robed men filled the screen — hacking the sand-filled air with long curved swords.

She sighed. Yes, she knew it looked as if Dad had something wrong — in the head she thought sourly.

Across the other side of the river a police launch ploughed the water into curdled waves, its red light flashing.

*　　　*　　　*

May packed him a small case.
Tests they said. Come in for tests.

In the end she had taken the afternoon off to go with him.
She had known it was no use asking Patsy.

They sat for two hours in a crowded waiting room.
Nurses and orderlies — young doctors, their pockets split and bulging with stethoscopes and notebooks — young women in skirts and jumpers carrying piles of files, breezed in and out.

Opposite a woman sat with her daughter.
Papery yellow, her hands stiff saffron claws.
'They shouldn't make sequels,' she said.
'We thought you would like it,' said the daughter, forcedly cheerful. 'You liked the first one.'
'It's never the same,' said her mother. 'The girl was all wrong. She was too tall.'
'Well it must be difficult to get it just right,' said the daughter.
She wore a short blue jacket and navy blue court shoes.
'They shouldn't have bothered,' said her mother. 'The girl was all wrong.'

May fetched Ernie a cup of tea from the canteen. He didn't drink it. He held it on his knee, slopping it in the saucer.

An African gentleman had lost his appointments card. He kept repeating, 'They told me to come here — Clinic 7.'

The receptionist hitched up her skirt and tapped at the computer,

getting off her chair to search through the pile of files.
'You should have come yesterday Mr Kionja,' she said at last holding up a form. 'We'll have to give you another appointment.'
Mr Kionja thumped the floor with the rubber ferrule of his stick and started to shout.
May couldn't understand a word he was saying.
'Next Tuesday,' said the girl.
'They told me to come here,' he shouted. 'Clinic 7.'
'Next Tuesday 2.30,' said the girl.
She handed him the card.

He searched his pockets for his glasses, putting them on.
He stared at the card in disbelief. 'They told me today,' he shouted. 'Clinic 7. Today — Clinic 7.'

He dropped the card, his gloves, and a folded copy of *The Sun* on the floor.
The young man standing behind him, his flesh ghostly pale, bent painfully to pick them up. May could hear him breathing, like a door creaking.
Mr Kionja continued to shout incomprehensively — backing out of the waiting room to harangue two nurses carrying trays of blood samples and a man in green overalls pushing a trolley of bottles.

The receptionist unwrapped a piece of chewing gum — screwing the silver paper up into a tiny ball and dropping it in the tin waste paper basket.
'Next...' she said.

Ernie was sent for x-rays.

They sat for another two hours in a large hall, like a hotel foyer — with round tables of scientific magazines.
Nurses and men in white coats wandered to and fro carrying x-ray plates and cups of coffee, stopping to chat.

She became increasingly fidgety. It was something about the way they were ignored — all of them — the hall was so full they had run out of chairs, leaving some people to stand uncertainly wondering what to do.

Ernie paid no attention. He sat staring fixedly — uninterested — saying nothing.

They waited forty minutes for the bus home.

May had taken Ernie in a cup of tea and two digestive biscuits overlapping on the blue-flowered plate that had been her mother's. She had all her mother's china.
May had lived here with her mother until she had gone into Hospital after her stroke.

It was one of those long old fashioned wards, with narrow high beds, tall windows, and screens on wheels, overlooking the entrance to Casualty where the ambulances came and went and nurses hurried, arms folded under their short cloaks.

Her mother lay with her face turned to the wall — a dribble of saliva dampening the pillow.
She had brought a box of her favourite chocolates — Cadbury's Milk Tray.

'Feeling a bit for sorry for ourselves today, aren't we dear?' said the Staff Nurse, hauling her up a little against the pillows, the blue armpits of her uniform dark with sweat.
'Better not give her those dear, they'll make her choke.'

May left them for the nurses.

She washed out the teapot in the sink — looking unseeingly into the dismal backyard.
The window faced onto the side of the bicycle shed. It had been the outside toilet until they had had a bathroom put in upstairs — the bicycles just fitted crossways.
The dustmen had dented the dustbin lid so that it didn't close properly — there was a bucket of rainwater and a broom with most

of the bristles missing…

Doug had given her a nice piece of calves liver.
She didn't think Ernie would eat it. He hardly ate anything these days…
She would do some mashed potato and open a tin of carrots — he might eat a little mashed potato and a few carrots.

He was to go in for tests Thursday morning.

She had packed his things today because tomorrow was Wednesday, early closing — and she would be late home.
Wednesday afternoons she went with Ida window shopping in Bethnall Green Road.
They had tea in the cafeteria of the British Home Stores.
They used to have tea in the ABC Tearooms — closed long ago.
In their place a branch of Littlewoods and Currys.
They stopped to look at the washing machines.

Ida had a Bendix washer/drier.
May didn't have a washing machine.
She washed most of their things by hand — taking the sheets and towels to the launderette in Swanfield Street once a week — dropping them in on the way to work and picking them up on the way home.

She had put in a towel and two pairs of pyjamas — the pair with the green paisley pattern and the warmer ones with the blue and grey stripes.
She'd put his slippers and shaving things in on Thursday morning.
She put the case in her bedroom so as not to upset him.

She opened a tin of luncheon meat, scraping off the jelly — to make sandwiches for tomorrow.
She left Ernie's on one of the blue-flowered plates covered with a napkin in the fridge — putting hers in the Tupperware sandwich box to eat in the packing room at work.
Now they had to wear white mop caps to cover their hair and thin surgical gloves when they handled the meat.

At first Ernie seemed alright after Lilly died.
He left the flat they had rented in Peckham, and moved back to live with her — going on Saturdays to watch Millwall when they were playing at home.
He went for a week's holiday to Bognor and on the works outing to Blackpool to see the lights.

And then he was made redundant. Just like that.
'We won't need you from Monday, Mr Wilson…'
Friday afternoon — half past three — a month's wages in his pay packet — not even a handshake after 18 years.

He tried to get another job — writing letters in his slanting handwriting with the looped tails — waiting anxiously for replies — shrinking from the rejection.

He ceased to go to the Prince Albert for his nightly pint — or to the football, becoming unable to cope with the unfamiliar change of buses at Liverpool Street — from 8 to 78.
He didn't even go to the Oval for the last test match against Australia when Stan got tickets.

He sat in the front room by the window, Great Sea Battles unopened on the table with the round plastic-lace mat — its pages marked with torn strips of blotting paper — watching the lonely skeletal heads of the one-armed grey and orange monsters lumbering back and forth behind the beautiful couple on the hoarding.

The street was deserted.
The house next door — squashed against the railings of a wasteland of nettles, rusting tins, old cookers — a Ford transit van — its doors and wheels torn off — the stuffing of its seats spewing out — had been empty for years, ever since Rose had gone to live with her daughter in Leigh-on-Sea, after Ted had died.

On the other side old Mrs Fish — well over 90 — encased in elastic bandages — the room stinking of bodily functions — sat immobile — waiting for the twice-weekly visits from the black District Nurse, and the daily Meals on Wheels lady in her Hush Puppies and sensible raincoat, carrying the tray of foil-covered dishes — shouting cheery greetings.

Mrs Fish was stone deaf.

Further along an elderly Polish couple — neither having mastered the English language beyond the simplest of phrases — in spite of their British citizenship, and nearly forty years of residency. Contributing to the life of the street with an occasional flick of the grey net curtains in their front room window.

The shop on the corner had been boarded up a long time. Advertising placards for Craven A and Bisto still leant against the wall beside the waste bin with its Wall's Ice Cream lining.

Their father had walked away down this street, his ankles bent by the black laced boots — humped by the heavy knapsack and tin hat — carrying his kitbag. His forage cap too small — his tunic too big, hanging loosely on his bony shoulders. Like Ernie he had never filled his clothes.

He was killed on the beaches of Normandy — still seasick from the rough crossing — gunned down as he waded ashore from the landing craft.

Life came late in the afternoon — with the kids on their bikes, squeezing through the gap to play football on the building site. The sound of young raucous voices replacing the thudding and whirring of machines — the deafening rattle of drills.

May had never thought she would always live in this house — that she would be here with Ernie.

Sitting on an empty crate at the back of Mr Withers' greengrocers — eating meat paste sandwiches and reading the *Woman's Own* — she had dreamt of other things.
They had thick cracked mugs of strong tea.

Mr Withers allowed her to have a fruit to go with her lunch — and apple or an orange — sometimes in the summer, a handful of glistening cherries or some damaged strawberries — squashed at the bottom of the punnets.

She would dream wistfully of a tall, dark, handsome young man filling her arms with roses — slipping a sparkling ring on her finger — folding her in his arms.

There was a short fat man in a striped city suit who came every Friday to buy four oranges and half a pound of black grapes. He called her 'sweetheart' in a jocular way and pressed a half crown into her hand with his fleshy fingers.
Every morning, just after they opened the shop — a tall young man with curly hair walked by — eyes down — hands in pockets. He would stop and buy a paper from the newsstand on the corner before disappearing into the Underground station.
She wove fantasies round him — hoping one day he would look up and see her — that it would be love at first sight! He never did.

She still read *Woman's Own*.
The stories were much the same — the love scenes rather more daring — referring to parts of the body May did not really like to think about — but the end was always the same — the final passionate embrace.
Instead of 'How to Keep Romance Alive in Your Marriage' — with the discreet use of perfume, the purchase of a new negligée and admonitions about 'not leaving your curlers in' — there were articles on Homosexuality and Sexually Transmitted Diseases.
No longer 'Six Irresistible Ways with Stewing Steak' — now 'Jambalaya with Rice and Fried Bananas'.

She started to peel the potatoes for supper.
She wished she had Ida's confidence — swinging her satchel at the boys from King Edward's Grammar — as they waited at the bus stop in their maroon blazers and maroon and black striped ties.
Ida said it was ridiculous girls wearing ties as May sheltered behind her. 'And this Bloody Awful colour!' The boys had black blazers.

The gangling boy with the thin mouth and grease-slicked hair tried to bribe Ida for a kiss. 'Two packs of chewing gum and three Senior Service,' he said. 'Come on Ida, be a sport!'

Ida caught him across the chest with her satchel. 'Shove off, grot face!' she said. 'I'm not that desperate.'
The other boys crowded round jostling them.

'What about half a bar of Fruit and Nut?'
'I can get a record of Jonnie Ray...'
'Buzz off you little twerp!' said Ida disdainfully. 'Would you mind getting out of the way. WE would like to get on this bus.'

Even the conductor swinging on his silver pole flirted with Ida.
'Are you getting on this bus luvvie?' he asked. 'Or are you practising signalling?' He put out a hand to help her up. 'On top only — thank you! And no messing about! Young Hooligans!' He stood aside to let the surge of dirty, dusty, sticky youth fight their way up the stairs.

Ida got a job in C&A at Marble Arch — sophisticated in nylons and high heels.
'You've always got earth under your nails,' she said to May. 'Why don't you get a job up West like me?'

May's mother didn't approve of her going up West. She didn't approve of Ida either. 'Flighty!' she said. 'All that muck on her face. She'll come to no good, just you wait and see.'

It was only a sense of duty which made May stay at home with her mother.
When Ernie married Lily, she couldn't very well leave her mother on her own.
She spent a lot of her free time babysitting for them, so that they could continue with their Ballroom Dancing.
That's how they met, waltzing an 'Excuse Me' to the tune from the Moulin Rouge.
After they got engaged, they all went to see the film — about a stunted artist with a beard who painted half-clothed girls, and

dancers who kicked their legs very high and did the splits.

They went to a cafe and had egg and chips and bread and butter. Lily gulped her food. She had an engagement ring with a tiny blue stone, and wore a yellow polo neck jumper, which helped to hide her rather long neck.
Ernie, as always, picked at his food — carefully dividing the white and yolk of his egg, and folding the bread and butter neatly in half.
Conversation was never their strong point.
Not like Ida, she never stopped talking.
She said May was stupid. 'Fancy wasting your Saturday nights looking after someone else's squalling brat. How do you ever expect to meet anyone?'
May, in her terrible shyness, didn't really mind. It was quite a relief not to have to worry about making a fool of herself. Ernie and Lily had a television, and she was quite happy to sit and watch and dream, and knit little garments for Patsy in loose, uneven stocking stitch.

She lit the gas under the potatoes.

She would wear her fair-isle cardigan and rose brooch tomorrow. She shouldn't have washed the cardigan — it had gone all felty.

*　　*　　*

Geoff had brought Kentucky Fried Chicken and a 4-pack of Foster's lager.
He had had to climb the five flights to the flat, because the lifts were out of order (again!).
The wall by the staircase liberally decorated with graffiti — obscene and otherwise.
Somebody had drawn a castle in yellow chalk — black birds swooped — an elongated red London Bus — hearts pierced with arrows — 'Death to the liftman' in purple felt-tip — a purple figure hanging from a purple gallows.

He ate the chicken straight from the cardboard box — and drank the lager straight from the can.

Patsy fetched pink plates and paper napkins — and glasses — but Geoff was already eating. He bolted his food without looking up — complaining about the lifts — his boss, Marvin who was a shit — and the present job.
They were wiring new flats in Docklands.

Patsy transferred her chicken leg and chips from the box onto a plate, and helped herself daintily to salt and ketchup. She wished Geoff was a bit more refined — licking his fingers and wiping his hands on his jeans — and he really didn't have to drink out of the can.

'It would be like living in a bleeding greenhouse,' he said. 'All that glass would make me fucking nervous.' He took a long swig of lager.

Patsy told him about her father.
'They're lucky not to have been burnt to death,' said Geoff. 'That house is a fucking fire hazard — the wiring is a fucking joke.'

Patsy wiped her mouth on the pink paper napkin — wishing his language wasn't so coarse.

She had envisaged romance somewhat differently to her real life experience with Geoff.
He didn't gaze into her eyes, or whisper endearments whilst holding her with tender strength — rolling off her to lie inert as if he had been on a trampoline — mouth open.
She felt cheated.

She most definitely didn't want to visit her father in hospital. If he were only in a few days, she wouldn't have to… and then what?

The awful trek — walking up to Vauxhall Bridge and over on the other side to catch the 44 to Guy's when her mother was dying.

Lily had had thick wavy hair — black streaked with grey.
As her illness progressed it became flat and thin, as if already dead — her nails brittle and flaking.

The hospital smelt of vegetable water and disinfectant.

'I'm never coming out,' she said, pulling at the ribbons on the blue open-work bed jacket that Auntie May had knitted.
'Oh don't be silly, Mum,' said Patsy.
'I would have liked to see you settled.' The brown mole on her cheek seemed to have grown larger.
'People don't get married nowadays,' said Patsy... And now her father — disappearing before her eyes. Auntie May said it was his kidneys — there was always a slight whiff of urine.

Auntie May had fed her mother with a spoon — some kind of porridge.
'Nice and sweet, just how you like it'... scraping the bits from around her mouth with the edge of the spoon — like feeding a baby.
'Just a teeny bit more — There's a good girl!'

Patsy willed him to die. He clutched his chest and keeled over, like on TV — the awful brown trousers revealing Auntie May's spongy pebbled Christmas socks.
She didn't want him to stay smelly, with frothy mouth and gummed-up eyes.

The London Hospital was even more difficult to get to — right down Mile End Road. She thought the 25 went up that way. She could catch one at Victoria. What a drag!

*   *   *

Ida had skin the colour of boiled ham, and fashionably short bleached hair.
Dr Jephta said her blood pressure was too high — she could stop drinking — lose some weight.
She had been having dizzy spells.
Of course she wouldn't go to Dr Jephta for anything Personal. She didn't fancy him touching her with those brown hands. She would ask to see Dr Poole, even though they said he drank.

She was Manageress of the Carvery at the Mulberry Arms in the Old Ford Road, near Victoria Park. It was very popular for business lunches. the men liked to buy her a drink.

She had told Kevin to be generous with the soda.
She didn't stand any nonsense from lecherous patrons — slapping away straying hands with just enough provocation to keep them interested.

She had long parted company with her husband Bernie — they never divorced — it was too expensive in those days.
She thought he had moved to Birmingham.
Probably bald as a coot now. He had been losing his hair even then — rubbing in Coconut Oil — supposed to promote hair growth. She used to joke him about growing mustard and cress on an old flannel!

Wednesday was her day off.
She sat in the faded flower-patterned armchair in front of the TV, varnishing her nails Venetian Violet. Her hands were broad — the nails thick and long.

She had tea and ginger biscuits on the table with the polish remover and orange sticks — bits of cotton wool in the ashtray.

She had the occasional cigarette — usually when she was 'entertaining'.
She tried to extricate a ginger biscuit without smudging her nails.

May's mother had always eaten ginger biscuits — Old Bag! Poor May! then Lily! Now the weedy Ernie!

They had gone on the bus to Peckham. May was going to babysit for Lily and Ernie. They were going Ballroom Dancing.
It was Saturday. Ida had wanted May to come with her to the Palais de Dance.
She had a peacock blue circular skirt and had bleached her newly permed hair.

May's mother wouldn't let her have a perm. Her hair was cut straight all round — straight and stringy. Her face blobby as the putty the plumber had used to mend the waste pipe in the sink — not even a hint of face powder to relieve the pallid shine.

Lily was sewing sequins on a dress of tangerine net — her black hair falling over her angular face — her lumpy joints protruding — invisible hinges working her hands and feet. The flat smelt of nappies and yesterday's dinner — Patsy grizzling in her carrycot by the window — streaked with condensation — the ineffectual one bar electric fire. She remembered it as clearly as if it were yesterday. You kept your coat on when visiting Lily and Ernie.

Ida screwed the cap back on the bottle of varnish.

May's mother didn't like her to go dancing.
'It's only a bit of fun,' Ida had said — mentally sticking her tongue out — silly old bag — about as sexy as a stuffed boulster. She and May were unlikely friends. She had taken her under her wing at school — protecting her from the rougher girls. A surrogate sister.

She had been going out with Melvyn at that time — hair heavy with Brylcreem — determined — forcefully passionate.
Swept along to some extent by his fervour, she drew the line at entering a new, important phase of womanhood flattened against a torn poster of Jane Russell, down the side of the Odeon.

She had found she was always in control — never carried away, drunk or sober.

The woman on the television was making a stew. She had the ingredients laid out on a scrubbed pine table.
Courgettes and some yellow knobbly things, and the inevitable string of garlic, — grinding liberal quantities of black pepper into a Pyrex dish of cubed meat.
Lily was always dumping Patsy on May — spoiled brat!
Lily dressed her up like Little-Bo-Peep — embroidered smocks and ridiculous frilly bonnets.

The woman put on a purposeful striped oven glove and placed another dish on the table. She took the lid off, smiling, sniffing appreciatively.

Now May was stuck with Ernie.

Lily and he had made a bizarre couple. Chasséeing across the bare hall, meagrely heated by oil stoves.

Lily in the sequinned net, the tails of Ernie's black frock coat flapping, as they jerked briskly to the music of Victor Sylvester — heads thrown back in studied abandon.

How could May stand working in that awful butchers?
She got up and went into the white melamine-surfaced kitchen and put her cup in the sink.

There were some kids kicking cans about down in the car park. Why weren't they at school? Kids nowadays! and their language!

May was late. Doug had had a last minute order for pork chops, and then the whole place had to be scrubbed down. Doug kept everything as clean as an operating theatre — briefly she saw Ernie laid out under a white sheet, a tray of silver saws and hammers — long pointed knives — gleaming in the dazzling spotlight over the bed — surrounded by masked men. She stripped off the thin rubber gloves, and went to get her coat.

She had taken Ernie in his morning tea — the stairs made her knee hurt.

He lay under the bronze shiny eiderdown, his brown and white striped pyjamas buttoned to the neck. She drew back the thin rayon curtains — they did not quite meet in the middle. On the bare dressing table with the winged mirror — photographs of Lily and their Mother faced each other. Lily smiling toothily — their Mother, her mouth clamped shut in a thin line — her hair set in concertina waves.

'It's Wednesday,' she said, 'so I'll be a bit late.'
'Give Ida my regards,' said Ernie.
They said the same things each week. Ernie didn't like Ida much —
thought her 'fast'.

She didn't take her bike on Wednesdays. She walked down to the
main road to catch the bus.

*　　　*　　　*

She could hardly recall the street as it used to be.

The streets behind had been flattened by a V2 — silently tearing the
sky to explode its venom among the terraced houses, swallowing
them in its vast crater — leaving scattered blackened bricks — bits
of fence and the stubborn staircase of No. 15.

All the windows in their street had been blown out — some of the
houses opposite suffered more serious damage — slates clattering
from roofs — walls collapsing. Much later the bulldozers and
swinging steel weights came, reducing them to instant rubble.

She and Ernie had been sent to stay with Auntie Annie, their
Mother's sister, who lived in a small village in Norfolk. They had
enjoyed it there — the open fields — juicy yellow plums — small
sour apples fallen on the warm-smelling grass, and long green
runner beans with little scarlet flowers. Auntie Annie made flat
scones on the top of her old black stove, and there was home-made
blackberry jelly and butter from the farm.

A scary woman in dungarees who smoked a cigar sometimes came
with pale green duck eggs and a rabbit wrapped in newspaper — in
the basket of her flat-tyred bicycle — bumping along the road, She
would sit in Auntie Annie's kitchen in muddy gumboots — drinking
tea, going on about 'This damned war' and 'The bloody Huns'.

Uncle Ted didn't come back either.
He was killed at Monte Cassino.

Now there was a large board at the end of the street, proclaiming Parker and Millets — Building for the Future! There was a picture of posh flats with white balconies, surrounded by trees, and a yachting marina.

She doubted that was what they were building here.

*   *   *

Patsy had a streaming cold. She had caught it on Sunday on their trip to Margate.

It had not been a success.

Geoff had invited Ken and Cheryl whom she didn't care for it at all. Ken's language was worse than Geoff's — and Cheryl! Well! Talk about common!

She had to sit with Cheryl in the back of Geoff's pale blue Ford Escort. It was none too clean in the back.

Cheryl wore tight black pants, high-heeled boots and a black leather jacket — her hair an uncombed frizz.

She rattled with chains and medallions and bangles. Her fingers — the nails bitten to nothing — obscured by rings.

She was trying to give up smoking — so she chewed gum noisily between fags.

It had poured with rain. They stopped for coffee at a Little Chef, and got very wet just crossing the car park.

When they reached Margate, the front was deserted in the driving rain.

Cheryl refused to get out of the car.

They had spent most of the day in a pub with a bright pink plaster mermaid hanging over the bar. Ken made lewd comments about her rather oversized bust. Some of the green scales had fallen off her tail. There were strings of plastic shells hanging from the ceiling.

They ate indigestible food. Geoff and Ken consumed quantities of beer. Cheryl drank lager and brandy.

She had one gin and orange, and toyed with some lemonade.

They had all ended up in her flat, and drank all the sherry she kept for special occasions.

Ken and Geoff went to get a Chinese take-away.
They were gone a long time — stopping off at the King's Arms.
Patsy had to sit and listen to Cheryl complaining about Ken, telling her intimate details about their relationship she didn't want to know.
Ken spilt a plate of spicy noodles on her acrylic Persian rug.

Now Debbie had messed up the post.
It was difficult to be haughtily disgusted at her stupidity — or suitably soothing to the irate customers, phoning to say they had been sent the wrong invoice — with a running nose and distorted voice.
She sent Debbie to get some Lemsip, and dabbed her nose with pink tissues.

She ought to phone Auntie May this evening to see if her father was prepared for his hospital visit.
She felt vaguely guilty about not going with him.
She really couldn't take any more time off.
She couldn't leave Debbie in charge.
He was only going in for tests.

She rather hoped Geoff would not come round tonight.
She just wanted to go to bed with a hot water bottle, and that certainly wouldn't suit Geoff.

*   *   *

Ida tried to conceal her annoyance at May being late.
She could have gone into Saxone and tried those shoes she had seen in the window — black high-heels with a gilt trim.
She stood inside the doors of the British Home Stores — inspecting a stand of woven lurex tops — £29.99 — perhaps next month she would get one.
May had a navy blue belted raincoat and flat brown lace-ups.
'You ought to get your hair done,' said Ida. 'You look a fright!'

They had a pot of tea and slices of Black Forest Gateau.
Ida poured the tea.

'Why can't Patsy help?' she said, knowing what the answer would be
— too busy — got her own life — Geoff wouldn't like it. There was a
man to steer clear of, if she'd ever seen one!
'You should insist,' she said. 'After all, he is her father.'

*   *   *

Ernie was not in the sitting room.
His glasses case lay on the table by the window beside the precisely
placed *Daily Mirror.*

She called up the stairs — but there was no answer.
She mounted the stairs painfully — pulling herself on the banisters.
His room was empty — bed neatly made — pyjamas neatly folded
on a chair.

He was not in the house.
Where could he be?
He never went anywhere anymore.
She thought of phoning Patsy, but he would certainly not have gone
there.
She put her coat back on, and went out into the street.
Perhaps he had gone to the Prince Albert.

There was hardly anybody in the bar.
The barman in a pullover with the head of an Alsatian knitted in
browns and blacks, large on his chest, polished the counter with a
dirty cloth. There was a glass-domed dish of sandwiches.
An unshaven man in a black donkey jacket swayed drunkenly on a
bar stool, talking loudly to the barman.
A few scruffy men in shabby overcoats sat together at a table.
There was a heavy smell of stale beer and cigarette smoke — an air
of dejected seediness — the worn lino showing patches of board.

He wasn't there.

She retraced her steps.
It had begun to rain.
There were two boys running — breathless — urgent — their anoraks shiny with water.
They had come from the building site.

Somehow she squeezed through the gap in the fence — her shoes sinking in the cloying mud.

Work had stopped for the day.
A lunar wasteland of mustard yellow mud — the cranes and diggers silent, their unwieldy limbs drooping wearily over the waterlogged earth.
A group of boys stood silent and still in the cold rain, looking down — one carried a football.

He lay face down in a ragged hole, half full of muddy water.
A discarded suit of clothes — arms floating sideways — his freckled scalp a giant bird's egg.

It was strange she felt so little.
Ernie had left life some time ago.
The only surprise was that he had been capable of doing such a thing.

Ghosts crowded round her — her father in khaki battledress — her mother petulant in the coat with the moth-eaten collar of rabbit fur — Lily, her streaked hair coarse in Death falling over the empty-socket eyes.

She was shivering.

Suddenly there was a squad car and two policemen and an ambulance.

Someone was getting in the hole, lifting Ernie's puppet body — the strings broken — his arms swinging loosely.

He was put on a stretcher, covered with a red blanket, and carried away over the lumps and pools of squelching mud.

She followed slowly — unable to speak — the ghosts walked with her.
One of the policemen took her arm, guiding her to the car.
'Shock,' she heard him say. 'Perhaps it's her husband... Come on luvvie...' Helping her into the car. 'You'd better come with us to the hospital — and you can tell us what happened. We'll see you safely home.'

The ghosts crushed in beside her — forcing her into the corner. They would move in with her now, and fill the house with quarrelling voices. They would demand her attention — disturb her sleep.

The police car reversed into Walsall Street, and followed the ambulance towards the hospital, where white-gowned figures would take Ernie away to join the others.

Safer Under the Stairs

The train was very crowded — full of soldiers with bulky kitbags and clumsy boots, and worried looking young women with untidy hair — Lucy said they were probably Land Girls, going to drive tractors, she said she wouldn't mind driving a tractor if she couldn't drive a tank...

She and Lucy had to stand in the corridor outside the compartment where Auntie Maud had managed to get a seat.

The nice lady in the green uniform with red badges in the Church Hall, had found them clothes from lots of cardboard boxes scattered round the hall. She had found Maisie a rather large dark green blazer, a cotton frock with faded yellow flowers and a pink cardigan. Lucy had a navyblue raincoat which was much too big, a grey pleated skirt, white boy's shirt and a rather shrunken fairisle jumper. The nice lady found them both white plimsolls from boxes and boxes of shoes and boots, and said they would be given extra coupons as they had been bombed out. They didn't need coupons for secondhand clothes.

Auntie Maud was very upset. 'They've nothing,' she said. 'Is there no more underwear — and nightclothes — they haven't got any night clothes...'

They nice lady was very soothing, and hunted in the boxes for some pyjamas...
There were other ladies pouring tea from large brown teapots, and piles of bread and scarlet jam on thick white plates...
'They will be reissued with coupons and gas masks,' the lady told Auntie Maud.
'Let's hope there isn't a gas attack today,' said Auntie Maud.
She was flushed and near to tears. Maisie took her hand, she didn't like Auntie Maud to be upset.

Their mother had been taken to hospital.

Auntie Maud said she wasn't well enough to see them at the moment.
They would be able to see her when she was better.

The train journey was very slow and very long. There was an air raid,
and the train had to stop until it was safe to continue.

Auntie Maud had brought meat paste sandwiches and some biscuits,
which she passed to them in the corridor.
They were on their way to stay with Aunt Harriet.
Maisie had not wanted to go and stay with Aunt Harriet, even
though she had a really big garden with lots of trees to climb.
Aunt Harriet was very different from Auntie Maud.
They always had to be on their best behaviour when they visited
Aunt Harriet.
She was very fussy about things like crumbs, and washing your
hands, and sitting properly, but now they had no choice.
There was nowhere else to go.

*   *   *

Auntie Maud had said it was safest under the stairs.
She had heard it on the wireless.

Auntie Maud said they were very lucky to have such a nice house —
in such a nice street — so near Hyde Park and the nice girls' school.

It was a nice street.
There were shops with bright windows — a baker's with round,
crusty loaves, doughnuts oozing jam, and little cakes with hundreds
and thousands. A newspaper shop that sold sweets, jars of candy-
striped peppermints, tins of toffee, colouring books and celluloid
dolls with stuck-on clothes. The grocer's was full of pickle jars and
tins of biscuits with pictures on the lids, and you could see the lady
with the white coat cutting slices of bacon with the big slicer, and
wrapping it in waxy white paper.

The house still felt strange and smelt strange.
The room at the top of the house she shared with Lucy had no

carpet on the bare boards. Their mother had put a rug between the beds, worried they might get splinters in their feet… Downstairs the rooms were still full of unpacked crates and boxes. Auntie Maud said there was plenty of time to see to all that.

They spent most of their time in the shabby basement kitchen, and small, dusty servants' sitting room, only, of course, there were no servants.

The Park was beautiful — huge trees weighed down with thick, rustling summer leaves, and the glittering water of the Serpentine, with people rowing boats, laughing and getting in muddles with their oars.

But the War hung in the summer air, a faint menacing whisper, a malevolent breeze.
The Park was zigzagged with trenches, and there were gun emplacements among the rhododendrons, mounds of sand bags, and soldiers everywhere, nearly everyone was in uniform, and high above, the cumbersome, silver barrage balloons danced an elephantine dance in the hazy summer.

The wireless crackled with warnings.
They had to carry their gas masks and identity cards at all times, even when they went to Lyons Corner House to buy pork pies…
Maisie loved the Corner House. The counters with whole hams and golden wheels of cheese, baskets of eggs and pyramids of fruit. The man in the tall white hat selecting what was required with a long silver two-pronged fork.

Auntie Maud said that would all change soon — now they all had ration books — there were shortages — the real jars and tins in the grocer's window replaced with 'pretend' jars and tins with nothing inside.

Auntie Maud came every Wednesday from Ealing where she had a flat with lots of ornaments and embroidered cushions. Solid and kind, bringing some little treat for them — a bag of humbugs — iced buns for tea — drawing books and crayons — a new knitted dress for Maisie's favourite doll, Susan.

The summer still spread warm fingers over the Park and the leaves on the magnificent trees had not started to change colour. Every afternoon they walked with their mother in Kensington Gardens, along little paths and round the big ponds with the fountains. There were not so many soldiers now — wandering in ones and twos, or sitting in small groups on the summer-parched grass smoking cigarettes. 'They've all gone to fight the Germans,' said Lucy.

The sombre voice on the wireless spoke of losses and retreats, and of bombing in Croydon.

Auntie Maud said maybe they wouldn't get this far — but her usual cheerfulness seemed a little false.

The air was strung with invisible wires — wires pulled tight to breaking point.
And then, when the leaves had begun to fall in golden swishing bronze heaps in the Park, the bombing began.

Every night they huddled on the basement stairs, wrapped in rugs, as the house shook with the barrage of anti-aircraft fire — seemingly ineffective against the swarms of swooping, whining planes, like angry gnats, the faceless, goggled pilots with leather gauntlets, releasing their deadly load of fire and destruction, dodging the red tracer bullets and the hunting beams of the searchlights.

Lucy made shadow patterns on the wall in the torchlight — all the lights had gone out — they were always going out. Their mother kept a supply of candles in the kitchen drawer.

Their mother said she didn't know what to do. She had heard nothing from their father. Lucy rushed for the post every morning, but there were only dreary brown envelopes — occasional letters from their grandparents — a card from cousin Edith holidaying in Scarborough. 'Pleasant, but very windy — not able to go on the beach — nice hotel…'

All the beaches were mined.
'Round balls with spikes,' said Lucy. 'It's to stop the Germans, if they try to land they'll all be blown up…'

There were also letters from their mother's friend Margaret urging her to leave London.

'If only Bill were here,' their mother said to Auntie Maud. 'I don't know what to do. I can't just leave the house…'

Maisie wished their father was there too — wished he was still going every day to his ink-stained office with the swivel chair, in his dark suit and careful tie.
'He's Captain of a battleship,' said Lucy, and then added, 'Perhaps he isn't Captain just yet — but he will be soon…'

But Maisie didn't want him to be Captain of a battleship.
They had waved him off, when there were purple and yellow crocuses carpeting the Park, carrying the battered brown suitcase kept for holiday visits to the seaside — now somewhere on a bullet grey, gun-spiked ship, slicing through the dark secret waters of a distant ocean — not the gently lapping white-crested waves curling on their holiday beach. Maisie didn't want the salt-splashing sea to be floating with round, spiked mines.

Auntie Maud said she was sure the War wouldn't last long. He would be back before he had time to get seasick…

'Look at my rabbit,' said Lucy, waggling her fingers in the torchlight. 'It really looks like a rabbit…' and she waggled her fingers some more. 'Look at the ears…'

'I can do a rabbit too,' said Maisie. 'And I can do a tortoise…' And she closed her small fist with the thumb sticking out between her fingers.

The trees in the Park were now hauntingly bare — the mounds of leaves dark and wet. Nobody rowed boats on the still waves of the lake. They were tied up, jostling woodily together by the deserted jetty — and the bombing got worse.

They had tried to play I Spy, but in the intermittent darkness on the basement stairs there was really nothing to Spy, so Lucy said they would do the Alphabet — think of as many words as possible for each letter.

Their mother told Lucy not to use the torch too much — it was difficult to get bulbs and batteries now — it was difficult getting anything.
Lucy said they should have a lantern — with a candle — but their mother didn't answer — there was also a shortage of candles…

Auntie Maud had suggested then that perhaps they should go and stay with Aunt Harriet, and Maisie had hoped they wouldn't have to. She was very severe, not smiling and jolly like Auntie Maud.

Their mother was having trouble with the stove — it kept going out. She was not used to lighting stoves and cleaning.
They had always had Mrs Parsons at their old house, nice Mrs Parsons in her flowered overalls who smelt of peppermints. She had scrubbed the floors with a hard bristly brush and yellow bars of soap. She had mopped and dusted, and peeled potatoes, and often made a sponge pudding or an apple tart for supper before she left. Maisie wished nice Mrs Parsons could come here.

They became quite friendly with people who lived in the street.

Mrs Burton, who lived two doors away, sometimes came and had tea with their mother. She always wore a fur coat and a close-fitting purple velvet hat. She had two cats, a big ginger one and an old tabby. She was very concerned that they did not have gas masks. She talked a lot to Lucy about books, and brought her a copy of Little Women to read. She said she would try and find a nice book for Maisie, she thought she had a copy of The Water Babies somewhere…

And there was the young man at the newsagents. He couldn't join the Army because he had a withered arm. Auntie Maud said it was a mistake when he was born. Maisie wanted to ask why there had been a mistake, but she decided not to. He was nice anyway, and she was sorry about his arm. He limped as well, but she didn't know what was wrong with his leg.

Auntie Maud got on very well with the lady in the grocer's — often getting little bits of extra this and that — 'end bits', she called them — but a paper bag of crumbled cheese made really good cheese on toast or a nice sauce for macaroni, a bit of bacon rind cooked with vegetables made a very nice soup.
Auntie Maud was very good at that sort of thing, which helped their mother a lot.
She seemed to get daily thinner and paler.
'The children never get enough sleep,' she said. 'None of us are getting enough sleep.'

And Auntie Maud would encourage her to go and have a lie down, and their mother would say, 'I still haven't heard from Bill...' and Auntie Maud would say, 'Well, if he's at sea, he won't be able to write will he?' and she would persuade their mother to go and rest.

They had to take a bus to their father's office in the City.
Their mother had papers to sign.
It took a very long time.
The bombing had reduced whole streets to piles of rubble — scraps of twisted metal and cloth, amongst shattered bricks — spikes of glass — odd baths and broken bedsteads.
Giant skeletal staircases still stood — grimly defiant against collapsing walls and toppled chimney stacks.

Auntie Maud was right. It was safest under the stairs.
Lucy said they should be very safe. They were under three flights of stairs.

Some of the ruins were still smoking. There were firemen with hoses. ARP men with stretchers, and grey, dazed people carrying bits and

pieces, bags and blankets — a saucepan — a chair...
The bus had to keep stopping, having to find a way round deep, ragged craters.

They were so tired when they finally got home, their mother sadder and whiter than ever. Lucy went round the house closing the thick, ugly blackout curtains.
They had soup and bread and ham for supper, and went straight upstairs.

Under her bed the goblins lurked — restless among the balls of fluff and mislaid hair slides.
The coldness of fear made her legs stiff, so that when the flashing blue hysterical wail of the siren gyrated in the darkness, she was slow to reach her slippers — laid out ready with her dressing gown — Lucy telling her to 'Hurry up!' as they slipped and slithered down to the basement.

It was a bad night.
It was cold on the stairs.
The whole house was cold.

They had to be very careful with the coal.
Their mother tightened the tartan rug round her shoulders and closed her eyes.
Even Lucy was silent.
They didn't make shadow figures on the wall.
It was very noisy — noisier than usual.
The whole house shuddered — there was a terrible tearing sound, and then an avalanche of tumbling walls — a thundering cascade of cracking timber and breaking glass — a fearsome, exploding darkness of choking plaster. The house collapsed around them, deadening the sounds of blasting guns and screaming aeroplanes — trapping them in engulfing blackness.

Maisie couldn't breathe — she tried to call out to Lucy — to their mother — she couldn't move — the weight of the massed rubble held her down.

She didn't know how long it was before she heard voices. She tried to call out, but her throat and nostrils were full of dust, and then she heard Lucy shouting 'Help' — a feeble shout — muffled and distant.

It was the young man from the newsagent's with the withered arm who pulled her out — lifting her with his good arm — there were firemen — and Mrs Burton in her fur coat and velvet hat saying, 'I knew that's where they'd be — They always sat under the stairs…'

Their mother was taken away on a stretcher in an ambulance. They were taken to a First Aid Post — covered with plaster dust — scratched and bruised. Lucy had a gash on her leg which was bleeding.
Then the grocer lady came and took them to her flat above the shop.

It was still the middle of the night.
The street had been badly hit.
Many of the houses were still on fire…
Flames scythed the sky with scarlet and yellow blades — umbrellas of sparks, a showering tinselled arch, against a sky livid with explosions — spiked with tracer bullets — swivelled with searchlights.
There were a lot of people in the street, their faces strangely reflected in the glow of the fires — shocked — surprised — angry.

'It's like Guy Fawkes,' said Lucy. 'There should be a Guy…'
Maisie had always been a bit scared of Guy Fawkes — the shabbily clothed dummy burning on a bonfire, and the whizzing, exploding fireworks.
This was even more scary. There were no jolly fathers setting off rockets and Catherine Wheels in leafy gardens, finger burning charred potatoes cooking in the glowing embers, and children dancing round the bonfire.
This was really, really scary and she was very cold. She was shivering all over, her teeth chattering. Amazingly she still had Susan, clasped tightly to her chest, her new pink knitted frock all torn and dirty.

The kind grocer lady wrapped her in a blanket and gave her a mug of hot Ovaltine.

In the grey, chill dawn, they saw their house, a charred ruin.
The top staircases had been destroyed, hanging like mournful, broken ladders, but the lower staircase was still there.
It had kept them safe.

A policeman came and asked them questions.
They had both memorised Auntie Maud's telephone number, and Lucy told the policeman 'She's our Auntie Maud — she'll know what to do...'

They stayed with Auntie Maud for a few days, whilst arrangements were made for them to go and live with Aunt Harriet.
The nice grocer lady, whose name they now knew was Mrs Cox, had given Auntie Maud a bag of nice things — eggs — ham — butter — some sausages... tut-tutting over the 'poor little things', whispering together about their mother. Lucy kept asking when they could see her, but Auntie Maud said she was not well enough yet, but that she was in a very nice hospital.

The young man from the newsagent had also been taken to hospital. He had badly gashed his good leg going back to free Lucy before the fire took hold.
He had saved their lives.

Maisie closed her eyes tightly and prayed very hard. 'Please God make him better — make Mummy better — bring Daddy home — stop this horrid, horrid, War...'
She was probably too insignificant for God to take any notice, but they had always been told to say their prayers.

Maisie slept on the sofa, and Lucy had cushions on the floor. Auntie Maud only had a small flat with one bedroom, that was why they wouldn't be able to stay with her. Lucy said she didn't mind sleeping on the floor. They wanted to stay with Auntie Maud, but she said they would be fine with Aunt Harriet.
'She has plenty of room, and a really big garden. You'll like it in the country. There won't be any air raids, and your mother will come as soon as she's better...'

Lucy said she didn't think Aunt Harriet liked children. She was very fussy, but Auntie Maud said that was how she was — she couldn't help it.
And then they had sausage and egg for supper and played Happy Families.

*　　*　　*

It was late afternoon before they finally got off the train.
They didn't have much luggage, just a few bags and Auntie Maud's small suitcase.

The station was deserted — one old man outside who said he was the taxi — his car, old and creaky with broken springs.
It had been raining, and the air smelt fresh and wet.
The taxi man had been expecting them. Aunt Harriet had arranged it.

As they got out of the car among dripping bushes in front of the square, grey house, Aunt Harriet opened the door, dressed severely in navy blue, with lace-up shoes, her hair in a neat bun.
'I thought you'd never get here,' she said. 'The train must have been very late…'

Auntie Maud started to cry, large tears rolled down her cheeks.
'Oh Harriet,' she said. 'It has been so awful — so awful…'
'There, there,' said Aunt Harriet, reaching out her hand. 'Come along in — the supper's nearly ready — I've got a roast chicken — come along children — come out of the wet — those shoes don't look very waterproof — come along Maud, you'll feel better after a nice glass of sherry…'

And then they were in the house — in the drawing room with large comfy chairs and a log fire burning, and Auntie Maud was telling Aunt Harriet all that had happened. Aunt Harriet told them to go and wash their hands ready for supper, and took them upstairs to their bedroom, all ready for them with pink eiderdowns and flowered curtains over the horrid blackout ones, and Maisie started to cry like Auntie Maud. They were going to be alright with Aunt Harriet. She couldn't help being stiff and serious, she was just like that…

'What are you crying for?' said Lucy. 'It's going to be fine — there's a huge garden, and Mummy will be here too as soon as she's better.' And she pushed Maisie in front of her into the bathroom. 'Hurry up and wash your hands — I'm starving…'

And Maisie shut her eyes, and fervently thanked the man on the Wireless for telling Auntie Maud it was safest under the stairs.

The Scent of Peaches

Eleanor had fallen in love with France from the moment the misted coast was visible, and the dreary shabby boat docked at battered Dieppe.

As the train lumbered through the flat countryside, smuts flying through the open window, gritty black specks settling on everything, her spirits rose.
She experienced an unexplained euphoria.
She was thirteen years old. Isabel, her sister, was two years older and very grown up.
It was 1947, and Europe was gradually mending itself, concealing its scars with box-hedged gardens and precise rose trees — globes of soft brilliance on thin brown stalks — neatly mown squares of little white crosses among the fields of nodding sunflowers and apple-laden orchards.
Bulldozers now, instead of tanks, groping the ruins — levelling the rubble for new apartment blocks, with bright curtains and balconies of geraniums.
War wreaths withering against grey stone lists of names.

She would always feel the same on arriving in France.
The magic of the few golden summers would stay with her forever.
The tumbling mosaic of memories, glittering fragments returning to tantalise with remembered scents, sounds and colours.

The first sight of the Sacre Coeur's sugar white dome as the train approached the Gare St Lazare.
Cool-chaired cafes — pungent Gaulloise.

The air was different, the light was different — clear and floating — the sun baked her feet on the pavement.
A citron pressé under the trees in the Tuilerie Gardens, tart and thirst-quenching in a tall glass clinking ice, and a long spoon to stir the sugar in the bottom.

The round pond by the gates, alive with bright-sailed boats.
The sudden breeze blowing drifts of pale yellow dust.
Elegant gold-winged bridges.
Diamond-cool dazzling fountains in the Place de la Concorde.
The dark expanses of the Louvre — da Vinci's enigmatic Lisa.
The incredible luminous Monets in the Jeu de Paume.
The stark, dramatic Musée des Art Modernes.
The view from the top of the Eiffel Tower. It was possible then to
go to the very top. Scratching her intials among the many thousand
others.
Soft, lazy Chantilly, with its sparkling water and formal gardens, the
sweet spicy smell of box hedges — huge fish floundering for bread
crumbs.
Crunching the golden sandy gravel of Versailles.
The small cups of bitter coffee.
And always the soaring, jewelled interior of Notre Dame. She would
never return to Paris without visiting this beloved cathedral — so
splendid — so beautiful.

*   *   *

They stayed with the Biengris, old friends of their stepmother's
parents.
They welcomed them with pleasure, and treated them as part of
the family. Their elegant balconied house with high railings hiding
it from the street, was not far from the Lake at Enghien, where
creaking boats rocked, and motionless fishermen in rough blue
jackets sat on banks of reeds waiting for their slack rods to tighten.

Monsieur Biengris was voluble, jolly and busy.
He had his own small business manufacturing electrical components,
his fortunes fluctuating from year to year.
Madame Biengris, distressingly thin, with white ankle socks and
canvas sandals, ran the house with the help of a girl from the village,
who had a lot to learn about personal hygiene.
Madame was deaf.
Her hearing aid was erratic, tending to fail her in the middle
of dinner while her husband was speaking to her. He would

expostulate, waving his arms in exasperation as she fiddled with the controls.

The war had been a long weary struggle.
Their son Maurice, a weedy dreamy young man, had spent the fearful years hidden in his room on the top floor to avoid being transported to a labour camp. So many had been taken — so few returned.
A member of the Resistance had thoughtfully burned down the Mairie, destroying all the records, so he had escaped detection.
They lived with the constant dread of betrayal.
Leather-fisted hammering at dawn — black boots on the stairs.
Not to be see at the windows — keep away from the windows — don't look down…
He was indoor pale, dark haired, moustachioed, studying composition at the César Franck school in Paris.

He still spent most of his time in his room, where he had his own upright piano.
His music minimal and surrealistic, the large sheets of manuscript paper scattered with long-tailed notes and black breve rests.

Yvonne, the youngest daughter, was the same age as Isabel. Plump, placid and pretty.
The older girl, Thérèse, spiky thin like her mother, always being urged to 'mange, chérie — mange!'
She had a job as a vendeuse in a very expensive handbag shop in the Place de l'Opéra.

The food was wonderful.
Soups thick with vegetables, delicious, soft aubergines cooked in oil, crinkly juicy baked tomatoes stuffed with savoury rice, crisp salads, glistening wines.
The lightest possible pastry, layered and topped with flavoured creams — coffee, chocolate, praline — twisted and rosetted.
Bread fresh and crusty.

Lying in a shaded deck chair among the fruit trees, reading and

anticipating lunch.
An abundance of scented peaches weighing down frail branches.
The dining room though cool, smelt of heat, the blinds striping the
room with sunlight.

The grey austerity of England faded away — the cardboard dried egg,
the listless bread, queueing for the occasional sausage, wheedling an
extra chop from the butcher.

It was hard to believe the war had been here, except for the odd
bunch of dying flowers laid on the spot where someone had been
shot — and it was better not to think about the Gare de l'Est with its
pretty façade, where so many had taken their last terrible journey.

Their stepmother's mother was kind.
A simple, dutiful person.
She insisted they should meet some of the family.
'But chérie,' she said to their stepmother, 'it would look most strange
if we did not bring them with us...'

Their father and stepmother had travelled separately, coming on
the Golden Arrow, staying at Le Crillon — where their mother and
father had stayed before the war.
One of the grandest hotels in Paris, facing the feathered fountains of
the Place de la Concorde, all paid for, as usual, by their grandmother,
who had grudgingly conceded to her son's wishes.
'Really Bertie — Why do you have to be so extravagant? And why
Le Crillon...?' She was thinking of Naomi, as she supposed was
Francoise. No doubt she thought she could superimpose herself on
any lingering memories — stamp out the ghosts with her ugly feet.

She still refused to help them with their French.
'How lucky having a French stepmother,' people would sigh. 'Your
French must be perfect...'
They smiled and looked away feeling her cold blank stare.

Lunch at a cousin's, a solid, red-faced charcutier, in a tiny flat above
the shop in a narrow dark street, with uneven cobbles and flaking

shutters.
The perturbing palor of the child in the dim airless room, in its grey-sheeted cot.
The massive spread of charcuterie, the unshaded light bulb hanging from the ceiling, squashed round the table with a furry brown cloth. The lights went out, and it was so dark in the little room that somebody sat the baby on the Camembert. There was laughter — 'It will improve the flavour!' — and it was passed round.

Driving north to Compiègne. Up the endless straight heat-shimmered roads bordered with silver green poplars. Here, straggling lines of burdened people had trudged — the debris of their lives crammed into bundles and perambulators. A pathetically easy target for the marauding dive-bombers of the advancing enemy.

Lunch at an uncle's farm, the rough walls peppered with bullet holes. A sumptuous feast served at a long table. There were cousins and aunts and uncles. Course after course on huge platters. So much food that Eleanor had to leave the table half way through to be sick, her rationed stomach unused to so much richness.

Not far along the mud-churned roads to Montsel, a bare small village, where they had a house.
There were two rooms at one end, and a smoke-blackened room the other, where the toothless grandmère with long black dress and dirty fingernails lived.

She had lived through three invasions, the Franco-Prussian and both World Wars.
Soldiers had fought and died in the surrounding fields and forests, the wounded and dying and dead laid out on the muddy roads and in the waterlogged ditches.
A long wild garden stretched behind the house, where their stepmother's parents had grown vegetables during the war.
The journey from Paris, though not too far, had been difficult and dangerous, but they had come as often as they could, desperate for food.
The father had made the journey many times on his tyre-punctured

bicycle.
He was a clever little man — alternatively obsequious and violent —
very unlikeable.

There was no running water, and an earth closet in a small wooden
hut the size of a telephone box, standing solitary, facing the gate.
A magnificent walnut tree shaded the front of the house, which had
a rickety balcony opening on to the granary which ran the whole
length of the ramshackle building.

Water was fetched from the pump on the village square.
A scattering of houses, some rich, some poor.
A yellow-shuttered shop selling dusty sun-bleached sweets, paraffin,
large bars of brown soap.
There was a telephone in one of the larger farms, for emergencies,
and a bus stopped twice a day.

Outside the village stood the ancient tiny church, isolated among
fields of corn and cattle. The old boundary between leper colony
and village, its twin tattered spires lonely survivors of the battering
of three wars. Inside it was musty, spider ridden, the wooden pews
worm-eaten, heavy with incense.
It had no regular services now, sharing its priest with other villages.

*   *   *

Monsieur Biengris had a 'Maigret'-type black Citroën.
Eleanor travelled on the roof rack, holding a large tray of ripe
plums, while Monsieur Biengris drove erratically, one-handed,
pointing out objects of interest to her with the other, and shouting
conversationally above the noise of the engine.
All things were possible then.

She and Isabel shared a comfortable cluttered bedroom at the top of
the house.
There was a narrow cupboard-like room adjoining, with a wardrobe
and basin. It was decorated all over, including the ceiling and the
wardrobe with floral-patterned wallpaper. They were surrounded by

beribboned bouquets of full-blown roses.

They washed their scant supply of clothing in the basin, and hung it out to dry. It was so hot it didn't take long.

They had to share the wide bolstered double bed, the linen sheets stiff with starch.

Her first perm in the back room of the cramped village hairdressers, emerging frizzy and scarlet-faced, after several hours of heat and curlers.

They visited the macabre Catacombs. The dank dimly lit slimy underground passages lined with walls of bones, decorated with skulls.

Isabel managed to attract admirers in the queue, two young men eager to protect her.

Isabel collected admirers wherever she went. Eleanor was thankful she did not. She would not have known what to do about it if she had.

To the echoing Invalides to see Napoleon's monstrous tomb.

To the theatre to see 'French Without Tears' in French.

To the cinema to see 'Carnet du Bal', a haunting film, with a haunting melody weaving sad semitones, nostalgic and melancholy.

Buying supremely comfortable rope-soled espadrilles in the market, and a pair of blue and white loafers at Bally's in Paris. The ultimate chic!

*   *   *

They came again the following summer on the Golden Arrow.

Their grandmother had made over a large sum for their father to pay off his debts.

A sum he was to dissipate, debts unpaid.

To Dover in the polished luxury of the Pullman with pink shaded lights and linen cloths on the tables, and then the French dining car. They ate their way to Paris.

Pâté, roast veal and petit pois, arriving at the Gare du Nord slightly queasy, to be met, delightedly, by Monsiuer Biengris and Yvonne.

After a brief greeting, their father and stepmother departed in a taxi, and they were whisked off in the rattly black Citroën, feeling contentment spreading, effervescent bubbles of pleasure bursting in the liquid evening light.

This year they did not visit their stepmother's relatives.
Their father was pursuing a mysterious enterprise which was to restore his wealth.
It came to nothing.

The enchantment of Paris.
The clanging Metro, descending the twisting white tiled passages — the wooden slatted seats — the brass door handles — Porte de Clignancourt — Porte des Lilas — Châtelet — Gare d'Austerlitz.
They clung on open-backed buses with chains to stop people falling out — Place de la République — La Bastille.
They visited Thérèse in the swanky handbag shop in the Place de l'Opéra — the carpet deep-pile eau-de-nil. Bulbous flagons and sharp-sided bottles of perfume among the glossy handbags, silk scarves and smooth gilt-buckled belts.

They browsed among the bookstalls on the banks of the Seine, passing over the disagreeable chalky drawings of famous beauty spots.
'It's a pity we can't read French,' said Isabel. 'Look at all this stuff...'

They went boating on a lake in the Bois de Boulogne, dragging their oars in the tangled pink-flowered weedy surface — rocking gently beneath the shady surrounding trees — tall-trunked pines and graceful flowered limes — rowing slowly between hammocked bush-covered islands, wild flowers woven among the long grasses.
The heat idling the afternoons away.

Going on Sunday mornings in the black Citroën with Monsieur Biengris, noisily cheerful, to buy charcuterie for lunch from a special shop in a neighbouring village, the window filled with shiny jellied meats, beautifully arranged.
Assorted dishes of cubed red and green peppers glistening with oil, sliced pickled cucumbers, mushrooms in a chocolate brown

sauce, glass tubs of green and black olives, white platters of sausage artistically decorated with little pots of flowers and sprigs of parsley and chervil.

Monsieur Biengris would have a lengthy chat with the proprietress, a careful, smiling, short lady in black — lovingly wrapping their purchases in sheets of shining white paper, ladling salads into white waxed boxes.
Then to the boulangerie for an armful of long bread.

Isabel, prettier than ever, attracted a motley selection of admirers of all nationalities, eager to buy her coffee, or ice cream, or perhaps a gateau at one of the many tree-shaded cafes which spread over the pavements.
Eleanor followed dutifully at a reasonable distance, ready to extricate her if there were any problems.

They returned to England in the rain, on the ordinary boat train via Calais-Dover, with a large piece of beef their father had ordered them to smuggle into the still-rationed country. It was wrapped in brown paper and hidden among Isabel's clothes.
The Customs officer asked if they had anything to declare, white chalk poised, holding a placard for them to read.
Isabel said 'No' firmly. Eleanor could only shake her head.
He marked their suitcases and moved on to a trembling vicar, turning out the contents of his case onto the Customs bench.
'One day,' said Isabel, 'one day I shall say "Do your own dirty work. Tell your own lies" and I shall leave forever...'

*   *   *

It was three years before she was able to go back to France. That year, and the following years, a kaleidoscopic carousel of memories — translucent, gilded summers.

The Biengris had had their salon grandly extended. A dimly shuttered room, scented with plum, peach and lavender.
A black grand piano, heavy-legged, glazed and roughened with age,

standing on the sun-gashed parquet.
A few lazy wasps buzzing at the window, flopping down on the round glass-topped table burdened with a green-leafed plant, glossy and spreading.
There were a sofa and armchairs of beige mock leather, and a glass-fronted, diamond-paned cocktail cabinet, jumbled with syrupy liqueurs and jars of paper cocktail umbrellas.
Here she played Beethoven sonatas, and 'In a Monastery Garden', a copy of which she had found in the piano stool.
Sometimes Maurice would emerge to play duets with her.
They had a book of Beethoven symphonies.
He was a little more talkative.
Occasionally at meal times he would make a controversial statement, and then watch with bland amusement the inevitable commotion it caused, helping himself to tender steak and golden frites from the oval white dishes on the table.

Her father and stepmother were again in Paris.
Her father had another grand scheme.
She was invited, with the Biengris, to lunch at Montsel.
Madame Biengris excused herself.
She had some problem with her stomach, a condition exacerbated by the deprivations of the war. Bony thin, she ate small quantities at great speed.
Eleanor and Monsieur Biengris set off in the black Citroën, bumping along the neglected, poplared roads, through the flat, evocative countryside, the fields brilliant with poppies.

Monsieur Biengris told her how he and her stepmother's father had both been pilots in the French Air Force at the end of the First World War. They had been exciting times.

The village had not changed. Water was still fetched from the pump, no electricity or internal plumbing.
The aged grandmère in her dusty black dress and broken slippers stood grinning toothlessly in her blackened doorway.
The others had arrived already.
They drank smoky pastis, and nibbled slices of salami, sitting in the

garden in the thick midday heat, the table laid for lunch under the leafy walnut tree.

Suddenly there was an argument. Her stepmother and the father shouting abuse at one another.
Accusation and counter-accusation. Eleanor couldn't follow the fast, angry French.
The father leapt from the table, and hurled himself into his car.
He was going back to Paris to fetch the evidence.
The mother was distraught. She had just placed a selection of carefully prepared hors d'oeuvres on the table, sliced meats overlapping in a pink wheel, glass dishes of prawns in pink mayonnaise, tomatoes shiny with oil and black olives, a basket of bread…

Her stepmother would not stay.
She demanded that Monsieur Biengris should take them back to their hotel in Paris immediately. She was not going to wait for her father to insult her again.
They drove away, leaving the mother standing weeping beside the table of abandoned food.
They passed the father driving like a madman on his way back to Montsel.

It was a relief to reach the tranquillity of the Biengris home, and the comfortable old fashioned bedroom, to lie on the wide bed, and gaze at the calm floral wallpaper.

Yvonne had a boyfriend, who she had to meet clandestinely. He was a very nice, good looking, hardworking student of engineering.
Monsieur Biengris had forbidden them to meet or speak to each other.
He considered him unsuitable. He had, as yet, no position in life, and would be unable to support a wife.
No 'nice girl' was permitted to go out with anyone whose intentions were not serious.
Even a visit to the cinema or a walk in the park was not allowed unless vows had been exchanged.

Eleanor's visit was most propitious.
Nearly every day she and Yvonne went to Paris, sightseeing.
They walked across hot dusty fields to catch the train.
Jean would meet them on the train, and when they reached Paris,
Jean and Yvonne would go off together, and Eleanor would wander
where she pleased.

Walking the spacious length of the Champs Elysees, shaded by the
densely leaved horse chestnut trees, their autumn conkers already
forming pale green spiky balls.
To the top of the Arc de Triomphe to gaze down the branching
boulevards of the Etoile.
Re-visiting the now familiar pictures in the Jeu de Paume.
Degas' calm horses shadowing the paddock, reins loose in the
jockeys' hands.
Monet's dreamy bridge at Argenteuil, the masts of the white boats
reflected in the sun-touched water.
Renoir's gentle people dancing under the glass-globed lights among
the trees in Montmartre...

She walked beside the metallic, khaki waters of the Seine, crossing
the Pont Notre Dame, to inhale the beauty of the cathedral.
Sitting in the Tuilerie Gardens, at a café among the trees, sipping
the bitter coffee, watching the surge of people pass — tourists in
shorts and sensible lace-up shoes, slung with maps and cameras.
Mothers with small children in pushchairs, on tricycles, solemn and
obedient. Young girls with short pretty skirts and ridiculous ankle-
turning high heels.

She made her way up the narrow cobbled streets of Montmartre,
arriving at the Place du Tertre out of breath, to sit at one of the
rough wood tables and order a cool citron pressé. There were many
students up here, anarchic among the eager foreign visitors.
Shabby artists tried to sell instant portraits, producing mostly awful
pictures of the Sacré Coeur and Moulin Rouge in garish colours.

The Place Pigalle disappointingly drab in the daylight.
The streetwalkers loitering on corners smoking and chatting to each

other, ankle bracelets glinting, the pavements dirty and uneven, torn paper clinging to trees.
She never saw it at night when coloured lights and flashing signs smeared it with glamour.

So many blissfully somnambulant shimmering afternoons.

Thérèse had become engaged.
Patrick, her fiancé, was short and as thin as her.
He wore glasses and had a high laugh. He was a solicitor, and worked with a big firm in Paris. A most suitable match.

The engagement was conducted in the proper, formal way.
Large quantities of household goods had to be purchased for Thérèse's 'dot'.
Many sheets and pillowcases, piles of towels, tablecloths and linen napkins to be monogrammed with their entwined initials.
Much kitchen equipment. Sets of saucepans and frying pans, a fish kettle, a bain-marie, various sieves and choppers. A canteen of engraved silver cutlery, and a set of cheaper cutlery for everyday use. Sets of glasses — for champagne, white wine, red wine, liqueurs, long drinks — crystal vases and desert bowls…

The hall was full of boxes.
Madame Biengris became increasingly thin and nervous, her hearing aid letting her down in the middle of crucial discussions, much to her husband's exasperation.

A suitable apartment in Paris was searched for, and eventually found.
They went to a heavily curtained musty flat, looking with dark furniture, and drank sweet syrupy drinks whilst the lease was signed.
The flat was small but perfectly adequate, with a view of dappled roofs.

She had to return to London before the wedding to continue her studies.

Seven months later, as spring struggled to ice the London parks with pink and white cherry blossom, and thousands of yellow crocuses carpeted the corner of Hyde Park where the morning horses trotted down Rotten Row, Patrick died suddenly of a heart attack. Thérèse was five months' pregnant.

Eleanor received a thick creamy black-edged envelope containing the announcement of his death, and an invitation to the funeral.
She was unable to attend.
She could not afford to go.
So ended the golden summers.